Men and women cau_____ . . .
The man whose ve_____ f

Ben Davidson—A chance encounter in a small Mississippi town plunges him into the heart of a frightening conspiracy.

Lisa Smith—Rich, beautiful, fearless—and determined to avenge a terrible, unforgivable act of violence.

Johann Smith—Prime Minister of South Africa, a man whose appalling debt to the *Adlerkinden* must soon be redeemed.

Stangl—A blond, blue-eyed killing machine who will commit any atrocity in the name of pleasure.

Dr. Eugene Croft—His deranged experiments are the culmination of the *Adlerkinden*'s legacy of terror.

Jan Leander—The South African Intelligence chief who has a personal stake in destroying the *Adlerkinden*.

Now, turn the page for an exciting excerpt from . . .
A CONSPIRACY OF EAGLES

THE BLAST FROM THE SHOTGUN CAUGHT THE GUARD SQUARE IN THE CHEST, HURLING HIM BACKWARD DOWN THE CORRIDOR...

Ben kicked in the door to the room where Lisa was being held. She was standing, fully dressed, by the bed. Tears of relief filled her eyes. He wanted to embrace her, but there was no time.

"Otto's dead. Let's get out of here!" He ran into the corridor, and in a moment Lisa was right behind him. Ben led her toward the roof exit. When they had almost reached it, the door to Stangl's office opened, and an armed man emerged. Ben noticed a jagged scar on his cheek. The shotgun exploded again, and the man ducked back inside. Ben didn't know whether or not he'd hit him.

He broke open the gun and reloaded. Smoke hung in the corridor, obscuring his vision. Ben took out the road flares, and in moments the corridor was filled with dense smoke and hissing flames. The carpet caught fire immediately. Ben grabbed Lisa and ran toward the staircase.

The fire began to spread rapidly, and the brothel became a madhouse. From behind his back, Ben heard a shout from the top of the stairs. "That's them. Stop those two!"

Ben turned, saw the man raise a gun, and fired at the same moment. The man's face disintegrated, and his body fell over the railing.

"Get out. Now!" he yelled to Lisa.

She ran in front of him. A shot passed by Ben's head, and he turned and fired the other barrel, blindly. But he could see nothing amidst the smoke that filled the building... until he felt the barrel of a gun in his side and turned to face the scarfaced man...

A CONSPIRACY OF EAGLES

BART DAVIS

BANTAM BOOKS
TORONTO • NEW YORK • LONDON • SYDNEY • AUCKLAND

A CONSPIRACY OF EAGLES

A Bantam Book/August 1985

Article by Jane Brody copyright © 1972 by
The New York Times Company. Reprinted by permission.

ISBN 0-553-17159-3

Published simultaneously in the United States and Canada

_____

Bantam Books are published by Bantam Books, Inc. Its trademark,
consisting of the words "Bantam Books" and the portrayal of a
rooster, is Registered in U.S. Patent and Trademark Office and in
other countries. Marca Registrada. Bantam Books, Inc., 666 Fifth
Avenue, New York, New York 10103.

_____

Printed and bound in Great Britain by
Cox & Wyman Ltd, Reading

H   0 9 8 7 6 5 4 3 2 1

To Sharon
First critic and best friend

Acknowledgments

It is with the deepest sense of warmth and gratitude that I acknowledge the contributions of Robert Gottlieb of the William Morris Agency to the writing of this novel.

My thanks and gratitude to Steve Weiss. Also:

To Conrad Bergmann and Mary Lacoste for their research assistance, and to Gerard Lanigan, John Prin, and Bob Harwood of Grumman Aerospace;

To Brandon Davis for his editorial assistance;

To Pat Plevin at NBC Television for his kind encouragements;

To Lorraine Kutzing for her amazing ability to decipher my scrawl;

To Daniel J. Comerford III for his friendship;

And, to Barbara Alpert of Bantam Books for her enthusiasm, her support, and her superb editorial advice.

"The most decisive influence on the Führer during the war . . . was exerted by Martin Bormann. The latter had . . . disastrously strong influence. That was possible only because the Führer was filled with profound distrust . . . and because Bormann was with him constantly and described to him all matters."

Hermann Göring
Testimony at the Nuremberg Trials.

Prologue

South Africa, October 1936

The wind blew dry and hot and smelled faintly of desert as it whipped across the landing strip. Johann Smith waited patiently while his younger brother, Hans, fidgeted in the limousine's rear seat.

Johann, a twenty-seven-year-old Afrikaner with sharp, aristocratic features and gray-blue eyes, ran his fingers through his closely cropped blond hair. Reaching into a pocket of his suit, he took out a package of cigarettes and offered one to Hans.

"I don't want one," said Hans, who was two years younger and looked enough like Johann to be his twin.

"Now, don't be petulant," said Johann coolly. "Relax. They will be here soon."

"I can't stand waiting any more. I'm hot and tired, and I need a drink," said Hans, and he shifted his position once again as the smoke from Johann's cigarette made his eyes burn.

Silence settled in the huge black car again. In the front, the black chauffeur sat as motionless as the dry, grassy plains of the Transvaal that surrounded them. Separated by a closed glass partition, even the sound of his breathing was absent.

Hans's voice seemed to burst from him. "Johann, maybe they're not coming. Let's tell the others to go home—that it's been canceled. Let's go home, Johann. Please?"

Johann spoke without looking at his brother. "I don't wish to discuss it again, Hans. We've been through this before. It's too late. We are committed."

"But the others look up to you. You could stop it if you wanted."

Johann spoke without anger, as if to a child. "It's too late. Accept that."

"But it's treason," Hans moaned. "We'll be shot if we're caught. Have you thought about that in your grand schemes?"

Johann was unruffled.

"We are Afrikaners, Hans. Our ancestors were Boer, not British. Our actions remain loyal to that tradition. It's beyond mere national ties. We aren't traitors to anyone but the British whites in our country who would like to take from us everything we have built. Do you want that?"

Hans looked away.

"Answer me," snapped Johann.

"No," muttered his brother.

"Good. Then listen again. There is a war coming, and we will be forced to fight on Britain's side against Germany. We will have to fight for those people who would give our country to the blacks, coloreds, and Jews. That contradicts our very existence. We have to break with the Commonwealth and end the influence of the British if apartheid is ever to succeed. Do you understand that?"

Hans held his head in both hands and pressed against his temples as if to bar his brother's words from entering.

"I don't know, Johann. I'm scared every time I think of someone finding out. What will we do?"

Johann looked at his brother, put a hand on his shoulder, and rocked him gently.

"Don't worry, Hans. I'll protect you. I always have. I'll make it all right. Haven't I always?"

"Yes, Johann," nodded Hans, lulled by the rocking motion.

"And when the war is over and Britain lies defeated, we will be in control of our country once again. Someday we will control all of Africa. A white Africa. Now wouldn't that be nice, Hans? No more blacks and no more coloreds. Wouldn't you like that?"

"Yes, Johann."

"Then you see who our allies must be? You'll be one of us?"

"Yes, Johann," Hans muttered as he buried his face in his hands.

Johann Smith smiled at his brother. "That's good. Very good, Hans."

Johann looked up as the sound of airplane engines reached the car.

"It's time, Hans. Compose yourself."

Johann went to the rear of the car, opened the boot, and

withdrew a Very pistol and two flares. Walking to the center of the air strip, he loaded and fired the pistol into the air. First, a red flare. By now the plane was circling. Johann fired a white flare, and the plane began to descend for a landing.

The roar grew louder, and Johann retreated toward the car as the four-engine Focke Wulfe Kondor hit the runway, slowed, and taxied to a halt thirty yards away.

Halfway down the fuselage a hatch opened and retractable steps emerged. Johann stopped a few paces from the steps, prepared to meet the men he had been waiting for. An observer would have noted no change in his outward appearance but, internally, Johann's pulse quickened appreciably.

The first man to descend the steps was tall with skin as pale as ivory. His light brown hair was brushed straight back from a high forehead, and large, bushy eyebrows stood out over eyes so deep a blue as to be shocking against his white skin. In his left hand he held a black medical bag.

Dr. Ludwig Stumpfegger, Adolf Hitler's personal surgeon, extended his hand, and Johann grasped it firmly.

"It is good to see you again, Herr Doctor."

"And you as well, Herr Smith. Everything is ready?"

"Yes. Everyone is waiting."

"Excellent," said Stumpfegger.

Smith's eyes moved to the top of the stairway as the second man began to descend. He was almost impossibly wide for one so short, and his heavily jowled face seemed to grow directly from his torso. His thin hair matched the color of his muddy brown eyes. Seeing him, Johann felt a vague unease for the first time.

"Good day, Herr Smith," said Martin Bormann, Reichsleiter of the Nazi Party.

"Good day, Herr Bormann," echoed Johann Smith.

Bormann's large hand and thick fingers surrounded Johann's lean one. It was an unpleasant feeling.

"It is a pleasure to meet you at last, Herr Reichsleiter," said Johann.

"For me as well, Herr Smith," said Bormann, his voice harsh and guttural. "I have been kept abreast of your activities by Dr. Stumpfegger. You have made the correct decision."

"We believe it to be."

"Where is the rest of your party?" asked Bormann.

"A few miles from here at one of my hunting lodges. Shall we go?"

"Yes," responded Bormann. "I want to be on my way as soon as possible."

The three men walked to the limousine. As they approached, Hans got out and hastily smoothed his wrinkled clothing.

"This is my brother, Hans Smith. Hans, this is Herr Bormann and Herr Doctor Stumpfegger."

Later, Hans stared out the window as they drove, his hands moving constantly in his lap. Bormann was the first to break the silence.

"These men of yours, you trust them absolutely?"

"I do, Herr Bormann. They are all Afrikaners and committed to our cause. Each opposes the Prime Minister's pro-British position."

"Being anti-British and being pro-German are not necessarily the same thing, Herr Smith."

"In this case it is," responded Johann. "We would support the devil himself to end Britain's power in South Africa."

"The comparison is hardly flattering," said Stumpfegger.

"But the dedication is commendable," finished Bormann. "I think our aims coincide."

"That's the right term, Herr Bormann, 'coincide.' Germany can have the rest of the world. We will be quite content with South Africa. Back in its rightful hands, of course," said Johann.

"And you will have it," said Bormann. "That is our agreement. Do your men know the full extent of our contract?"

Johann took a deep breath and looked steadily at Bormann. His voice was angry when he spoke.

"They know that apartheid will die under British rule and survive only if Germany defeats Britain. Since the Great Trek in 1835, we Boers have been trying to escape the British. We've fought to be separate from them many times and to live our lives the way we want to. When diamonds were discovered, they made war on us and took them. When gold was discovered, they took that from us as well. It's taken us thirty years to recover from their last war. Their 'Scorched Earth' policy left every farm in the north a burnt-out ruin. Twenty-six thousand of our women and children died in refugee camps, and six thousand of our men died on the

4

battlefield. We have fought them for a hundred years, but each time we have lost.

"This time we won't lose. To this cause my men have pledged their lives, and their fortunes. That is sufficient, is it not?"

"That is sufficient," said Bormann.

In the distance a dark speck grew into a low, stone structure as they approached. Three other limousines were parked around it, and smoke rose from the chimney.

"When will they know it all?" asked Bormann.

"When it's necessary, Herr Reichsleiter," said Johann evenly.

"You are a man of style, Herr Smith. I like that."

"Thank you. We are here, gentlemen. Come, Hans."

The four men entered the lodge. Three others stood talking quietly, drinking wine from crystal goblets. The room was filled with objects of the hunter's skill. Animal heads decorated the walls and skins adorned the floors. It was a man's room, a conqueror's domain. Johann moved to the center of the room and spoke to Bormann.

"May I present my colleagues: Herr Pieter Van Dyne, whose family owns one of the largest diamond exchanges in Amsterdam; Herr Walter Hauptman, who is the sole heir to one of the largest diamond-producing mines in the country; Herr Franz Voorstein, who represents in Parliament, as I do, a large number of Afrikaner districts. Gentlemen, Reichsleiter Martin Bormann and Herr Doctor Ludwig Stumpfegger."

Johann walked to a table on which sat seven identical documents and spoke over the conversations that had started.

"It is time," he announced. "Let us begin."

The men in turn signed each of the seven documents. When they were finished, Johann handed one to each man. The last went to Bormann who spoke directly to him.

"The Adlerkinden have been born today, Johann Smith."

"We are only the first of the Eagle's Children," said Johann. "Many more will follow," and he nodded to Hauptman, who placed his hands on a wooden chest that lay on the table. Reinforced with black iron bands, its primitive appearance was not at odds with either the room or its occupants. He opened the lid of the chest.

Packed against black velvet and blazing like stars in a winter's night were tray after tray of perfect blue-white diamonds.

"Ten million rands, Herr Reichsleiter. Our birthright," said Hauptman.

Bormann's eyes seemed to shine as brightly as the diamonds. He looked around the room, and his voice shook with emotion as he spoke.

"What starts here will never end. We who leave here will never forget. The lesser races of the world will tremble before us, before the Adlerkinden. At war's end, we will meet again, my friends."

Black servants were called in to take the chest to the limousine that would transport it back to the airfield. Stumpfegger followed it outside to the car at Bormann's command.

The Reichsleiter smiled for the first time and raised his arm in a salute that would soon echo throughout the world.

"Heil, Hitler!" said Martin Bormann.

One by one the men returned to their cars and were driven away, raising dust in their passing. A strong wind came up that obliterated the signs of their passage, returning the dust to the earth from which it had come.

Obersalzburg, Germany, October 1939

Martin Bormann was notified of the Führer's arrival by the SS guards at the perimeter gatehouse. They called over a private phone line that ran directly to the Berghof Adler high on the mountaintop of Obersalzburg. Berghof Adler, the Eagle's Mountain Castle, was Bormann's brainchild and in it, with the exception of the Führer, he ruled absolutely.

Bormann replaced the phone and walked to the huge picture window in the living room. The enormous view down the mountainside extended past the Untersberg to Berchtesgaden and Salzburg. From the window he watched the procession of limousines, led by Hitler's twelve-cylinder Dusenberg, slowly wind its way up the mountain road. The road had cost twenty million marks to build and ended in a steep cliff whose face was ascended by a 165-foot elevator, blasted from solid rock, the only entrance to Berghof Adler. He poured himself a glass of wine from the bar on the side wall.

It would take a while for the procession to move from the

outer perimeter, with its identity checks at two gates, to the inner perimeter and its third check, up the long, winding road that could only be traveled by one car at a time. Though identity checks would obviously be waived in the Führer's case, the guards would want to impress Hitler with their thoroughness and discipline, and that would take more time.

Like a king, Bormann surveyed his creation from on high. There had been a few landholders on the mountain who had refused to sell their property. He had sent his SS troops to tear down the centuries-old buildings and farmhouses and then sent the owners to the death camps. After all, he thought, was it not a crime against the state to refuse the Führer? He had done the same to the numerous chapels on the mountain and, finally, had confiscated state forest lands and transferred them into Hitler's private holdings. The resultant estate was almost three square miles and covered the mountain from its sixty-five hundred foot peak to the valley below.

In the distance, Bormann watched hundreds of trucks filled with construction materials flow over the network of roads he had built. He had turned forest paths into concrete arteries. They had already completed a barracks, a huge garage, a hotel for the Führer's guests, a housing complex for the growing number of servants and maintenance workers, and a dormitory building for the hundreds of construction workers. Several greenhouses had been built to provide the Führer with fresh fruit and vegetables for his vegetarian diet. Even at night, lights glowed at new construction sites. Blasts of dynamite occasionally woke guests in the middle of the night.

Standing at the window, Bormann experienced a warm glow of pleasure due, only in part, to the wine. A trade school drop-out and an ex-convict, the son of a military musician, he had done quite well for himself. Buttoning up the tunic of his plain brown uniform, he prepared to meet Adolf Hitler.

The elevator was waiting at the top of the shaft, and the descent was rapid. Smoothing down his thin hair, he waited for the motorcade to come to a stop before him. He had timed it well. The Führer's car was just topping the final slope. "What would happen to me," he wondered, "if the Führer discovered the real reason for Berghof Adler?" The thought made his massive frame shudder in the cool moun-

7

tain air. By the time the Dusenberg rolled to a stop, however, he was smiling, his arm raised in salute.

Hitler emerged from the car wearing a long leather coat to ward off the cold air. He was flanked quickly by two aides carrying briefcases. Hitler paused for a moment to breathe deeply and then raised his arm to acknowledge Bormann's salute. He appeared tired, his face drawn.

"It is good to be here again, Martin. Things go well?" he said.

"Yes, my Führer. With your presence here, how could things go otherwise?"

Hitler seemed pleased by his remark and gestured for the rest of the cars to disgorge their occupants. Immediately, a crowd grew on the mountain slope. Bormann knew them all, with the exception of the drivers and low-ranking aides. Dr. Otto Dietrich, Hitler's press chief; Albert Speer, Hitler's personal architect and Minister of Armaments; old familiars like Joseph Goebbels, Minister of Propaganda, and Franz Schwarz, the party treasurer.

Hitler and his aides rose in the elevator first, and then, in groups of four, the rest of the party ascended. Some nodded to Bormann in greeting, others in ill-disguised hostility. He ignored them. Soon, he stood alone.

A few minutes later, a comparatively inconspicuous Mercedes sedan pulled to a stop on the plateau in front of the elevator. Three women emerged, and Bormann stepped forward to meet them. The first two were Hitler's secretaries.

"Good day, Fräulein Wolf and Fräulein Schroeder. You may go straight up to the house."

Both were young and pretty with blond hair and heavy makeup. They smiled at Bormann as they passed.

The third woman to emerge from the car was less pretty than the other two. Pleasant and fresh-faced with mousy-colored brown hair, her modest air did little to betray her position in life. She was Eva Braun, the mistress of the man who would make war on the world.

Bormann stooped to help her from the car. He thought it absurd that she still had to arrive separately from the Führer when their relationship was common knowledge. But Hitler had willed it so, and so it must be. Even in his daily walks to the "teahouse" at the mountain's summit, Eva Braun walked many paces behind him with the rest of the party, never at his side. It was, he knew, a constant torture for her to be the eternal mistress and never the wife. The daughter of a conservative school teacher, her sense of morality was constantly strained.

"Good day, Eva."

"Hello, Martin. How are you?"

"Very well. And you?"

Eva sighed. "I am well enough. It was a long, lonely ride with only those two idiots for company."

"You have made it many times before. No?"

"But it grows longer every time."

"Have you spoken to him about it?" asked Bormann.

"Just last night. There can be no change, he says. He is very unhappy about it, too."

"I know he must be."

"It puts such a strain on him, Martin. He has the whole world on his shoulders. I don't want to make it worse, but I can't seem to help myself..."

Bormann reached for his handkerchief as Eva started to cry.

"It's so... public," she finished, sobbing.

"I am sure the Führer has his reasons."

"You know his reason, Martin. It is the same as always. If he married me, the leader of the greatest Aryan nation in the world is terrified of the child he would produce."

"But he is the Führer," protested Bormann.

"Yes, I know that," said Eva, wearily. "Perhaps it is better this way, unless you can help us as you promised."

"I am trying, Eva."

Only a few inches shorter than Bormann, she looked at him steadily and took his hand in hers.

"It must be soon, Martin. I am no longer so young. And I am afraid."

"Be strong, Eva. He needs you to be."

"Remember your promise, Martin. A wedding gift."

Eva Braun turned away from Bormann and entered the elevator. Soon she was high overhead and would be entering the Berghof.

In the gathering dusk, Bormann rubbed his face in his hands to soothe tired muscles. Glancing about to make sure he was alone, he walked quickly from the plateau. About a hundred yards from the elevator shaft, he came to a group of high hedges that screened from view the beginning of a path known only to him and a few trusted others.

The path continued around the mountain and then began to rise sharply upward. Bormann began to breathe heavily from his exertions in the thin, cold air. He finally came to a large steel door, large enough to admit a truck. Set in its corner was a smaller door, sized for a man.

Removing a key from his pocket, Bormann opened the door, entered, and relocked it behind him. He stood in a chamber twenty feet high and fifty feet deep that was lit by a series of naked bulbs hanging from the ceiling. A loading dock was built into the solid rock wall, and Bormann was pleased to see that one of the SS guards had his rifle trained on Bormann's head. One guard had failed to go through the proper entry code, and Bormann had had him tortured to death. His screams had filled the labyrinth of tunnels for hours. No one forgot again.

"Authorization?" barked the guard.

"Reichsleiter," responded Bormann.

"Code?"

"Number One."

"Password?"

"Adlerkinden."

The guard had finished the process. He snapped to attention and called for the other guards to do so as well. Bormann returned their salutes casually.

"My compliments to the guard. I am pleased."

The tension left the guards' faces as they resumed their posts. Bormann left the dock and entered a tunnel that would take him to his office. He had chosen the guards for two qualities—loyalty and fanaticism. Drawing from the ranks of the SS, he had selected those who not only had killed countless times but those who enjoyed doing so. From the guards of concentration camps, from the death squads, from the assassins, he had picked these men to guard his secret. Here alone he walked at ease.

All the Adlerkinden were housed in incredible luxury. The finest Austrian chefs worked in the kitchens. The tapestries that appointed the walls had last hung in great museums. The living quarters were furnished from the great hotels of fallen cities, and the rate of pay was three times above normal. In a lower level was a brothel for the men's use. New girls were brought in regularly to replace those "damaged" or used up.

Bormann came to a door at the end of the corridor. Opening it with another key, he stepped into the central section of the complex. It was code-named "Adlernest," the Eagle's Nest, for it was here that what Bormann sought would be born.

In sharp contrast to the rough rock walls and naked bulbs of the entry chamber, the walls here were tiled, the floors were carpeted, and the entire impression was one of a modern hospital facility. Orderlies in white lab coats seemed to be everywhere, carrying racks of test tubes or pushing medical machinery from room to room.

A single guard station, in which sat two of his SS troops behind a glass enclosure, surveyed the operation with machine pistols held ready. But the staff that walked by with brisk efficiency seemed hardly to notice them. The guards noted Bormann's entrance and saluted sharply.

Bormann returned the salute and headed for the main nursing station where a male nurse sat filling out reports and overseeing the movements of food and medication to the "patients" in the huge dormitory-style room behind him.

The head nurse was named Erich, and he snapped to attention as he saw Bormann approach. He had dark, curly hair that sprang out in tufts over his body and emerged over his white T-shirt and white jacket. His blunt features twisted into a hesitant smile as he saluted.

"Heil, Hitler!"

"Hello, Erich," said Bormann. "Any problems?"

"None at all, sir. Everything's running smoothly."

"And our patients?" asked Bormann.

"We are down to fifteen in the dorm, sir. Eight died this morning. I think Doctor Stumpfegger was trying something new. Here's the chart, sir." Erich made a move to hand a clipboard filled with papers to Bormann, but he stopped him.

"That won't be necessary. I'll get the report from the doctor himself. Where is he?"

"At this hour, he's usually in Lab Seven. Do you want me to call him?"

"No. I'll go there myself."

Bormann walked away. Pausing to peer into the patients' dormitory, he received a salute from the guards stationed inside who noted his entrance. Thirty-five beds, formed neatly into seven rows of five, ran the length and width of the room. The patients were women. Some Oriental, some Negro, some Indian, and some Caucasian. A few were pregnant. Most were in bed, but a few wandered the room aimlessly under the scrutiny of the guards. Bormann walked to one woman who was lying in bed. Her eyes stared emptily up at him. He recognized her as one of the girls from the brothel he had transferred here a week ago. Some of the men had been careless with her. He was sure she could still be of use.

He casually flipped off the bed covers and stared at her. Her gown was open, and her body was exposed to his view. There was no motion from her. He reached out to one of her breasts and pinched the nipple between his thumb and forefinger. Still no response. Bormann beckoned to a guard who came rushing over.

"If she is still in this condition in forty-eight hours, use her as fertilizer in the greenhouse."

Borman left the room and walked down the main corridor. In reality, he understood little of what took place here. He was an administrator. Focus enough resources and talent on any problem and a solution could be found. He believed in that premise completely.

In Lab Seven, Doctor Stumpfegger was stooped over a series of beakers pipetting red liquid from one to the next. He was so engrossed in his work he failed to notice Bormann's entrance.

Bormann's gaze wandered over the lab. The entire stock of a Belgian pharmaceutical company was housed in the Adlernest, brought by train across Europe. Long slate-topped tables covered with racks and glassware, test tubes, and other equipment filled the room, and the whirrings of centrifuges and the hiss of autoclaves filled the air with the sounds of exotic mechanical birds.

"How goes it, Ludwig?"

Stumpfegger almost dropped his pipette but recovered quickly.

"Martin? You startled me. I didn't know you were here. Is the Führer in the Berghof already?"

"He arrived an hour ago."

"And Eva?" asked Stumpfegger.

"A short while later," responded Bormann. "She's very upset and wants us to hurry. Can we?"

Stumpfegger put his equipment on the table and sighed. "We are closer every day. But the task is enormous. So many new techniques. Each step requires new inventions, almost a completely new technology. Even the new data from the camps helps only a little. She must be patient."

Bormann's hand wandered to a test tube.

"She is close to breaking, Ludwig. It is an enormous strain for her. And for him."

"I know, Martin. For the last three years I have thought of nothing else. I'll try and push the staff faster," said Stumpfegger.

"Good. If there's anything you need . . ."

"There's already a list on your desk," said Stumpfegger.

"I'll get to it right now," said Bormann, and he turned away as Stumpfegger returned to his work.

Bormann left the lab and went straight to his office. Seated at his desk, he cleared up a stack of reports and correspondence. One troubled him greatly, and he reread it three times. Frowning, he pressed a button on his desk and began to write out orders. A few minutes later there was a knock on the door.

"Enter," he called.

SS Captain Heinz Stangl entered the room and stood at attention. Stangl, twenty-one, with his blond hair and fine features, looked sixteen. His looks were deceiving, as many had discovered. Stangl killed with a pleasure that was almost sexual in its intensity.

He had found Stangl in a unit assigned to the Warsaw Ghetto. His favored pastime was to line up men in a row and see how many he could kill with a single bullet from his luger. Bormann had watched him at it all afternoon. Stangl had been completely undisciplined, but Bormann had changed that. He handed the letter to Stangl who read it quickly.

"Who is this Johann Smith?" he asked.

"It is of no importance to you. It's enough for you to know he serves our ends," said Bormann.

"He wants you to kidnap his brother and his wife?"

"His brother is becoming unreliable and may talk of things that must remain secret. If he talks, Smith and others will be shot as traitors. We cannot allow that."

"But to kidnap them and hide them until we win the war—"

"Is absurd," finished Bormann. "Smith does not have the stomach for what has to be done. But you do, don't you?"

"Yes, Herr Reichsleiter," said Stangl, smiling.

"A sub will be waiting for you at the pens at Bremerhaven. You will be taken to South Africa. A man named Pieter Van Dyne will meet you there. I will arrange it all by the time you arrive. Kill them. No one in authority must suspect anything, but Smith must know that it was done by us. Do you understand?"

"The first part but not the second. Why must he know?"

"He will hate us, but he will fear us. And that fear will bind him more deeply to us. The same with Van Dyne. Now do you see?"

"Yes, Herr Reichsleiter."

"Then go."

Stangl left the office, and Bormann, happy in his work, began to write another report.

The submarine surfaced off the coast of South Africa at ten o'clock at night ten days later. There was no moon and the seas were calm. Stangl, in black sweater and pants, carrying a pack on his back, put his booted feet onto the rungs of the ladder and climbed down to the foredeck. Two sailors helped him into the rubber dinghy, and he quickly paddled to the shore a half mile away. Looking over his shoulder, he could see the sub begin its plunge back beneath the surface where it would wait until he returned.

Coming to rest on shore, Stangl deflated the raft and buried it, using the oar as a shovel. Ten minutes later he was crouched in the tall grass that lined the highway. Shortly, a car slowed down, blinked its lights three times in succession, then paused and blinked them twice again.

He ran to the car. Pieter Van Dyne, the driver, was dressed in a bush jacket, jodhpurs, and high leather boots. On the way to Johannesburg, he briefed Stangl on the layout of Johann Smith's home. Stangl listened intently and then repeated the details almost word for word. Van Dyne nodded when he was done.

"How are you going to transport Hans and his wife out of Johannesburg?" he asked.

"It is arranged," said Stangl. "Do not worry."

"I'm sure it is, but..." protested Van Dyne, but he was cut off by Stangl.

"Please take me straight to the home of Smith. Wake me when we arrive," and he promptly went to sleep.

Van Dyne stifled further questions and continued to drive.

Hours later, he tapped Stangl who woke, totally alert. It had been daylight for some time. "We're in Jo'burg. Five minutes to the house."

"Drive near the woods at the rear of the house and let me off. Then wait. I wish to reconnoiter the property."

"Fine," said Van Dyne.

Soon Stangl stood in the woods behind Smith's mansion. On the back lawn a man and a woman were playing with a small infant. They were alone. The descriptions of Hans Smith and his wife Greta clicked onto the screen of his mind. He removed a silenced English Webley .38 caliber pistol from the pack. He was totally at peace.

Hans and Greta were engrossed in their daughter Lisa's pleasure with the butterfly they had given her. Only six months of age, she was too young for words, but her joy was evident in her excited cooings.

A shadow covering the group caused Greta to look up into the sky. The last thing she saw was Stangl's face, outlined by the sun's radiance, before the bullet caught her full in the chest, hurling her backward onto the grass. She was dead before her head hit the ground.

Hans, taking in his wife's body and Stangl's presence faster than Stangl had anticipated, leaped at him from the ground. But he had forgotten about his daughter and, trying not to step on her fragile body, tripped and fell headlong into the grass. It was all Stangl needed. Reversing the gun in his hand, he clubbed Hans once on the side of his head, and he lay still.

Putting the body on its back, Stangl took the gun, wiped it clean, and put it into Hans's hand. He pressed each finger down hard onto its surface, then lifted Hans to a standing position by holding the body close to his own. He freed one of his arms by taking most of the weight on his chest, took the gun in Hans's hand, and placed its muzzle against his head.

When he pulled the trigger, very little of the brains and blood got on him. Stangl liked to be neat. He let the body fall as it would in the grass.

Frowning, he looked at the baby. He did not have instructions. He never acted without instructions. Bormann had taught him that to do so would mean his death. She was so little and defenseless he wanted to crush her. But he had no orders. He left the child playing happily on the grass with her butterfly, unaware that she was now an orphan.

The specially made silencer for the octagonal barrel of the Webley came off easily.

For a final time Stangl reached into his pack, replaced the silencer, and took out a book. He placed the book on the grass by the body and made his way back to the car. He had been gone for only ten minutes.

"All finished?" asked Van Dyne as he reentered the car.

"Yes. Drive me back to the coast."

"The coast? But aren't your orders to . . ." The light began to dawn on Van Dyne at last. Horrified, he shrieked at Stangl.

"You bastard! You filthy rotten bastard! There was never to be a kidnapping at all. You set us all up. They're dead, aren't they?"

Stangl said nothing.

"Aren't they?" yelled Van Dyne.

"Yes, they are dead. Would you rather he had exposed you? Then you would be dead. You are a traitor, you know."

"Bastards!" was all Van Dyne could say. Finally, he started the car for the drive back. It was a long, silent ride.

Johann Smith got the call from one of the servants at eleven o'clock that morning in his offices at Parliament. He almost toppled his secretary rushing to get to his car and then almost ran over several others in his race home. His usually clear face was frozen and pale, and tears marred his vision. He had thrown his chauffeur out of the car and had driven it himself.

At eleven-thirty he was standing on his back lawn over the dead bodies of his brother and sister-in-law. In one arm he cradled Lisa, who, having lost her butterfly, was content to play with the flower in his lapel.

In his other hand he held a book. He knew it was not one that his brother would have read. He therefore knew what had happened. He also knew that he alone had set in motion the terrible chain of events that led to what lay before him.

The flower had fallen off his lapel, and Lisa had begun to cry. Her wailing echoed off the distant house and came back to him to mingle with the sounds of his own tears. He held her tightly.

"Don't cry, my little one. I will take care of you. Always. You are all I have left, and I am all that's left for you. I am your father now."

Slowly, he turned away from the bodies and walked toward the house. Inside, he ordered a servant to call the police. His position would assure only a cursory investigation. Suicide would be the verdict. No one but he would know that it was murder. No one but he, the killer, and Martin Bormann.

The sirens began to wail in the distance. Smith paused by a fireplace in which a roaring fire was burning. He tossed the book into it and watched as it caught fire and flames began to curl and blacken the edges. He continued to watch as *Mein Kampf* by Adolf Hitler was reduced to ashes.

Book One

One

Mississippi

Having been a city person all his life, Ben Davidson was totally unprepared for the rural South. It seemed almost inconceivable to him that the sophistication of New York City could exist in the same country as the backwoods of Mississippi, and even more difficult to think of each small town he passed as more than a neighborhood crowd.

The drive down from New York had been a leisurely one, and Ben was glad he had decided not to fly. Each state seemed to have only a slightly different character than the one before as he drove through it, but the cumulative effect as he reached Mississippi was huge. The large shopping malls and frequent fast-food places had given way to lone general stores and one-pump gas stations, and the songs on the radio shifted from rock to gospel and country & western. Ben recognized his feelings as those of a stranger visiting another country, and he tried to lose himself in the miles of back roads.

It sure as hell was different than the South Bronx, Ben thought as he drove, where the dozens of different ethnic groups had fought for every inch of their own turf, where a young white boy learned to be fast with his fists and his mouth to survive. Samuel Davidson, Ben's father, had been a doctor dedicated to serving the community of the poor and forgotten. Ben had loved to sit among the tools of his father's trade, the stethoscopes and syringes, bottles filled with different medicines, charts and diagrams on the walls—some in Spanish—and the old gray leather examining tables with the endless rolls of crackling paper.

It would have been a happy time for both Ben and his father but for Ben's mother Eleanor, a wealthy Connecticut girl who couldn't understand why Samuel insisted on "wast-

21

ing" himself on the urban dregs when they could have lived comfortably elsewhere. Her bitterness pervaded the apartment and all of Ben's childhood, and her harsh raving at both men caused Ben to leave home as soon as he possibly could. And now she was dead...

The blaring of a truck's horn brought Ben's attention back to the road. Slowly, he pried his hands from the wheel of the rental car where they clung white-knuckled and sweaty. Shaking them to relieve the cramping, he realized with some annoyance that he had driven miles past his intended exit on the highway. He began to breathe deeply, evenly, filling his lungs with fresh air—an old trick to relax himself, expunge the hurt and anger, and drive away old ghosts.

Ben ran his fingers through his thick brown hair and concentrated on relaxing his arms and legs. His lean, six-foot frame had become cramped in the car, and he flexed his back and shoulder muscles to relieve the cramping there. Reaching up to adjust the rearview mirror, he caught a glimpse of his face reflected in it. Large, heavy-lidded brown eyes stared back at him, their whites reddened with exhaustion and emotion. It had been only two days since his mother's funeral, but he felt no release, no grief, just hollowness. His father's funeral seven years earlier had overwhelmed him with sorrow, but he felt nothing now.

He forced himself to think about his latest project, the reason he had come to Mississippi. His literary agent and friend of many years, Bill Gottbaum, had suggested it. When they returned to his office after the funeral, he had spoken firmly.

"Look, Ben, I know your mother's death has been upsetting for you. The best way to deal with it is to go right back to work."

"I don't know, Bill," Ben replied, looking at Gottbaum with affection. At sixty, he looked seventy, with stooped round shoulders, heavily lined face, and suit that, although expensive, seemed two sizes too large for him. His eyes, however, were bright with energy and intelligence, and the corners of his mouth were perpetually turned upward, giving him the look of an aging leprechaun. Ben went on, "I appreciate everything you've done for me, but I'm not even sure if writing's what I still want to do."

"Why the hell not?" Gottbaum demanded. "You've become

Jennifer Crusie

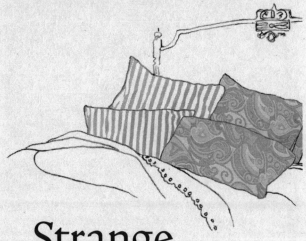

Strange Bedpersons

"Wonderfully fresh, funny, tender and outrageous...
Crusie is one of a kind" —Booklist

Published 17th September 2004

M385

International Bestselling Author

BARBARA DELINSKY

Threats and Promises

Someone to watch over her?

Published 15th October 2004

MIRA™

Susan Andersen

hot

& bothered

"Bright, smart, sexy,
thoroughly entertaining."
—Jayne Ann Krentz

Published 15th October 2004

an outstanding investigative journalist, and your work sells. *The New York Times* thinks you're the only one to do this particular piece. Think about it before you chuck your career, okay?"

Ben sat back in his chair and looked around Gottbaum's office. Reams of paper spilled out of every drawer in his large desk, piles of manuscripts supported piles of books that supported, in turn, more manuscripts. He closed his eyes, then looked at Gottbaum. "I'll think about it and call you tomorrow, I promise."

Ben had spent the night in his apartment thinking about the assignment. It was the subject of the article that finally decided him. The *Times* wanted an article on the Ku Klux Klan.

When Ben was ten, there was a group of boys who used to taunt him on his way to and from school. It was the leader of the boys, a big, obnoxious thirteen-year-old, who would steal his lunch money or throw his briefcase in the gutter. Other boys would stand and jeer, and for months the humiliation sent Ben home in tears.

In the end, he had to fight. He mentally rehearsed it for weeks, and each time, he emerged unscathed and victorious.

After the fight, Dr. Davidson set Ben's broken ribs and assured him that the missing teeth were not permanently lost.

"How did it feel to fight back?" his father had asked.

Ben's lopsided expression grew thoughtful. "Almost as good as winning would have," he had replied.

He looked forward to writing the article on the Klan. When he wrote, he won more often.

He had an appointment in Natchez in the morning with Nathan Armstrong, the Grand Dragon of the Klan. "But," he thought, "I'll never make it if I don't find the damn road." He was heading south on Interstate 55 and had already missed the turnoff for 84 to Natchez. Turning off the interstate, he began to backtrack northwest, hoping to intersect with 84. It wasn't until several hours later that he had to admit he was totally lost. It had been dark for some time, and all roads looked alike and took him further into the backwoods.

After a few miles, he came upon a collection of three dwellings that only in the loosest of terms could be called houses. With roofs made of corrugated tin sheets and walls of ill-fitting, overlapping plywood, these homes compared unfavorably with caves. Bright moonlight cast strange shadows across the yards strewn with broken glass and the wrecks of old cars.

As he turned off the car's engine and stepping outside, the silence hit Ben like a hammer blow. City people are never used to the silence of the woods. He hadn't expected it. Neither was he prepared for the gut-wrenching scream that emerged suddenly from the nearest cabin, nor for the door bursting open and a large black man coming toward him with a shotgun held in his huge hands, like a vision of death and destruction.

Ben came to a dead halt, the threat of the shotgun stopping him as effectively as the edge of a cliff. He carefully held both hands in full view of the man whose gaze never moved from a spot about twelve inches above Ben's abdomen.

"What you want here?"

"Look, I mean you no harm. I'm on my way to Natchez, and I got lost. I'm looking for Route 84. Can you help me?"

The man's response was cut off by another piercing scream from inside the shack. The scream seemed to turn the man's attention back inside, and for a moment, he was staring through Ben and not at him. The first movement from Ben, however, and his attention returned in full force, though Ben could see the strain clearly written on the man's face. "This here's Waylin," he said.

"Is there something wrong? Is someone hurt? Perhaps I can help."

"You a doctor?" the man asked.

"No. But I have had some medical training. Is someone sick?"

The man seemed to hesitate, as if trying to decide something. The gun wavered for an instant and then returned to a steady position.

"We don't need yoah help. Back in yoah car and git."

Ben began to retreat to his car. The shotgun could blow away half his body even at this distance. He moved as slowly and carefully as he could.

Then came a scream so agonizing that Ben thought the man might pull the trigger simply from clenching against the onslaught of that pain. He half expected to die if the scream didn't stop. He was almost at the car. Three more feet.

"Hold up, mister," said the man. "You say you got doctor trainin'?"

This time the man's eyes held a different light. Ben noted the change in the man's attitude, and the use of "mister" for the first time.

"I've had two years of medical school and a lot of experience in Vietnam. If someone's sick and it's not too serious, maybe I can help till we can get him to a hospital. I'm willing to try, but you have to point that gun the other way. Please."

The man seemed to stiffen at the mention of the gun, and Ben wondered if he had spoken too much or too soon. Then the screaming began again.

"Shit!" said the man, clearly in conflict. Then, "Shit," again. Slowly the gun began to lower until it was pointed at the ground. Ben began to breathe again as the man broke open the shotgun and rested it on his shoulder.

"My name's Wilcox. James Wilcox. I'm sorry 'bout the gun, but we don't get many white folk round here. If ya'd help us, I'd be mighty thankful."

"My name's Ben Davidson. What's the problem?"

In response, Wilcox turned toward the shack and entered, leaving the door open. Recognizing that now he was free to run to his car and leave, Ben still turned resolutely toward the shack after wondering if he was foolish not to run like mad.

The source of the screams became evident as Ben entered the shack. Lying on the bed was a young black woman who, to Ben's anxious eyes, looked hugely pregnant. He could see that the woman was in labor and the baby due any moment.

"You done birthin' before?" Wilcox asked.

Ben moved to the woman's side. Her face was glistening with sweat and her body taut with the spasms of muscular contractions. After checking her pulse and repositioning her on the bed, Ben turned to her husband.

"Do you have a family doctor?"

"We been havin' Dr. Croft. He's a white man's doctor. Like you."

Ben smiled, "I'm sorry, but I told you I'm not a real doctor. Half maybe. Plus you could throw in a few deliveries in the rice paddies in Nam. Where is Dr. Croft?"

Wilcox gestured toward the road. "I sent my cousin Rawlings to fetch him." He scratched his head. "Don't know what's keepin' him. He's been awful good to us. Don't charge us nothin'. Gives us all kinds a shots and stuff for Annie here. Says he's got the callin'."

As Ben gave orders for the preparation for the delivery, he began to build up a mental picture of Dr. Croft. Probably someone his father would have liked—a kind man, who did the work others would not stoop to do. A good man. He hoped he would be able to meet him.

James fetched a pot of water and was boiling the swaddling clothes, string, and the knife that Ben would use. Then he went to sit with his wife. Both seemed relieved to have Ben with them. Annie's eyes followed Ben around the room while she tightly gripped James's hand.

Ben smiled at her when their eyes met, and he went to sit by her.

"Now listen, Annie. My name's Ben, and I've delivered so many babies that yours is going to be as easy as falling off a log. Just hold tight to James as the contractions hit. You look like a strong lady, and that's the best kind. Now you both listen carefully, and I'll tell you what we're going to do." He hoped he sounded more confident than he felt.

As Ben explained the contractions, the timing, and the process they would use, he saw the anxiety in both James's and Annie's eyes begin to dissipate. Slowly, as he had seen his father do so many times, he wrapped them in a spell of soft words and charm, and let them draw on his strength for theirs.

Though it was chilly outside, the cabin began to heat up with the wood stove at full blast and the exertions of all three filling the air with sweaty exhalations. James was constantly mopping Annie's brow, and his breathing became as labored as his wife's. The contractions grew closer.

Annie screamed, "James, oh God, it hurts me so bad." James held her face in his huge hands.

They soon ceased to be separate people and became one single pulsating sweaty unit. The men became mere extensions, prodding, soothing attendants to the miracle occurring at Annie's center. A comradeship emerged, no less deep for the unlikeliness of the comrades.

James at the head, Annie in the middle, and Ben between

her outstretched legs, the unit writhed to a litany of pushes and cries.

"Push now. Now. Again. Breathe."

"Good girl. That's my girl."

"Oh God, oh God, oh God!"

"Push again, harder, keep it up. Breathe."

"My God, my God, my God!"

"Now, Annie. Now. Push!"

But at the instant of birth, as a bloody child fell into his outstretched arms, Ben knew that something was horribly, inexplicably wrong. Shielding the screaming infant from his parents' view, Ben cleaned him as best he could, thinking it was an illusion. But as the blood came away, he was forced to accept the harsh fact that he had just delivered to Mr. and Mrs. James Wilcox an impossibly white-skinned, blue-eyed baby boy.

Ben's mind was a mass of dark confusion as he finished his tasks. Slowly, after covering his wife, James rose and reached out to Ben for his son. In his eyes was a gratitude that made Ben wince from the shock he was about to deliver. But he had no choice. He handed the screaming infant to its father.

The sounds of joy that had begun emerging from the throat of James Wilcox turned into a long-strangled cry of rage, confusion, and betrayal. Annie looked up terrified. Before Ben could act, James ran to his wife and thrust the infant into her face.

"What is this?" he screamed at her. "Who you been sleepin' with? He's white. Damn yoah black ass, he's white!" He sank down to his knees, still clutching the child, sobbing.

"Easy, James," Ben cautioned. "Maybe there's an explanation."

"Easy? For what? For that whore?" Annie, almost too weak to speak, began to cry with painful sobs.

"Never, James. There's never been no one but you. I swear, James. I swear to God. Never. No one but you. Never. I swear it. Please. You gotta believe me."

"Then how, bitch?" James yelled, his hands clenching convulsively so that Ben began to fear he might hurt the baby, so tiny in James's hands.

"How do you explain this? Shit!"

The rage in the room grew so strong that Ben knew it must soon explode. He started to reach for the infant but was unprepared for James's huge fist smashing into the side of his head. He crashed heavily onto the floor and rolled under a table.

From then on it was like being underwater. Every motion seemed slowed, far away. His arms and legs wouldn't move. His head lolled in the dirt. Annie's screams sounded as far away as those remembered from a dream.

In agonizing slowness he watched an insane James grab the baby from the blanket and take its legs in his fist.

Before consciousness left him, he heard Annie's pleading moans and saw her clutch at James, fall, and rise again to stop him. With his last seconds of vision, until his mind crossed into the void waiting to protect him from the shock of what he knew was to come, he saw James swing the infant over his head and bring the child's head down on the table like a hammer in the hands of a crazed, maniacal carpenter; and as the blood washed over his eyes, it was only slightly ahead of the darkness that took him completely.

Two

Ben awoke slowly, hardly feeling the hands under his shoulders and legs which lifted him to a sitting position. Still groggy from the blow to his head, he felt as if he were emerging from a dream and remembered only fragments of it.

A sharp acrid odor brought him to full consciousness, and with it, the sequence of events reordered itself into clear, horrible memory. He struggled to stand but a distant voice spoke.

"Easy now. You've had a nasty head injury. Slowly. Can you see anything?"

Ben struggled to open his eyes and, when he did, had to struggle again to clear them and establish focus. As he tried to see, the vague outline of a man leaning in front of him began to form. Ben nodded.

"That's good. Let your eyes focus slowly. You're in for an enormous headache as it is."

Details began to become more distinct as time passed. At first, Ben could only be sure it was a man in front of him, but this impression was more strongly conveyed by his voice than by visual detail. Slowly, he began to see that the man was sixty or seventy years old at least, with thinning white hair and a benign, wizened face. He fainted again.

The sharp odor of smelling salts awakened him once more. This time his head cleared more quickly. Ben looked at the face in front of him.

"Who are you?" he asked in a voice not much louder than a croak.

"I'm Dr. Eugene Croft. Can you sit up now?"

Ben nodded and was helped to a sitting position on the bed. He realized that there were other people in the room, though he could not clear his vision enough or move his head to see them.

"What happened?" he asked.

"Yes, indeed, what happened? We were hoping you could tell us."

Ben felt better now. His head was clearing rapidly. He remembered. Moving his head was an effort, but as he did so, he glanced into the corner of the room. What was left of the infant, battered and smashed, was lying there. Ben's stomach heaved. He rushed to the door and made it outside to be suddenly, violently sick onto the dirt in front of the cabin.

Two men helped him to his feet and helped him back inside. He sat down weakly on the bed. Dr. Croft had quickly covered the infant. Neither James nor Annie Wilcox were to be seen.

"My name's Ben Davidson. I'm a writer from New York. I'm here to do a story..." Slowly, hesitantly, he described the night's events, from his getting lost to the awful rage of James Wilcox that had almost crushed in his head along with that of the baby's.

"Where are they?" Ben asked.

"Annie has been taken to my clinic. She's in shock and has lost a great deal of blood. Evidently, he hit her as well. We are doing our best for her. I am only sorry I didn't get here sooner. I might have prevented..."

Ben shook his head numbly. "Why did he do it? How could it have happened?"

Croft laid a hand on his shoulder. "Surely you have heard of this before. A light-skinned child that grows up to 'pass' as white. Many of these people consider it a blessing. What you did was quite noble. I'm sorry to see you repaid so poorly."

Ben felt his sleeve being pulled up and a sting in his left arm.

"Sleep now. Rest. In the morning we shall discuss it. You will be my guest."

Ben began to protest, but Croft stopped him firmly.

"Nonsense. I will not hear of it. Please put Mr. Davidson in our car," he instructed his assistants.

And then it was too late for anything except falling down the long dark tunnel where there is no pain and no memory.

Three

Successive shocks numb. As such, all Ben felt when he awoke in a strange bed in a strange house was mild interest in the fact that his pajamas were much too large and that their design was atrocious. Then he realized that he never wore pajamas regardless of their design, and suddenly other memories began to filter back into his battered head.

He reached up to scratch an itch on his scalp and discovered that someone had bandaged his head. Moving from the bed to look in the mirror over an old oaken dresser, he saw a face reflected back that would have made him rich as a Grade B horror-movie star—eyes red and bloodshot, chin unshaven, cheeks sunken, and large bags beneath his eyes.

Someone had placed his suitcases by the bed with a note pinned to the largest. It read:

> Dear Mr. Davidson,
> If you are feeling better, then by all means dress and join us for breakfast. Your clothing is being cleaned. Please do not remove your bandage as you have a nasty bruise which I will look at later.
> Regards,
> E. Croft

"Wonderful," Ben said aloud. "Who the hell is E. Croft?" Deciding, however, that it was better to unravel this mystery when cleaned and dressed, he took his shaving kit from his bags, showered, using a shower cap someone had conveniently provided, shaved, and felt immensely better.

The long, hot shower also had the effect of bringing the previous night and E. Croft back into clearer focus. But it was like the events had occurred in a movie or a book. He could remember the events but not his own part in them. It all seemed unreal.

Ben left the bedroom and headed downstairs. He wandered through a hallway into a big, old-fashioned kitchen, complete with fireplace and brick baking oven. The stove was an old gas model, though the refrigerator was large and modern. A large pine table was littered with baking implements, and the smell of hot bread filled the room. Looking out the window, Ben saw a well-kept garden with tomato plants on stakes and other vegetables he was unable to recognize.

The living room also had a fireplace and was furnished with large colonial, overstuffed pieces. It was a comfortable room. There were few knickknacks but many books. Ben tentatively decided there was no Mrs. Croft.

At the end of the hallway was a door marked "Laboratory—Private." Unable to pass it by without looking inside, Ben pushed the door open while trying to appear casual about the intrusion.

It was as well stocked a lab as he had ever seen. Racks of test tubes, centrifuges, autoclaves, beakers, and such were arrayed in vast profusion. Seated at a desk in one corner, making notes of some kind, was Dr. Croft, too absorbed in his writing to notice Ben.

"Good morning, Dr. Croft."

Croft's head shot up and seeing Ben, he rose. "Mr. Davidson?"

Ben smiled. "I woke up and felt much better. I didn't see anybody in the house so I wandered in here." Ben gestured around. "Quite a setup for a country doctor."

Croft smiled. He spoke easily. "Come, let me get you some breakfast. You must be famished."

"As a matter of fact, I feel terrific. Getting smashed in the head must agree with me."

"Come here. I want to check your pulse and temperature, and then take a look at your skull."

Ben allowed himself to be led into an adjoining cubicle that served as an examination room. Croft closed the door to the lab and checked Ben's vital signs. Then he replaced the head wrapping with a smaller bandage.

"No wonder you feel so good, Mr. Davidson. Your pulse is high; you have a bit of a fever. Technically, you're still in a state of shock. You are like a light bulb that burns most brightly before it burns out. You need rest and nourishment. Come, we'll eat."

"I want to tell you how grateful I am for your kind hospitality, Doctor. I've been a great imposition."

"Don't worry about that. It's the least I can do for a man who was so unselfish as to help one of my patients. From what I could tell, you did an admirable job. You cannot hold yourself responsible for the actions of a maniac."

Ben was uncomfortable with that description of James Wilcox. He could not accept that the same man who had comforted his wife for all those brutal hours was a maniac. Yet neither could he accept what that man had done. It was a paradox, and he said as much.

Croft settled back in his chair. He removed a pipe that he filled, lit, tamped, and relit until a gray-white cloud of smoke curled around his head.

"I have worked in this section of the country for many years. I have seen things which would shock and appall any sane man. What happened last night has happened before; another mouth to feed that cannot be fed and therefore must be destroyed; the results of incestuous unions between fathers and daughters; mothers giving birth to children whose only connection to the father is the money he received for the prostitution of the woman. I've seen it all before."

"It seems so hard to believe. I mean, I saw the look in her eyes when she saw the baby. She seemed as shocked as he was," said Ben. "Was there anything in the prenatal care that might offer an explanation?"

Croft's benign face clouded over. "Please remember, Mr. Davidson, that you are my guest. I find that insinuation most offensive."

"I apologize, Doctor. Please forgive the ramblings of a writer with limited knowledge of the subject. You've been wonderful to me, and I thank you."

The speech had the desired effect. Croft's face softened, and he retook his seat at the table, still puffing on his pipe.

"Apology accepted," Croft said.

"Thank you," Ben replied. "Is it possible for me to see Annie to say good-bye? I'll be leaving shortly." Although Croft looked as if he were going to deny permission, he agreed and beckoned for Ben to follow him to the lab.

"She is still in shock, Mr. Davidson, and very weak. Also, she has already been interviewed this morning by the police, to whom I had to report the incident. I left you out of it, or it might have taken days for you to be free to leave."

"Thank you, Dr. Croft. I appreciate your concern."

"Just don't agitate her," he cautioned.

Annie was lying in a bed in one of the other examination rooms near where Croft had looked at Ben's head wound a short while earlier. Her breathing was shallow, and beads of perspiration dotted her forehead and upper lip. Croft excused himself.

"I have work to do in the lab. You may have five minutes with her, no more. I will be right outside the door. If she has trouble breathing, call me immediately."

"I will, Doctor."

Croft left and closed the door behind him. Ben pulled a chair closer to the bed and sat down.

"Annie?" No response. He tried again. "Annie? It's me, Ben. I was with you last night. Can you hear me?"

He was rewarded by the flutter of her eyelids and then with her eyes opening. She could see him but made no move to talk.

"Do you remember me, Annie?" Ben asked. She nodded an affirmation.

"Good. Are you strong enough to answer some questions for me?" Again the nod and then, in a voice that came from far away inside her, "Where's James?" Tears formed in her eyes.

"I don't know, Annie. Dr. Croft said he ran away. I can't remember anything after he hit me."

Annie looked frightened. "James's strong."

"Yes, he is. How do you feel?"

She smiled weakly. "Not sick no moah. Carryin', I was always sick."

"Didn't the doctor give you something for that?"

Annie nodded. "Made me feel sicker."

Ben reached out for her hand. "You'll be fine now. A few days of rest, and you'll be fine. You're strong, Annie. You can have more children."

The mention of children was a blunder Ben instantly regretted. Annie's face contorted with pain. She shook her head violently.

"No moah babies. Not without James. No moah." She began to cry. Ben squeezed her hand.

"I'm sorry, Annie, but I've got to ask you one question, and you've got to tell me the truth. It's very important, Annie, and I promise you that whatever the answer, no one will ever know or hurt you. But you've got to tell me the truth, okay?"

Annie was silent for a moment, but eventually nodded agreement. Her eyes were wide and frightened. Ben took a deep breath.

"Annie, in the last year, did you ever make love with a white man?"

Annie's eyes never clouded nor did she avert her gaze. She simply said, "No, Ben. Never at all." And the truth in her voice and in her eyes, for Ben, was unquestionable and undeniable.

"Thank you, Annie. I have to go now. I came to say good-bye."

Annie's eyes had closed, and for a second Ben thought she was asleep. He turned to go.

"Ben?" It was a whisper.

"Yes, Annie?"

"Bye."

"Good-bye, Annie."

Ben turned and left the room. Dr. Croft was seated at his desk. He looked up as Ben entered.

"Is she all right?" he asked.

"She's sleeping. Thank you for letting me see her."

"Come, I'll take you to your room. You may rest before leaving."

"I appreciate your help, Doctor."

"It's nothing. I will leave directions and a map in your car. I am leaving on my rounds shortly."

He offered his hand to Ben.

"Good-bye, Mr. Davidson."

"Good-bye, Dr. Croft."

Later, as Ben packed his things in the upstairs bedroom, he

reviewed the conversation. It was probably true, he thought, that he had not really seen the blue eyes. Everything about the night grew hazier as time went by. At this point, he could visualize the baby with blue, brown, or even red eyes if he tried hard enough.

Engrossed in thought, he failed to hear the door open behind him until the click of its reclosing caused him to turn. Standing with her back to the door was one of the most striking women Ben had ever seen. Her long brown hair cascaded past her shoulders in large soft curls onto her simple button-front sleeveless dress. The dress stretched tautly over upturned breasts and flaring hips, and the legs that emerged beneath it were long and beautifully tapered. High cheekbones set off perfectly her large brown eyes, and her white teeth were surrounded by rich red lips that were moist and full. But by far the most striking feature was her skin. The color of deep amber, it was flawless and unmarked by even the slightest blemish. In the warm afternoon light it seemed almost translucent, and Ben found himself staring into its depths. She appeared to be no older than her late teens, yet she returned his stare, and her hips seemed to jut out enticingly.

"Who are you?" Ben asked. He was still holding a folded shirt destined for the suitcase. A smile crossed her face.

"What's your name?" Ben asked again, disturbed somehow by the smile.

"Heidi," she replied. "What's yours?" The smile was covered as her hands came up to her mouth to stifle a giggle.

"What are you doing here, Heidi? Did Dr. Croft send you?"

Now the smile changed into a deep frown. Her eyes looked down at the floor, and she began to pout. Ben grew more uncomfortable.

"Nope," she said. "He didn't send me. Everybody's gone, and I had nobody to play with. So I came to visit you. Are you a nice man?"

The coquettish smile had returned, and her eyes were once more focused on Ben. She moved away from the door until she was standing closer to him. One hand toyed with the buttons on her dress. The first two came undone, exposing the inside curves of her breasts. He moved past her and

35

opened the door to the room. Walking out to the landing he called, "Dr. Croft? Are you still home? Dr. Croft?"

"I told you he's gone," she said petulantly. "They're all gone. All the men. Everybody but you."

He turned back toward her. Another button had opened, and as she swung back into the room, the redness of her nipples was open to his view. Her hand moved inside the dress and stroked them until hard points poked at the thin fabric of the dress. He followed her back inside.

Ben tried to concentrate. "What do you mean 'everybody's gone'? I saw only Dr. Croft in the house. Are there others?" he asked her.

She nodded. "Lotsa men here. Mostly at night. Doctor calls them ordel . . . odal . . ." She looked at Ben helplessly, confusion on her face.

"Orderlies?" Ben asked. He was rewarded with a grateful smile.

"That's it. That's what they are. We have lotsa fun. They're smart, like you. But not so handsome."

She sat down on the bed and mashed his clothing into a disordered pile. Like a child she began to bounce on the bed, using her feet to push off the floor. Ben returned her smile of pleasure, sadly. He knew what it was now that made him uncomfortable. The girl was proof of nature's talent for compensation. Like the blind man whose hearing was acute or the small man whose strength was enormous, the girl before him had beauty beyond belief to compensate for the fact that in her mind she would forever be a child. She had stopped bouncing, and her hand had opened the last of the buttons. The dress opened like the petals of a flower as she spread her legs open wide. She wore nothing underneath.

"Heidi, please . . ." Ben protested, but her eyes were closed, and her tongue flicked over her lips as her hand roamed freely over her body.

As her left hand stroked her shoulder and neck, and then slowly moved to caress her breasts, her breathing became more and more ragged. Her right hand played over the soft tautness of her belly until it dropped lower to caress the smoothness of her thighs. Her back began to arch as she played lovingly along the inside of her thighs, and Ben could see moisture begin to glisten amidst the soft brown hair between her legs. Finally, her index finger found its mark as low crooning moans began to emerge from her lips.

Suddenly her eyes opened, and she looked up at Ben. Her hands left her body, and she stretched out her arms toward him.

"Please," she moaned. "Do me. Please, I need it."

Ben shook his head.

"I'm sorry, Heidi. I can't."

Her fingers returned to the moistness as she spread her legs wider apart.

"Please. I'll do anything you want to. Please . . ."

Again, Ben shook his head sadly.

"I can't."

He turned away as her eyes closed again, and her fingers flew faster and faster. Loud moans followed him onto the landing outside the room until finally one long, protracted scream filled the empty house.

Ben's hands gripped the staircase railing tightly. He had not been unaffected by Heidi's sexuality. But for all her womanly attributes, it would have been like making love to a child. The sounds had stopped now. He wondered what her role was in the house and who the orderlies were that she had talked about.

Ben turned at a sound behind him. Heidi was standing there, her dress buttoned up once again. Her face was a study in childish innocence as she walked past him and went down the stairs. Somewhere in the house he heard a door slam shut. He returned to his room.

Ben finished packing and brought his suitcase down to his car, which was waiting outside. The keys were in the ignition. Some field hands were working in the rows of plants adjacent to the house, and Ben had his first real look at Croft's residence.

It looked like any other three-story house of its kind. Painted white with green shutters, it was straight out of American Gothic. On the main floor a large, windowless structure had been added, which Ben assumed to be the lab and the examination rooms.

It was a cloudless, beautiful day, and in the bright sunlight Ben's curiosity began to seem morbid. What use was it to pursue this whole thing further? He had helped out some poor folks, gotten beaten up for his trouble, and spent the night in the local doctor's house. Nothing more. He stretched out his six-foot frame and decided that his next stop would be Natchez. He got into his car and drove off.

Ben kept telling himself this all the way down the road. He almost succeeded in convincing himself. Then, with a smile that was half self-mockery, he turned the car around and stopped.

The problem was that he had no idea where he was, or where the Wilcoxes lived. He smacked his head with the palm of his hand to jar his memory and almost passed out. When his vision cleared, he realized self-abuse was not going to do any good at all. Rating? Waiting? Waylin! That was it. He searched the map but could not find it.

Ben began to drive back in the direction he believed Waylin might be. In less than an hour he was totally lost. The afternoon shadows began to lengthen, and Ben had almost decided to give up when he passed a sign which read "Waylin," and underneath, "Unincorporated Village, Population: 216." He had found it.

He experienced a strong sense of déjà vu when he stopped his car in front of the shack. So much had happened in so short a time.

Ben paused at the front door. If James were inside, he wanted to be ready. There was no telling what he might do, and Ben's head still ached from last night's blow. He kicked the door open and went in low and fast. It was unnecessary. The shack was deserted. He stood up and looked around in bewilderment.

Not only was James gone but so too was every piece of furniture, every personal item, every pot and pan. Even the bed and stove were missing. As if some fanatical maid had scrubbed everything out of existence, there was nothing left to indicate that anyone had lived here, merely four walls and a ceiling. There was even a hole in the roof where the stove pipe had been.

Ben tried to remember where the table had been. He located a spot from memory. Even scratching the dirt floor he failed to find any trace of the blood that must have fallen there. Only dirt caked under his fingernails.

Ben ran to the other shacks but found an identical situation. Four walls and a ceiling. Nothing else. He wandered back to his car. None of this made any sense to him.

But then again, Ben thought, neither did a white baby with blue eyes born to James and Annie Wilcox. Ben got in his car and drove away, a direction beginning to emerge from his confusion.

He never saw the sedan parked a few hundred yards away nor heard the man inside call on the car phone to Dr. Croft to report Ben's visit. Nor did he hear Croft's terse command to follow Ben.

Dr. Croft was indeed quite busy, but not with his rounds. He had not yet left the house. Before him, on an operating table, lay the body of Annie Wilcox, whom Croft was patiently, methodically, dissecting.

Had Ben opened the doors to the other rooms, he also would have seen James Wilcox, sedated and restrained on another identical operating table. The sedation had been necessary after James broke one of the straps to get to his wife when he saw what Croft was about to do. Now he lay, head lolling, only a few feet away.

Croft was smiling as he reached through an incision to the ovaries and removed them from the body. "Perhaps," he thought, "she may not be a total waste at that."

Four

Copenhagen

The entrance to Tivoli Gardens glowed with light from the thousand naked bulbs which formed a lofty arch over it. It was unlikely that any passerby could fail to turn his or her head and not peer past the gateway into the magic land that beckoned within. A few long-haired youths who could not afford the price of admission loitered near the ticket booth, frustrated that magic was not without price.

Ivan Koenig was surprised to see Walter Hauptman buy a ticket and enter the park. It seemed out of character to

Koenig that Hauptman, the owner of South Africa's Raelord Mine, the second largest producer of diamonds in the country, would decide to enter this amusement park, or any amusement park, for that matter.

Koenig didn't mind. Tivoli might be a welcome diversion in his boring, arduous task. He hoped Hauptman would decide to eat something. His feet hurt, and he was hungry. As he had all day, Hauptman ignored Koenig's following him. Stiffly Hauptman strode past the booths and rides, carrying an attaché case. He didn't even appear to notice the full-breasted Danish girls who seemed as numerous as the flowers bedecking the walkways and cafés. Koenig sighed and trudged after him. Happy screams floated down from the giant roller coaster.

Many of the men he had followed had been rather nice about the whole thing. It was a simple security precaution, after all. The lack of such security, in this age of international terrorism and kidnappings, would have been conspicuous and careless beyond belief. The owner of a diamond mine would be a prize for any of a dozen groups of terrorists who needed money to carry out their threats.

Koenig shifted the holster under his armpit; it was causing an irritation that made him itch when he sweated. He sighed again but, thinking of the pension that awaited him in six months, continued his rapid walking. On his last assignment he had been taken to dinners by the man he followed, which enabled him to eat in places he could never afford and even pad his expense account when he palmed the dinner check. No such luck here, though. "Stuck-up son of a bitch," he swore to himself.

Koenig knew well that his was a posting given to agents who were old, used-up, or has-beens. In Koenig's case, he was simply too old for more active field work. He was proud of his past and looked forward to retirement, which he accepted with the grace of one who knows that it is no crime to give way to those younger and stronger, and folly not to. He had done his part; now came the peaceful rest.

Both of his sons were grown, married, and held good jobs. He and his wife saw them on alternate weekends, and the grandchildren were a constant source of delight. Of course, everybody in the family, with the exception of his wife, thought that he sold medical supplies. He often smiled at the thought of what his grandchildren would say if he could tell them the truth. They'd never believe "grampy" was a secret agent. Koenig smiled at the thought.

He passed the groups of men, with shirt sleeves rolled up, proving their prowess at the shooting galleries, and noted the crowds losing money at the games of "chance." The open air theater at the center of the park was occupied by only a few young people holding hands. The show would start soon, now that it was fully dark. Idly, Koenig noticed that Victor Borge was appearing. Perhaps he could catch the show later in the week. His wife would like that. Hauptman still walked quickly ahead.

Scratching his scalp through the little hair that grew there, and soothing his empty stomach through the layers of fat that had recently taken over a once well-developed body, Koenig watched Hauptman pause by two girls standing by a tree. They were obviously prostitutes on the Tivoli equivalent of a street corner. Hundreds of prostitutes roamed the park looking for customers among the thousands of sailors and merchant marines who sailed daily into Copenhagen, one of the world's busiest ports. Was this why Hauptman had entered the park? he wondered. But no, Hauptman strode away again.

Koenig was relieved. What use could so rich a man have for common street girls? He had simply to lift his hotel phone and call any of a dozen high-priced call girls. Such a move as he had thought Hauptman about to make could presage something more deviant. That could be trouble, and Koenig wanted none of that.

Hauptman came to rest once again, stopping near one of the many fine cafés in the park. This one had both indoor and outdoor tables. Pretty waitresses bustled about serving the patrons, and Koenig's throat began to ache for a glass of Tuborg beer. His wish seemed about to be granted as Hauptman entered the café. He took an outdoor table, in a corner, next to a low brick patio wall whose top was adorned with boxes of bright flowers. Koenig followed and took a table on the other side of the patio. He nodded to Hauptman when their eyes chanced to meet, but got no nod in return. Just as well, thought Koenig. If he smiled, I'd have to eat with the son of a bitch.

A waitress came and took his order and shortly a cool beer met his grateful throat. A few minutes later an excellent salmon steak with boiled potatoes graced his table, and he dived into both with relish. Keeping an unobtrusive eye on Hauptman, he noticed that the man had downed his third beer, and only a tray of finger-sized sandwiches had been placed in front of him.

Won't be long now, Koenig figured, and sure enough, a few seconds later, Hauptman stood up in obvious need of a men's room. He heard the quick question to the waitress and saw her point inside the cafe. Hauptman, case in hand, hurried inside while Koenig, smiling devilishly, made a silent wish that he wouldn't make it. He knew he should follow Hauptman, but his fish and his beer and his tired feet all persuaded him otherwise. Let the man have his privacy, he thought.

But Koenig, old and tired as he was, was one of that rare breed of men who does a job well simply for the pride taken in doing so. So when the little voice inside said, "Relax," it was met by the internal imperatives of a man who had had no tolerance for sloppiness of any kind in his work for more than thirty years. He could not know how much Hauptman counted on the laxness that all the other agents had shown nor how much the absence of that quality would cost him.

He rose from his table and followed Hauptman inside to the men's room. Koenig was quite surprised to see him exit a side door out into the night.

His first thought was that Hauptman was bolting on the check, but that thought was patently ridiculous. Hauptman could buy the whole café should he want to. Instincts trained by years of covert service caused him to slip quietly into the bushes just outside of the door through which Hauptman had left. Koenig could see him clearly illuminated by the strings of light bulbs that hung between the trees next to the walkway.

Hauptman walked quickly to three men who were apparently waiting for him. One of the men was tall, blond, and appeared to be in his late forties or early fifties. The lines around his eyes, forehead, and mouth belied his curiously boyish face. Koenig was too far away to see the color of his eyes, but in a man of so fair a coloring, he guessed they were blue. He was wearing a dark blue blazer with a yellow shirt and a lighter blue ascot at his neck. His slacks were light gray, and he was wearing cordovan-colored loafers on his feet. "Like he just walked off a yacht," was Koenig's impression.

The second man was much younger, midtwenties perhaps, with a face that had been on the receiving end of too many punches. Koenig recorded the man's misshapen nose, with its crooked central line that indicated it had been broken several times, as well as the scar on his cheek where the skin had grown white when it healed. Koenig had seen the type countless times in his career—the professional thug whose muscle was available for hire to anyone who could pay his price. Men like that could be found on any dock or in any professional gym in the world where business was conducted over the sound of breaking bones. He was holding an attaché case identical to the one Hauptman carried.

The third man was much older and shorter than his companions, and even his advanced age and well-cut suit failed to mask his massive frame and bullish face. From the way the other two seemed to hover around him, Koenig got the distinct impression that he was in charge. Koenig was still too far away to hear their conversation as he watched them. He mentally compared the faces of the three men to the endless list of agents stored in his memory. Although the leader of the group seemed somehow familiar, he could not place him; and he was sure he had never seen the other two.

Koenig was already moving to establish a closer position. He knew he was watching an exchange. The elements were as obvious as the identical cases. He tried to be soundless but was well aware of his stiffness and hoped he would be covered by the sounds emanating from the café. He got to within five feet of the men, covered by the screen of bushes in front of him. He was breathing heavily and tried to quiet himself. His armpit itched.

It was to the man in the blazer that he watched Hauptman hand his case. After making the exchange, the youngest promptly left the group and strode away. Koenig ignored his leaving and concentrated his attention on the remaining three. In his mind he called the blond man in the blue blazer "Ascot" and the short, bullish man "Suit."

"You are prompt as always," said Ascot.

"I've got to go quickly before that fool of a bodyguard suspects," said Hauptman.

"Please, open the case," asked Suit in a harsh, dry voice.

"Still? Do we have to go through this every time?" protested Hauptman.

"Open the case," ordered Suit, and Ascot complied.

Koenig watched as the case was opened. In the stark light from overhead what he saw was unmistakable. Like a hundred separate, sparkling rainbows, in the case lay a king's ransom in diamonds. Their brilliance reflected light onto the faces of the men, and Koenig could see them smile.

"Very good, Herr Hauptman," said Ascot.

"Van Dyne will be kept busy," agreed Suit. "You still serve the Adlerkinden well. Your job is done. Have a good flight home."

Hauptman turned to leave. Koenig was so entranced by the implications of what lay before him that he failed to hear the noise behind him until it was too late. He struggled in vain as the arm that encircled his throat crushed his windpipe. He heard only the sound of his own tortured attempt at breathing, and then the knife entered his ribs with a hot, searing pain. Then there was nothing but the moist earth under his face. Nothing at all.

Koenig was mildly surprised to find himself alive when he awoke several hours later. Sloppy, he thought. I should be dead. Something in the thought amused him, and he laughed until the pain hit him, and he almost blacked out again. Touching the wound was agony, and the amount of blood on his hands told him he was dying. That he was alive now was a minor miracle. They must have believed him dead. That was a mistake.

Sitting up was unbearable. Standing, a vision of purgatory. Walking was simply impossible. He managed to stagger against a tree, as afraid to move his hands from his wound as the Dutch Boy was to take his finger from the dyke. In either case, sure destruction would follow.

He stood eventually, using the tree as a support while the world tottered crazily around him. After a while, the world steadied somewhat, but he was too weak to move. "The young one," he thought. "I should have watched the young one. A few years back this wouldn't have happened. Too damned noisy. Too damned old!" He cursed himself again. Only one thing kept him alive, the need to report. For thirty years he had reported. He could not let go now. He had to report. The world began to spin again, and he wanted to cry.

The old whore was named Elsa, and like all her evenings past, she had come to ply her trade to the mass of sailors and tourists in Tivoli Gardens. Things were not going so well tonight, but it was early yet, she told herself, and the show was due to let out soon. She would find someone then. Maybe two.

When she saw Koenig leaning heavily against the tree, she assumed he was just another tourist who had had too much to drink. Pushing her breasts up in their wired bra to expose a deeper décolletage, and moistening her lips, she failed to notice his blood-stained clothing until she was next to him, and his hand shot out to grab her arm. She almost screamed, but his voice stopped her.

"Please," he gasped. "A phone. Just get me to a phone. A thousand kroner. Please . . . a phone."

The whore had been a pro too long to accept words or promises.

"The money now. Then the phone."

"In my pocket. But please, quickly. I can't make it much longer. Take it all."

Elsa quickly transferred the money to her bra. Then, putting his arm around her shoulders, she walked and carried Koenig to a public phone a few hundred feet away. The bargain completed, she started to leave. Koenig could barely stand.

"The number. Please! I can't dial. You must. I beg you . . ."

Then he was silent. Even the old whore knew he was a dead man. It was merely a matter of minutes. But he had paid her well.

"What the hell," she swore, and dialed the number he recited. She held the phone against his head impatiently. Koenig held on, each ring a death knoll.

"Koben Imports. Good evening."

"Look . . . no time . . . please. Tell Leander . . ." God! Hold on just a little longer. His tongue felt like wood.

"Who is this?" the voice asked. "Do you have an account with us, sir?"

Accounts, codes, too much energy.

"Tell Leander 'Hauptman . . . diamonds . . .'" He knew this time he would not awaken. He could not feel his body.

"Van Dyne . . . Adler . . ."

"Sir! Please, your account number. Sir? Hello?"

It was the old whore who hung up the phone. Koenig had died.

Five

The ultra-modern communications center for the Bureau of External Operations was housed on the second floor of a four-story, white stone building on a side street just a few blocks from the Union Buildings that house the administration of South Africa. A small brass plate by the front door bore only the numeral 27. No one who worked for Ex Op needed any other reminder. And no one who didn't work there could ever pass through its portals, even by accident.

Renovated by security experts on loan from the Israeli secret service, the building itself was as secure as a submarine on the ocean's floor. Its communications systems and computerized data processing units were among the most modern in the world.

When the high-speed coded transmission from Copenhagen came into the Comm Center without the proper identification codes of its originator, it was immediately sent to a computer, which converted it into a voice print and then compared that print to all of the prints of those who worked for Ex Op. A few milliseconds later a match was found, and that information, along with the original message, was forwarded to the terminal in the office of the Director, Jan Leander.

Leander, who was sipping a cup of tea at his desk when the report came in, read it and punched a button on the console at his desk. The "file" was immediately electronically transferred to the Assistant Director, Peter Dreyer. Pressing a second button, Leander spoke into the microphone built into the console.

"Investigate and preliminary report in one hour."

This information was instantaneously added to the "file" that would appear on Dreyer's terminal. Then Leander called in his secretary and repeated the order because, after thirty-

46

five years in intelligence work, he didn't trust the computers worth a damn.

Leander was fifty-six years old. The gray in his close-cropped light brown hair was beginning to show more predominantly, and his once flat abdomen showed signs of increasing roundness. Shorter than most, but not overly so, Leander continued to work out daily, but the years of sitting behind a desk were no substitute for the rigors of field work. His hazel-colored eyes scanned the terminal again, and his high forehead and fine features creased in concern.

One hour later he was frowning at Dreyer, whose dark hair, nondescript features, and medium build made him an ideal field man, and who held the print-out from Copenhagen in his hands.

"It's definitely from Koenig?" he asked.

"We have a voice print match. No question about it," responded Dreyer.

"This is all we received from him?"

"Yes, sir. He must have been dying at the time. It boils down to these four words: Hauptman, Diamonds, Van Dyne, and Adler."

"Any problems with the police?"

"No. They were very cooperative and quite happy to have us take the matter out of their hands. The body is being shipped out today."

"Damn!" said Leander.

"Yes, sir," said Dreyer. "The arrangements will be handled by the department. Pity of it is that he had only a few months left to pension. This assignment was only to let him finish up his time. One of the easy postings. Bloody waste."

"He was a good man," said Leander softly. Then, "Has coverage on Hauptman been reinstated?"

"Yes. As soon as we got the report on Koenig. I've stepped it up."

"Cancel that. Reinstate normal coverage. We don't want Hauptman to think that we connect him in any way to Koenig's death for now. Fact is, if we didn't have Koenig's phone call, we wouldn't have. Let Hauptman continue to believe that he is above suspicion."

"With his wealth and connections, he's not far from wrong, sir."

Leander glanced at the man warmly. "That's really quite enough 'sirs' for today. Don't you think, Peter?"

"I've always thought it was good for your sense of security, Jan."

The rapid promotions that came to Leander filtered through to Dreyer also. Long ago, Dreyer had realized that Leander was the key to his own rise in the ranks; and as their friendship grew, any thought of competition or jealousy was obliterated by shared goals and shared successes. Dreyer spoke again.

"You know that Hauptman is thick as thieves with our beloved Prime Minister. How do you think he'll react to an investigation of Hauptman?"

"Hauptman is clearly one of the boys. That's why this operation stays in house. I want no interference from Mr. Smith."

Dreyer nodded at the phrase "one of the boys." It was a term they had first used over cold beers on the terrace of the apartment they shared during the war. It denoted the very powerful South African businessmen and politicians whose entire purpose was to continue a policy of racial separation—apartheid.

Both Leander and Dreyer had been pleased to learn that each hated apartheid and felt that the country could be a paradise without it. A commitment to social justice was only the first of many shared values in their long friendship.

"What, then, is our next move?" asked Dreyer.

"I want Hauptman's house searched. Let's see what we come up with."

Dreyer was staring. "You are going to conduct an illegal entry search of one of the most powerful men in the country? Even knowing our charter does not allow us to operate within our own borders. If Internal Security gets wind of this, it will be your head on the block. I don't want your job that badly."

"Then guarantee I don't lose it. Don't get caught."

Leander began to read. The meeting was over.

Six

Walter Gerstein woke to the silky feel of the down comforter that surrounded his twelve-year-old body and to the smell of warm bread. Though he had been in his uncle's house for only two days, he knew that this smell of bread would forever be associated with his Uncle Franz, whose bakery on the first floor of the house had become a constant source of delight. Soon the sweeter odors of pastries baking rose into the room, causing him to throw off the covers and race out of bed.

His father Otto, a schoolmaster in their small hometown of Dahlenburg, had brought the family to his brother's house on vacation during the school recess. Walter was fascinated by so huge a city as Berlin, as was the rest of the family. It seemed to him that they had walked over a thousand miles since arriving. The streets and shops possessed a variety of luxury that made the whole city seem like a fairyland. He rubbed his sore feet in anticipation of the new day's walk.

By the time he had washed, dressed, and arrived at the breakfast table, the adults had already begun to drink their morning coffee. He slid happily into the one remaining chair at the table, next to his cousin Brita who, though only two years older, seemed infinitely more sophisticated and worldly than he.

"Good morning, Walter," said his Uncle Franz. "Did you sleep well?"

"Yes, sir," mumbled Walter between mouthfuls of hot bread and butter.

"The boy can't get enough of your bread, Franz," said his father. "I suppose he should have his fill. We may not eat this way again if the inflation continues. Half our town is out of work."

"Politics," complained his mother Gerda. "Must you always talk politics? Enjoy your breakfast and be thankful."

Franz looked up from his bread. "Otto is right, Gerda. It is getting bad even here in Berlin. Someone has to do something. Hitler has said . . ."

"Don't mention that madman at this table," said his father, red in the face. "Isn't it enough that he despoils the city with banners and posters, and his thugs roam the streets? Would you elect him to power? How do you think we Jews will fare under the Nazis?"

"He's not as bad as all that, Otto. He promises to end the suffering and restore Germany to its rightful place in the world. Who would not like to see that? Tell me, who?"

"Hush, papa. You'll give yourself a fit," said his Aunt Helga.

"I would not like it if it costs us our honor and our self-respect," said his father quietly. The silence that followed made Walter uncomfortable. He looked up at his father and his uncle. It had surprised him at first how different they were, though they were brothers. His father was a small, frail man with hair growing only on the sides of his head. His spectacles sometimes made him look like a big bug, Walter thought. His uncle, on the other hand, was much bigger, and his fat arms had big muscles on them from kneading dough all day. He had all his hair, and Walter had been shocked to discover that his father was the younger brother. His mother broke the stony silence.

"We are on vacation. Let us not argue on so fine a day. Come, Helga. We will clean up, and then we'll all go for a walk. Walter, go put on your coat. You too, Brita."

It seemed to Walter that his father and uncle were still angry, but the prospect of another walk through town happily obliterated all other thoughts. He dressed quickly, munching on a crust he had secreted away from the table.

By the time he made it back downstairs, the entire family was assembled and waiting. Uncle Franz put a sign on the door that said, "Closed for One Hour," and locked the shop door. Walter slipped his hand around his mother's arm. Her arm in turn slipped into his father's. Franz, Helga, and Brita walked the same way.

Many of the shopkeepers in the crowded Jewish section of the city waved hello as they walked past. Some were sweeping the street in front of their shops; others were busy behind counters cutting meat, weighing fruit, selling hats, or working at any of a dozen trades. One little old man whom Walter had met the day before, Herr Swartz, tossed him an apple from his stall. He ate it as they walked.

The two- and three-story, gray stone buildings that lined the streets seemed so large compared to the wooden houses of his town. The women in elegant coats with fur collars and men in suits dazzled him. The big cars that flowed by were an endless source of pleasure as Walter counted the different makes and models. He wondered why his father couldn't teach school here. Surely, they would want an intelligent man like his father. Then they could have a big car and shop in department stores. He would like that, he thought, as he tried to ignore the beggars in the street.

His reverie came to a halt when his mother stopped abruptly, pulling him backward by her rigid arm. They had come to a park, a small square of grass and trees between two street corners. This, he thought, we could see at home. Why are we stopping? His mother pushed him behind her, but he poked his head around her big body to see what was going on.

A group of ten or fifteen men were parading around through the park. Walter was amused by their stiff-legged strutting walk. Like the ducks we have in our pond at school, he thought, and this made him giggle. Their clothing was funny, too. Each man was dressed completely in brown: brown shirt, brown cap, and brown trousers with funny-looking wide tops on the leg. He liked their boots, though, all black and shiny. Each man carried a short stick with a big metal tip on its end. He wondered who they were and why his mother kept shoving him behind her as they approached. Did they work for the circus?

He heard his Uncle Franz say to his father, "Let them pass, Otto. They are the Sturmagteilung. It is unwise to anger them."

"I have heard of these Brown Shirts, these Storm Troopers. Bullies and thugs. This is a part of your new Germany, Franz. I am disgusted."

"It is not the time to argue this. Lower your voice. If they hear you . . ."

Walter was surprised to hear a strange quality in his uncle's voice. It sounded like he was afraid. But of what? It seemed to him that the family had moved closer together somehow, like a big knot with him at its center. Even Brita seemed to be less assured than usual. She had hidden behind her father. The column of marching men drew closer, and Walter saw that they would pass directly in front of them.

"Otto, I beg of you. Get out of their way. We have our families with us. Please, Otto."

His father looked like he was very angry. He had the same look as he had had when Walter had showed him a kitten he had found in the woods. Some boys had shaved it and left it hanging from a tree by its tail. His father's eyes had seemed to grow tired, and his facial muscles sagged like weights had been tied to them. He had said, "Walter, there is enough cruelty in the world already. Harsh winters and fierce animals and many people who starve without reason or die without cause. It is no business of children to add to the misery. This poor kitten who never hurt anyone demeans us all by its suffering. Never be a person who adds to the world's misery, Walter, lest it demean you, too."

Walter sensed the same mood in him now as, reluctantly, his father stepped back to allow the column to pass. Walter saw the same tired look on his face. Suddenly, the entire column turned, and the family was once again directly in its path. Only a few feet remained between the two groups.

The leader of the brown men called the column to a halt. He was a short, stocky man whom Walter thought looked like a bull. The folds of flesh on his face caused jowls to sag beneath his chin. He, too, carried a metal-tipped club. He is too ugly for the circus; he would frighten everyone, thought Walter.

He realized that the Bull, as he thought of the leader, was talking to his father. The voice was harsh and guttural, and Walter felt tiny chills ripple up his back. The men of the column surged forward until the family was surrounded by them. Brita began to cry, and his mother and Aunt Helga held their coats closed tightly against their chests and did not look at her. Suddenly, nothing was funny. Walter became afraid.

The Bull was speaking, gesturing with his club, and he could see his father strain not to move back from its assault. The rest of the family was silent. Only his father spoke. Uncle Franz looked away.

"You are in our way, Jew," said the Bull.

"We have done nothing to offend you. Kindly let us pass."

"Your presence offends us, Jew."

"That cannot be helped."

"We can help it, Jew."

"We are loyal German citizens. You have no right to molest us."

"What are rights, Jew?"

"They are what separate us from animals."

His father's voice was calm and soft. For no reason he understood, tears sprang into Walter's eyes. He had never thought of his father as a brave man, and he did not do so now. But his twelve-year-old emotions experienced a burst of fierce pride that rolled through his body and made his muscles knot in response.

Having never experienced brutality, he was totally unprepared for the metal-tipped club that came smashing down into his father's face. Nor for the sound of ripped tissue and broken bone. Nor for the blood.

He stood transfixed by the sight of the Bull and his father. The club came down again and again. Blood ran through his father's fingers, which clutched his face. Then the violent chaos spread to the rest of the men, who moved into his family with clubs swinging, came at them with the relentlessness of a tidal wave.

A great weight came crashing down on him, and he struggled against it as it threw him to the ground. It was his mother's body. Rolling out from underneath her, he could see his Uncle Franz locked in struggle with two men. He had one man's neck in his big beefy hands and was choking him to death. He saw the other man's club rise and fall in a vicious arc, and his uncle toppled like a felled tree. Three of the men had thrown Brita to the ground and were tearing at her clothes. Her tiny breasts emerged as her shirt was ripped from her body, and the small dark patch showed between her legs as her skirt was torn away. One of the men leaped on top of her. Then Walter was grabbed suddenly by one of the men. He could see his blazing eyes and hear his hoarse breathing, and as the club began its final deadly descent, Walter knew he was about to die.

But something he had never known or felt before burst within him as the deadly club sped toward him. Perhaps all the hatred had come together now, or the fear had come full circle in him; but in the terrible onslaught of emotion, he had

53

no time or reason to understand. He kicked out with all his might at the man who wanted to kill him, and it saved his life.

He felt his foot go so deeply into the man's groin that it met bone. In a scream of pain and rage the man released his hold. The club missed his head and smashed into his shoulder. Walter could feel bone break and hear that awful internal crunch. The pain almost caused him to black out, but he was free! He ran in panic from death, blood surging from his shoulder, his left arm dangling uselessly.

He wanted a weapon. Any weapon to fight back with, to smash and rend and tear and kill. But when he looked back at the square, there was no one left but the brown men kicking lumps of flesh, and the Bull watching and smiling.

The pain in his shoulder seared him again with an agony almost as great as that in his heart. There was no one left. He had to run before they came after him. He had to leave every person he had ever loved. But he would not forget the Bull.

The next few hours were a maze of fear and pain. Later, as darkness began to close around him, he could run no longer. There was no place to go. Utterly spent, he fell exhausted to the cold cobblestones of a residential street. It occurred to him that he was going to die there. It also slowly occurred to him that he didn't care. His last conscious thoughts were confused and unreal. He was hurt knowing that the Bull would survive, and then he hurt no longer. The long, slow slide into oblivion was a gift and a blessing.

Walter Gerstein did not hear the tall man stoop over him nor the questions that he asked. He did not feel the man lift him up nor, later, the soft bed underneath him. He was unaware of the doctor's visit or of the tall man's bedside vigil. He slept, and for three days the world's madness passed him by and let him live.

On the fourth morning, Walter awoke. He tried to sit up, but the pain that met that movement tore a cry from his lips. There were bandages on his shoulder strapping his arm to his side. The terror was still fresh for him, only a few hours old, and he began to tear at the restraints. He had to run.

He heard footsteps approaching the room and tore faster to free himself before his captor arrived. He fell to the floor in his struggles, on his left side, and passed out from the pain.

Walter awoke with a man standing over him. His first

thought was that the man had no brown uniform. Instead, he was dressed in black slacks with a white turtleneck sweater. The man had strong clear features, thick wavy brown hair, and a full beard. Gentle brown eyes, like his father's, peered down at Walter, and the man's voice was soft and warm. His strong hands held Walter to the bed.

"Who are you?" asked the man, but when Walter didn't answer, he asked, "Can you speak? What happened to you?"

"Where am I?" Walter croaked, his throat sore and dry.

The man smiled. "You're in my bedroom."

Walter noticed that the man had an accent, foreign but not unpleasant. The sound of his voice was soothing. He handed Walter a glass of water.

"Who are you?" Walter asked.

"My name is Captain Paris Leander, Master of the ship *Portstar*, of South African registry. I mean you no harm. Please believe me, boy. Ask yourself, would I have tended to your wounds if I meant to hurt you? I think not."

"Why did you . . ?" Walter had to sip the water to continue.

"Why did I what, boy?" interposed Leander.

"Help me?"

"What choice did I have? You practically fell at my feet in a grand heap, broken and bloody. You looked like you'd had a bad time of it, but you were too far gone to talk about it. I brought you up here, called a doctor, and he said you were in shock. Not to mention your busted shoulder. Would you have preferred me to leave you where I found you? I think not, boy."

Walter felt himself relax. This man would not hurt him.

"Can you tell me what happened to you? Where do you belong? Is there family near here that I can send for?"

Walter didn't want to tell him. He tried to seal it up behind a wall of silence. But the pain was too fresh, too recent, and he had no defense for it. He couldn't even lie. He had never learned the art. Finally, in a long, sobbing rush he told Leander about his family. And about the Bull.

He noticed a change come over Leander as he listened quietly. The gentleness left his eyes to be replaced by a hardness. His large calloused hands clenched and unclenched and clenched again. Soon Walter had told him everything. The effort made him sleepy, and he said so. Leander smiled at him.

"That's all right, boy. You sleep now. No one can hurt you here. I'll look in later. Go to sleep." And Walter did.

But it was Walter who came to Leander the next morning. He was sitting at his breakfast table reading the newspaper and drinking coffee. He looked up, surprised.

"You shouldn't be out of bed, boy. Your bones have to heal. You don't want to be a cripple, do you? I think not. Hungry?"

Walter nodded. Leander brought him some bread and milk. He ate slowly as it made him queasy.

"Are you French?" he asked Leander.

"No, South African. You mean because of my Christian name?"

Walter nodded. Leander laughed, and the sound filled the room. But the blackness inside Walter could not be penetrated by it. Leander noticed that.

"Try and forget it, boy. Move past it. Seal it up and get on with your life. It's a shame you've got to grow up so fast. But life is a hard thing sometimes, cruel and indifferent." He stood up to clear the dishes but kept on talking.

"You asked about my name. Well, my father always felt that one of the things a man ought to be able to do well was be a good judge of women and of war. He was certainly both. Remind me to tell you the story about when he . . . but some other time. Anyway, he named me after the judge of the world's first beauty contest, a man he admired deeply. Do you know the story of Paris, boy?"

Walter shook his head. "No."

"You ever learn about the ancient Greeks in school?"

"A little bit. Some of the gods and goddesses."

"That'll do just fine. Well, one day they were having a big feast, these gods and goddesses, but they forgot to ask one of their number, Eris. Eris was a nasty sort. She was known as the Goddess of Discord. She was always disagreeing with someone or other. Well, Eris got mad at this slight and decided to muck up the party. Follow? Good.

"She made a golden apple and wrote on it the inscription 'To The Fairest.' Then she tossed it into the center of the party.

"Now you have to remember that all those goddesses were a petty and jealous lot, so they started to squabble about who the apple was for and who was the fairest. Pretty soon the world's first beauty contest was held.

"They needed a judge, but all of the gods were too smart to choose between the three goddesses who claimed the apple: Hera, Queen of the Gods; Athena, Goddess of Wisdom; and Aphrodite, Goddess of Love and Beauty. So they chose a mortal, Prince Paris, from a city named Troy, to be the judge. Got it so far?"

Walter nodded, entranced by the story. Somehow, when the captain talked, he didn't feel so lonely.

"Well, the goddesses proved to be pretty tricky, and they each offered Paris a bribe to ensure a quick win. Hera offered him the rule of Europe. Athena offered him great victory in war. But Aphrodite offered him Helen, the most beautiful woman in the world."

"What did he pick?" asked Walter.

"Well, boy, he chose the lady. My father always said any man who'd rather fight than fool around had a loose cannon on his deck. So he named me after a man he admired, Paris of Troy. There's more to the story, but we'll save it for another time, okay? You go back to bed now."

Walter started for the bedroom, but stumbled. Leander reached out to steady him. Walter looked up into the kind face, and suddenly flung himself into the big strong arms and cried with breathless abandon.

"Easy now, boy. It's all right. Let it go. Just let it go. It's too big to leave inside."

And then Walter felt himself lifted, stroked, and put to bed where he slept without dreams.

The next few days were strange for Walter. When Leander was away, he explored the apartment with its high-ceilinged rooms, glass doors, and painted woodwork. He built a fire in the hearth in the sitting room and stared into it for hours at a time. Once, he was gazing out the window and saw a brown-uniformed man in the street below. He shut all the windows and sat with the shades drawn, a poker in his hands. When Leander returned, he said nothing but held him close. Later, they talked long into the night.

Ten days after he had awakened in Leander's apartment, Walter found Leander packing a huge trunk that sat in the middle of the living room. When he entered the room, Leander beckoned him into a chair and then sat opposite him.

"Walter, we've come to a crossroads, you and I, and there are some weighty decisions to be made."

Walter felt fear rising hot in his throat.

"You're leaving me," he said.

"Well, my business in Berlin is done. The *Portstar*'s loaded and ready to sail for home. You're a fine boy, Walter, but I've got no room for you in my life. Most of my time is spent at sea. That's why I've never married nor had a family of my own. You can see that, can't you?"

Walter tried hard to hold back his tears. He had known this moment would come. He realized how much Leander had done for him, and he refused to be angry or hurt. He resolved to go back to his village, to his neighbors. Maybe someone would take him in. If not, he would find a job. As an apprentice to some tradesman, maybe. Then Leander was speaking again.

"I am not a rich man, but with no one to spend money on but myself, I have a goodly sum put away. I've come to think highly of you, and maybe I can help."

"How, sir?"

"I'm prepared to pay for your tuition at a boarding school in Switzerland till you're of age. You can continue your education, and they'll take care of everything you need. With no other family, I think it the best way. You don't want to live in the street, do you? I think not."

Walter was taken aback by his generosity.

"But how will I pay you back?"

"There's plenty of time for that when you graduate and find a trade. We'll keep in touch, boy. Maybe I can visit if I'm ever back this way. How about it?"

"It's very kind, sir."

"Well, then? You accept?"

"No, sir."

Leander's breath blew out in a loud snort. "No? Why the bloody hell not? What will you do?"

"Survive."

Leander looked at him sharply, thoughtfully. "Where?"

"I'll go back home. Someone'll take me in. I can't leave yet anyway."

"But why not?"

"I'm going to kill him, the man who killed my family."

"You're crazy, boy."

"I've thought about it, sir. I'll watch for him all over the city. I'll find a gun, and when I see him, I'll shoot him dead."

"That's no plan. The rest of his bunch will get you and kill you. Do you even know how to shoot? I think not."

"It doesn't matter what happens to me. I've got to pay him back."

"You don't even know his name."

"I'll find out."

Leander looked furious. "That's it, boy. I've done everything I can for you. You've made your decision. Now get dressed. We're leaving in an hour," and he stomped off to the kitchen where Walter heard pans clattering.

Walter dressed slowly. A funny feeling in his stomach spread through his chest. Even at twelve, he knew that the loneliness had started. If Leander wasn't too angry at him, he resolved to borrow some money. Just enough for a few days. That will be all right, he thought. He sat down on the bed to think. When he looked up, Leander stood in the doorway. Walter met his gentle brown eyes and fought down tears.

"Come home with me, son."

And then he was off the bed and wrapped in the strong arms, and the tears flowed freely. A long time later Leander spoke.

"Now listen to me. We've only got a few minutes before my mate arrives to take us to the ship. Then we've got customs and emigration checks to pass. This damn country will never let Walter Gerstein go. They may even be looking for you if they've identified your parents. You understand?"

Walter nodded. He felt the loneliness go far away, and he felt alive again.

"From now on Walter Gerstein is dead. You are my nephew, Jan. Jan Leander. Your parents were South Africans on holiday, killed in a car crash; and I've come to take you home. When we get to South Africa, we'll change the nationality of your parents back to German. As my nephew, you'll have no problem applying for citizenship. List your religion on any forms as Protestant and not Jewish, and if anyone questions you, let me do the talking. Just look distant and grief-stricken. Got that?"

"Yes, sir. Jan Leander, Protestant, and look distant."

A loud knocking came at the front door. Leander hugged him.

"Let's go then. My mates are here."

Walter picked up the bundle of new clothing that Leander had bought for him days earlier. On top was a torn and bloody shirt. Leander took it.

"You can't take that. Too many questions if they search the baggage. Put the rest in my trunk."

Walter went into the sitting room and did so. Leander tossed the shirt into the fireplace. Walter watched it burn. He thought about the Bull. Leander caught his expression and read his mind.

"Forget about him. Maybe someday you'll get a chance. For now, you've got to forget."

"I think not," said Jan Leander.

Cape Town, 1939

The Operations Center for Military Intelligence was a madhouse as usual. Large glass sheets with engraved grid projections of the major theaters of war were being modified every few minutes as orderlies delivered new information on troop movements and supply shipments. Over large tables the general staff moved miniatures of ships, tanks, and battalions using long sticks with the ease and skill of gambling house croupiers. Orders flew through the air to the accompaniment of Morse code sendings and the crackle of radio static.

Captain Jan Leander, seated at his desk in a cubicle off the main room, was studying a German transmission that had been intercepted and decoded only moments before. He lifted his phone from its cradle.

"Get me the Air Marshall's HQ." Thirty seconds later he was speaking to a staff officer.

"This is Captain Leander at OCMI. Please take the following message for Brigadier Rawlings. Start: Jack, you were correct. A strike is anticipated on the base at Tsumeb. Change over to the refueling station at Walvis Bay. Good hunting. Stop. Please repeat that."

The officer did so to Leander's satisfaction.

"Very good. Get that to him immediately."

Leander hung up the phone, pleased. He looked around at the frenzy of activity in this room that had been his home since 1938 when he had enlisted against his Uncle Paris's objections.

"For God's sake, boy," his uncle had said. "You've got only a year left at the university. Finish up before you get into this stinking war. It won't go away. You owe it to yourself to finish a degree."

"I owe it to Walter Gerstein to be in this war," Leander had said, and it had effectively ended the argument. It had been so long ago that he had come to South Africa that any other life seemed dreamlike and unreal. Even speaking German sounded strange to his ears, and he had thought only in English for years.

"Besides," he had said, "who are you to tell me not to join when you'll be wandering across the oceans playing tag with Nazi U-boats? You don't have to go either. I saw the letter on your desk that asked you if you'd take a training position at the naval base. You volunteered to go to sea."

"I am an old fool," his uncle had said, and there had been mirth in his eyes as he fingered his beard, which had been showing gray for some years.

"I never thought I'd see the day you'd rather fight than fool around," Jan had agreed.

Paris had grinned. "Chalk it up to early senility." And the tension was dispelled with their laughter. Then his uncle had turned serious again.

"I understand what you have to do, Jan. I know it's been brewing deep inside of you ever since we met. I had hopes for a while you might forget about it, but every time I convinced myself you had passed it by, I'd see a look on your face, and I knew it wasn't over for you yet. It's a heavy load to carry, boy."

Jan had touched his uncle's shoulder. "You've made it easier, Paris. No one could have done more than you have."

"Every time I came home and saw how you'd grown, every time I saw you achieve some success at sports or," and his uncle's eyes had twinkled, "with the young ladies, I was very proud to call you my nephew. You knew that, didn't you?"

Jan had tightened his grip. "I knew that. I've been very proud to call you uncle; father's more like it." Jan paused and took a deep breath. "You would have liked each other a great deal, you know."

"I think we would have. You're a fine man, Walter Gerstein, and . . . I love you."

Tears had sprung into Jan's eyes as they embraced.

"I love you, too, Uncle Paris."

A few days later Paris had shipped out on the *Portstar*. Jan had seen him off at the docks. The rain had been coming down in sheets all morning, and the tarps covering crates to be shipped slapped sharply in the morning wind. His uncle had been in good spirits, anxious to sail.

When the loading was finished, they had turned to each other and clasped hands.

"Come back safely, uncle," Jan had said, and Paris had laughed. It was a good laugh, from deep in his belly.

"The *'Star* takes good care of me, boy. I'll be back. Just make sure you don't outrank me when I do."

And then there was nothing left to say but things that needed no saying. Jan watched his uncle turn away, mount the gangway, and vanish over the railing. Deckhands began to loosen the thick rope that bound the ship to the dock.

"Come back safely, uncle," Jan had said to no one but the wind and the sea. Then he walked slowly away and did not look back even when the huge fog horns on the center stack blasted the final song of his childhood over the gray-white waves.

The following day Jan had arrived at army headquarters. He took aptitude tests until his head swam. His fluency in German and knowledge of German idiom and custom had overjoyed the officer at the recruitment center and made him a natural for intelligence. Officers' schooling had followed immediately, and he had been promoted to section head with the rank of captain in less than a year and a half. He was proud of his skill and his victories. One officer had commented about him, and he had overheard: "A nice enough bloke, really. But he takes the whole thing so bloody personally." More than just a wartime occupation, Jan Leander had found an avocation.

He watched his friend, Lieutenant Peter Dreyer, walking toward his desk. The expression on his face worried Leander. It was unlike his friend to be anything but jovial.

"Hello, Peter," he said.

"'Lo, Jan." Dreyer was holding a communiqué.

"Something for me?"

Dreyer seemed to hesitate a moment before handing the paper to him. Then he looked at him sadly.

"I'm truly sorry, Jan. The *Portstar*'s down. Happened this morning off Finland. Sub got her. All hands lost." Dreyer placed his hand on Leander's shoulder. "I was awfully fond of him, too, Jan. I'm very sorry."

Leander thought of his uncle, carting munitions across the treacherous North Sea. He had last seen him eighteen months ago. They were both well aware of the risks. Now the odds had run out. Tears blurred his vision as he stared at the picture of his uncle on his desk.

He reached into his desk and removed another picture from inside it. It had been duplicated and enlarged from the endless files in M.I. storage. The face of the Bull stared back at him. He had put a name to the face of his enemy over a year ago—Martin Bormann, Reichsleiter of the Nazi Party. Other officers kept pictures of their wives or families close to them. In a way, so did Leander.

Seven

Pretoria

Leander was just finishing his nightly glass of wine before bed when the phone rang. Cursing under his breath, he grabbed the receiver from the nightstand as if it were a reptile poised to bite. There was no such thing as a simple call this late at night.

"Hello?"

"Jan?"

"Yes."

"This is Peter. I'll be by in ten minutes."

Before Leander had a chance to respond, the connection was severed.

Leander dressed quickly in slacks and a pullover shirt. Walking downstairs to the kitchen, he put on a pot of coffee. He barely had time to light the stove before his doorbell began ringing.

Peter Dreyer was standing on the floodlit porch dressed in coveralls and tapping his foot impatiently. Leander let him in. The whiteness of Dreyer's face stopped the rebuke that was half out of Leander's mouth. Dreyer's words came out in a rush.

"Look, Jan, I'm awfully sorry to get you out of bed at this hour, but we found something that I want you to see."

Leander settled into a chair in the living room and bade Dreyer do the same. It was obviously a physical effort for Dreyer to restrain himself to sit. Visibly, slowly, Dreyer calmed down.

"We ran the entry into Hauptman's house tonight," he said.

"Problems?"

"No. None at all. We did a simple electrical stoppage from the street line and took a crew in posing as municipal workers. Simple and straightforward. No snags."

"Good," said Leander, relaxing.

"Jan, look at this." Dreyer handed him a photograph of a document dated October, 1936.

It seemed to Dreyer that Leander aged noticeably in the few moments it took him to read the document. It was a Leander that he had seen only a few times before who looked up from the paper. It was his eyes, thought Dreyer. They are seeing somewhere else.

"Where was this?" Leander asked.

"In one of three safes in the house. Bitch to get into."

Leander's eyes scanned the document again.

"It could bring down some of the strongest supporters of apartheid in the country," said Dreyer.

Leander read from the piece of paper each name that had been signed there, "Johann Smith, Hans Smith, Pieter Van Dyne, Walter Hauptman, Frank Voorstein...And two others—Dr. Ludwig Stumpfegger and Martin Bormann. My God, Peter. There's more to this document than just politics."

"Jan, it would be almost impossible to prove the authenticity of that document. Its only potential use is to create a big enough scandal to topple the present government and force a moderate into power. What are you thinking of besides politics?"

"Look again at the list, Peter. Smith is the Prime Minister; Van Dyne is the president of our largest diamond exchange in Amsterdam; Hauptman owns the richest mine in the country..."

"And Voorstein died of natural causes in 1968 at the age of sixty-seven. Hans Smith committed suicide in 1939. The

Nazis have been dead for thirty years. So what?" interrupted Dreyer. "What are you digging for?"

Leander was having a hard time breathing. He felt a ghostly hand clutching at his chest. He stared intently at Dreyer.

"You still don't see it, do you? Think of Koenig's last message. Hauptman, Van Dyne, Diamonds, Adler... Think, man!"

The significance struck Dreyer almost like a physical blow. "It's still going on..." and his voice was a whisper. "It's still going on." He looked at Leander, who seemed to be talking more to himself.

"When the Allies held the trials at Nuremburg, Martin Bormann was tried 'in absentia.' His body was never found. In '67 it was reported he was living in a Nazi colony in Brazil. It was never substantiated. In 1971 they thought they'd found his skull during some rebuilding in Germany. Also unsubstantiated. All we know is that he, Stumpfegger, and a few hundred others tried to escape from the Reich Chancellory on May 1, 1945. Under protection of a tank they crossed the Weidendammer Bridge out of Berlin. The tank was blown up by the Russians advancing into the city.

"In 1953, one Dr. Werner Neumann was put on trial. Adenauer had him extradited from the British Zone where he was working for an import-export firm and had started a new Nazi cell. It came out that he had escaped on the same night as Bormann and had stayed with him until the next morning where they parted company.

"Neumann made it to Frankfurt where he worked as a laborer for five years before getting to the British Zone. Bormann was never heard of again, except in rumor."

"Why do you care so much about Bormann? You know too much for a casual interest," said Dreyer.

Leander looked directly into the eyes of his old friend.

"He was a monster."

Dreyer stared back. "No other reason?"

"No."

"And you believe..."

"I believe only that his name is on this paper. But I tell you this, Peter. If he's alive and connected somehow to this country, I'll find him. There's never been a plan that Bormann was involved in that wasn't loathsome. We've got to know what connects these people to him."

"I still maintain," said Dreyer, "that the blow this would give to the people who support apartheid is more important than Bormann. We may never get this chance again. Merely leak it to the newspapers, and Smith and all his people come tumbling down..."

"To be replaced by more of the same. First, I want to know why and where and how. Bormann was a plague, and a plague must be stamped out at its source," finished Leander. He went on in a gentler tone. "There are larger issues here. We must not move until we know what's at the root of all this. We can't take the chance of exposing it prematurely."

Dreyer let his breath out in a long, slow sigh.

"Jan, I've trusted you for thirty years, and you've always come through. You've earned this one."

Leander sat back in his chair. His head hurt from the strain he was feeling. He glanced at the list of names again.

"What do you know of Hans Smith's death?"

Dreyer spoke as if reciting. "Smith's brother died of apparent suicide in 1939. He shot his wife as well. Only the daughter, Lisa, an infant at the time, survived and was adopted by her uncle, Johann Smith. No motive was ever uncovered for the deaths."

"I remember now. It was during the war. Strange rumors at the time; no history of business failure or emotional problems."

"Does it strike you as odd?" asked Dreyer.

"It didn't then with the war on and so many other priorities. But in the light of this," he shook the document again, "perhaps it was not a suicide."

"You mean murder? Smith wouldn't have killed his own brother, nor would he have allowed one of the others to do so. It makes no sense."

"Maybe Hans became unreliable. Maybe he changed his mind and wanted out. Maybe his wife became a problem. We don't know—but it's a start," Leander said.

Dreyer had the feeling that Leander was moving too quickly for him. He had seen him in this state often over the years, making insightful leaps on a problem that stripped away the endless questions, leaving a course of action obvious, apparent. Only in the retracing did it become clear that Leander's genius for analysis was responsible.

"It's got to be a crystal operation, Peter."

It was a private language between them. Many years earlier, as a school child, Leander had watched a science teacher perform an experiment with what he called "supersaturated solutions." In this case the solution was sugar dissolved in water. The water looked ordinary, even though it was filled with dissolved sugar. When the teacher suspended a string dipped in sugar into the water, over a period of several hours the dissolved sugar was "pulled" out of the water to form large crystals on the string. The boys were all delighted to learn that they had created rock candy—solid sugar.

Leander had summed up the operation succinctly. The conspiracy members were like the dissolved sugar, hiding. They had to be brought out from their hiding places by introducing something that they would form around. Something, or someone, to "pull" them from the "water"—the crystal.

They had run this type of operation successfully before. The only real danger was to the crystal—the bait. Often it was destroyed.

Leander ticked off his fingers. "First, if we use a pro, we run the risk of sending them running if he's spotted. It must be someone we can follow but who isn't linked to any known service. Second, it must be someone whose motives, ostensibly, have nothing to do with diamonds. Third, it must be someone they might not destroy out of hand, as they would an agent. Fourth, it must be someone we can program."

"And who might that be?"

"Isn't it obvious? Our crystal has to be Lisa Smith, the Prime Minister's daughter."

Eight

The Union Buildings in Pretoria gleamed in the noonday sun. Set on a hill overlooking the city, the huge three-story Grecian-style building housed the administration of South

Africa's government when Parliament was not in session in Capetown. The ministerial offices, state archives section, and reading rooms were scenes of constant activity as people sped down long corridors on countless errands. The clatter of typewriters and the buzz of telephones filled the air as the nation's business was transacted.

The windows in the offices of the Prime Minister looked out over the succession of garden terraces that descended from the building's front in a profusion of sculptured shrubs and trees. Lunchtime picnickers were spread out over trhe acres of grass and gardens from the Delville Wood Memorial, a tribute to the South African troops of World War I, past the Garden of Remembrance, to the vast sweep of lawn ending at the equestrian statue of Louis Botha, the first Prime Minister of South Africa.

The outer offices housed countless assistants and secretaries attending and recording the state's business. The inner offices were assigned to those of higher rank, advisors close to the center of power. The Prime Minister's office and attached apartment were decorated simply. Pictures of past political leaders—Jan Smuts, Louis Botha, and others—adorned the walls. A huge desk and assorted chairs for visitors were arranged with the simplicity only great wealth can achieve.

The usual quiet of the inner office was shattered by the sound of voices raised in anger. Johann Smith, the sixty-five-year-old Prime Minister of South Africa, was furious.

"I can't even begin to understand your attitudes, much less condone them," he shouted at the beautiful young woman gazing placidly up at him.

Lisa Smith sat unflinching in a large leather chair, becoming rapidly bored as his rhetoric, as usual, failed to impress, intimidate, or frighten her. She ran a casual hand through her long blond hair and remained calm in the face of his anger. Her finely chiseled features bore no expression, which provoked him even further. Lisa liked games, and this was one of her favorites.

"Your behavior is intolerable. Have you no sense of your position? Or mine?" Smith said, exasperated.

"I couldn't care less what you or any of your friends think of me," Lisa said complacently.

"You cannot continue breaking rules and standards with

impunity. My position can only protect you so far. Do you understand that?"

"I choose my friends as I please."

"Wonderful, this independence of yours," said Smith sarcastically. "Let me read you a list of your recent accomplishments."

Smith riffled through the papers on his ornate desk. Finding the one he wanted, he began to read.

"This month you were arrested in a raid on a club that specialized in live sex shows. Charming. I can only hope you were one of the audience and not in the show itself."

"You don't have to worry, uncle. My tits aren't big enough. They wouldn't have me."

Smith blanched. Lisa knew that her vulgarity shocked him, conservative that he was. Further, she knew that using "uncle" instead of "father" drove the hurt deeper, made it more personal. Losing his composure, Smith responded in kind.

"You have, over the past several years, made a complete shambles of a life that anyone in her right mind would have cherished. You use both men and drugs indiscriminately. You gamble and associate with the filth of the world. If your parents were alive to—"

"Don't mention my parents!" yelled Lisa, and then she immediately regretted her display of emotion. If she let him know that it still hurt, it could be used as a weapon to penetrate her defenses. But Smith, a veteran of a thousand personal and political skirmishes, had his own games to play and probed deeper.

"Your parents loved you. In their name, I ask you to reconsider your actions."

But Lisa's defenses were back in place.

"My parents are dead. They are incapable of loving anyone."

"They loved you, I say."

"And I say they left me!"

"This last episode is too much, Lisa. I can overlook many things, protect you from your own idiocy in the hope that you will come to your senses." His voice hardened. "But if you are ever seen in the company of that man again, even by accident, I will disown you forever. We will never see each other again. Never!"

Lisa saw she was close to losing the game. She knew full

well that all of her trespasses but this one could be forgiven. For the man of whom her uncle spoke was undeniably, unforgivably, a black. She knew, too, that this transgression carried a penalty so severe that no one in any position of power, no friend of the family, and certainly no one with any regard for his political future, would lift a finger to save her. She had lost this round, and the game, and both knew it. Smith smiled and pressed his advantage.

"I have taken the liberty of telling your servants to pack your things from your apartment. They are in a car outside. The driver will take you to your home in Johannesburg where you can come to a decision."

"I won't go there," Lisa protested weakly.

"You will go where I tell you to go. You will make no trouble, no scene. You will meditate there on your sins. When you return, and think long and hard on this, dear daughter, you will either reform publicly as well as privately, or you will be disowned. You may go now. I will call for your car." Smith smiled again in dismissal.

"Uncle?"

"Yes?"

"You are a total prick." She strode from the room savoring the anger on his face and relishing even the smallest of victories.

In the privacy of the car, Lisa permitted herself the tears she would never show her uncle. She cried until the sobs wracked her body, but it brought her no true relief. She watched the countryside roll by, absorbed in her own thoughts.

Lisa knew why her uncle was sending her to the family home in Johannesburg. It was the scene of her parents' suicide and, without a doubt, the most painful place on earth for her to be. It was a punishment, a reminder that, were she to continue her present ways, she would again be left totally alone.

Her problems with her uncle, her adoptive father since her parents' death, began at an early age. She understood only intellectually what countless psychiatrists had told her: that she took out her anger at her parents, whose suicide she viewed as deliberate abandonment, on her only living relative, Johann Smith. Nothing he tried to do for her over the years mattered. Lisa could be close to no one. For in every relationship that meant any kind of commitment, she was the one who broke it off before getting close enough to be hurt. People would abandon her, she knew they would. Consequently, her friends and lovers had no choice—when nothing they gave was returned, they went elsewhere.

It was a vicious cycle, a self-destructive cycle, but she was unable to break out of it. One psychiatrist told her that she would never be happy until she had killed herself and joined the parents she had never known. Lisa had never actually attempted to kill herself, but she realized that her taste for fast cars, sordid people, and depraved affairs, were a form of it.

The drive of only sixty miles or so from Pretoria to Johannesburg went quickly. Soon she could see the gate to the estate and the black servant who attended it. Lisa's sense of dread increased as the car entered the private road leading to the house.

As on most South African estates, the house was built of stone. It was an imposing structure two stories high with separate barns, sheds, workhouses, and servants' quarters scattered around the property. The sight of it made her ill.

As the car stopped, one of the house servants ran to open the door. Lisa emerged into the hot, afternoon sun. The servant, Amad, had been born on the estate and had served the family for fifty years.

"Welcome home, Miss Lisa."

"Thank you, Amad. I'm not feeling very well. I think I'll go to my rooms. Tell the cook I'll want only a light supper."

"Very good, Miss Lisa." Amad began to assist the chauffeur in unloading the car.

The house was virtually unchanged since Lisa had last been home years earlier. The floor of the huge foyer was inlaid with ceramic tile over which were strewn area rugs of brilliant design. The furnishings were wooden and massive. Large armoires, carved in bas-relief, stood on both sides of the room and added to its medieval presence. "This house is an anachronism," she thought to herself, "like everything else in this country. God, I need a drink."

Lisa entered the main room off the foyer, where guests were greeted and that contained a bar. The room was carpeted in a deep maroon with chairs and tables done in rich leather of the same color. Floor to ceiling glass doors looked out over the garden, and this afternoon, light was streaming through them adding gold highlights to the reds. Lisa went directly to the bar.

"Make mine straight scotch, please."

The voice from behind her startled her, and she dropped the glass onto the bar. Turning, she saw a man sitting comfortably in one of the chairs, holding out his glass for a refill.

"Who the hell are you?" she demanded.

"I'm surprised you don't remember. We have met, you know."

For a moment, Lisa could almost connect a name with the face, but it slipped away.

"I'm sorry, your name escapes me."

The man smiled. "When a beautiful woman forgets me, it is I who am sorry." He rose and walked to the bar. "My name is Jan Leander. We met a few months ago at your uncle's dinner party. You were quite a hit."

Lisa remembered the night. She had tossed her salad into the face of a guest who had made a pass at her, not out of anger but because she had wanted to. It occurred to her now that she could as easily have chosen to go with him.

"I was a bit smashed, and he was an offensive little man who was also a bigot."

"You don't like bigots?" asked Leander.

"Who and what I don't like are none of your business." Lisa smiled scornfully; she had it now. "Or has External Operations decided that girls throwing salads are threats to our security?"

"Very good, Miss Smith. You recover and counter quickly. Like a pro."

Leander had said the last three words in a different tone of voice, and Lisa noted it. In South Africa it was unhealthy to be accused of anything. Even lies had a way of being "proven."

"Did my uncle send you?"

"No. He knows nothing of my visit."

Leander filled his glass from the bar, then filled another and handed it to Lisa.

"Come, come, Miss Smith. We are not amateurs. You know who I am, why I'm here, and what I want. Let's not muddy up the waters with foolish questions."

Lisa took a deep breath.

"I sincerely do not have the slightest idea what you are talking about, Mr. Leander."

Leander sighed. "I did hope we could work this out calmly. But, if not..."

Leander moved toward the phone, but Lisa blocked him.

"Mr. Leander, I may be a bit frivolous, perhaps even depraved, as my uncle insists. But I am not stupid. If you pick up that phone and call some unlisted number, I am going to be in for a rough time, regardless of my family connections. I know how these things are done. So you must believe me when I say that if you want to frighten me, you have succeeded."

Leander sat down, then removed an enormous cigar from inside his jacket pocket. He toyed with it in his hands, slowly removing its nine-inch length from its gray metal container. Lisa watched it slowly emerge, an inch at a time. It was so brown as to be almost black and at least a full inch thick. When Leander's hands were almost a foot and a half apart, it suddenly popped from the tube with a strange sucking sound.

Like a bird transfixed by the sway of a snake, Lisa's eyes followed Leander's movements with the cigar. He placed a small square, gold object on the table in front of him and then reached into his pocket and produced a matching gold lighter.

Slowly, he placed the tip of the cigar against the gold square. Like a miniature guillotine, the upper half of the square held a diagonal blade whose cutting edge rested a half inch above a hole in the lower half's center. Deliberately, Leander placed the rounded end of the cigar at the mouth of the hole and began to turn it inward. Lisa felt her throat constrict, and her breathing grew sporadic as Leander began to press downward on the blade. She could hear a sound like wet straw being squeezed. With agonizing slowness, the blade bit into the tip, until, all at once, the blade fell home and a small piece of cigar fell into Leander's lap. An involuntary gasp was drawn from her lips. She felt beads of sweat gather under her arms. Her knees drew fractionally apart. Leander spoke, but her eyes never waivered from the black rod in his hands.

"What I am about to tell you, Miss Smith, is classified under the highest rating of national security."

Lisa could feel a trickle of sweat run down her side and her face grow hot. Leander had begun to draw the length of the cigar over his lips in long, slow strokes. His tongue licked each surface till moisture gleamed along its length. He pushed the table aside and drew his chair closer to hers. Her legs grew weak, and she fought down the urge to be sick. But she could feel her breasts strain against the fabric of her shirt and could not look away.

Leander had picked up the gold lighter. With a click the top sprang open, and he fanned it into flame. He pointed the cigar at her like the muzzle of a gun ready to shoot. Lisa strained to shift her concentration to his face, but her eyes were riveted to the huge black cigar and the flame.

"What significance does the name Walter Hauptman have for you?"

Lisa stared at him, trying to concentrate. The room felt close and stuffy.

"He owns the Raelord Mine, and he is a friend of my uncle's. I don't understand."

"Nothing more?"

"No, truly. Why?"

"And the name Pieter Van Dyne?"

"He owns the largest diamond exchange in Amsterdam. He is also a friend of my uncle's. Please tell me what this is all about."

Leander ignored her. "Nothing else?"

"No."

"What does 'Adler' mean to you?"

Lisa paused. "I don't know anyone by that name. I swear it."

Leander appeared to think for a long moment, then handed her the document Dreyer had found in Hauptman's safe.

"Read this," he demanded.

In the few minutes it took Lisa to read the page, her expression went from fear to shock to total disbelief. Leander, the questions, this house, the cigar, and finally the awful document, were too much. Blackness engulfed her and she slipped to the floor.

Leander gently lifted her back into her chair. He hated doing this to a confused young girl like Lisa Smith, but he steeled himself to continue. He had no choice—she was the crystal, his only lead. He grasped her by the shoulders and

74

shook her, calling her name. She awoke with a start, trembling and uncertain.

"You are lucky that I am a patient man," he told her. "Now sit up and talk to me."

"What does this mean?" she asked, pointing to the paper. "How can this be?"

"Stop acting the innocent, Miss Smith. We know about this agreement between the Nazis and these men in 1936. We know that your entire family was and is involved. *Still* involved, Miss Smith. One of my agents was killed a few weeks ago." He paused for added effect. "You are involved, Miss Smith, or you would be dead, just like your parents!"

Leander's last words had almost the same effect as if he had pulled the trigger of a gun.

"What are you saying?" Her voice was a harsh whisper.

Leander continued, his voice like a whip, cutting at her already flayed emotions.

"Did it never strike you as odd that your parents committed suicide for no apparent reason? No history of the slightest problem? Rich, healthy heirs to power and position. There was no reason—except this." He pointed to the paper. "We believe they wanted out, or proved unreliable, and were killed. These people leave no loose ends, especially a loose end like you. You are too close to it all. I repeat—either you are a part of this or you would be dead!"

Lisa sat unmoving, rigid. She was far away, in a different time, a different place. Her eyes looked weakly at Leander.

"You are saying that my parents were murdered? By whom?"

"We don't know. Of these conspirators, Van Dyne was your father's closest friend and confidant. Has he never told you? I can't believe he wouldn't have."

"They told me . . . they all told me my parents killed themselves. I believed it. How could I not? You were lucky— you had parents who loved you, who took care of you. Mine deserted me. They loved each other more than me. They even loved death more than me."

Lisa felt hot tears course down her cheeks. "How could you or anyone else know what that's like? I never even knew them . . ."

Her voice finally broke, and she buried her face in her hands. It was too much too fast, and her mind could not handle what she had learned. Lisa tried to regain some kind of control. She looked directly into Leander's eyes.

"I didn't know. I swear to you."

After some minutes of silence, she watched Leander put out his cigar and replace the document in his jacket. Leander went to the bar to pour a drink for each of them.

"Here," he said. "Drink this."

Lisa accepted it gratefully. Its raw fire burned and numbed her throat, and she began to feel steadier.

"Do you believe I'm innocent, Mr. Leander?"

Leander took a deep breath, then answered.

"Yes, I do."

"Then what can I do?"

"Do? You can do nothing," he said. "You are an amateur. Where would you go? What would you do?"

"You could tell me."

"And see you dead in a week? No. You will do nothing but keep this to yourself. If you tell anyone at all about our talk or about the conspiracy, then you will die. I may have made an error in accusing you, but do not think that you are totally cleared. If you attempt to warn your uncle, you will never reach him alive. You will be watched night and day. Do nothing, Miss Smith. Nothing at all. Good-bye."

Leander left Lisa sitting openmouthed at his departure. The sun streaming through the windows had turned deep amber. Lisa began to cry but for the first time in many years, with a feeling of release.

As Leander reached the front steps, Dreyer started the waiting car. Once inside, Leander sagged into the cushioned seat and let his body go limp. He was tired, physically and emotionally, from the ordeal he had put the girl through. So little truth, so many lies. He wondered, idly, if he was getting too old for this business. Perhaps I should retire, he thought. But not till after this one, was the thought that quelled all doubt. Dreyer interrupted his reverie.

"Did she buy it?"

"I think so. She even passed out once."

"You hit her?" asked Dreyer incredulously.

"Don't be crude. From the shock. The profile we have of her is essentially correct. She's a mass of confusion. At the center of Lisa Smith is the need to exonerate her parents and thereby herself. I think she'll be our bait. I hope we all find what we're looking for."

Dreyer assumed the remark referred to the conspiracy.

"We'll know in a few hours."

Leander nodded, his eyes heavy. "Wake me in Pretoria."

Dreyer nodded and continued to drive as the last rays of the sun made the sky catch fire.

Nine

Lisa sat in the room long after Leander had gone, until the deepening shadows turned to dusk. The drink she had poured earlier for herself remained untouched on the table beside her.

Leander's words kept ringing in her mind, over and over again.

> *"You are involved, Miss Smith, or you would be dead, just like your parents!"*
> *"We believe they wanted out, or proved unreliable and were killed!"*
> *"Van Dyne was your father's best friend!"*

She kept seeing him there with that awful cigar pointed at her head, but in her mind nothing compared to the possible relief from the burden she had carried for so long.

How odd, she thought, to find comfort in the belief that my mother and father were murdered. But if that was true, then they didn't leave me. They didn't! And that ray of hope shone in her mind like a beacon dispelling years of despair.

But in its place there grew a feeling of hatred so strong that it was like nothing she had ever felt before. It wiped away the depression and the helplessness she had always carried with her. They didn't leave me, she thought again, but now I have something to hate; something I can punish. Something that's not myself, she thought in a flash of intuitive understanding.

There was no doubt about what she would do. She had

decided hours ago. She couldn't go to her uncle, that much was clear. He was one of them.

"Van Dyne was your father's best friend!"

He would be first. Leander might decide to identify the men in the conspiracy. She didn't give a damn if it ruined the whole damn country. She'd pay them back. If what Leander said was true... that thought stopped her cold. The more she thought about it, the more she wondered. But in the end it really didn't matter. The hope was enough. To prove her parents innocent of suicide was enough. She would go to Amsterdam and get the truth from Van Dyne.

Leander had warned her that he would have her killed if she attempted to contact any of the men on that list. She realized he would have her followed. If she could "accidentally" slip her tail, though, it could be days before Leander located her. Enough time to get to Van Dyne. Enough time to find out.

Lisa reached for the phone and called the airport. A few minutes later she had the information she needed. A direct flight to Paris took off at 10:00 A.M. the following day. She made a reservation in the name of L. Salister, the first name to come to mind. A reservation in her own name might show up on security checks. The plane was nearly booked, but she got on.

She left the room and went to find Amad, who was in the kitchen with the cook. He rose from the table as she entered.

"Amad, please put my suitcases back in the car. I'm going back to Pretoria tonight."

"But..."

"Just do as I say, please."

"Yes, miss."

"I've got some supper for you, Miss Lisa," said the cook.

"I'll eat it here. I want to be on my way as soon as Amad is done."

"Yes, miss."

Lisa sat down to eat, rehearsing her plan in her head. It seemed fine to her. Nothing too tricky. Finishing what was on her plate, she went into the living room and called a friend in Pretoria. The phone rang several times before it was answered.

"Hello?"

"Jane? It's Lisa. Can I see you first thing in the morning?"

"Isn't it a little late? Where are you?"

"Never mind. I need your help with something. Can I count on you?"

"Is it illegal?"

"Not a chance," Lisa lied.

"Okay, then. I'll leave the door open. You can let yourself in."

"Fine. I'll be there soon."

The ride back was unrelieved in the pitch black of the night. Lisa found, against her will, that her eyes finally closed, and she slept most of the way back.

She was awakened by the driver on the outskirts of Pretoria. He announced that they were being followed and asked for instructions. The matter of a car following the Prime Minister's daughter was not to be taken lightly, and he was confused when Lisa ordered him to ignore the car. She gave him Jane's address and told him to proceed.

Jane was already up and drinking coffee. She looked up, bleary-eyed, as Lisa entered.

"What are you up to, my dear girl?"

"Jane, it's frightfully complicated. Please just help me and do what I say. I promise you won't regret it nor get into any trouble. Will you?"

"I suppose so," Jane replied. "Now tell me what you want."

A few hours later, Lisa was in Powell's, an exclusive dress shop downtown. She had bought a new brown dress with a matching scarf and light brown jacket. On her head she wore a deep, wide straw hat which covered most of her face.

At precisely nine o'clock, Lisa left the store, walked outside, and ran smack into Jane, who threw up her hands and hugged Lisa warmly. The two women were being watched by the man seated in the parked car across the street, but he noticed nothing more than that they chatted and reentered the store.

A few minutes later, he saw Lisa emerge once again, get into her car, and drive off. He accelerated quickly into the morning traffic to follow.

Lisa watched him pull away. Dressed in a new suit that she had purchased after dressing Jane in her other clothes for her role as decoy, Lisa went to the curb and took a cab to the airport.

On the way she checked the purse Jane had given her that contained, among other things, her passport and three thousand rands in traveler's checks, which Jane had picked up from Lisa's apartment.

At the airport, Lisa noted with satisfaction that the plane was listed as full. Entering a phone booth, she called the reservation desk and canceled her prior reservation in the name of Salister. Then she made a dash for the counter, where she bought a first-class ticket to Amsterdam on the now unfilled plane.

As the last boarding call was made, Lisa raced to customs; and as her passport was a diplomatic one, she was shown directly to the plane.

Twenty minutes later, she was in the sky, chuckling to herself at the fools she had made of everybody. She ordered a drink to celebrate and almost spilled it, as the plane hit a pocket of turbulence, on the man reading his paper next to her.

He had good reason to laugh as well, but Peter Dreyer disliked doing so in public. He had said good-bye to Leander at his office earlier. Leander had been very excited.

"She's done it, Peter. She's on her way. Thinking she's rather clever, no doubt."

"Amateurs always do," Peter agreed.

"She's using a double reservation and will probably use her friend as a decoy. I've just had a report from the surveillance on her apartment. Her friend picked up the passport and money."

"Did you have her phone bugged?"

"Of course," said Leander.

"And her friend's apartment?"

"Ten minutes after she called."

Dreyer smiled and picked up his suitcases. "I'll be going now. Take care, Jan."

"And you, Peter. And take care of our crystal, as well. She's got to be alive to attract sugar."

Dreyer had snorted at that. Keeping an untrained amateur alive long enough to attract anything was no easy job.

He thought about it again as the plane bounced repeatedly. This is not going to be an easy ride, he thought, and hoped it was not an omen. He snorted again.

Lisa Smith offered him a tissue.

Ten

With the notable exception of the French Quarter, New Orleans is not a pretty city, or so Ben thought as he drove into its downtown area.

Although the drive south had sped by quickly and without incident, Ben felt weak and his head ached. Croft's prediction about his burning out had been correct, and he decided to find a room with a soft bed and rest before proceeding further.

It was only midafternoon, but the Quarter was filled with people. There were housewives carrying baskets of groceries or laundry, store owners hawking their wares, and teenagers intent on the opposite sex. It was, as yet, too early for the bands in the clubs to begin playing, and the only music in the streets erupted from jukeboxes in the dark bars as doors swung open and closed.

Ben entered the St. Charles Hotel, its lobby decorated with deep brown carpets, white wrought-iron tables and chairs, and walls of white marble.

"I'd like a room, please," he said to the uniformed desk clerk.

"Certainly, sir. Will you be staying with us long?"

"I think just one night will do," said Ben.

"Very good, sir."

"My car is being held by the doorman, and the luggage is inside. Here are my keys," Ben stated as he signed the register. The deskman smiled professionally.

"I'll have it sent up immediately." He rang the bell at his side, and a young, dark-haired boy sprang to the desk.

"Please get Mr. Davidson's luggage from his car and bring it to room two-sixteen." The boy exited, as the bell rang again and a second boy reported to the desk.

"Please escort Mr. Davidson to his room." He turned back to Ben. "I trust your stay with us will be pleasant, sir."

"I'm sure it will be."

Arriving at the room, the bellhop opened the door, entered,

and began describing the television, air conditioning, and hotel services, hoping for a large tip. Ben gave him some money, and the boy left quickly.

Moments later his luggage arrived. Ben tipped the boy and shut the door to the room. In less than ten minutes—his wound cleaned and dried, and his clothing scattered around the room—Ben lay fast asleep.

Downstairs, the man who had followed Ben from Mississippi waited a few minutes longer before leaving the lobby. He had heard Ben's room number quite clearly.

Quietly he ascended two flights of stairs to the hotel's second floor. Unnoticed by the staff, he noted the number and location of each room as he passed it until he came to Room 216. This was a corner room, in the back of the building, and a view of its door could be commanded by the rooms numbered 212, 214, 218, and 220.

He paused to tie his shoe and, in doing so, noted the location of elevator, staircase, ice machine, linen closet, and Room 216's position relative to each along the long corridor. Twenty seconds later he walked casually through the lobby and out the front door to the street.

From his car, which he had parked on a side street, he took a black attaché case and locked it in the trunk. Then he drove for a few blocks until he found a small luggage store. There he bought two suitcases, one small enough to fit inside the first. He paid cash, ending the entire transaction in a few moments. At the car he placed the small suitcase inside the larger to give it weight.

He drove back to the St. Charles, allowing the doorman to take his car keys and lift his suitcase into the hands of a waiting porter.

"Good day, sir," said the desk clerk as he approached.

"I would like a room," said the man.

"Very good, sir."

"Just a moment," said the man as the clerk reached for a key. His cold blue eyes fixed the clerk like a butterfly on a specimen board.

"I have a great aversion to noise and would like a room away from the rattle of the elevator and people tramping to those idiotic ice machines. Further, I would like to be on a lower floor, close to the stairway in case this firetrap of a building should choose to burn down. Can this be arranged?"

The desk clerk had been at the hotel far too long to take offense at a difficult customer.

"Will the second floor be acceptable sir?"

"Yes."

"Room two-eighteen is at the end of the corridor, facing the rear courtyard of the hotel and should be very quiet. The elevator and ice machine are at the opposite end. Will that suffice, sir?"

For the first time the man seemed pleased.

"That will be fine," the man replied. He turned toward the elevator as the clerk directed a bellhop to pick up the suitcase and guide him to Room 218.

"Have a pleasant stay . . ." called the clerk, but the man was already out of earshot.

The bellhop was disappointed with the small tip he received as the man cut his speech short and ushered him from the room immediately after he had unlocked the door.

Inside the room the man neither turned on the television nor approached the big bed. Instead, he took one of the chairs, placed it by the door, picked up a newspaper which he had bought from a stand downstairs, and began to read. Every so often a noise in the hallway would cause him to put down his paper and open the door a crack to check, but the door to 216 remained closed, and the man went back to his paper.

Ben awoke, feeling tired and drained, shortly before seven o'clock. After a long shower, he felt better, dressed, and left the hotel in search for a place for dinner.

Outside he was struck by the amazing transformation that befalls New Orleans' French Quarter at night. The many people had given way to crowds so dense that even the streets were filled with the overflow from the sidewalks. Music blared from countless open doorways, from jazz to bluegrass, and all of it hot, loud, and sweet.

Walking through the streets, Ben stepped into pools of sound that surrounded each doorway until he felt like the needle on a radio dial spun through the stations picking up short bursts from each. It was a strange way to pick a restaurant, by its music, but Ben was caught by the sharp sound of one jazz quintet and followed it inside to find, he hoped, food as palatable as its music.

It was a minute or two before his eyes grew accustomed to the darkness. The maître d' told him that his table would be ready in a few moments and suggested he step into the bar for a drink while he waited. Ben took a stool at the bar, a long slab of mahogany with brass fittings on the corners, bordered by brass rails on the floor. The bar was well stocked and barmaids moved swiftly about the room serving small tables crowded with people.

"Can I get you something, sir?" asked the bartender, a big man dressed in a striped polo shirt and black sailor-type trousers.

"Scotch, please."

"Right away."

The drink appeared at his elbow a scant five seconds later. For a while Ben watched the man work. It pleased him to watch someone really skilled at his trade. In the old neighborhood he had often eaten at a diner a few blocks from his house on those nights his mother refused to cook and his father was working late. Sitting at the counter, he would watch the short-order cook preparing ten meals at once with hands as fast and as sure as a symphony conductor's. Giant piles of home fries, frying onions, eggs, steaks, all were grilled to perfection on the spotless griddle. Ben had been sorry when the diner was sold to make way for one of a chain of radio stores.

His reverie was interrupted when a voice beside him observed, "Good hands, no wasted motion, and he sets up his bar well, don't you think?" Ben turned to the woman on the next barstool, surprise showing on his face. She smiled and asked, "You *were* watching the bartender, weren't you?"

"Are you taking a poll or do you work for the restaurant?" Ben answered her question with one of his own, feeling uncomfortable at her directness.

"Neither, I'm a stewardess for American. My name's Amy Cassidy. What's yours?"

"Ben."

"First time in New Orleans?"

"No."

"Look, Ben, this is called conversation. First, I speak and

volunteer information; then, you speak and do the same. Get it? It comes easier with practice." She smiled again, with real warmth, and Ben visibly relaxed.

She was very attractive, in her late twenties, he judged. Blond hair in a mass of curls framed her pretty, green-eyed face. Thin, dressed in a bright blue skirt and blouse, she looked fit and athletic.

"I'm sorry," Ben began. "I'm not especially good at repartee. I'm a writer here doing research."

"How exciting. For a book? Or a movie?"

"Originally for an article. I do freelance work for magazines and newspapers, but I've gotten a bit sidetracked."

"Go on, I'm intrigued. Is that how you hurt your head?" she asked.

"No," he lied. "I hit my head getting out of the car." He quickly tried to change the subject. "Do you always talk to strange men in bars?"

He knew he'd blown it the minute the words left his mouth. The look on her face changed to one of scorn.

"That has to be the dumbest thing I've heard in years. All I offered you was conversation, not an invitation to bed. You think you'd be a little more sophisticated for a writer. Forget it, I'm sorry to have bothered you."

She turned away, back to the bar, and finished her drink. Ben wanted to kick himself for putting her off with a thoughtless remark. He always felt awkward dealing with women in social situations; rarely had a relationship lasted more than a few dates. He wanted to make contact, but his emotions seemed sealed up inside, protected by years of self-control and frustration. Determination replaced anger as he turned to intercept Amy as she left.

"I'm sorry. Could we please try that again?" he asked quietly.

Amy turned back to him, her bright smile again in full force.

"Sure, why not?"

Ben caught the maître d' signaling that his table was ready, and he decided to invite Amy to join him.

"I know we just met, and I haven't distinguished myself conversationally at all, but if you'd have dinner with me, I think I'd be better company after some food."

Amy nodded her acceptance. "I'd like that very much,

Ben. I did overwhelm you a little, and I'll try not to do it again."

They followed the maître d' to a table in the corner of the large room, where the jazz quintet continued to play. In a few minutes, they were served the house specialty, shrimp jambalaya, and Ben began to relax and open himself to Amy's gentle questioning.

"I've always wondered about writers," Amy said, spearing a morsel of shrimp from her plate. "It must be such a thrill to see your name in print. Instant ego gratification."

"It's funny you should mention that," Ben said, "because my first things published were under a pseudonym. I didn't start using my real name until a few years ago."

"Why not? What made you use a pen name?" Amy asked, intrigued.

"I was a lieutenant in 'Nam in 1971, when I first started writing, and what I wrote would have gotten me court-martialed. So I sent the work to an agent friend of mine who got it published under another name."

"How did you get the stuff out of 'Nam? I thought the army censored what came in and out."

"They did. But I gave it to a friend who smuggled it back into the states on a furlough."

"Sounds very complicated."

Ben laughed. "Not really. The army was so uptight about dope smuggling they never checked for anything else. He simply stuck the papers in his underwear and walked through. We both thought it was a fitting vehicle."

"Weren't you scared of getting caught? I would have been."

Ben sobered for a moment. "Did you ever feel anger so deep, or were you so appalled by something, that it just didn't matter what the cost was and that you had to strike out against it? I'm no martyr. I saw guys get so crazy that they would frag the officers' latrine or mess tent just to get back at somebody."

"Frag?" Amy interrupted.

"Blow up with fragmentation grenades."

"Oh, how dreadful."

"The whole thing was dreadful. I'm not unique. I was able to get it out by writing rather than by shooting an officer in the back. Maybe I was doing the same thing. I guess it depends on how you look at it. Anyway, I came back to find I had a bit of a nest egg and offers to do more. I took them, and here I am." Ben glanced at his watch.

"You have an appointment?" Amy asked.

"I have some time, but I need to do some work for an hour or two. Could I see you later?"

"Of course."

"Good. Now tell me about you before I go."

Amy flung a few curls from her face and laughed. "There's very little to tell. I'm from Cincinnati, Ohio, where I went to school. I studied theater at the university and was twenty-three before I realized that Hollywood wasn't looking for me. I fell into this job because it seemed like a good thing to do. But I've never had to take over for a dying pilot or copilot, or shoot terrorists. Most of my job is really being a glorified waitress in the sky for obnoxious tourists who think we're running a hotel instead of an airplane."

Ben winced. "Remind me to behave myself next time I fly."

"I don't mean that. We're paid to serve the passengers. What makes me angry is the guy who expects me to answer for the pilot and the weather, go out shopping at thirty thousand feet up, and then tuck him in and smile when his hand goes up my skirt."

"I see your point," he said, and signaled the waiter for the check. "I'm staying at the St. Charles. Where can I meet you later? Say eleven or so?"

"I'll meet you in the lobby. Okay?"

"Fine."

Ben paid the check over Amy's objections, and they walked outside. The streets were still mobbed. Amy stretched in the night air.

"I'm going back to my room to change. I'll see you later, Ben. Thank you for dinner."

"Thank you for coming. I'll see you at eleven, at the hotel."

Deciding it would be easier to find a cab outside the Quarter, Ben began to walk. The mosaic inlays of street names on every corner glinted blue and white in the light from the street lamps. The meeting with Amy had affected him, and Ben was glad for a chance to examine his feelings while walking.

He had long since given up hoping for the breathtaking, pulse-quickening, love-at-first-sight meetings that he had read and heard about, but it was nice to feel something again. He had begun to think of himself as an emotional cripple, since every woman he had taken to bed had left him feeling lonelier and emptier than ever. He had to find someone with whom he could express himself as he did in his writing, someone who made him feel whole again. Maybe nothing would happen with Amy, but he felt like he'd made a first step toward something, and he picked up the pace of his steps.

A few minutes later he saw a cab and hailed it.

"Tulane Medical School," he told the driver.

What Ben wanted was the Medical School Library, for in it, he believed, were the keys to some of the puzzles presented by Dr. Eugene Croft. From his own experience, he knew that medical students studied at odd hours and sometimes all night. The library would be open at least until midnight, and he thought he could find the books he needed without help.

Arriving at the school, Ben paid the driver and walked up the broad concrete steps to the entrance. Pausing to ask a student for directions, he was directed to the library. Even at this late hour groups of students stood together talking animatedly about some new facet of their training. The scene took Ben back to his own school days, and for a time he felt sadness overtake him. Then he was at the door and entered.

"May I help you?" The librarian behind the desk looked up at him.

"Yes, please. I'm a student at New York University here on vacation. Can I get reciprocal privileges to do some work in the library?"

"You know you will not be able to remove any books from the library."

"That's okay. I just want to do some research."

The librarian smiled. "I'm sure that will be fine. Let me make out a temporary pass to the stacks."

Armed with his pass, Ben entered the main room and went straight to the card catalog. Finding the listings for what he wanted, he went to the reference desk to ascertain their locations. A student working there showed him the way, and soon he had two of the books he needed spread out before him: the *American Medical Association Medical Directory* and the *Directory of Medical Specialists*.

The first volume yielded nothing, which did not especially surprise him. It was not unusual that a doctor with a backwoods practice like Dr. Croft's would not be a member.

In the second volume he hit pay dirt. Croft was listed, but what Ben found was totally at odds with the "simple country doctor" Croft had claimed to be. He was listed in the section on "Research."

Croft, Eugene R.
   b. 1902 Heidelberg, Germany
Education—B.A.—1920 University of Heidelberg
             M.D.—1925 University of Berlin
             PhD—1954 University of Chicago
Specialty—Genetics Research
Publications: See Bio Abstr acts, 1937, 1953, 1966,
          1968, 1970.
Awards—
   Chapman Fellowship, Latham Committee Scholar
Positions—
   Visiting specialist Alabama State Board of Health;
   San Antonio Childrens Hospital, Assistant Direc-
   tor of Research; New York Veterans Hospital,
   Geriatrics Research

Ben returned to the stacks to find *Biological Abstracts*, which functioned as a kind of index to the hundreds of research articles published yearly in the field of biology and described them briefly. He found the volumes for the years listed under Croft's name quickly and returned to his seat.

An hour later, drenched with sweat, he closed the last of the volumes on the book-littered table. It could not be true, but the coincidences were impossible to disregard. There was only one last bit of corroboration required.

Totally shaken by the monstrosity of what he had uncovered, Ben went to *The New York Times Index* and crosschecked his findings against their articles. Soon he was finished, and the last piece of the Croft puzzle fell into place.

He picked up the article by Jane E. Brody from *The New York Times* that he had photocopied from the microfilm viewer and read it again. It was dated July 27, 1972.

It was a scientific experiment. For 30 years Federal health officers allowed 400 poor black men known to have syphilis to go untreated despite the discovery that penicillin could cure their devastating disease.

The study, which began in Tuskegee, Ala., in 1932 (ten years before penicillin) to determine the course of untreated syphilis, has raised once again a major dilemma for medical research that concerns the ancient issue of means and ends: Assuming that some experimentation on human beings is necessary to medical progress, how can these studies be performed in a way that does not violate the basic rights of man?

Ironically, the Tuskegee Study, as it is called, was begun in the year Hitler came to power. It was Hitler's atrocious "experiments" done in the name of medical science which led after World War II to the promulgation of the Nuremberg Code, a series of ethical guidelines to be applied to all human experimentation. It was ignored in the Tuskegee research.

None of the men in the study were ever treated for their disease, and at least seven eventually died of the late effects of syphilis. Even before penicillin, none of the patients were given the admittedly toxic therapy of the day—injections of metals like arsenic, mercury or bismuth—to see if they fared any better or worse than those untreated. The study's subjects may never have been told in terms they understood what was wrong with them.

One of the study's 74 survivors, Charles Pollard, an intelligent although uneducated farmer in Tuskegee, told a reporter, "they never mention syphilis to me—not even once."

The ethics of the study would have been questioned regardless of who the subjects were, but the fact that Federal doctors had selected poor, uneducated men—and not one of them a white man—further inflamed the issue. As one white Southerner remarked, "The worst segregationist in Alabama would never have done this."

Even with a score of proclamations, codes, declarations, statements and guidelines formulated since the Nuremberg code that are now supposed to be applied to all human experimentation, many questionable studies have been done in recent years and, to loud cries of "human guinea pigs," several have become embroiled in public controversy. Almost without exception, they involve members of minority or disadvantaged groups.

● Eight years ago, as part of a study of immunity to cancer, a leading New York cancer specialist injected live tumor cells into chronically ill patients without ever telling them in plain English what they were being given and why. The researcher was found guilty of "unprofessional conduct" by the state Board of Regents. Fortunately, nothing went awry in the subjects, all of whom rejected the tumor cells.

● Nearly 400 poor women—most of them Mexican-Americans who had already borne many children and had come to a San Antonio family planning clinic for contraception—were enrolled in a study a few years ago to determine whether oral contraceptives did in fact cause psychological changes. All of the women were given identical-looking drugs, most of them active contraceptive agents. But 76 women received a "dummy", or placebo, drug. Seven pregnancies occurred before the study was ended, six of them in the placebo group.

● In 1969, coercion was charged in conjunction with a study in which live hepatitis virus was injected into mentally retarded children at Willowbrook State Hospital on Staten Island. Parents, who were said to have a poor understanding of the study, were allegedly being forced into consenting to their children's participation by way of getting them into the crowded hospital.

The controversy dissipated after changes were made in the consent procedure and the medical rationale was thoroughly explained. But to this day, many scientists are still objecting to the use of mentally defective children in research, subjects who themselves cannot possibly give informed consent to what is being done to them.

● The question of informed voluntary consent has been raised repeatedly regarding research on prisoners, who many believe are under a subtle form of coercion—the hope for a shorter term, earlier parole, easier duty—when they agree to be subjects in medical studies. Three years ago, this newspaper exposed an extensive network of highly questionable studies of drugs and donations of blood plasma in Southern prisons. Many prisoners were stricken with serious illnesses and some of them died. All were given substantial monetary rewards for their participation, and thus many failed to report illness for fear they would lose their only source of income.

In the last four or five years, concern over the ethics of human experimentations has mounted. Nearly every issue of the leading medical journals contains some comment on the subject and a number of physicians and ethicists have put together book-length discussions.

In reading them, one thing becomes clear—even among the most concerned and conservative, there is to this day no universal agreement on what is and what is not an ethical experiment.

During the Tuskegee Experiment, Croft had been listed as a visiting member of the Alabama Board of Health and in 1937 had published an article entitled "The Effect of Spirochete on Spermatozoa Production of Gamete Pairs." Nearly 400 black people were injected with the disease or allowed its infection remain untreated, and Croft did research into the effects on their reproduction! He had followed it up with similar research in his doctoral thesis in 1953.

In 1965, Croft had been a staff researcher in New York at the same hospital where chronically ill patients were injected with cancer, unbeknownst to them, and Croft had published research in 1966 on the effects of that cancer on reproduction and genetic structure.

In 1967, Croft had been at the San Antonio Children's Hospital where women were given placebos instead of contraceptives, and Croft published a study on the psychological effects of that deception in 1968.

And in 1969, Croft was back in New York in the Veteran's Hospital on Staten Island, only a few miles from Willowbrook State Hospital where retarded children were injected with live hepatitis virus. Only six months later, in 1970, Croft published another article entitled "The Structure and Function of DNA Protein Changes as Effected by Viral Infection." Further, his proximity to the southern prisons could not be ignored.

Ben carefully replaced the books after making copies of what he'd read. He put all the material in his jacket pocket, knowing that the wisest thing was to go to the attorney general. He looked at his watch and suddenly remembered Amy waiting for him. He would go back to the hotel, see her, and then get some sleep. His hand brushed his forehead and found it hot, the result of mental exhaustion and too little rest. He sat for a moment to clear his head.

The blue-eyed man, seated a few tables away, rose and walked to the phone booth. His call was brief, and afterward he left the library and began to walk quickly toward the St. Charles. Halfway there he flagged down a taxi and rode the rest of the way.

At the hotel he went out to his car, parked in the hotel garage, and removed the black attaché case from the trunk. He walked quietly and without haste. In his room he rested the case on the bed and removed four items: a thirty-eight caliber revolver, a small strip of plastic, a silencer, and six cartridges in a quick-load plastic holder. After loading the gun, he placed it, with the silencer, into his coat pocket.

Making certain there was no one in the hallway, he crossed the hall to Room 216, used the plastic deftly, and opened the door to Ben's room. Inside, he relocked the door, pulled a chair directly opposite the entrance, and sat down to wait, the assembled gun resting lightly on his leg.

Downstairs, Ben had just entered the lobby. He was surprised to find Amy waiting calmly in one of the wrought-iron chairs.

"I'm really sorry, Amy, but I got totally hung up on the research. I didn't think you'd still be here."

"I'm not sure why I am," she said. "You look terrible," she added.

"I feel that way," admitted Ben.

"Did you find what you were looking for?"

Ben shuddered inwardly. "I suppose I did. I'm truly sorry I didn't call."

Amy looked at him for a long moment and then seemed to decide something. Her smile returned.

"Forget it. You don't look like you were having a very good time either."

"I wasn't."

"Well, then, we can make it up to each other." They entered a nearby bar and ordered drinks. Ben sipped his slowly, knowing it would not take much to make him drunk in his weakened state. His brain was still reeling from what he had learned. Visions of James Wilcox's last act replayed in his brain like a movie in slow motion.

"You seem to be very upset by whatever you were working on this evening," Amy observed gently. "Do you always get this involved in your work?"

"Usually," he answered. "I have to feel that it's personal. Otherwise, there's no real force behind my inquiry, no passion in the words that I write. The difference between good investigative reporting and mediocre storytelling is usually the writer's personal commitment. And . . . what I'm working on now is something I sort of fell into. But the deeper I dig, the more I find I don't know. And what I've found already scares the hell out of me."

"I wish I could help you, in some way," Amy said after a moment.

"We've known each other such a short time. Why would you want to become involved, knowing so little about me?" he asked warily.

"Call it a whim, maybe, Ben. But there's something about you, something in the way you watch people, and your intensity when you talk about your work, that makes me want to be part of it, want to do something more vital than what I do."

Ben found the thought of Amy's companionship a tempting one. He had felt so alone for so long, unable to share even his simplest feelings. He wondered if he dared take her up on her offer . . . but he had no right to involve her in what he'd discovered.

"I think we should take this slowly," he said, not wanting to hurt her with outright rejection.

"But you will think about it . . ." her voice trailed off.

"Yes, but I have to be honest with you. Partnership, especially emotional partnership, is difficult for me."

"Okay, I won't push. Tell me more about your work."

Ben relaxed, the subject postponed for a moment.

"The articles I've done fall somewhere in between investigative journalism and exposés. The Vietnam pieces were just the beginning, really. I like to dig deep into whatever subject I take on. And, after all this time, I've developed a good ear for inconsistencies, which usually cover up lies, which usually cover up more heinous activities.

"Since I'm not tied to any one paper or magazine, I've got a little wider latitude to choose my stories. I've played some very strange roles at times to get the background for the story I was chasing. One time I pretended to be a medical administrator, to investigate services and staff in the city's hospitals; another time I was a fisherman on a piece about corruption in the wholesale fish markets. I've been a diamond buyer, a long-haul trucker, and a nightclub owner. I've even had to be a chickenhawk."

"Come again?"

"A man who finds young boys to sell into prostitution. It was a lousy assignment, but helping to put some of those people away for a long time was pretty good compensation."

"It begins to sound more like police work than journalism," Amy said. "I never realized it could be so dangerous."

"It isn't, much of the time," Ben replied. "But sometimes you've got to take some chances to get your story. It can be very lonely, not to mention violent. I had enough of violence in Vietnam," he added reflectively. "For a number of not very good reasons, in retrospect, I enlisted with the Special Forces—the Green Berets. I did a lot over there I'd like to forget, and I hoped when I got out I could put it behind me. Most soldiers do, and I tried to, God knows. But I've needed those skills more than once since the war, so I've tried to accept it as part of my work. I don't know, maybe I seek it out—it seems that a lot of my stories are pretty dangerous." Ben looked uncomfortable, not sure he wanted to continue the conversation.

"Look, nobody—at least no sane man—likes violence," Amy told him. "You use it if you have to—to survive." Ben looked surprised that she understood that. It was an awkward moment. Conscious of being together, conscious of a growing attraction, neither Ben nor Amy wished to jar their fragile relationship with suggestions of deeper involvement. Yet that very suggestion hung in the air between them like Amy's perfume, alive and inviting. And both Ben and Amy were aware of it.

"In the normal course of events..." she began tentatively.

"I'm... unsure," he said, pulling back.

"Maybe I can be sure for both of us. For now, Ben," she said.

He reached over and brushed his hand gently over her cheek. There was greater risk for him, he knew, in being intimate with Amy than in all the dangerous assignments he could think of. Yet something stirred within him and, knowing he could not have what he did not risk, his hand slipped down to hold hers.

"For now, maybe that's enough," he agreed.

They walked through the lobby. The elevator was empty, and Ben pushed the button for his floor, acutely conscious of Amy's quiet presence next to him.

They stepped into the carpeted corridor. Their feet made almost no sound as they walked past identical doors and from pool to pool of light cast by each overhead bulb. At his door Ben leaned down to pick up the newspaper placed there by the hotel.

He reached into his coat to search for his key, fumbled it out of a pocket, and almost dropped it. When he placed it against the lock in the knob of the door, it slid in with bumpy ease. Ben felt his hands tremble a bit with mounting tension, and he drew a deep breath as the door opened inward a small way when the lock released it.

He stepped aside for Amy to enter. It was a gentlemanly gesture that saved his life.

He saw the flash of gunfire and Amy fall almost at the same time. Vietnam-trained reflexes took over, and Ben dived to the floor, throwing whatever he had in his hands, in this case the newspaper, simultaneously. He was lucky, as the paper burst open in a shower of pages. A man Ben didn't recognize struggled to get out of a chair.

Ben leaped at the man and struck viciously at his exposed neck with the edge of his hand. The man grunted and buckled but did not go down, and Ben saw the silenced revolver in his hand turn toward him.

Grabbing the wrist that held the gun, Ben threw his weight backward and brought the man's gun arm under his right armpit. With his left elbow, he struck backward as hard as he could and felt the point of his elbow strike the man deep in his ribs. Ben twisted again and, locking on the man's wrist, used his leverage to turn it around and press it backward against the arm. It broke with an audible snap, and the gun clattered to the floor.

The man tried to swing at Ben's head, but pain and confusion caused him to miss. Ben kicked him in the groin, and when the man went down, followed through with a final stomp to the back of his head. The man lay unconscious at his feet. Ben picked up the gun and went to where Amy was sprawled limp on the floor.

She was dead, a gaping hole under her left breast. Whatever might have been, whatever could have been between them was over before it began. Enraged, Ben leveled the gun at the still unconscious man and struggled not to kill him. He almost lost.

The door was still open; the entire fight had lasted only a few seconds. Ben shut and locked the door. He looked at the man with a cold rage devoid of all feeling but hatred. He shifted the gun into his left hand and searched the man who lay silently at his feet.

There was nothing in the man's pants pockets save for some cash and a room key to 218. Ben found the man's wallet in his jacket pocket. A Mississippi driver's license made out to Henry Schmidt; assorted credit cards in the same name. Emptying the cards onto the table, Ben noticed an inside flap in the wallet. Prying apart the leather fold, Ben took out a plain white card embossed with black lettering. On it was the picture of an eagle with wings spread over what appeared to be a nest. Underneath was typed Henry Schmidt, and his signature appeared directly below. Above the eagle, in Gothic script, was one word: ADLERKINDEN.

Ben looked at the card for a long while. Adlerkinden— Children of the Eagle.

The coincidence of the Mississippi license and his recent visit there was impossible to overlook. If Croft had had him followed, then the man had seen him go to the Wilcox place and later to the medical library. His visit to the library would have convinced Croft that he had not forgotten Annie and James. Croft had little to fear from either event separately, but together the conclusion was inescapable.

Ben mentally kicked himself for having failed to predict what now seemed obvious. And because of his stupidity, Amy was dead. At that moment he hated Croft even more. With a clarity that wiped away all other emotions, he realized he had to destroy Croft; not only for Amy or Annie or the hundred others Croft had abused, but for himself, too.

Schmidt began to stir. Ben pulled the chair a few feet from him and sat down with the gun pointed at Schmidt's chest.

Schmidt rose to a sitting position before he saw Ben and the gun and froze. Ben saw Schmidt's eyes take in the empty wallet on the table and the I.D. card that Ben held in his left hand. Ben cocked the trigger of the gun, the click audible throughout the room.

"Who or what is the Adlerkinden?" asked Ben in an ice-cold voice.

"I don't speak English," said Schmidt in German.

"I speak German. It's all the same to me. What is the Adlerkinden?" demanded Ben in fluent German.

Schmidt said in English, "I don't know."

"You're lying. Who sent you here?"

"No one."

"Why did you try to kill me?" Schmidt was sweating visibly.

"Did Croft send you? Tell me."

Schmidt leaped from the floor at Ben. The mad lunge almost took Ben by surprise, but in a reaction faster than conscious thought, Ben squeezed the trigger, felt the vibration of the exploding shell, and saw the hole blossom in Schmidt's chest as the body came crashing down on him, knocking him from the chair.

He picked himself off the floor and pushed Schmidt's body

aside. The first shock of reaction was beginning to set in, and Ben was shaking.

He sat down to think. He had to be free to get Croft. Nothing else mattered now.

He picked up the key to Schmidt's room and went across the hallway with the gun concealed in his jacket. In one move he opened the door and burst in, gun ready, but the room was empty.

It was two o'clock in the morning, and the corridor remained deserted. Ten minutes later, Ben had carried both bodies into 218. He wiped the gun and replaced it in Schmidt's hand. Picking up the room phone and muffling his voice, Ben called the desk. He asked for an extension of Schmidt's stay for three days and canceled maid service. It would not fool anybody for very long, but he hoped it would buy him enough time to get out of New Orleans. He left, locking the door with the "Do Not Disturb" sign in place.

Returning to his room, he cleaned up as best he could.

Fully dressed, he lay down on the bed. He knew sleep would not come for many hours, if at all. He would have to face his pain and anger and despair—for Amy, and Annie and James, and somehow find a way to avenge them.

Eleven

Ben checked out of the hotel at 9 A.M. the following morning. It was not until he had crossed the state line back into Mississippi that he began to feel he had avoided pursuit. He kept the radio turned to an all-news station and, in between weather and livestock reports, hoped that he would get some notice of the discovery of the two bodies in the St. Charles.

I killed a man last night, thought Ben, realizing that he felt almost no remorse. He had always been taught by his father that life was sacred. Now he found he disagreed. It was the quality of life that was sacred, not the life itself. Those who deliberately did evil to others lost the right of protection under the law. He knew he was being simplistic and that the shades of differences in situations always had to be taken into account; but in the case of Croft, and the men who worked for him, he felt the issue was clear: They had to be stopped.

There comes a point, he thought, when a man has to stop saying, "Why doesn't somebody do something?" and do it himself. He had reached that point. Now there was no turning back, or the ghost of Amy and the specter of Annie's baby would haunt him till he died. He focused on that thought to strengthen his determination.

Ben still had the map Croft had given him, and tracing the route back to Croft's house was a simple matter. He was unsure as to exactly what he would find, but he knew that some form of tangible evidence would be necessary to convince the authorities of Croft's activities.

Some rest, he decided, was the first step to take. He pulled off the main highway into a seedy-looking town that met his two needs: a hardware store and a motel. He stopped at the store first and picked up the items he thought he would need, then drove to a motel called the Avon.

An old man with few teeth, little hair, and great rolls of fat tossed him a key, grunted, and returned to his television.

The room itself was furnished in Poverty Modern. Even the plastic flowers on the table were wilted from the countless cigarette butts that had been used to feed them. Ben lay down on the bed, and the springs groaned in protest. He reached over to the phone, called the manager, who answered after fifteen or so rings, and placed a wake-up call for eight that night.

All at once the adrenaline that had kept him going was replaced by a soporific, and he could barely keep his eyes open. Finally, he stopped trying and drifted into a deep, dreamless sleep.

The raucous buzz of the phone woke him several hours later. He answered the call and then rolled off the bed into a sitting position. Eye-level with the mirror over the dresser, Ben paused to stare at himself. His features looked drawn and haggard. He ran his fingers through his hair and tried to rub the sleep from his eyes, then headed for the bathroom.

The shower, like the room, was decrepit—stained white metal walls and a head so low he had to stoop to get his six feet under it. Ben cracked his head a few times while grabbing for the soap, which kept falling out of the grimy holder.

He shaved and dressed in a sweater, jeans, and sneakers and put his recent purchases in the pockets of a nylon Windbreaker. Then he repacked his bags in the car, drove over to the adjoining diner, and ordered breakfast. After two cups of coffee and a hasty trip to the men's room, he paid his check, got into his car, and drove off.

An hour later Ben pulled the car off the road half a mile from Croft's house. He parked it on a dirt path he had noticed the day before while leaving. It was eleven P.M. The moon was half full and gave him enough light to walk by. He stopped for a moment to fix some landmarks in his mind in case he was moving fast when he got back here. He hoped the precaution wasn't necessary.

Walking alone on the road at night felt strange. Ben grew conscious of the wind that whipped through the trees, of gravel that crunched under his sneakers, and of every stirring in the brush alongside the road. He wasn't afraid of the dark, only afraid of what the dark might hide. In Vietnam the dark hid death. Here, Ben hoped, the dark would hide him from death.

A hundred feet from the house Ben stopped to reconnoiter. He had seen only the front door, but surely there had to be a back door and a separate entrance into the examining rooms. If he could find it, that would be his safest entrance. There were no lights on in the house.

He found the door without incident. The glass panel next to it cut easily when Ben applied the glass cutter he had bought in town. Reaching through, he released the bolt lock and opened the door. No one stirred, and he stepped inside.

Ben waited until his eyes adjusted to the lack of moonlight. He did not want to use the flashlight until he was inside the lab, which had no windows. He entered the lab through a short corridor and played the flashlight over the room.

"Who's that?" growled a voice, and Ben jerked the light in the direction of the voice, preparing to strike at it and run. The beam showed James Wilcox, strapped to a table, and Ben almost cried with relief. He played the beam on his own face.

"Quiet, James," Ben whispered frantically. "For God's sake, hush up. It's me, Ben. Don't make any noise, or you'll bring the house down on us."

James remained quiet as Ben unstrapped him from the table. The sense of warmth that flooded through Ben felt strange to him, but he realized he was glad to see James, in spite of everything. He had long since stopped blaming James for his actions. He was a victim. Croft's victim.

"What you doin' here?" whispered James.

"Listen. I got it all worked out. I know what Croft's up to. Why your baby . . ." He let the sentence trail off when he saw James's eyes. "You gotta help me stop him, James. Please. Where's Annie? We'll get her out of here, too. You both can testify to—What are you doing?" Ben whispered hoarsely, but James had twisted the light from Ben's hand and shone it on the corner of the room. Ben followed the light and saw, to his horror, the body of Annie Wilcox behind the glass of a cold box. Her naked body still bore the incisions Croft had made earlier, and her face, with eyes wide open, was a mask of terror and betrayal.

"He made me watch, Ben. He did it 'cause he said I ruined his 'speriment," moaned James hoarsely. Ben was mute with shock.

"I'm gonna kill him," James rasped. "Now."

Ben recovered quickly. "Please, not now. Let me get what I came for, and the law will get him. Please, James. We can't take him now. Listen to me!"

But it was too late for James. The light in his eyes was that of a man on a mission from Hell. He was past anything human. He would go straight for Croft like an avalanche speeding down a mountainside, unstoppable, terrible in its race to reach the land below. Ben put up his hands to stop James, but James sent him sprawling with a push. He went crashing into a table covered with beakers and test tubes, and Ben knew that the cacophony would be heard all through the house.

He struggled to get up. He could hear James's bullish roar as he ran through the house in an effort to get to Croft. Ben knew he had only moments before he was discovered. He ran to the desk at which he had seen Croft working earlier and pounded on it in frustration. No journal. The drawers were locked, but he took a screwdriver from his pocket and, heedless of noise, pried one after another open and threw their contents to the floor. In one drawer he found a metal box that resisted his efforts to open it.

Suddenly, the unmistakable crack of a gunshot sounded in the house. Then another and a third. There were yells and orders being shouted.

Ben could waste no more time. Without regard to what he was taking, Ben crammed papers into his pocket, grabbed the metal box, and ran for the door. He flung it open and raced into the night air. The only hope now for James, if he wasn't already dead, was to get the police.

Without warning, a shape loomed in front of Ben—one of the guards from the house. Ben saw the moonlight glint off something shining in the man's hand.

Acting on reflex, he swung the metal box at the man's head. The impact jarred his arm straight to the shoulder, as the man went down with a heavy thud onto the damp earth. Ben spun away in what he hoped was the direction of the road. It sounded like all hell had broken loose behind him, and the lights in the house cast crazy shadows in front of him, making it hard to see where he was running.

His foot slid into a depression, and he went down in a crash. Rolling onto his back and then his stomach, he managed to right himself and realized he had fallen into the drainage ditch which ran along the road.

With pain throbbing in his left shoulder from the fall, Ben raced into the night. Though he had not run like this in a very long time, fear was a great incentive. Finally, after what seemed like hours, he found the landmark he had selected earlier. A few feet away he saw the dirt road where he had parked the car, unlocked and with the keys in the ignition.

Throwing himself into the front seat, he tossed the metal box into the back and gunned the motor to start.

Pulling out of the dirt, he headed as fast as he could down the road to get help. It was ten miles or so to the sheriff's office he had seen on the map. Ten miles were an eternity that night on a dark road with only James's last screams for company. His heart pounded as if it would burst from his chest, and his face and hands stung from cuts he had gotten when he fell.

Gradually, as he fought for control, his heart slowed down, and his breathing steadied. If he rushed like this into the sheriff's office, they would think he was a madman. Slow down. Relax. Rehearse what you are going to say, Ben told himself.

Out of the blackness the sheriff's office loomed suddenly, spotlighted against the night—a low, brick building with two police cars parked out front. Ben pulled over, took a deep breath and walked to the entrance.

Inside, there were two men in uniform playing cards. They looked up with vague hostility when Ben entered.

"Yeah?" said one who was about thirty-five, with thin, blond hair and a huge belly overriding his pants. His right hand moved a few inches toward the .38 strapped to his side. He was clearly in charge.

"Officer, I just passed Dr. Croft's place, and there seemed to be a huge ruckus going on. Lights were going on and off, and they were chasing someone. I thought you'd want to know."

"Who are you?" asked the other man. He was younger and leaner, and had a face that had not yet outgrown its pimples.

"I'm a writer from New York interviewing Dr. Croft because of his fine work here. I drove up to the house, saw the chaos, and hurried over here. I think I heard gunshots."

The older man eyed him suspiciously, and Ben tried to look as relaxed and innocent as he could. But every second brought James closer to death, if he were not dead already.

The man seemed to make up his mind.

"Okay, Billy. You stay here on the radio, and I'll go check it out." He nodded to Ben. "You can follow me back in your car."

"Sure, Sheriff. Let's go."

They left the office. Ben's pulse was racing, and he nearly rammed the back of the police car as the sheriff seemed to insist on driving at thirty miles an hour. Ben kept up a steady chant in his head: "Let's go, let's go, let's go, let's go," and pounded his hand on the wheel in frustration.

It was all unnecessary. The house was a mass of flames shooting fifty feet into the sky. As Ben pulled his car to a stop, he watched small explosions blow out windows and doors as the conflagration grew like fire in a haystack. Already, the roof of the lab had fallen in, and the sides of the house began to collapse as the upper stories fell into the lower ones. Built almost entirely of wood, the house would be embers long before any help could arrive.

Ben watched the sheriff circling the blaze, looking for bodies that Ben knew he would never find. As a funeral pyre for James and Annie, it was almost beautiful. As a source of evidence to indict Croft, it was hopeless. Ben spent a few minutes watching the flaming cinders curl upward and then, without looking back, drove away.

An hour later he checked into a room at the Hilton Hotel at New Orleans Airport. His only hope now lay in the metal box and the papers he had stolen. So far it did not look promising.

Most of the papers were simple receipts from pharmaceutical companies for drugs and lab equipment. The rest were notes or reminders of appointments. Disgusted, he threw them on the bed and took the screwdriver from his jacket to pry open the metal box.

The box contained personal correspondence to Croft, some of which was years old and mostly written in German. Ben read them, but they revealed little more than reports of friends' whereabouts over the years. No names rang a bell, and most were just signed with initials anyway. They were from all over the world, according to the postmarks, but they had only box numbers as return addresses, which he could not trace. He tossed these onto the bed, too.

Next he brought forth the first item of interest. Bound together by a thick rubber band were several letters that indicated that large sums of money had been transferred into an American bank for Croft's use. Ben's heart beat faster. This could tell him who funded Croft's research. The stationery was very expensive and bore the letterhead Van Dyne Diamond Exchange Ltd, 216 Herengracht, Amsterdam, N.L. Whoever was paying for Croft's work must have funneled the money through Amsterdam to the United States. It wasn't much to go on, but it seemed likely that, wherever Croft had gone, he would contact his source of money to set up a new account.

Ben picked up the final item in the box. It was a snapshot, yellowed with age, which showed two young men. One Ben assumed to be Croft, although he could not be sure—the years had faded the photo considerably. But the shape of the face and the eyes looked to be very similar. He was dressed in a business suit of 1930s vintage and standing next to another, similarly dressed man. The other was considerably shorter and stockier than Croft, with almost no neck and a large head with thin hair brushed straight back from a thick, wide forehead. Ben could not place him and simply tucked the photo away in his wallet.

Before he could sleep he needed to make some phone calls. First, he dialed the airlines and booked a morning flight for New York. It was almost three A.M. when he dialed again, and it took many rings before Bill Gottbaum answered his phone.

"Hello?" the groggy voice said.

"Bill? It's Ben Davidson. I'm sorry to get you up at this hour, but I'm on to the biggest thing of my life, and I need your help."

"Ben? What the hell are you talking about? It's God knows when in the morning. Where the hell are you?"

"New Orleans, and I know what time it is, and I already apologized."

"New Orleans? What the fuck is in New Orleans? I got eight different phone calls from Natchez that you didn't make your appointment. What happened? Are you all right?"

"Yes. Look, it's too complicated right now, but you've got to trust me. I need some favors. Ready?"

"You're insane."

"Probably. I'll fill you in when I see you."

"Okay. Okay. What do you need?"

"Go to my apartment. The landlady will let you in. Get my passport from my top dresser drawer."

"Passport? Why?"

"Stop asking questions. I'll explain later. *Please*. Then I need some cash, about three thousand. I'll convert it to traveler's checks at the airport."

"Airport?"

"Stop sounding like an echo. There's a ten A.M. flight on American to Kennedy that gets in at 12:30, your time. Meet me there. And pack me a suitcase or two, with enough for two or three weeks. Everything from formal clothes to my running shoes. Okay? I know it's asking a lot, but you'll understand when I see you."

"Passport, cash, clothes. Is that all or do you want me to get a fucking picnic basket as well?"

"Won't be necessary, but thanks anyway. See you in the morning." Gottbaum's acrid response was cut off as Ben hung up the phone. He knew Bill would be there.

He called the airlines again and arranged a second flight.

Then, with a weariness only partially abated by his new lead, Ben slept the sleep of the totally exhausted.

In the morning, feeling considerably more refreshed, he left the hotel, returned the rented car, and caught the plane to Kennedy.

Gottbaum was waiting. Ben ignored the searing look he got as he dragged Bill toward a restaurant. He refused to answer questions until they had ordered lunch. It came promptly, and they talked as they ate.

"What is this all about?" Gottbaum demanded.

"Did you get what I asked you to?"

Gottbaum handed him a heavy envelope. "It's all here, and the suitcases are in a locker." He handed over the key as Ben relaxed and pocketed it.

"You always come through for me, don't you?" Ben said warmly.

"Lord knows why," said Gottbaum, somewhat mollified.

"I do," said Ben. "You're one of the good guys."

"Good guy, my ass. Now tell me this instant what this is all about, or I'm walking."

Ben took a deep breath and told the story exactly as it had happened: from getting lost in Mississippi up through the events of the previous night. He handed Gottbaum the envelope containing the research he had done.

"It's all here, Bill. Read it for yourself. The rest of it you have to take my word for. It all happened."

Gottbaum was sitting wide-eyed. His hand began to tap nervously against the table. Ben reached out and put a hand over his to steady his friend.

"I know, Bill. I feel the same way. That's why I'm going. There's no other choice. Who would believe this? I have no proof, really. At least none that would stand up in a court or with the F.B.I. You're not even sure you believe it, are you?"

Gottbaum frowned, and he looked away. "No, Ben. But at least I'm sure you believe it. I suppose that will have to be enough."

Both men had finished eating, and the remains of their lunch lay before them. The loudspeaker was announcing the boarding of KLM flight 726. Ben stood up to go. Gottbaum stood also, and Ben could see he was severely shaken. The men shook hands for what seemed to Ben to be a long time.

"Thank you, Bill."

"Forget it. Good hunting."

And Ben strode away toward the plane that, in a mere six hours, would take him to pick up the trail of the man he had learned to hate. He was on his way to Amsterdam.

Book Two

One

Ben flexed his left shoulder again in an attempt to work out the stiffness that had come in the last twenty-four hours. He was sure that the fall outside Croft's house had done no permanent damage, but it had been an irritant on the long flight from New York to Amsterdam.

Though it was late at night and the airport was uncrowded, there was still a line of taxis, most older Mercedes, in front of the Arrivals Terminal. He flagged one down and gave the driver his luggage to stow in the trunk.

"Hotel Pulitzer, please," Ben directed the driver.

Ten minutes later, as the car sped along the highway beside a wide river, silver in the moonlight, Ben could see the lights of Amsterdam shining on the other side. The cab crossed the river over a bridge to the city's center. He watched the road signs marked "Centrum" lead the way, until the broad streets gave way to the tiny cobblestone lanes that ran alongside the canals in the oldest section of the city.

He loved this part of the city. The streets were narrow, bordered on one side by the tall, narrow canal houses—some dating back to the early 1600s—and on the other by the canal. On the opposite bank the same pattern was repeated.

Often the taxi slowed to a halt to allow another car to pass rather than to risk a dunking in the canal. Ben saw that the city fathers had added guard rails alongside the canal and that lines had been added to allow cars to park side by side. When he had visited Amsterdam as a college student, he had met a man who ran a thriving business pulling the cars of foreigners, who were unused to parking so close to an edge or who were too drunk on Dutch beer to do so properly, out of the canal waters.

During the sixteenth century, most goods brought in and out of Amsterdam came by way of the canals into the city. Merchants vied for space along them to build their houses and businesses. Land became so expensive that only a few could afford more than a narow tract. Thus, houses were built only one room or so wide to accommodate the largest number of people per foot of canal. As a result, some of the staircases in the houses were on a pitch equal to those in naval ships; and often tourists had to push their bags ahead of them up the stairways, unable to carry them at their sides.

The Pulitzer had taken sixteen of these houses and restored the facades to their original beauty. Then it had gutted the insides and rebuilt them into a bright modern hotel of almost two hundred rooms, each of the rooms shaped a bit differently.

When the taxi pulled to a stop in front of the hotel, Ben tipped the driver and took his bags inside. The night clerk had no trouble giving him a room overlooking the canal. A bellboy was summoned to carry Ben's luggage, and a few moments later he was safely ensconced in his room.

Ben was exhausted. He slipped off all his clothes and took a long, hot shower, hoping to relieve his tension.

Dressed in only a towel wrapped around his waist, Ben turned off the large overhead light and sank wearily into a chair by the window. Parting the heavy drapes, he stared out at the canal below. A sense of loneliness and disconnection began inside him which failed to be dispelled by the scene.

A small boat passed on the canal. Its lone occupant, a young boy, stood at the controls at the boat's middle. Occasionally, he put a bottle of beer to his mouth and took a long pull at it. Ben watched him float by until he was lost to sight.

Ben knew he couldn't risk going to Van Dyne and being honest—the likelihood of some collaboration with Croft was too great. Further, a frontal attack such as he had made on Croft's house was out of the question. He had no connections in Europe, and the exchange would be much more secure than Croft's old wooden house.

The only solution that presented itself to his tired mind was to try to get close to Van Dyne, and then to play it by ear. Through Van Dyne, he might get a chance to trace Croft. If, he added to himself, Croft had been in touch with Van Dyne. *And* if he were not recognized. *And* if Van Dyne did not see through him. Too many ifs and too few choices.

But his skills lay in his ability and experience as an investigative journalist. It was on these he would rely. He had arranged with Gottbaum to cover any inquiries raised.

Ben reached over to the bedstand for the various folders

placed there. He always read before bed and, with no book, these would have to do.

The first folder turned out to be a four-page newspaper of sorts printed by the hotel, which announced its facilities and even included a fairly good map of the city. Ben studied it carefully.

The next folder was an invitation to visit the Den Mopet Diamond Polishing Works. A car would even be sent to the hotel to pick him up. He thumbed through the next few; all diamond centers throughout the city—same pitch.

Then a flash of excitement ran through him. He stared at the card for a long moment—the Van Dyne Diamond Exchange, 216 Herengracht.

Ben dialed the front desk.

"I would like to visit the Van Dyne Exchange in the morning."

"No problem at all, sir," responded the clerk. "I'll leave a note for the day clerk who will have it all arranged as soon as the exchange opens."

"Make it eleven o'clock if that's not a problem."

"No problem, sir. Eleven o'clock. Is that all, sir?"

"Just a wake up call at nine A.M.," said Ben.

"Nine A.M. it is, sir."

Ben hung up the phone and settled his head on the pillow. It begins tomorrow, he thought, and then he slept.

Ben felt considerably more refreshed after breakfast the next morning. He was seated in the lobby reading a newspaper when the car arrived precisely at eleven o'clock.

Leaving his newspaper on the chair, Ben smoothed out the jacket of his dark blue three-piece suit. He folded his raincoat over his arm, picked up his attaché case, and walked out of the hotel. A green Mercedes 450 sedan was waiting in front, its driver standing and holding the door open.

They drove over the Kiezersgracht canal and turned onto the Herengracht. Residences here had been converted to businesses, and bright brass plaques adorned the buildings. The streets were spotless, the windows clean and bright, and flowers sprouted from a hundred window boxes in profusions of color. People on bicycles sped along, sometimes faster than cars in the narrow street.

The car stopped at number 216. Ben walked up the short flight of black, wrought-iron-bordered, stone stairs to the entrance alcove. A well-dressed salesman stood at attention in the foyer poised to greet those who entered. On the left was a guard station with a uniformed guard inside. Ben ignored the well-dressed salesman and stepped directly to the guard station.

"Good morning. My name is Ben Davidson. I'm a journalist from the United States, and I'd like to see Mr. Van Dyne. I have no appointment but will wait if necessary."

Ben watched the face of the guard closely. It seemed unlikely that any alarm concerning him would have been spread from Mississippi to Amsterdam; but if there had been, he wanted to be able to bolt quickly.

His name seemed to bring no response at all from the guard, and Ben relaxed.

"What is the nature of your business, sir?" asked the guard.

"I'm doing an article on diamonds for an American magazine. The reputation of this house is international, and I thought it would be a good place to start. Would you relay my request, please?"

The guard nodded politely and pointed to a group of chairs. "Would you have a seat, sir?"

"Thank you," said Ben.

He watched the guard pick up the telephone in his booth, dial a series of numbers, and speak for a few moments. Ben watched the crowds of tourists swell through the exchange as he waited.

"Mr. Davidson?"

Ben turned. Standing before him was a man in his middle to late thirties, Ben judged, dressed in a well-cut suit of European design. The flared waist of the jacket accentuated the man's trim build, and his stylishly groomed short brown hair and pencil-thin mustache bespoke an executive on his way up the corporate ladder. His brown eyes were clear and intelligent. The man extended his hand, and the grip was firm.

"I'm Gees Rikkers, Mr. Davidson. I understand you are an American journalist. How can we be of service?"

Ben gave Rikkers his most forthright smile. "It's very kind of you to see me on such short notice, Mr. Rikkers. I'm in

114

Europe doing a series of articles on the capital cities. Just the other day I received an offer to do an article for *The New Yorker* magazine on diamonds; and, being in Amsterdam anyway, I thought I could do much of the preliminary research right here. Again, I'm sorry I couldn't give you more notice, but I only just heard from my agent myself, and I didn't want to pass up this opportunity. *The New Yorker* has a circulation of a million, and it seems hardly prudent to turn it down. Of course, if you'd rather I went elsewhere..."

"Our company would figure prominently in this article?"

"Absolutely," Ben stated. "Especially if I can get some usable quotes from Mr. Van Dyne himself. It would give the piece greater credibility. Don't you think?"

Rikkers was all smiles. Credibility meant trust. And trust translated into dollars.

"I do indeed, Mr. Davidson. I'm sure Herr Van Dyne will enjoy meeting you."

Ben saw a small frown crease Rikkers's lips.

"You do understand, however, that we must, ah...obtain some...ah...validation?"

"No problem at all. I'm registered with the Guild in New York; and if you'd care to call my agent, his name is William Gottbaum, in New York City. He's probably in his office about now. The address is Avenue of the Americas, and his cable is GOTTAGLIT."

It was the correct thing to say. Rikkers waved his hand in a gesture of dismissal, but Ben was sure the call would be made anyway.

"Excellent. Would you please excuse me for a few minutes? I'm going to speak to Herr Van Dyne," said Rikkers, and he left and ascended the stairs.

Ben resumed his seat and looked around the room. The tiled floor was a series of alternating squares or diamonds, depending on your viewing angle, of black and white. The walls were painted white, and six-inch mouldings lined the intersections of walls, ceilings, doorways and windows. The staircase itself was a beautiful curve of wood, which rose about five feet from the floor to a first landing, and then ascended to the second. In the center of the room a dark, ornate table stood on an oriental rug. On the table was a huge brass cachepot filled with bright, fresh flowers.

Ben saw Rikkers returning.

"Mr. Davidson? Won't you please step this way? Klaas will be happy to hold your coat and case."

They walked down a gray-carpeted hallway, its spotless white walls and finished ceiling indicating that the building had been refinished on the inside as well as out. They emerged into an ultramodern open room that housed a dozen secretaries seated at their desks. Each seemed to be busy typing or filing, and the room presented an active, efficient organization. At the far end of the room was another corridor through which Rikkers led him. He explained as they walked.

"That room houses the general secretarial staff and our junior executive staff. The offices at the end of this corridor are for the more senior people. Herr Van Dyne's private office is located here." Stately below and modern above—interesting corporate metaphor, thought Ben.

They had stopped in front of a solid wooden door on which the panels were carved in bas-relief. Rikkers opened the door, and they entered a room well-furnished in tones of blue. A secretary was seated at her desk. She was an attractive, dark-haired woman in her late thirties.

"Good morning, Katherine," said Rikkers. "We are here to see Herr Van Dyne." Rikkers moved to a door on the far side of the room. Katherine reached under her desk, and a sharp buzz sounded. The door swung open. Ben followed Rikkers into the next room.

It was similar to the previous office with a desk, lamp, tables, and another secretary, but accented in yellow this time. The secretary was a much older woman who had been a beauty in her youth. Ben thought the term for her now would be handsome. Her gray hair was coiled tightly into a bun on the back of her head. Her clothing was simple, a gray blouse and skirt, but of expensive cut. She wore no jewelry save for a small diamond pendant and a gold wedding ring. Like the offices, she represented unostentatious wealth.

"Mr. Davidson, this is Mrs. Stoelin, Herr Van Dyne's private secretary."

Rikkers smiled warmly but deferentially at the woman, and Ben took his cue from that. Mrs. Stoelin accepted Ben's hand, but both her smile and tone of voice were cordial.

"Won't you have a seat, Mr. Davidson. Herr Van Dyne will be with you shortly." She glanced back to Rikkers. "Thank you, Mr. Rikkers."

It was a firm dismissal, and Rikkers had obviously heard it before.

"I hope to see you again, Mr. Davidson. I'll leave you now in Mrs. Stoelin's very able hands. Good morning."

"Thank you, Mr. Rikkers. Have a good day."

Ben sat in a comfortable leather chair and browsed through a magazine. After only a few minutes he heard a tone buzz on Mrs. Stoelin's intercom, which she spoke into in tones too low for Ben to hear.

"Mr. Davidson? Herr Van Dyne will see you now."

Ben thanked her, rose, and walked into Van Dyne's office. He had begun to have feelings of anxiety at his planned deception even though his cover was a familiar one.

"Good morning, Mr. Davidson."

Ben's first impression of Van Dyne came from his voice. It was smooth and mellow, and his English was spoken with a clipped, upper-class accent. It was a voice that could, with equal ease, have ordered an execution or a loaf of bread, a glass of sherry or an invasion.

Van Dyne himself was standing behind a huge, modern, marble slab desk; a large picture window behind him back-lit his form and made it impossible to distinguish his features from any distance away. Ben squinted against the Apollo-like effect of the sunlight behind the man and walked forward to meet him. The psychology of the device was obvious, and Ben refused to be intimidated by it. Rather, he walked directly to the window and looked out.

"Good morning, Herr Van Dyne, It is very kind of you to see me on such short notice. What a splendid view this window provides. I've loved the canals since I first visited Amsterdam some years ago."

With the window at his side, Van Dyne turned toward him, and the axis of their meeting shifted both into the sunlight.

Ben thought Van Dyne must have realized his intent when he saw a slight narrowing of Van Dyne's eyes; eyes which he could now see were blue.

"It is a pleasure to meet you, Mr. Davidson," said Van Dyne. Within the office was a modern sectional couch and two chairs around a glass coffee table. Van Dyne motioned Ben to the couch and took one of the chairs for himself.

In the normal light in this part of the office Ben looked closely at Van Dyne. The face and figure fit the voice. Van

Dyne's features were those of an aristocrat: from his sharp, acquiline nose to his polished and manicured fingernails. The hair above his high forehead was pure white and only slightly longer than a crew cut. Ben guessed his age at sixty to sixty-five. His suit was of dark silk and fit him perfectly. His French-cuffed white shirt sported cuff links of diamonds inset into gold squares. His handmade tie matched his suit, and a diamond stick pin pierced its center.

"How can I help you?" asked Van Dyne. "Can you give me some idea of the scope of your article?"

Ben was ready. Keep it general, he had decided.

"Millions of people in the United States own diamonds: engagement rings, pendants, and the like. They're a source of pride and an emblem of wealth. Now, with the current exodus of American travelers to Europe, everyone is talking about the great buys in diamonds to be found. Especially here, in London, and in Antwerp. The magazine would like to do a general piece, primarily educational in nature, for the average lay buyer. It's a high interest piece this time of the year before the summer tourist season starts." Van Dyne nodded. The explanation apparently made sense to him. Ben continued.

"I know that Amsterdam is a center for diamonds. I even toured one of the works when I was here a few years ago. I'm working on other pieces, but this one is a bit of a rush due to the timing. I'm sorry for the lack of notice." Van Dyne waved away the apology.

"You've been to Amsterdam before?" was his only question.

"During my college days," said Ben. "You have a wonderful country."

"*They* have," corrected Van Dyne. "I'm South African, not Dutch."

"I didn't know that," said Ben, as he reached into his pocket, brought out the tape recorder, and placed it on the table. "I assume? . . ." started Ben.

"Quite all right," said Van Dyne.

"You were saying that you're South African," prompted Ben, switching the tape on.

"Indeed," continued Van Dyne. "During the nineteenth century, after diamonds were discovered in South Africa, we needed to assure adequate representation in the world market. My grandfather came to Amsterdam to set up an exchange. Although we've prospered here, we've never lost our ties to the motherland."

"Was your mother South African also?"

"She was. As was my wife." Van Dyne noted Ben's eyes raise at the use of the past verb. "My wife died three years ago. Our children are currently in South Africa. When I die, this will pass to them. Van Dyne's is a family enterprise, a closed corporation in the legal terminology."

"In these days of multinationals, why do you remain small, relatively speaking?" asked Ben.

"To guarantee quality," was Van Dyne's quick response. "Gem diamonds are not like steel, where the more you produce the better off you are. Although, realistically speaking, even a glut of steel could drive prices down on a worldwide basis. Diamonds of gem quality must maintain their rarity and their quality, or they cease to have any value at all."

"Is the supply controlled then?"

Van Dyne looked a bit uncomfortable.

"You ask incisive questions, Mr. Davidson."

Ben smiled at Van Dyne to take any sting from his next words.

"You're evading my question, Herr Van Dyne."

Van Dyne accepted the barb gracefully, but shifted position in his chair.

"It is a bit of a sore topic. Many will say that the diamond supply in the world is free to rise and fall with demand. Others claim that the supply is deliberately limited, and excesses stockpiled, to create demand and keep prices stable and, ultimately, rising."

"What would you say?" asked Ben.

Now it was Van Dyne's turn to smile.

"I would say that there are two sides to every story."

Ben accepted defeat. Deeper questioning would disturb their tentative relationship. Besides, Ben thought, this is only a means to an end: Croft. He shifted the thrust of his questioning.

"This may seem basic, but where do diamonds come from, anyway?"

Van Dyne's response was again automatic.

"Simply put, diamonds are crystallized carbon, carbon that has been subjected to great pressure over a long period of time. An American friend once told me you had a cartoon character who used to make diamonds from coal by subjecting it to intense pressure between his hands."

"Superman," Ben interjected. "He used to say, 'a million pounds of pressure for a million years.' I always thought it would be a neat trick."

"Rather," said Van Dyne dryly. "But essentially he had the right idea. Diamonds occur naturally and are mined underground, in open pits, or alluvially, which means in river or seabeds."

Ben had learned long ago that an interviewee liked nothing better than to talk to someone he felt did not understand the subject. It catered to a common flaw among professionals who had a tendency to believe that layman was synonymous with moron.

"I understand that South Africa is the largest producer of diamonds. Is that correct?" he asked.

Van Dyne smiled. Ben had risen above moron level.

"Over half the supply of gem diamonds in the world comes from South Africa. The alluvial diggings along the Voal River and the Kimberly Mine's volcanic pipes are the richest in the world."

"That's the 'blue ground' I've heard so much about at Kimberly?"

"Correct, Mr. Davidson. Diamond crystals form in the volcanic magma. The magma flows to the surface along the tubes or 'pipes' that feed the volcano. Some crystals flow out with it. When the lava decomposes, the diamonds are left, imbedded in the ground, in stream beds and the like.

"At the turn of the century, the deposits in the Kimberly Mine were thought to have been played out. The workers continued to dig through the surface earth and also through a yellow claylike rock. When they hit a soft blue rock, the blue ground you spoke of, they figured they had reached the end of the source and that the mine was played out.

"You've heard the name Cecil Rhodes?" Van Dyne asked, and Ben nodded agreement.

"Cecil Rhodes and Barney Barnato, two Englishmen, had a stroke of genius. They thought that the blue ground might not be the end of the source but the source itself. They bought up the supposedly worked out claims and began to dig. When they broke down the blue ground, they discovered the largest source of diamonds ever found. The blue ground is a tube extending downward from an ancient volcano. You have a blue ground pipe in the United States in Arkansas, but for many reasons, it doesn't produce as much."

Van Dyne now was warming to the task.

"Rough diamonds are usually octohedral shaped, and the faces are often rough, curved, or pitted. There are usually growth markings on the crystal, which are triangular indentations called trigons. Sometimes we even find twin crystals grown together. These are called macles. Is this too technical?"

"Not at all. But I'm still trying to get an overview of production. Is mining the stones as easy as just pushing aside some mud or dirt next to a river?" Ben asked, becoming interested in spite of himself.

"No. Tons of earth have to be moved to find even a single crystal. You might be interested in the separating process, though." Ben indicated with a nod of his head that he was.

"The earth is poured over giant vibrating trays of grease. Plain, ordinary grease. Diamonds have an affinity for grease and stick to it when the earth is washed away. The smallest stones, ones not trapped, are caught in a sieve," Van Dyne explained.

"It seems oddly poetic that one of the rarest and most precious things on earth is attracted to the most common, ordinary sludge," Ben pointed out.

"It has always seemed so to me," Van Dyne agreed.

"What happens after that?"

"From the mines, the stones are sent to the De Beers Central Selling Organization in London. They grade the stones according to weight, color, and clarity. This establishes a price." Van Dyne paused a moment. "In partial answer to your earlier question about the market, you should be aware that the De Beers organization controls over eighty-five percent of world production. All of us buy our uncut stones from them. You may draw your own conclusions."

"The conclusion seems inescapable," said Ben, hoping for Van Dyne's support. However, Van Dyne looked at his watch, abruptly stood up and crossed to his desk. He paused with his finger over an intercom switch.

"It is past noon, Mr. Davidson. Lunch is an old custom here. Would you care to join me? It will be sent in for us."

"I'd be delighted," Ben said.

Van Dyne called his secretary and ordered lunch. He moved with the ease that wealth and power give a man. Within these walls he ruled absolutely. Van Dyne had turned to stare out the window.

The door opened, and Mrs. Stoelin appeared, wheeling a cart draped in a white tablecloth. The dishes on it were topped with room-service-type covers. A carafe of white wine and two wine glasses stood on the cart next to a small vase of yellow tulips.

Mrs. Stoelin uncovered the plates and placed the dishes before them; filet of sole with almonds, small boiled potatoes, and asparagus. Then she poured the wine into the delicate crystal.

It was now Ben's turn to be interrogated as he turned off the recorder. "You must lead an interesting life; what other writing have you done?" asked Van Dyne from across the room.

"My first articles were about Vietnam. It was easy to write about it, having been there," said Ben. "I've done others on political topics; others on travel. I prefer to free-lance."

"Were you for or against the war—if that is not too personal to ask?" Van Dyne peered at Ben closely.

"Not really. I was against it. It was a stupid, bloody waste."

"Apparently a great many of your young people thought so too," said Van Dyne.

"Enough to make a difference," responded Ben.

"America is such an interesting country to those of us who are not American. Take your 'hippies,' I believe you call them. Come here a moment, would you?"

Ben walked over to the window. Van Dyne pointed to a group of young people on the other side of the canal. Both male and female had hair past the shoulders. They were dirty and barefooted and dressed in motley.

"That is one of America's gifts," said Van Dyne, and there was scorn in his voice. "Beggars and clowns. And it's spread to Europe, too. They come here by the thousands, lured by Dutch tolerance. A useless generation who contribute nothing of value. Parasites who live on the leavings of others. You disagree?"

Ben didn't think he was being deliberately baited. The entire youth movement would be alien to a man like Van Dyne. Although parts of it were attractive to Ben, he too had never been truly comfortable with those who "dropped out." But he believed in their message enough to defend it in part.

"They're looking for answers to some important questions. Questions we need to ask."

"Such as?"

"Who we are, and what the hell are we doing here? Why does there seem to be cruelty and injustice, and why do we accept it so easily? They're not unreasonable questions, Herr Van Dyne."

"Perhaps not, Mr. Davidson. But they are personal questions that each man must answer for himself. In their groups and communes and bands they are as similar as cattle. And then to attack their government that has given them the society which they feed off? I don't understand," said Van Dyne.

"My country was founded on the right to question. These kids take the right seriously, if a bit naïvely."

"I think America is a naïve country," said Van Dyne with a smile. "You seem to have an enormous penchant for publicly baring and examining your political and social soul. Take your Watergate scandal. In the rest of the world it would have been a minor item. A few articles in the papers, an inquiry, a resignation or two, and back to business as usual. Why did you make such a fuss?"

Ben drew a deep breath before speaking. "Because America is more than a country. It's a standard."

Van Dyne looked intrigued. "Of what?" he asked.

"Maybe of excellence, of honesty, of integrity. Or maybe it should be described as an honest attempt at those things. And when we screw up, we're bitter and disappointed. I don't want to sound like an avid flag-waver or superpatriot, but the stakes are too high to sweep our garbage under the rug. Those who govern must be accountable. Sometimes it takes a lot of people yelling to make that happen. As I said before, it's not perfect. It's just an attempt at something better."

"Then you believe that the 'people' should rule and not the leaders?" said Van Dyne as they ate.

Ben wasn't quite sure whether or not he heard disdain in Van Dyne's voice, but he thought it time to turn the issue back to Van Dyne. He picked up the last bit of fish from his plate.

"Don't you?" Ben asked.

Van Dyne raised his wine glass and peered into its depths. "I think it's a ridiculous notion. Just as no factory can run properly unless there are managers, no country can run properly without skilled leaders making decisions. Anything less is pretense and obscures the issues."

"But can't you question those leaders and their decisions?"

"Would you question your doctor without the slightest medical knowledge yourself? Even his answer would be meaningless to you. Do you think my job and yours are interchangeable, and would you buy stock in this company if it were? Governments are like businesses in that way. I think..."

Abruptly Van Dyne stopped speaking. He covered the pause neatly with a sip of wine. The simple discussion had turned into something different, more intense. Both men realized it. Ben broke the uncomfortable silence after Van Dyne's withdrawal.

"Lunch was marvelous. Thank you for inviting me."

"My pleasure," mumbled Van Dyne as he strode to his desk and called Mrs. Stoelin in to clear away lunch.

Ben saw that the office had its own private bathroom off a short corridor, which he noticed through a door that was slightly ajar. He wanted to get a closer look at what lay beyond it. Van Dyne was bent over some papers on his desk.

"Herr Van Dyne?"

Van Dyne looked up. "Yes?"

Ben made a slight grimace. "At the risk of being indelicate, do you have..."

"Oh yes. Right through there."

Ben opened the door and swung it shut behind him as he passed through. He passed by the bathroom door, shut it, and quickly strode down the corridor.

At the end was a brightly lit room filled with filing cabinets, most four-drawered and steel gray. Ben counted ten against the walls. All had locks on the upper right hand corner.

It was time to get back. He walked to the bathroom, entered, and flushed the toilet. Van Dyne was seated in the same chair, and Ben retook his seat on the couch and snapped on the recorder.

"I didn't think this would take so long. You're an interesting man, Herr Van Dyne."

"This is my life," he gestured around the office. "And the lives of my family for three generations. But you, too, deserve a compliment. I have rarely enjoyed an interview as much."

Ben smiled. "Thank you. Can we continue?"

Van Dyne looked at his watch and frowned. "I have some pressing business to attend to this afternoon. Tomorrow morning I'm free, and I can give you a tour of our facility. Would that suit you?"

Ben nodded. "That would be terrific. What time tomorrow?"

"Ten o'clock?"

"Perfect. And thank you again." Ben and Van Dyne shook hands, and Ben turned to leave the office, but Van Dyne spoke again.

"Mr. Davidson, I'm having a few guests to my home this evening for a dinner party. One of my nieces from South Africa has just arrived to stay with us. I'd like to extend an invitation to you to join us if you'd care to. It is formal, of course." Van Dyne had moved to his desk, his hand poised on the intercom. Ben could hardly believe his good fortune. The closer to Van Dyne, the closer to Croft.

"I'd be delighted, sir."

"Good. Eight o'clock, then. Mrs. Stoelin will give you the address. Good day, Mr. Davidson."

"Good day, Herr Van Dyne."

Ben walked out of Van Dyne's into the bright sunlight of midafternoon. The car that had brought him was waiting at the foot of the steps.

"Please take me to the nearest car rental agency," Ben directed the driver.

The rental process was quick, and he drove a compact Fiat back to the hotel.

In his room, Ben located his tuxedo and decided it needed pressing. The desk obligingly sent up a porter who promised that he would have it back in two hours, upon receipt of a tip.

Ben stripped off his clothing and lay down on the bed. With the drapes opened, the strong afternoon sunlight felt good and warm on his body. He reached over to the phone and asked the desk to call him at six-thirty. That would give him plenty of time to dress, and Van Dyne's home was only a few minutes away.

Two

Ben stepped out of the shower and briskly toweled his body dry. He ran a comb through his hair to separate the tangles. He had always been meticulous about his appearance, especially when preparing to play a role for one of his stories. By the time he was dressed and ready to leave, it was almost seven-thirty.

He put on an old but well-cared-for raincoat, checked his reflection once more in the full-length mirror, and left the room, locking it behind him.

His car was parked out front, and Ben squeezed his body inside. Van Dyne lived as well as worked on the Herengracht, but on the opposite side of the city as the Exchange.

Van Dyne's residence was a three-story canal house, one of the largest he had seen in the city. The facade was entirely of brick, and each of the oversized windows in the front was bordered by large black shutters. The double entrance door was also black, and its brass hinges, knob, and door plate were gleaming and unmarred by a single fingerprint.

The brass knocker felt cold in Ben's hand as he rapped on the door. He was not surprised to see, as the door swung open, a liveried butler standing in the foyer beyond. The sounds of a party—conversation, laughter, and glasses tinkling—rushed out and filled the air.

"Good evening. My name is Ben Davidson. I believe I'm expected."

The butler turned and glanced briefly at a list on a table inside the hallway.

"Good evening, sir. May I take your coat?"

Ben handed over his raincoat and turned toward the sounds of the party. Before he stepped even a few steps forward, he saw Mrs. Stoelin approaching.

"Hello, Mrs. Stoelin. I'm happy to see you again so soon."

"Good evening, Mr. Davidson. We are pleased you could come tonight. I have been serving as Herr Van Dyne's hostess in the years since the death of his wife. Please come inside and join the other guests."

Ben followed her through the antique-filled foyer. Mrs. Stoelin's appearance had changed dramatically from her earlier office garb. The skirt and blouse had been replaced by a strapless, pale blue evening gown of a chiffonlike material that, as she moved, revealed a stunning figure. The severe bun had been replaced by a style of fuller, free-flowing loose curls; and she had added makeup. Once again, Ben thought she was a handsome woman.

"You look lovely, Mrs. Stoelin. Herr Van Dyne is both a privileged employer and a lucky man."

He saw a faint rush of color to Mrs. Stoelin's cheeks, but she took the compliment well, and for the first time, Ben saw her full smile.

"Such charm from one so young is rare. Thank you," she said.

"I meant every word," said Ben, and he mentally patted himself on the back for not screwing it up.

Mrs. Stoelin turned, placed her hand over Ben's arm, and directed him inside. They passed through a large archway that separated the foyer from the living room. The living room had an intricate hardwood parquet floor and oriental area rugs. The furniture was expensive: mahogany armoires and heavy velvet drapes. The couches and chairs in the room were varying shades of pale brown with blue and burgundy accent pillows that picked up the colors in the rug. It was a beautiful room, high-ceilinged with exposed beams, and in a fireplace on one side, almost the width of the room, a fire glowed and crackled.

There were a dozen or so guests already in the room standing about with drinks in their hands and talking in small groups. Uniformed waiters circulated with trays of drinks and hors d'oeuvres. Mrs. Stoelin motioned to a waiter who promptly came over with a tray of champagne glasses. She took one and handed another to Ben. He took a small sip. It was excellent, and he said so.

"I'm glad you like it. Let me introduce you to the other guests."

With Ben's arm still in her own, they approached the first group of guests. Mrs. Stoelin interrupted the three men and two women talking.

"This is Mr. Ben Davidson. Mr. Davidson is a journalist from America who is working on a project with Pieter."

The people raised their glasses in greeting. Mrs. Stoelin indicated the first of the three men, an elderly, white-haired gentleman whose well-cut tux could not conceal a large pot belly.

"Mr. Davidson, this is Mr. Geoffrey Devonsheen of London, England. He is a senior partner with Lloyd's."

Devonsheen shook hands with Ben and indicated a beautiful raven-haired woman.

"This is my wife, Margaret, Mr. Davidson."

Ben took Margaret's outstretched hand and smiled. "Ben, please," he said.

Mrs. Stoelin turned to the next man.

"Signor Alonzo Fredericci of Rome, Italy, of the export firm of Fredericci and Sons."

Fredericci was in his late forties, Ben judged, and his black hair was slicked back to accentuate the distinguished gray at his temples. His dark eyes and clean features made him a handsome man. They shook hands, and he introduced his wife, Maria, a short, buxom brunette on whose jewelry alone Ben could have retired.

The last man was large enough to play fullback for the Los Angeles Rams. He was at least three inches taller than Ben and a hundred pounds heavier. He had large features, a big nose and jaw. His blue eyes were clear and intelligent-looking. His reddish hair had touches of gray in it down to his thick, bushy sideburns. His most dramatic feature was a huge walrus-type mustache of flaming red that extended across his upper lip and down to his chin. Ben's hand was almost swallowed in his grasp.

"Monsieur Georges Delacroix of Paris, France, Director of the Première Banque de Paris."

"*Bon soir, Monsieur Delacroix,*" said Ben. "*Ça va tout bien? C'est un plaisir de faire votre connaissance.*"

Delacroix was delighted to be addressed in French; to a Frenchman there is no other language. It wasn't so much a conceit as a conviction. Delacroix smiled warmly and pounded Ben on the back.

"*Et un plaisir de vous connaître, aussi. Votre français, c'est très bien, monsieur.*"

"I studied in school. And I've traveled in France twice before. It's a beautiful language and country."

"D'accord," said Delacroix.

"You should have been a diplomat instead of a writer, Ben," said Mrs. Stoelin as she led him to another group and replenished their drinks. A waiter passed by, and Ben snatched some hors d'oeuvres. He was hungry and needed food to counteract the alcohol. He saw Van Dyne on the other side of the room talking to a young, blond woman Ben's age. He caught only a glimpse before the introductions started again, but he wanted to see more. The feeling surprised him.

The rest of the introductions read like a list of Who's Who. He met two counts, one Spanish and the other French, another bank president and his wife, and a stunning woman who was the senior editor of a financial newspaper in Austria. Other guests had arrived by now, and the room held about thirty people. Ben met a member of the Dutch government, two Dutch stockbrokers, and an Australian movie star, who was so handsome that even Ben was impressed.

Mrs. Stoelin left him to welcome the latest guests. He found himself standing near Delacroix and Devonsheen.

"Join us, Ben," boomed Delacroix. "Geoffrey talks incessantly about business. It's his raison d'être." He looked relieved to be free of debentures.

Geoffrey frowned. Ben judged a sense of humor was not a priority at Lloyd's.

"I never miss an opportunity," said Devonsheen primly, like an annoyed teacher.

"What are you currently working on?" asked Delacroix of Ben.

"An article on diamonds. That's how I've come into contact with Herr van Dyne. He's been very accommodating," said Ben.

"Solid bloke," said Devonsheen in some sort of agreement. "Company's solid as a rock."

"Should be," said Delacroix. "When your friends own the country that owns the mines that own the diamonds. Don't you think? Better than the oil business."

Ben extended a cautious probe. "What friends?" he asked.

"The crowd that runs the RSA. Van Dyne's an Afrikaner, and it's the Afrikaners who run the show there. Prime

Minister's one and so's half the Parliament and business people," said Delacroix.

Ben was familiar with the term Afrikaner, but not with its fullest meaning.

"Afrikaner. That's a political party, isn't it?"

Delacroix snorted. "More like a damn religion. Great Trek, white supremacy, apartheid, and all the rest. They're anti-British, too," he added to needle Devonsheen, who took the bait.

"That is totally untrue. Britain has the best of relations with the RSA," he said with a pout in his voice.

Ben had finally figured out that RSA meant Republic of South Africa. Also, he found Delacroix's comments interesting in the light of Van Dyne's political comments over lunch. Racism and fascism tended to fit together very easily.

"Have you known him long?" asked Ben of both men.

"Lloyd's has handled the high-risk shipping insurance for the Van Dyne Exchange since its inception," said Devonsheen proudly. "I took the account over personally fifteen years ago. I believe I can safely say we are friends as well as business associates."

"How nice for you," said Ben, looking to Delacroix.

"I barely know him," said Delacroix. "He does a bit of banking with us. Nothing extensive. We just concluded some stock negotiations, which is why I flew up."

"What's your impression of him?" asked Ben.

Delacroix laughed. "He's a shrewd businessman. And a pleasant enough fellow for a man whose politics are to the right of Genghis Khan's." Ben laughed too. He liked Delacroix's forthrightness.

A waiter stopped with more champagne, and all three men took another glass. Devonsheen wanted to turn the conversation back to business.

"The main issue in these types of bonds is liquidity," he was saying. Delacroix snuck a wink at Ben and said between Devonsheen's words, "If you are ever in Paris, lunch perhaps?"

"Absolutely," Ben agreed as Delacroix picked up the issue of liquidity.

Ben wanted to make contact with his host who was still conversing with the blond woman. He wondered if he should just walk over, but was saved the decision by Mrs. Stoelin, who appeared at his side.

"Have you seen Pieter yet?" she asked.

"I was just going to go over," said Ben.

Neatly propelled by Mrs. Stoelin and fueled by another glass of champagne, he walked over to Van Dyne. And almost stopped dead in his tracks.

He found himself staring at her. He had never before experienced an impact quite like this. It was not that she was beautiful, although she was. Her blond hair hung straight and free down to strong, white shoulders; and her low-cut gown revealed high, small breasts and a trim waist. She was almost too thin, but he found himself thinking that was very sensual. But it was, in part, her face that made the strongest impact.

Her features were clean and sharp. High cheekbones jutted prominently from clear, white skin. Her jawline was even a bit too strong and her mouth a bit wide, though that, too, conveyed an impression of sensuality. But there was a look that seemed to cross her face from time to time as she talked to Van Dyne. It was a look of pain, of vulnerability. It was a look of deep wounds, and it made Ben want to reach out and put his arms around her. Something inside him responded to the pain amidst her beauty. The champagne, he thought to himself. But the feeling persisted and even intensified.

Van Dyne had turned toward them as Mrs. Stoelin approached.

"I'm glad you could come, Mr. Davidson. May I call you Ben?"

Ben nodded, trying not to stare at the girl. For her part, she had not even noticed him.

"Fine," continued Van Dyne. "Then please call me Pieter. I have no need of formality in my own home. I'd like to introduce my niece. Ben Davidson, this is Lisa Smith of South Africa. Her father is one of my oldest friends and is with the government there."

"Hello, Lisa," said Ben, totally at a loss. He had never felt anything like this before. It occurred to him that he had not felt very much of anything before.

Lisa turned to Ben and mumbled a greeting too low and disinterestedly for him to hear. He was devastated and didn't even know why. "Ben is a journalist, Lisa," Van Dyne added.

"Oh?" said Lisa absently. Finally her eyes came up to meet Ben's. He felt the same impact. Only stronger.

Mrs. Stoelin and Van Dyne were silent. Ben thought he must appear ridiculous, suddenly tongue-tied. Out of the corner of his eye he saw more guests enter the room, and Mrs. Stoelin eyed Van Dyne. Lisa had looked away again.

"We have to see to our guests, Pieter. Shall we?" and she reached out her hand to him.

Van Dyne obliged her. "Would you escort Lisa to dinner, Ben?" he asked. "Everyone here is either too married or too old." Ben nodded, and Van Dyne and Mrs. Stoelin left to join their guests.

Lisa was staring at him now. A smile twitched at the corners of her mouth as if she sensed his discomfort. Without the presence of Van Dyne and Mrs. Stoelin, he had no choice but to look at her directly. It seemed to him that her eyes swallowed him up, and he felt something stir in the pit of his stomach.

As their eyes met again, he saw something for the first time happen in Lisa's. For a moment, he sensed a connection, a kind of rapport. Something seemed to pass between them that was personal, recognizable.

The vagueness seemed to leave her face to be replaced by interest. Her attention was focused on him now, and her chin had lifted toward him. It was an intimate gesture, a prelude. She seemed to sense it and withdrew, but still their eyes held.

"Who are you?" she asked.

"My name is Ben Davidson. I'm from the United States. We were just introduced by your uncle."

"He's not my real uncle. Just a friend of the family." Why did I tell him that? she wondered.

She was experiencing unfamiliar deep feelings. She thought Ben attractive, but he was gazing at her so strangely.

"Have we met before?" she asked, frowning.

"I don't think so. I would have remembered," said Ben. Your unc... Herr Van Dyne is helping with a project. I'm a journalist."

"I've known quite a few writers," Lisa said, and Ben heard a tinge of sadness in her voice.

Abruptly, Lisa's mood seemed to change. It was replaced by one of coldness, almost hauteur. She flipped back her hair.

"Most writers I've met are either pompous or boring. They're not real. It comes from playing word games all the time," she baited him.

Instinctively, Ben knew she had just run from him.

"Why are you pushing me away?" he asked softly.

Lisa was unprepared both for the question and the tone of voice. It caught her off guard.

"I don't know." She paused. "Habit, maybe," she said. Surprised by the honesty of her response, it was Lisa's turn to stare. Her reaction to Ben puzzled her, put her on her guard. I have something to do here, she reminded herself, and he can't be a part of it. She heard Leander saying, *"Van Dyne was your father's best friend. He never told you?"* I can't think about you now, she addressed Ben in her mind.

Many of the guests had gone, and the room was half empty.

"I think dinner is ready. Shall we go inside?" Ben asked.

"All right," she said as he escorted her.

Van Dyne's dining room was enormous and looked like a baronial hall. The table was set for more than thirty people.

Van Dyne, seated at the head of the table, caught Ben's eye and indicated two places next to him. Ben held Lisa's chair as she sat next to Van Dyne. His smile to her was not returned, and Ben wondered why there was tension between "uncle" and "niece."

Van Dyne stood and conversations ceased.

"A toast," he said and raised his glass. Everyone followed suit. "To our continued health and prosperity. I am glad to welcome you all to my home."

The first course was large icy shrimp, which Ben learned were prawns, covered with a spicy yellow sauce. Waiters poured white wine.

"I didn't realize I was so hungry," he said to Lisa and speared another shrimp.

"What are you working on with Pieter?" asked Lisa.

Ben felt a pang of displeasure at having to deceive her.

"An article about diamonds and diamond buying. It's sort of an educational piece for the summer's tourists who've heard about the great buys in Amsterdam."

"Are there?" asked Lisa.

"Sure. Beating the excise tax in the States is a buy in itself."

"Don't they pay it at customs?"

Ben laughed. "Only if they declare it. Most don't, and it's really impossible to catch. Who's to say where a ring or a bracelet came from? Besides, you could just put it in your pocket. No one is really searched. Even in a pinch, there's usually a 'cousin' who's a jeweler who'll swear she bought it from him."

Lisa's response was lost to him as the lady on his right, the Italian importer's wife, yanked on his arm and started to discuss the political situation in the U.S. Ben was trapped into a debate.

By the time Ben could disentangle himself from the political debate, which got less coherent as the volume of wine intake increased, dessert was being served. He turned back to Lisa and found her talking to Van Dyne. He heard the words "father" and "feud" and decided it was personal. He sat watching the other people and wished he could talk to Lisa.

She must have felt his gaze because she turned and spoke to him.

"Would you like to take a walk, Ben?"

"I would. My head's beginning to spin."

Outside, the city was silent. It was almost midnight and the air was crisp and cold, a welcome relief after dinner.

They walked together in silence at first, along the canal. Their shoes made sharp clicking noises against the cobblestones, loud amidst the quiet. Most of the windows were dark, and few pedestrians or cars passed them.

Lisa slipped her arm into his, and he felt her shiver against the night chill.

"Cold?" he asked.

"A little," she responded.

He brought his arm tighter against his side to bring her closer. In spite of the chill, he felt warm and alive.

"You didn't seem as if you were enjoying the party given in your honor," Ben observed carefully.

"These people bore the hell out of me," she admitted freely. "All they ever talk about is money and power; how to get more or how to safeguard what they've got. It's an obsession. But you didn't appear to fit in at tonight's gathering either."

"I've never mastered the art of endless talking and saying nothing."

Lisa laughed for the first time. It was warm and unrestrained, and Ben was delighted.

"If that's so," she said, "you're one of the few who hasn't. Most of the people I know are as vague and weak as their conversation."

"Why continue to know them then?"

Lisa shrugged. "Convenience, I suppose."

"We justify so many things under that heading," he said quietly. "Staying in unfulfilling jobs or in unhappy relationships; letting others run our lives because it's just too damn inconvenient to fight back and make a commotion."

They crossed over the canal, and Lisa paused at the center of the bridge to peer down into the dark water below.

"And where would you rank loneliness?" she asked softly.

"For the world ... or for me?"

"For both," she said, turning back to look at him, eyes searching.

"Most people stop looking before they've found what they really want," he said slowly.

"And you? Have you found what you want?"

She was only inches from him now, and he felt drawn to her. But he held back, unsure of himself and of the emotions he was suddenly feeling.

"No. I haven't found it yet," he said, choosing his words carefully. "For me, that's a function of the past."

He saw her sudden move and realized that he had touched on something painful to both of them. But, acting on instinct alone, he again drew back. They began to walk, both silent, and her arm slipped into his again.

A small café offered shelter from the night, and they ducked inside. Dark, polished wood caught the reflections of tabletop candles in the dimly lit interior. Ben chose a private booth and ordered coffee for them both.

"You're the first person in a long time who doesn't seem to mind my being quiet," Lisa said abruptly. "Most men panic if I'm not chirping brightly every second. You must be pretty sure of yourself."

"Right reaction, wrong reason," Ben smiled ruefully. "It may seem strange, but your quiet makes me feel unpressured.

If we had to be witty and charming every minute, I don't think either of us could stand the strain."

Lisa's appraisal of him was long and thoughtful. "You're comfortable to be with, Ben. I usually don't feel that with a man."

"You're not alone," he answered honestly. "I tend to avoid moments like this."

"But you're not avoiding this one," she said.

"Neither of us is, it seems," Ben replied, hearing the surprise in his voice echoed in hers.

Neither was aware when their hands first touched, as their conversation made the world outside and the reasons each had come to Amsterdam a distant memory.

Ben had never learned the countless small lover's deceits and empty promises; he had no pat lines or quick answers. And that was good, because Lisa had heard them all. Declarations of love and testaments to her beauty, her sensuousness, left her cold. Few men had ever touched her emotionally, and even those who had she had rejected, unable to face the betrayal she knew would eventually come.

But Ben's simple honesty affected her, and she found herself opening up to him as she had to no other person, not even her closest girlfriends. His quiet strength allowed her to feel safe and protected for the first time in so long.

For Ben, the flame that glowed so suddenly inside warmed him, driving away old fears. Here were the feelings he'd feared himself incapable of, and the chest aching with desire for this woman.

They left the café, walking close together along the canals back toward Van Dyne's; Lisa's head was pressed against Ben's shoulder, his arm tightly around her.

"When can we see each other again?" he asked.

"There are . . . things I have to do," Lisa responded. "Things that can't be put off. Tomorrow, I think. Is that too soon?"

"Not soon enough," Ben admitted. "But it will have to be."

They had wandered into Westermarkt Square, past the old church whose spires and towers housed the giant bell that hourly rang out over the city. A gentle wind spread Lisa's hair against her face, and her mouth quivered, upturned and beckoning.

Ben's arms encircled her waist and crushed her to him. His lips brushed against hers lightly, and he felt her strain toward him in response. Her arms laced around him and pulled him closer, as they kissed once again, harder this time, and he felt her taut, high breasts against his chest.

For minutes they just stood there, ignoring the wind that swept around them. A bargain had been sealed between them, a promise to begin here next time they met.

Each had pushed aside the nagging voices that claimed them. Briefly, Ben had forgotten Croft and Mississippi, Amy lying dead in a New Orleans hotel hallway; Lisa had shoved away Leander's voice insisting that Van Dyne knew, that he *had* to know. Now, slowly, they separated.

"Tomorrow," Lisa said softly.

"Tomorrow," Ben agreed.

He held her tightly as they walked slowly back to Van Dyne's. Outside the house he kissed her once again, gently and longingly, as the bells of the Westermarkt Church chimed again and again and again.

Peter Dreyer knew that the bells would ring. He had checked his watch. He wanted the bells to cover the sound of the motorized Nikon that he used to photograph Lisa Smith and the man she was with.

He had already taken pictures of all of Van Dyne's guests and copied down the plate numbers of their cars. Some, like this man's, were rented. It made no difference. They had the computer codes for the rental agencies and could tie in at will. This man's given name, as well as the others, could be obtained in minutes.

Dreyer was tired. He had been ready to turn over the watch to one of his agents and turn in for the night when Lisa had emerged from Van Dyne's.

Hurry up, he thought to himself. Are you going to stand there bloody forever? Dreyer hoped they would go to Van Dyne's and not to some hotel. Complications would mean he'd have to stay awake.

He sighed with relief. They were now standing outside the door. Dreyer walked unnoticed on the other side of the canal to the van that housed his men. The specially built side door opened noiselessly, and Dreyer got in.

"Get the shots?" asked Max Pilsten, one of their local

people assigned to the consulate here. Of slight build, he was pale-skinned and fair-haired.

"No problem." Dreyer turned to the other man in the van, Henry Gerroff, who was watching the house through binoculars.

Dreyer wasn't very fond of Gerroff. Though Gerroff had years of field experience, he lacked the maturity and wisdom to go with it. He had trouble with the more mundane elements of intelligence work and fancied himself a man of action. An undisciplined hothead was more like it, thought Dreyer.

"You see the man with her?" he asked Gerroff.

"Yes," Gerroff said.

"Put him under surveillance."

"No sweat," and Gerroff was out the door a few seconds later. Dreyer picked up the binoculars and watched him, through the van's one-way side window, take a position where he could watch the man and Lisa.

Lisa was going up the stairs. Good. He could relax. He watched the man walk to his car in a daze, it seemed to Dreyer, who watched him drop the keys twice. Soon, he drove away. Gerroff, already in his car, followed.

"How many guests left?" he asked Pilsten.

"All gone," was the response.

"Fine. Call me if you need me," said Dreyer, and he left the van and walked to their hotel, which was located a few hundred yards away. He could be back at the van in under two minutes. He rubbed his eyes with his fingers. God, he was tired.

Leander was due to arrive in the morning. That troubled Dreyer. Leander had been too intense about this operation from its inception, as if there were something personal in it for him. Dreyer didn't like the thought. Agents, even the best agents, made mistakes if they thought emotionally and not rationally. He tried to put the thoughts from his mind as he trudged up the narrow stairs at the hotel.

Three

Lisa felt as if she were being torn in two. New feelings flowed through her, and she realized Ben Davidson was the cause.

In the living room the servants were cleaning up the debris of the party. A half-empty bottle of champagne lay on a table. Lisa picked it up and, finding a semiclean glass, poured herself some.

It had been hard for her to be comfortable with her "uncle" for the two days since she had arrived. She had tried to keep it under control, but she was sure he had noticed a strain when they spoke. She had wanted to grab him by his lapels and have him tell her what he knew about her parents. She tried to put Ben from her mind and to concentrate on why she had come here.

The idea that Leander had planted had grown into conviction. She was sure that her uncle knew something. If, she reminded herself, there was something to know. But there *had* to be. So much depended on it.

She took another sip of champagne and wandered into the den, her emotions at war.

A servant came to the door. "Can I get you anything, miss?"

"Yes, please. If Herr Van Dyne is still awake, ask him to join me here. And bring some brandy, please."

She could wait no longer. He had been at the office all day yesterday and last night had attended meetings. He had left this morning before she could catch him, and the party had taken any chance away for the evening.

The servant returned to the den carrying a tray with a bottle of brandy and two Waterford snifters on it. He informed her that Van Dyne would be joining her in a few minutes.

Lisa's pulse began to quicken, and her chest felt tight. Anticipation was causing her to fidget in her chair. She tried to control it, wanting to appear casual with her uncle. It was important to control the dialogue, to spot inconsistencies if he gave them to her.

All hope of control vanished when Van Dyne entered the room. He was wearing bedclothes and a floor-length dark green velvet robe. His first words were, "I just spoke to your father."

Lisa experienced a moment of fear. She had not forgotten their last meeting. He had ordered her to Johannesburg, and she had gone to Amsterdam. Van Dyne noticed her reaction.

"Lisa, you may find this hard to believe. I know there have been problems between the two of you in the past, but Johann is genuinely concerned about you. He said if you're happier here than in Johannesburg, then it's all right. He loves you deeply."

"I'm his dead brother's daughter. Nothing more," she said.

"Nonsense," replied Van Dyne. "You are his child. He lives for you. That is what it means to be Afrikaner. Everything we do is for the future generations—for the children. Never forget that, Lisa."

"Everything you do is for power, uncle. Have you forgotten what it is to be black in our country?"

The barb hit home, and Van Dyne's face turned scarlet.

"I have not forgotten that a hundred years ago the blacks lived in the jungle. They were illiterate and impoverished. We've been in Africa for three hundred years and have earned what we've got. The blacks have their homelands, and we have ours."

Lisa watched him grow livid. These were unquestioned beliefs.

"How many diamond fields are in the black homelands, uncle? How many?" she demanded.

"Better ask how many schools and hospitals. We've given them a civilization," said Van Dyne.

"And ruined theirs at the same time," she shot back.

"Why are you doing this? What is the point? You've been given everything. How could you be so ungrateful? No wonder your father is so exasperated with you," said Van Dyne.

"He's not my father!" yelled Lisa. "My father and mother died thirty-five years ago. Suicides in your Garden of Eden."

Van Dyne looked uncomfortable for the first time. He started to speak in quieter tones.

"Hans was a sensitive man. We were very close as boys. He was my best friend, Lisa. You know this is painful for us both."

"Why did he kill himself and my mother? Why, uncle? You must have known something."

"He killed himself, Lisa. That's all there was to it. Let it lie." He looked at her with pain in his eyes. "Let it lie," he said again.

Lisa fixed his stare with her own. In her softest voice, barely above a whisper, Lisa said, "You're a liar, uncle. My parents were not suicides. You know that, and so do I."

Van Dyne's entire facial expression changed, and Lisa sensed fear. But he recovered quickly. "What do you think you know, Lisa?" he asked.

"That my parents were not suicides," she answered, and almost added, "that they didn't leave me," but didn't.

"What brings you to this conclusion, now, after more than thirty years?"

Lisa decided to keep Leander's name out of it. If Leander came after her as he had threatened, the only coins she would have to trade were her position as Smith's "daughter" and that she had kept his identity secret.

"I have good reason to believe it. Accept that," she said.

She saw Van Dyne gearing up for a series of denials. It was time for a last desperate shot. She said, "Tell me about the Nazis, uncle. Tell me about 1936."

Van Dyne froze. A look of pure shock came over his face.

"How did you find out, Lisa? It's very important," he asked her.

"I found some old papers of father's. He spoke about it. He mentioned your name. You were his friend," she lied again. "It made me look at the suicide in a different light. It started me thinking. I came here for the truth."

Van Dyne sat back down in his chair. Something had changed in his face, and Lisa was unsure.

"Can I see those papers?"

"No. They're in a safe place."

Van Dyne seemed more comfortable now.

"I have never wanted to tell you this, Lisa. I'm truly sorry you brought it up. Please forgive me for having to tell you because I know how much you'd like it to be otherwise."

Lisa felt bile rise in her throat. Van Dyne continued.

"In 1935, Hitler's Germany was already on its way industrializing and rebuilding militarily. But the Reichsmark was still weak in the world market. The Nazis needed hard currency: gold and diamonds to make their paper currency stable and curb inflation. Without a stable currency, Hitler couldn't hope to reorganize Germany into a world power or complete the reforms on which his party had come to power.

"Now, contrary to what many believe today, the governments in England and France were aware of Hitler's ambition. He had just assumed the offices of president and chancellor and became 'der Führer.' He also renounced the Treaty of Versailles. It was obvious what he intended, but they needed proof. Proof implies intelligence networks, and there were none at the time.

"In 1936, we were approached by the Nazis. They came to South Africa to buy hard currency. Do you know who was approached?"

"No," Lisa said. The specter of Leander hung near by. "All I know is that you and my father were involved. Were there others?"

"There were," said Van Dyne, "but I can't tell you their names. This is still classified." He looked at her through narrowed eyes, and then rose and poured her some brandy.

"Here, take this. The rest is not easy. It was decided by British Intelligence that we would accept the offer in order to begin a network inside Germany. Supposedly, we would be allies. In reality, we would spy on them. The pressure was enormous. Every time we traveled, we faced death if we were exposed. We were double agents and the game took its toll. We could tell no one. Again, Lisa, you must understand the pressure."

"What has this got to do with my parents?" But she knew what was coming. Her throat constricted.

"Most of us made it through. Some didn't. Your father cracked, Lisa. He took his life to get to the one place no one could hurt him. And he took your mother, too. I'm sorry. It was thought better for you not to know." There was sadness in his voice.

Lisa believed him. She took the bottle of brandy, walked out of the room, and didn't look at Van Dyne as she left. The weight was back again, and the world was an ugly place.

Van Dyne watched her go dazedly up the stairs. She had

believed him, he knew. He raised the brandy glass to his lips and drank deeply. His hand shook. For the first time in a quarter of a century, he was frightened to the depths of his soul. He took another drink and then another. Five minutes later he had calmed down.

Van Dyne summoned a servant.

"Yes, sir?"

"First, go upstairs and get my clothing. Something casual. Second, call a taxi and have it meet me on the corner of the Utrechtstraat. Third, stand by my niece's room. She is not to leave under any circumstances. Use force if you have to. Do you understand?"

"Yes, sir. I'll get your clothing right away and make the call while you dress. Will that be all, sir?"

"Yes. Yes. Snap to it." Van Dyne let irritation creep into his voice. He knew it was caused by fear. He had never shouted at his household staff before.

Ten minutes later, dressed in black slacks and gray sweater with suede rubber-soled shoes, Van Dyne left his house through a rear concealed entrance. He wore a raincoat and an old beat-up hat and was indistinguishable from a million residents of the city.

In the van across the street from Van Dyne's home, Pilsten vigilantly observed the house through his binoculars. He remained totally unaware of Van Dyne's exit.

The taxi was patiently waiting two blocks away. Van Dyne got into the backseat.

"Ninety-six Terenstraat."

He saw a smile appear on the driver's face and knew what the driver assumed. The address was in the middle of Amsterdam's Red Light District, second only to Hamburg in its variety of sexual delights. Van Dyne sat back in his seat not wanting the driver either to recognize or remember him.

Van Dyne looked at his watch and saw it was almost three A.M. Regardless of the hour, the Red Light District was in full swing. Crowds of people packed the streets along the canals from building to edge without a break. The taxi slowed to a crawl, and the driver had to use his horn to separate the mobs of people and pass through. Legal here, prostitution drew huge crowds.

People, tourists mostly, browsed in and out of countless sex shops in which entire walls were devoted to sexual apparatus.

Vibrators of shapes and sizes and colors so varied as to make a gynecologist doubt his training were an endless source of amusement, as wives poked husbands in the side and whispered jokes into their ears. And there were sales for those who were not joking at all.

By far, the largest crowds gathered in front of the storefront-sized windows behind which sat one or two prostitutes clad in slips or gaudy, provocative gowns. Around most were erotic displays of whips, chains, and leather straps. Most of the people stopped and stared until the prostitute, seeing no paying clients, would rap sharply on the glass for them to move on. Girls unattached to a shop stood on the street.

Van Dyne watched the endless crowds swirl around the taxi, and his face grew ugly.

Number 96 was identical to the other three-story buildings around it. Next to its entrance were two windows behind which sat two prostitutes. A small crowd of men, mostly sailors, watched as they lowered the tops of their gowns to entice them inside the brothel.

Van Dyne ignored them and walked inside. A giant stood just inside the door. His name was Otto, and the tattooed arms that emerged from his black T-shirt writhed with hideous black snakes. Van Dyne smothered a shudder at the sight of him.

"Stangl?" asked Van Dyne, wishing to keep their conversation to a minimum.

"In the office," replied Otto, and Van Dyne walked away. He passed through a foyer from which a staircase led to the upper floors. Van Dyne could see into the parlor beyond. A dozen men, many with half-naked prostitutes on their laps, were seated on couches. In the room's center a naked woman lay tied on a dais while a second woman fucked her with a pink rubber dildo. While he watched, a man rose from the couch and put his penis into the first woman's mouth. Some of the other men applauded and threw coins. Van Dyne felt a wave of nausea pass. He wanted to be gone as quickly as possible.

The second floor contained private bedrooms. A cacophony of moans and slaps and sighs emanated from them. The building was old, and the carpet in the hallway was worn. Cracks ran across the walls and ceilings like spider webs. Van Dyne ascended the last flight.

The top floor had been refinished to some degree. A new coat of cheap paint had been spread over the doors and walls, which were now uniformly gray. It was quieter here.

The office was the last room down the hall. Van Dyne opened the door without knocking. The office was a suite of rooms: an anteroom that contained a desk, which held only a blotter and a telephone; a parlor; and a bathroom. Behind the desk sat a blond man dressed in shirt, slacks, and a jacket. The slacks were yellow, the shirt and jacket blue, and a gold ascot took the place of a tie. Van Dyne was struck, as always, by the youthful appearance of the man's face. It did not jibe with his age, and the lines near his eyes seemed like an afterthought of nature.

"Hello, Stangl," said Van Dyne. Stangl looked surprised to see him.

"This is an odd hour for a visit, Van Dyne. You want a girl?" It was an insult. Van Dyne frowned.

"Be careful, Stangl. I'm not one of your customers."

Stangl grinned humorlessly.

"I know that. We're comrades. That's even better," he said.

"Business associates is the term. Don't presume on our common affiliation."

"Cut out the high and mighty crap, Van Dyne. We're on the same side whether you like it or not," said Stangl.

"You are a matter of expediency, Stangl. Nothing more," Van Dyne said. He was annoyed at the verbal fencing. It served no purpose. Stangl, too, wanted to end it.

"All right. We've both bared our fangs. Something must be up, or you wouldn't be here. Let's stop the bullshit."

"We've got to talk. Are we private?" asked Van Dyne.

"No one is here but me. Come inside."

Van Dyne followed him into the parlor. It was as cheaply furnished as the rest of the building. The brown rug had numerous cigarette burns in it and was threadbare in several places. A couch and two armchairs were in similar condition. A small radiator, painted silver, hissed menacingly in one corner.

Stangl sat in one of the chairs and lit a cigarette. A standing ashtray was overflowing, and butts had dropped to the floor. Van Dyne sat on the couch. He felt its old springs compress.

"We have a serious problem," Van Dyne began. He didn't like Stangl, and the close contact disturbed him.

"What is it? A shipment late?" Stangl asked, and blew smoke out his nose.

"We've been penetrated," said Van Dyne. The impact on Stangl was instantaneous. "For the first time in over thirty years Lisa Smith is asking questions about her parents' death," said Van Dyne.

In short-clipped sentences, Van Dyne repeated his conversation with Lisa and her accusations.

"My question is," continued Van Dyne, "why now? Where did this information she claims she has come from? I don't believe the story about some of her father's papers surfacing. It's been too long. And Johann was too careful. Nothing would have escaped his notice."

"I agree," said Stangl. "Did she mention other names? Does she know about Smith or," here he hesitated and said in a lower tone, "Bormann?"

"She accused me of a collaboration with the Nazis. And she mentioned 1936."

"*Scheisse!*" swore Stangl. "What did you say?" he asked.

"I lied. I told her we were double agents working for Britain, and her father couldn't take the pressure. I think she believed it," said Van Dyne.

Stangl shook his head. "It doesn't matter, Van Dyne. For a woman in her position, it could be checked too easily. All you've gained is some time. And not very much of that."

"I know that. That's why I'm here. We've got to act quickly. The accusations alone are too dangerous to let her remain free."

"Kill her," said Stangl, and Van Dyne saw pleasure cross his features.

"Don't be a fool," he exploded. "She's Johann's daughter, at least in his mind she is. Kill her, and he'll hunt you down with every resource at his command. You aren't authorized to take such action!"

"I'm authorized to control this area!" snapped Stangl. "Why else would I sit in this cesspool day after day. I report only to Bormann. No one else."

"Think of the publicity, Stangl. You can't kill the daughter of the Prime Minister of one of the richest nations on earth and expect it to remain a private matter. In a foreign country the authorities would have no choice but to launch a full-scale investigation. Do you want Interpol on our hands? Think, man!"

Stangl slowly nodded assent. "All right. Besides, there are larger issues," he said.

"You're beginning to see," said Van Dyne.

Stangl was thinking out loud. "Assume that she could not have gotten such information on her own," said Stangl.

"Why?" asked Van Dyne, glad to be past Stangl's urge to kill.

"Because she knows too little and too much. She knows that there was a conspiracy, but she doesn't know its nature. She connects you to her father's death, but doesn't know about me. She cites the year 1936, but has no real idea of the significance of the date. And finally, she comes to you and knows nothing of the diamonds. It smacks of a fishing expedition."

Van Dyne nodded slowly. "You think she's been programmed."

Stangl nodded and lit another cigarette.

"I think she's being used. I don't know if she realizes it or not. I would suggest the latter."

"I spoke to Johann earlier today. He gave no indication at all of this. And I don't think she was acting. Perhaps someone *is* using her."

"And threw her at us," finished Stangl.

"To what end?"

"Because her control doesn't know much more than she does, I would guess. He or they are fishing, too."

Van Dyne felt a surge of fear. "How could this happen?" he asked. "After so many years?"

Stangl shrugged. "No organization is totally secure. We found that out during the war. Even the S.S. was rotten. And the Abwehr was a joke even after Canaris was killed." Stangl used a gesture to include Van Dyne in the present. "We learned from their mistakes. For forty years the Adlerkinden have remained secure."

"There must be something," insisted Van Dyne.

Stangl looked uncomfortable. Van Dyne pressed.

"You know something."

Stangl flicked his ashes onto the floor.

"A few weeks ago an agent bodyguarding Hauptman in Copenhagen saw the transfer. He was killed before he could relay any information. It was certain. Besides, it's too soon. It's not feasible to connect the two events."

Van Dyne was not as sure. He was, in fact, deeply worried. The world he had worked for for forty years was in jeopardy.

"Whose agent died?" he asked harshly.

"Ex Op's. He was a tired, old man. No coverage was stepped up on Hauptman. We watched. Smith received the report, and it was listed as due to street violence. The agent was old and slow. He was due to retire. The matter was closed," Stangl answered.

"You can't know that for sure," retorted Van Dyne.

"Smith runs the damn country. If he can't be sure, who can? It's *his* fucking service," said Stangl angrily.

"What do we do about Lisa?" asked Van Dyne, unconvinced.

"Maybe Smith could handle her."

Van Dyne shook his head in disagreement. "I think he would protect her. You of all people should realize his regard for her. You helped make her his only living relative."

Stangl got up and began to pace. The air was thick with smoke. It hung in the lifeless air of the room. Van Dyne was exhausted. I'm getting too old, he thought.

"Then we have to use her, too," said Stangl, "as someone else is."

"She can't be hurt," warned Van Dyne.

Stangl turned to him. "No need to," he said "We won't even inform Smith yet. When we have proof that even he can't deny, he'll be forced to deal with her. And we'll have her wrapped up nice and tight and ready to deliver."

"What do you want me to do?" asked Van Dyne.

"Send the girl here. And when the fisherman follows his bait, we'll catch the fisherman. I've got Otto and plenty of manpower. At night the district is crowded. We can use that to our advantage. The fisherman can't move as fast as we can."

Van Dyne got up. His years felt like so much weight upon him. He needed sleep. He put on his coat and hat and walked to the door.

Stangl still sat and seemed to be thinking. He looked up at Van Dyne.

"Be careful. Your house is probably watched, and I don't want the trap sprung till tomorrow. I'll be expecting our visitor," he said.

Van Dyne nodded and left the office. As he left the building, he saw the circus was still in full swing.

Four

Lisa's head hurt when she awoke. She opened her eyes slowly. They felt caked and crusted. A shaft of morning sunlight lanced through the curtains and made her blink several times. The motion increased the pain in her head.

Unwanted memories of the previous night's conversation with her uncle came flooding back. She shut her eyes as the pain returned. She had come seeking solace and had found only further hurt.

"Damn you, Leander," she said aloud, and it hurt her throat to speak. Tears flooded her eyes, but she was too enervated to cry.

The bottle of brandy lay empty on the night table. The rest of the night before was a haze of pain and alcohol. She wondered how much it would take to drink herself to death. It shouldn't be too hard, she thought, not if you added some pills . . .

It was too hard to think. Leander, Van Dyne, Smith, her parents—all blended together in a confusing mass. There was no hope, only despair.

Lisa rolled off the bed and stripped off the clothing she had slept in. She dropped everything into a pile on the floor. She felt like she was moving under water, each step an effort. Naked, she wandered around the room trying to decide on a direction.

"There's nowhere to go," she said to her reflection in the mirror over the dresser. "I could be anywhere, it doesn't matter. Maybe I'll tell Johann about Leander. That will pay him back."

But even spite was too much effort, and she let the thought vanish back into obscurity. Abruptly, Ben's image flashed into her mind. A sudden warmth flowed through her, jarring her with its intensity. For a moment, the warmth warred with her despair. She remembered his lack of pretense, his honesty. Like the hope of finding out about her parents, Ben had made her feel special and alive again.

But Van Dyne's explanation of her parents' suicide had left her so devoid of hope that doubt consumed her.

"They're all great the first night," she thought bitterly. "And in the morning they're all the same. He won't be any different. A quick fuck, a civilized agreement, and then each of us on to the next. It's always the same."

Her hand found a small bud vase on the dresser, and she threw it at the wall in anger. It smashed into a thousand fragments, and the water made a stain that ran down the wall like blood from a wound.

"Miss Lisa? Are you awake?" a voice asked at the door. It was one of the servants. She vented some of her anger on him.

"Yes? Yes, I'm up. What is it?"

"Herr Van Dyne is waiting for you at breakfast. He asks you to join him," Pers said through the door.

"I don't want to eat. I'll be down later," said Lisa angrily.

"Herr Van Dyne said to tell you it was a matter of some urgency."

"Tell him I'll be down in a few minutes. I want to wash," she said finally.

Lisa went into the bathroom and threw cold water on her face. The shock of it hurt but left her more clearheaded. She pulled on panties, then took a pair of jeans and a blouse from her closet and dressed quickly. She rarely wore a bra and did not do so now. At the mirror Lisa ran a brush through her hair and worked out the tangled mess until it was straight and shiny. Jamming her feet into a pair of running shoes, Lisa left her room and went down to meet Van Dyne.

Van Dyne was already dressed in his business suit. He was sitting at a table in the rear of the house in a room that looked out at the small garden between his house and the house behind. The table had large trays of ham, cheese, and fresh hot bread on it, and a coffee urn sent small puffs of steam into the air. Lisa sat down, and Van Dyne poured her a cup of coffee.

He looked at her with a deep, measuring stare. Lisa felt as if he could see through her. She attempted a nonchalant attitude and piled ham and cheese on the plate in front of her. The protective walls she had let down the night before were back in place. No one would get through again. She wanted Van Dyne to think that what he had revealed meant no more or less to her than the weather. It was a start at making the pain less acute. Van Dyne looked at her sadly.

"I think I hurt you very much last night, Lisa. I'm sorry," he said.

"Don't be," said Lisa. "It doesn't really matter."

"But I think it does," insisted Van Dyne. "I spoke to you harshly, and I should have been more sensitive. Your father was my best friend. It hurt me, too, to think of it after all these years."

"It was an absurd hope to think I'd find something new after all these years. Forget it, uncle. I have," she said.

"I think someone misled you, my dear. Perhaps someone who wanted to hurt you. Or me, for that matter. Won't you tell me who that was?"

"No, uncle. Let it lie."

"But I think your father should know about it. Anything that affects you affects him."

She began to get angry. "The matter is closed. I'll tend to my own affairs in my own way. I'll be leaving later today. I'm sorry for all the trouble I've caused."

"Lisa, where are you going? You know you're welcome here for as long as you like," said Van Dyne.

"I know that. But I'm going back home. That's final."

"What about Ben Davidson? It seemed to me you two hit it off quite well."

Lisa looked down at her lap. Thinking about Ben hurt.

"He means nothing to me," she said.

Van Dyne put his cup of coffee down and looked directly into her eyes. She noticed he looked tired. His face was drawn and haggard.

"There's more to Hans's death than I told you last night, Lisa," he said.

"What could there be?" she asked bitterly. "He killed himself and my mother. End of story."

"Not quite," said Van Dyne.

Lisa took a deep breath. The walls had begun to crack.

"It's not for me to tell, Lisa. There are promises, things

151

older than you are. It's very complicated. Do you trust me, Lisa?"

Lisa found his hesitancy infuriating.

"Yes, I trust you. Now tell me what this is all about."

Van Dyne nodded. "There's a man in this city who knew your father and mother . . ." he paused, looking for the right words, ". . . at the end."

"Who is he?" asked Lisa, the beginnings of excitement and fear mixed together in her.

"I can't tell you that." Van Dyne saw Lisa ready to shout, and he continued quickly. "But I called him this morning, and he agreed to see you. I think you'll find what he has to say important. Will you go see him? He's waiting for you."

With every fiber of her being, Lisa wanted to say no. Let it end here, she thought. Let it be over. No more false hopes, no more useless dreams. Say no, she argued with herself.

"I'll see him, uncle, before I leave," she finally agreed, defeated by her need to hear the man's story.

"Fine. Finish your breakfast, and Pers will call a cab. The address is ninety-six Terenstraat. You are expected."

Ben sat on the edge of the hotel bed, playing devil's advocate with himself about dropping the search for Croft. "Why the hell are the victims of the world more important than my feelings for Lisa?" he muttered. "I could cancel the appointment with Van Dyne and tell him I've got enough for the article. Maybe I'll even write one at that."

He postponed a final decision by picking up the phone and dialing Van Dyne's home number. A servant answered, "Van Dyne Residence."

"Good morning. This is Mr. Davidson. Is Miss Smith available to come to the phone?"

"I'm sorry, sir. Miss Lisa has left for the day. Would you like to leave a message for her?"

"Do you know where she went?" he asked.

"I'm sorry, sir. Miss Lisa is not here. Will that be all, sir?"

"Please tell her that I called."

"Very good, sir," said the servant and hung up.

Ben tried to convince himself again. It made perfect sense. Lisa mattered to him. Was anything worth risking losing her now? But the look in James's eyes as he stared at his dead wife, and the look of disbelief frozen on Amy's face forever, and the memory of the baby he had delivered lying smashed to a pulp on a dirt floor—Ben shook his head sadly. A great sigh escaped his lips, and his chest heaved. "Shit!" he said out loud.

Ten minutes later he walked out of the hotel. There were things he had to do before he kept his appointment with Van Dyne.

Gerroff, sitting quietly in the lobby, folded his newspaper into precise, even parts and stuck it into a basket by his chair. He followed Ben out into the street, trudging after him, cursing every other step. It was drizzling, and he'd left his raincoat in the car. He cursed again and kept walking.

Lisa was surprised when the taxi entered the Red Light District. It seemed an odd place for a friend of Van Dyne's. The sex shops were all closed at this hour of the morning, and the theaters were shut and barred.

Lisa had never been here during the day. It seemed to her that the section looked worse in the light, like an old whore seen, without the cover of night, in all her wrinkles and flaws.

Number 96 had nothing to distinguish it from the surrounding buildings. She hesitated before entering.

The rain had increased to a fine mist which the wind blew into her eyes and ears. But her feet moved forward of their own volition, and her hand reached out to grasp the doorknob. Her determination to leave faded, and she both dreaded and desired what she might find.

Lisa knew she was in a brothel. She had been to others. Now there were no sounds of music or laughter or passion. It was an eerie feeling, the quiet.

She walked into the parlor. It, too, was deserted, the dais in the center empty. Lisa knew from experience what took place there. But being alone here, like a ghostly presence observing the aftermath of some ugly battle, she felt a sense of self-deprecation and, for the first time, wished that places such as this had not been a part of her life.

"We're closed," said a rough voice behind her, and Lisa,

startled, almost jumped. The speaker was a big, burly man whose arms were covered with tattoos.

"We're closed," the man repeated.

"I am Lisa Smith. I believe I'm expected."

The man looked her over from top to bottom, his gaze lingering on her breasts. He nodded slowly.

"I'm Otto. Come with me."

At the top of the stairs Otto turned and walked down the hallway. Lisa followed until Otto stopped at a door. He gestured for her to enter, but she balked. The absence of people, Otto's menace, the house itself, combined to make her afraid.

"I don't..." she began to say, but it was too late. Otto grabbed her in his powerful arms, and she was helpless in his grasp. Holding her with one arm to his body, he opened the door to the room. She could smell his sweat. It made her ill. Otto threw her into the room, and she tripped over a rug and fell. She looked up, and Otto was locking the door.

"Please..." she said weakly.

Otto lifted her effortlessly, threw her onto the bed, and began to secure her hands and feet to its four posts. Lisa tried to kick at him, but he caught her calf in one of his large hands. He dug his fingers into the muscle, and she screamed in agony.

She tried to calm herself. Hysteria would be her enemy. She had no chance to beat Otto on physical grounds. He had proved that. Her only hope lay in rational thinking. Whatever reason she had been brought here, she was still alive.

She anxiously surveyed the room, which contained a bed, a dresser, and a washstand. The wallpaper was an old, faded flower print, and the drapes hung limply over an old greasy shade. The only modern feature in the room was a large mirror set into one wall. Lisa saw her body, spreadeagled and tied, in its reflection. Something about it struck her, but she couldn't bring the thought to full consciousness. She had no time.

Otto removed his shirt and pants. He wore only a black jock strap. Lisa gasped when she saw the bulge it made.

Casually, almost absently, he hit her twice across the face with his open hand. It caught Lisa by surprise, and she had no time to turn. The blows stung rather than hurt. She screamed curses at him, but he hit her again. Think! she told herself. Try to ignore the pain. Otto was looking in the mirror.

With both hands, Otto reached for her blouse and pulled it apart. The buttons popped off and fell to the floor. He opened her jeans and pulled them down. She was open and vulnerable. Again he looked at the mirror.

Otto leaned over her. One of his hands dropped to her breast and caressed it. Lisa felt her nipple stiffen, in spite of her terror. Otto pulled her head around with his other hand and forced her to look at him.

"Who sent you to Van Dyne?" he asked. Lisa's mind was spinning.

"No one," she said. It was the wrong answer. Otto squeezed her breast. She gasped in pain and writhed on the bed to get away. Otto looked in the mirror again and then back to her.

"Who sent you to Van Dyne?"

Lisa gave the same answer, and again he dug his hands into her breasts. The mirror, she thought, as the agony subsided. Why does he keep looking in the mirror?

Again the question. Lisa gave the same answer, and he hurt her again. Suddenly, two thoughts came almost as one to her pain-riddled mind. Leander didn't lie, and the mirror is two-way—we're being watched!

The pain came again. Lisa tried to blank it from her mind. She had to address those behind the mirror. They were in control. They could stop Otto.

Otto was reaching into her pants. Lisa tried not to lose control.

"Listen to me, whoever is behind the mirror," she yelled. "I am the daughter of the Prime Minister of South Africa. If you hurt me, there is no place on earth you can hide. If I die, you die. Whatever happens to me, happens to you."

She felt Otto's finger probe inside her. Lisa shut off her mind from her body and yelled again.

"Listen to me, whoever is behind the mirror..."

In the next room, Stangl watched Lisa's half-naked body writhe in pain. He heard her clearly through the speaker set into the wall. He turned to the man next to him and spoke. "She's tough," he said. "She won't break under this."

"I won't permit you to go further, Stangl. She's right. Smith would have our heads," said Van Dyne.

"It was only an attempt," said Stangl. "We'll proceed as

planned. If she was followed, we'll know in a few hours. They can't stay hidden in this district."

Van Dyne turned away from the scene inside. Lisa was still yelling.

"If I die, you die..." came the tinny voice from the speaker. Otto was removing his strap.

"Stop it, now," said Van Dyne. "Now!"

Stangl turned. There were four others present besides Van Dyne—three men and a girl. The man Stangl spoke to had a nose that had been broken too many times and had a long white scar on his cheek.

"Erich, tell Otto to stop," Stangl said, and the man left the room. To the woman Stangl said, "Feed her in an hour, René. Otto will stand guard at the door. She is to use the bathroom only after meals. You will escort her. If she escapes..."

René nodded; the threat was unnecessary. She already knew Stangl's moods and pleasures, though she had been in the house only a few months. He had allowed her to stay off the streets, but in order to stay, she had to suffer his demands. The alternative was the streets again. He owned her, and he knew it. She hated him. He knew that, too. It seemed to increase his pleasure. René nodded agreement. But she didn't want to leave yet. Not while the girl lay naked on the bed. The scene had brought a dampness to her groin. René imagined her hands on the girl's breasts, in between the girl's legs. She ran her tongue over her lips, and Stangl noticed it.

"You like the girl. Eh, René?"

René shot him a glance of pure hatred. He always tried to humiliate her. But she said nothing.

"Go take care of her now. She's not for you. Understand?"

Stangl spoke to the other two men. "Tell the girls it's all right to come out of their rooms. I want them in the streets in an hour. Someone will be setting up surveillance on the house. I want to know who. And where. They are not to interfere. Tell them only to pinpoint the location and report back to me." As an afterthought, he added, "Tell the girls there are five hundred guilders in it for the one who makes the spotting." Both men left.

Stangl and Van Dyne stood alone in the room. Van Dyne was again watching Lisa in the mirror. Otto had left, and

René was untying Lisa. Lisa hadn't noticed yet that Otto was gone. She was still screaming.

"If you hurt me...", came through the speaker, undiminished in its intensity.

"Did you enjoy seeing her that way?" asked Stangl.

Van Dyne's face lost its color. "You're a pig, Stangl," he hissed.

Stangl laughed. "And you're a hypocrite."

Van Dyne started to protest, but Stangl stopped him with a wave of his hand.

"Come," he said. "We have work to do."

"I've got to call my office and tell them I'll be late," said Van Dyne.

"You can use the phone in the office," said Stangl. "Get Rikkers to take care of business."

"All right," agreed Van Dyne, following Stangl out the door.

It took a while before Otto's absence penetrated Lisa's consciousness. She realized suddenly that her hands were free. She stopped screaming and heard someone speaking; a girl's soft voice crooned to her.

"It's all over, little one. He's gone. No one will hurt you now. It's all over, little one. He's gone..."

The girl untied her legs as well. Lisa's first thought was one of victory; then it turned to apprehension. The girl was pretty and dark-haired. She pulled Lisa's clothing together, tying her shirt at the bottom.

"Who are you?" Lisa asked.

"I'm René. I'm here to take care of you." Lisa felt René's hand brush her breasts.

"I'm leaving," said Lisa and got up to stand. Her legs were still weak, and her chest hurt.

"I don't think so, little one," said René. "There's a guard at the door. You'll be here for some time. Try and relax." René walked over to stroke Lisa's hair.

Lisa had known gay women before. She had even experimented once, years before, and she suddenly saw that René's interest in her was more than guard to prisoner. It was definitely sexual in nature. Her mind raced in high gear, desperate to use anything, any advantage to escape.

"I'll be back to feed you in an hour. You can use the bathroom then if you want," said René.

Lisa thought hard and stilled her disquiet. She tried an

experiment. Reaching out, she let her fingers wander over René's cheek and put on a pouting expression.

"Make it sooner. I'm so hungry." René hesitated, but Lisa continued. "We have so much to talk about. Don't you agree?" Her fingers caressed more deeply. A change came over René. Her eyes glazed a little, and her breathing deepened. "All right, little one. I'll be back soon."

René cast a last, loving look at Lisa's body. Still testing, Lisa let her blouse swing open to reveal her breasts. René nodded, her face flushed, then turned and left the room.

Even though trapped and betrayed, Lisa felt the despair of the previous night vanish. One thing was clear to her. Van Dyne had betrayed her, sent her here to this. He feared her questions.

"Leander didn't lie! Leander didn't lie!" It was almost a song inside her head. It was her uncle who had lied. And the search for her parents' killer was still on. They could want her here for no other reason than to silence her.

Lisa knew they would never let her go. She wasn't sure if they would kill her; in fact, she doubted it. But, free, she was too great a risk.

She went to the window and looked out. It had bars across it. No escape. She thought of smashing the mirror with the washstand, but she found it was nailed down when she tried to move it. Besides, Otto would hear it and come charging in in seconds.

She sat in the chair to think. Was there anyone she could trust? Anyone she could get a message to, who would come for her if she called?

The thought hit her like a physical blow. There was only one person she could think of. Why had she doubted that this morning? she asked herself. Because the world had fallen apart again, she answered. It would have to be Ben, she told herself. She would have to trust. Lisa began to think.

The morning rain had stacked up flights in the sky above Schipol Airport, but Leander's plane had military clearance and touched down on schedule. Leander's clearance bypassed the customs check, and Dreyer was relieved to see him come through the gates.

"Hello, Jan," said Dreyer, taking Leander's bag. "The car's outside. We've got to hurry. Lisa's moved."

After a brief greeting to Dreyer and a grimace at the weather, Leander remained silent until they were in the car. Dreyer gunned the engine and moved into the morning traffic.

"What's happening?" asked Leander.

In a concise report Dreyer told him of Lisa's contact with Van Dyne, her schedule for the past two days, the emergence of the man now identified as Ben Davidson of New York, and the morning's visit to the house at 96 Terenstraat. Leander listened intently until Dreyer finished.

"The girl is still inside the house?" he asked.

"As of ten minutes ago. Pilsten is on surveillance in the van, and I pulled Morgan from the embassy to cover the back. He can be released when we get there."

"Where's Gerroff?"

"On Davidson. He's due to report in a few minutes. Pilsten will take it in the van," said Dreyer.

"How do you figure Davidson?" asked Leander.

"He's an unknown, at present. There is some evidence of attraction between him and the girl. Look at these." Dreyer handed Leander the photos he had taken the night before.

Leander leafed through them. He pointed to Ben in one of the pictures.

"This is the man?" he asked.

"Yes. We have no active file on him. No one does. I checked with Central an hour ago. Research is doing a more thorough job, but that'll take a day or so. What we have came off the rental agency's computer. He lists his occupation as a journalist," said Dreyer.

Leander nodded, lost in thought.

"Do you think Lisa has confronted Van Dyne yet?" he asked Dreyer. They were approaching the city limits.

"I don't know. It's anybody's guess."

"Why did she go to a brothel? That's what you said the building is, right?"

"Absolutely," said Dreyer. "We're checking ownership now. I've already rented a loft across the street for a surveillance site."

Leander seemed pleased. "You've done a good job, Peter. Let's hope this brothel is significant and not just Lisa going to play with friends. Leave Pilsten in the van until we can establish a more permanent setup."

"Fine with me, Jan."

His thoughts of the night before were still bothering Dreyer. He decided to speak them.

"Jan, if I'm out of line, then tell me. But why the hell does the director of the agency come thousands of miles to take charge in the field? It isn't standard operating procedure, and you know it."

Leander seemed on the verge of speaking but apparently decided against it.

"Trust me, Peter," was all he would say.

Five

Transvaal, N.E. South Africa

Craig Ryerson stripped off his khaki work shirt and tossed it on a pile of steel girders that lay baking under the intense South African sun. He was so deeply tanned from working outdoors on construction sites throughout the world that his ordinarily fair skin was bronze-colored, and the hair on his arms had turned almost white. He swiped a lock of sweaty sandy-colored hair that had fallen into his eyes back under his steel hat and watched a team of workmen lay in a sixteen foot I-beam to cross-brace a new section of building.

"Watch the swing on that son-of-a-bitch. Lower it easy. Take your time with it," he called out in loud disapproval as the crane operator, responding to the hand signals of the workmen, lowered the I-beam too swiftly. It fell into place with a vibrating clang, and the whole massive three-story structure rang like a tuning fork in protest. The workmen looked sheepish. Others, in different sections, grinned and yelled catcalls.

"How many times do I have to tell you guys to take it easy?" Ryerson yelled again in frustration. "Kee-rist. This whole job is one bleedin' frustration after another," Ryerson cursed out loud.

One of the black native laborers standing nearby grinned but said nothing to Ryerson's outburst. He moved along with a load of brick in a wheelbarrow to where the skilled white masons were building an outer wall. Ryerson watched the native, a Zulu tribesman, whose earlobes were stretched to hold flat, wooden disks, drop the bricks in the wrong place, hearing the curses at the "ignorant Kaffir."

"What a bleedin' country," Ryerson moaned to himself as he began to direct the workmen in placing the next beam. The sound of jackhammers joined the melee.

At thirty-two, Ryerson was lean and hard and had the experience of a man twice his age. He had grown up in Sydney, the only son of a pharmacist and his wife. His parents had wanted him to be a man of science, a doctor or chemist perhaps, but early on, Ryerson displayed such an ability and an enjoyment in using his hands to build that it grew clear he was going to be a construction engineer.

Capitulating somewhat to his parents' repeated requests for him to live a "civilized life," Ryerson joined a prestigious Sydney construction firm after graduating from the university with his engineering degree when he was twenty-one. But soon he had had his fill of building two-story banks and mansions for the wealthy. In a move his parents still described as "patently irresponsible," Ryerson quit the firm after two years and joined a government team building roads and bridges in the Outback.

He loved the outdoors. The enormous vistas of land and sky pleased him as much as the scope of the projects on which he now worked. A desire grew within him to see the rest of the world; and so, after three years in the Bush, an accomplished engineer with an excellent reputation, he joined the construction section of the United Nations World Health Organization.

Ryerson celebrated his twenty-fifth birthday in Pakistan where the W.H.O. was building a hospital. At twenty-seven, he toasted his birthday in Caracas, where the W.H.O. was building clinics. He turned thirty on a boat crossing the China Sea to a new project in Taiwan. And by the time he was thirty-two, he reckoned he had built, balled, brawled, and boozed his way throughout half the countries in the world. Thinking back, he was hard pressed to remember an unhappy day since leaving Sydney nine years before.

But Craig Ryerson was unhappy now. This whole project had a strange feel to it. The W.H.O. had assigned him here six months before. When he arrived, only a small collection of buildings, W.H.O. labs, stood on this site in the North Eastern Transvaal of South Africa.

It was beautiful country though, he admitted to himself. The air was clear and sweet, and mountains reared up majestically in the distance. It was bush country, with thorn trees and the strange baobab trees that looked like they grew upside down in the orange earth. Wildflowers grew in red and purple profusion everywhere.

But the thought that something was wrong here still plagued him as he watched the next beam slide into place, not much more slowly or accurately. Where was Bourke, the foreman? Ryerson needed to get his directions for the next section. He had no blueprints of his own to follow.

That was a part of it, he decided. Things were so secretive around here. Who ever heard of the foreman being the only one to see the blueprints and not his assistant? Yet Bourke carried them around as if they were a map to buried treasure. Consequently, Ryerson had to work a step at a time, with no real overview of the project—like a bricklayer not knowing where the next brick was going to go or where the corner would start. And if Ryerson made a mistake, Bourke, a big, thick South African of mixed Irish and German descent, screamed at him maniacally.

And the project didn't look like a hospital, Ryerson reminded himself. After the 'dozers had cleared the land of bush, the first thing constructed were inner- and outer-perimeter, eight-foot fences. The site looked like a fortress, rather than a hospital.

"Watch it there, damn it!" yelled Ryerson as a workman carelessly clambered over the beam to release it from the crane's cable, and the crane arm started to take up slack too soon. It was hard to maintain discipline in his crew when its members kept changing. The foreman on the job constantly kept switching personnel from section to section for no reason Ryerson understood.

And why build the structure in sections anyway? It was a technique first developed in the prefab industry but made little sense in a structure of this size. Without the guiding hands of the foreman, workers were often like a roomful of drunks each with a separate piece of a jigsaw puzzle trying to put it together while stumbling around. No wonder it was going slowly, he thought.

It was a damn sloppy technique, Ryerson decided, and a frown creased his leathery-skinned face. He brushed the sweat from his forehead and wiped his palms on his faded blue dungarees.

The workmen on the upper story were having trouble again guiding in a beam.

"What the hell is wrong up there?" he yelled in exasperation. One of the workmen, a man named Jones whose black hair sprang in wiry tufts all over his back, chest, and shoulders, gave him a sour, challenging look.

"Stop bitchin', Ryerson," he yelled down to the ground. "Unless you think you can do it any better."

Ryerson knew that the challenge was childish and that accepting it was just plain dumb. If he lost, he lost control totally. Better just to stand on his authority. But, he realized, he had precious little of that left. And Ryerson had worked too many construction gangs in too many places not to know what happened when the boss lost his authority—chaos reigned, and people got hurt. These men were too tough and too self-sufficient to cooperate unless someone tougher took control.

In the final analysis it was probably the frustration of the job that caused him to leap onto the pile of girders and scurry up the structure like a spider traveling up his web. He got to the uppermost story traveling the last ten feet going hand over hand up the rope for the rivet basket. He faced Jones squarely.

"A monkey could do a better job than you," he said. He wasn't even breathing hard.

Ordinarily, each girder was pushed into place by two men as the crane lowered it. Weighing almost six hundred pounds, the girders had a tremendous inertia if they started to swing. Ryerson grabbed a pair of construction gloves from his belt and motioned the crane to start lowering the beam. He heard a snort of disbelief from Jones, and other workers stopped to watch, intent on the outcome. Power tools were shut off and hammers ceased pounding.

Ryerson braced his feet against the girder he was standing

on. The next beam would be set horizontally onto two vertical columns forming a section of roof. The crane started to lower it, and a shadow crossed Ryerson's face as it blocked out the rays of the sun.

It was moving too fast, and Ryerson motioned for less speed. Obediently, the crane operator slowed its descent. It came steadily downward. If the descent were not true, the beam would miss the lips of the vertical columns, and the procedure would have to begin again. It was the workmen's job to guide it true, using brute strength and hand-eye coordination.

Five feet from the lips, Ryerson saw that the beam was off true by about a foot. Jones saw it too, and Ryerson heard his pleasured grunt behind him. Someone below gave odds against Ryerson. Ryerson knew he had only one shot at this, and he tensed his muscles in anticipation. Jones laughed out loud, sure of his victory. It made Ryerson angry.

Ryerson grabbed the beam on both sides of its flanged top when it was waist high. In one convulsive movement he pushed against it with all the force he could summon from his hard, compact body. Though only five-feet ten-inches tall and a hundred and seventy pounds, that force was considerable.

At first there seemed to be no change in the beam's lateral motion as it continued downward. Ryerson reversed his direction and pulled as hard as he could. Slowly, the beam began to sway like a pendulum, through an arc. He heaved again, and the sway became more pronounced.

With one hand he motioned for the crane operator to pick up the speed. The arc had increased to almost a foot. Ryerson grabbed the beam with both hands and heaved against it to slow its swing. Muscles straining and bulging, and sweat pouring from his body, Ryerson strained to cut the momentum of the beam. He began to see black spots in front of his eyes. No one spoke, and the laughing had ceased.

In one final moment of descent the beam looked like it was going to miss completely. But Ryerson had aimed it just right. As the beam brushed over the one Ryerson stood on, it swung right over the lips of the columns and dropped precisely into place. Ryerson felt it slide home with a deep reassuring clang. He straightened up and looked at Jones who was silent. Ryerson realized he was grinning.

Then he realized that others were grinning, too. Someone

slapped him on the back, and another yelled, "Way to handle that mother, Craig." And even Jones finally grinned.

"Not bad for a college kid," he said and offered his hand. Ryerson took it.

"You can buy this college kid a beer later on. Deal?" he said with warmth in his voice.

"Deal," said Jones, and pulled on his gloves to get back to work.

When Ryerson got back to the ground again, he was in good spirits. It had been a victory of sorts. Not over the girder or the men, really. But for whatever the reason, it was a victory over the oppressive mood that this project seemed to generate in him. He felt lighthearted and content.

A native worker ran up to him to say that Bourke wanted him at the lab complex. Ryerson nodded and left his post to follow.

The main complex was a series of four, one-story, white stucco buildings, a quarter of a mile away inside the compound, which housed medical and laboratory personnel and their research facilities. When the hospital was completed, they would be vacated and serve some other purpose. Now they were the scene of constant activity and heavy security. Bourke's office was in Building Three, and Ryerson was ushered in past two armed guards.

Again he felt uneasy. Was this kind of security necessary? Bourke had explained it in terms of Black Terrorist groups, but Ryerson had seen nothing but wilderness animals in the area since he had been assigned here.

"On schedule?" Bourke asked gruffly and without preamble.

"More or less," said Ryerson. "Come and take a look for yourself."

"I'll do just that," said Bourke, and Ryerson followed him back outside. Three new girders had been placed since Ryerson had left. He was pleased his performance had had a positive effect. Bourke squatted on his heels in the grass native style and looked over the work. He plucked a stalk to chew as he spoke.

"Too slow, Ryerson," he said. "The whole North Wing has to be up in two weeks. It won't be at this rate."

"Under these conditions, I'm going as fast as possible," said Ryerson stubbornly.

"Use more niggers. Send a boy to the nearest village,"

165

growled Bourke unhappily. Ryerson found the racial slurs so common here distasteful.

"The only problem, Bourke, is that if I do that, the white workers go berserk if the black workers do anything of a specialized nature. They yell union at me. All they'll let the blacks do is cart and carry work," he said.

"They'll have to learn to..."

Suddenly, Bourke leaped up from his squat in midsentence and screamed at the top of his lungs. He clutched his thigh and tumbled headlong into Ryerson, who saw the cause at once. A long tan and black rope slithered away into the grass. Bourke had been bitten by a cobra. Bourke writhed on the ground in agony. Ryerson knew that the doctors would be the best bet, and he ran inside to get one. He had been bitten several times himself, in Asia mostly. He knew that though it was painful, if antivenom were handy, it was rarely fatal. Here antivenom would not be in short supply.

The labs were closed to any and all but staff. He saw an open door in Building One and ran inside. He was lucky. In Building One, Ryerson found a doctor he knew, named Wassermann, who had treated one of the workers for a broken arm a few days before.

"I need you, Doc," he said in short terse tones. "Bourke's been bitten by a cobra. Right outside Three. Got it?"

"Right," said Wassermann, a portly, balding man in his forties. "I'll grab my bag. I've got the antivenom in it."

Ryerson watched him run out the door and followed. Outside Building Three the doctor began to treat Bourke, who had lost consciousness. Ryerson started to offer his help when a thought struck him—the blueprints in Bourke's office were unguarded now. He might never have a better opportunity to see them. His sense of responsibility to help the doctor with Bourke conflicted with his sense of curiosity. A born engineer, his curiosity won. He sidled past the guards who were lifting Bourke onto a stretcher.

Feeling a little bit like a second-rate spy, Ryerson walked casually back inside. The blueprints were on Bourke's desk where he had left them. Ryerson flipped through them slowly, scanning each page completely before turning to the next. His trained mind began to build up a picture of the building as the drawings gave up their secrets.

Questions began to form in his mind. According to the

plans, the second floor of the hospital was supposed to be lab facilities. Ryerson double-checked the color-coded labeling twice to make sure. Yet, when he scanned the blueprints themselves, he found discrepancies in design so far-reaching that no labs he'd ever seen could be used there.

This is all wrong, he told himself. There were no conduits for wiring to any space but the walls. No lab stations could be added unless wiring was done beforehand through the floor. Plus the rooms were too big. The square footage was immense, almost ten thousand square feet per room. At that rate the second floor would contain only five rooms. What were they planning to put in there? he wondered. As a ward, it would hold two beds every ten feet; allowing for corridors between, each room could hold an average of three hundred beds. If that were the plan, it would be more like a dormitory than a hospital, he thought. None of it made sense.

On the top floor were more rooms that bore no relation to their color codes in the design. The interior walls were too thick, and each room had double entry portals that almost appeared to be airlocks from the data he read. The codes said that the rooms would be for Administrative Personnel. But on the plans, each room bore a "P4" designation, which Ryerson had never seen before. He wondered what the hell "P4" meant. These looked like no plans for offices he had ever seen.

He continued to see discrepancies as he probed further. The kitchens were way too big for the number of patients and staff the codes called for. As were the gymnasium facilities coded as Rehabilitation. Even the classrooms, coded as Staff Training Centers, were numerous enough to train three times the projected number of staff.

"Bourke, I need..." said a voice that halted in midsentence.

Ryerson looked up, startled, to see a foreman named Tamely, a thin, wiry South African, standing in the doorway looking at him through narrowed eyes.

"Where's Bourke, and who let you in here?" he demanded.

Ryerson let the blueprints settle back onto the desk and tried to appear as nonchalant as he could.

"Bourke got bitten by a snake. Doc Wassermann's got him. I came in to pick up the next workload while he's out. I've been trying to figure out where my section is in this mess. Can you give me a hand?"

Ryerson had on a face innocent enough to convince a hanging judge. Tamely scrutinized him closely. As if he were trying to sense some wrongness, Ryerson thought. He just kept up his innocent face and smiled benignly into Tamely's stare.

"You can't read prints?" Tamely asked, sarcasm in his voice.

"C'mon, Tamely. Give me a break. I can read them standing on my head." Ryerson feigned anger. "You know my credentials. But I got here ten seconds before you did, and it would take me an hour to figure out the damn color codes the bright boy architect decided to use. You know damn well that blueprints are as individual as flamin' fingerprints. Now are you gonna help me or what?" he demanded, a study in outraged innocence.

Tamely studied him for another few seconds. Ryerson kept up his act. Finally, Tamely seemed to soften a bit.

"Sorry, Ryerson. I was just worried about Bourke. You say a doc's got him?"

"If I were you, Tamely, I'd worry about the snake. It's probably died of blood poisoning by now," Ryerson joked.

Tamely laughed, a thin dry sound, and Ryerson figured he passed Tamely's test.

"Go back to the site, Ryerson," Tamely said. "I'll send over a replacement for Bourke in a few minutes."

"Right," said Ryerson, and he walked past Tamely who locked the door to Bourke's office behind him.

Back at the site, Ryerson watched the work with mixed emotion. His crew had shaped up nicely, and the smiles that greeted his return were not lost on him. Like a giant anthill, workers moved over the structure hammering, riveting, laying brick. Bulldozers lumbered in the distance on steel treads moving earth. Ryerson was at home in the middle of the endless cacophony of construction. It gave him a sense of security to build something that would outlast his own life. The question is, he asked himself, what in the hell are we building here?

Later that night he got stinking drunk with Jones and the other men. His feat that afternoon had grown into Herculean proportions, to be retold each drink. It was retold many times.

The next morning, Ryerson stumbled onto the construction site to find he had been transferred to the W.H.O. African

Regional Center in Brazzaville for reassignment. He had been fired for the first time in his life.

Six

Ben arrived a few minutes early for his appointment with Van Dyne. The rain had stopped, and the morning sun poked tentatively through the clouds. The steps to the exchange glistened wetly after the rainfall, and the floor inside was slippery from the comings and goings of customers and employees. Rikkers was waiting inside.

"Good morning, Mr. Davidson. I'm afraid Herr Van Dyne has been detained at a business meeting. He called a few moments ago with a request that you wait. Will that be all right?"

This was a stroke of luck Ben had not hoped for. It meant that no one would be in Van Dyne's office, and the exchange's file room would be unobserved. At last he could look for a link to Croft. Ben tried to hide his nervousness. It was a gamble, but one he felt he had to take.

"That'll be fine, Mr. Rikkers," he said.

Mrs. Stoelin sat behind the desk in her office as he and Rikkers walked in. She was dressed for business, and her manner was only slightly more casual for having seen Ben socially the previous night.

"Has Herr Van Dyne returned yet?" Rikkers was asking Mrs. Stoelin.

"Not yet," she said. "I expect him any moment. You may wait inside, Mr. Davidson."

"Thank you, Mr. Stoelin. By the way, I enjoyed last night immensely. Thank you."

"You're quite welcome," she said, and at her touch of the concealed switch, the office door swung open.

It had taken Ben almost all morning to find an office supply store that sold the same cabinets as in Van Dyne's office. Posing as a security-conscious buyer for an American corporation setting up an office in Amsterdam, he had the salesman

169

go over every inch of a number of cabinet systems. He was shown which ones were burglar-proof and which were not.

He now withdrew from his pocket a six-inch, flat iron crowbar with flanged ends that was only a half-inch wide, and a screwdriver, that he had bought in a local hardware store. Pulling the first cabinet out from the wall, he put his shoulder against the top and leaned it against the wall. It was heavy and he started to sweat, as much from anxiety as from exertion.

Reaching under the bottom lip of the cabinet, Ben found the locking unit bar. He maneuvered the flanged end of the push-bar into place and forced the bar downward. He felt the "click" of its release. Taking the screwdriver in his other hand, he pulled the bar further down, past the fulcrum point of the push-bar. A second "click" and the lock had been sprung.

He stood up and opened the first drawer. It contained records of purchase for quantities of stones from De Beers in London. Ben flipped through them quickly. The next contained the same kind of records, but for a previous year. The third and forth drawers were also useless.

He opened the next cabinet and began to go through the files. His shirt was damp across his back. Personnel files. Nothing of any use to him.

Ben pulled the next cabinet from the wall. His tools were getting slick from the moisture on his palms. The flange wouldn't catch on the bar.

"Stop sliding, damn it!" Ben muttered. It was no use. He couldn't release the lock. He pushed the cabinet back into position, grunting from exertion and went to work on the next.

Ben's back grew cold, and the muscles started to cramp as the sweat evaporated in the cold air conditioning. His shoulder began to ache.

The files inside were records of sales to jewelry houses all over the world. He began to feel desperate as he pushed the cabinet back against the wall and moved on to the next one.

"You're a very poor burglar, Mr. Davidson," said a voice behind him. "I didn't realize these files were so accessible. We shall have to rectify that."

Ben turned, and despair flooded through him. Rikkers stood in the doorway, a guard with him, gun drawn.

"There is a concealed video system throughout this entire suite of offices. It's operative when Herr Van Dyne is not here. When he comes in, he switches it off. You were picked up ten seconds after you started. Step inside, Mr. Davidson." Rikkers's tone was harsh.

Ben walked into Van Dyne's office under the watchful stare of the guard who moved to a position by the door.

"Who are you, and what do you want?" demanded Rikkers, pushing Ben into a chair.

"My name is Ben Davidson, and I'm doing an article on diamonds."

Rikkers's face showed disbelief and annoyance.

"Why break into our files?"

"I thought I could get a lead on the fixing of diamond prices on the world market. People would pay for that kind of story."

"You're lying," snarled Rikkers. "Give me your wallet."

Ben hesitated, not knowing what to do next. Rikkers looked to the guard. The sound of the gun's cocking was both audible and clear. Ben fought down the urge to do something, anything at all, and handed his wallet to Rikkers.

Rikkers spilled the contents onto Van Dyne's desk. Ben watched him pick up the items one by one and look at them. Suddenly, Rikkers's face changed completely.

Rikkers's expression was uncertain. The card, Ben realized, the card that he had taken from Henry Schmidt in New Orleans! The card that identified him as a member of the Adlerkinden, one of the Eagle's Children.

"Who are you?" asked Rikkers. His voice had a catch in it now. Ben uttered a silent prayer and took his only shot.

"I am Henry Schmidt," he said, *"von den Adlerkinden."*

The effect on Rikkers was instantaneous. Ben permitted himself a small hope.

"Who sent you?" Rikkers asked, a new element of suspicion growing on his face.

A fierce elation went through Ben. There *was* a conspiracy!

Ben sat up straighter in his chair and put command on his face and in his voice.

"Have your man wait outside unless he is one of us. And kill the cameras unless you want me to talk to your security people."

Rikkers was indecisive. He stared at the card and turned it

171

over in his hands. Finally, he turned to the guard as his hand threw a switch under the desk.

"Wait outside until I call you," Rikkers told the guard. Ben held his breath. The guard hesitated.

"But, Herr Rikkers, policy . . ." he said.

"Do as I say!" barked Rikkers, displeased by the disobedience of his employee in front of an unknown quantity. He came around the desk, and the guard holstered his gun and left the room, closing the door behind him.

Rikkers stood in front of Ben.

"Who sent you, Herr Schmidt?" he asked again. "And why?"

"The Eagle sent me," Ben said.

Rikkers's face changed abruptly, and Ben knew he had made his last mistake. Combat training took over as Rikkers's mouth opened to yell. In one swift movement, Ben's stiffened fingers hit him in the throat, and the scream died to a tortured gurgle. Ben let the momentum of his blow carry him forward, his elbow smashing into the side of Rikkers's head. Rikkers dropped to the floor, unconscious.

Ben listened for the guard. Long seconds ticked away until he was sure he was safe. The files were out. He had no way of knowing if Rikkers had turned off the cameras in the file room as well as in the office. He had to get out now. He pulled Rikkers's body out of sight behind the desk and looked at the intercom. He pressed the call button and muffled his voice.

"Mrs. Stoelin? Send the guard in. No problems. All a mistake."

The buzzer sounded as Ben got behind the door. When the guard was five feet into the room, Ben pushed the door shut and launched himself at the guard who, seeing no one, started to turn and reach for his gun. Ben hit him square in the groin with a front kick. The gun clattered to the floor as he doubled over. A hard blow to the neck, and the guard lay still.

Ben fought to keep calm as he put on his jacket and smoothed his hair. Stifling the need to run, he walked calmly out of Van Dyne's office. All he could do now was escape.

He glanced at Mrs. Stoelin as he passed her desk. She looked at him curiously.

"I need more tapes. Be right back," he said. Mrs. Stoelin looked to Van Dyne's office but made no move to get up.

The secretaries were still typing as he passed them. The hallways seemed longer than ever before. With each footstep he resisted the need to run. One step at a time. He got to the staircase and descended.

The guard in the lobby showed no surprise when Ben asked for his coat and case. The exit doors stood only five feet away. He walked toward them.

The fresh air blew into his face as he opened the outer doors. Ben wanted to cry with relief. He was out. He got into his car and almost drove into the canal before he realized it was in a forward gear.

As he drove, excited thoughts and new connections raced through his head. Before, the complex question of the Adlerkinden contained too many variables. Now, at least one of those variables had been identified, solidified, and a value could be fixed.

The card was the connection. For it to surface in New Orleans and also have the impact it had had on Rikkers was proof that a link existed. There was a conspiracy. Clearly, Rikkers had held the card in awe. And if not for that simple fact, Ben realized, he might still be at gunpoint in Van Dyne's office.

He turned the syllogism over and over in his mind. If Croft had invoked the Adlerkinden and Rikkers was a part of the Adlerkinden, then in some way Croft and Rikkers were connected. It also cast grave doubts on Van Dyne. His involvement could be deeper than Rikkers. Guilt by association was not proof. But Rikkers operated with the sureness of one whose position was secure and Van Dyne could provide such security.

But apart from this verification, Ben knew he had little to go on. Adlerkinden was a German word, yet thus far he had not stumbled over any connection to Germany. All he had were pieces of the puzzle. The overall design still eluded him.

Of one thing he was sure. It was time to check out of the Pulitzer. Van Dyne knew he was staying there, as did Lisa. He had to face the agonizing possibility that even she, too, could be involved.

The Amsterdam streets were alive with people on their way to lunch. Couples walked arm in arm by the canals. He tried to put all thoughts of Lisa from his mind. It was unlikely he could ever see her again, and the hurt of that seared through his chest.

Rikkers regained consciousness slowly. He could barely breathe, and a long spasm of choking and coughing caused him to pass out again.

When he awoke, his tortured throat had lost its swelling enough to sustain breath and consciousness. Tears poured out of his eyes, and his jaw hurt fiercely. What had happened? he wondered. He couldn't quite put it all together. He tried to stand, but his head swam. He made it into Van Dyne's chair.

He saw the guard sprawled limply in the center of the room. Davidson was gone. Davidson! He remembered now. Rikkers reached out and tried to focus on the intercom's call button. It took most of his strength to push the button down.

"Mrs. Stoelin . . ." he gasped.

The door flew open. Mrs. Stoelin took in the unconscious guard and Rikkers's bruised face in a glance. Her hands flew to her mouth to stifle an exclamation of shock.

"Call Van Dyne . . ." hissed Rikkers.

Seven

Lisa stared out the window and watched people in the street pass by. A sailor connected with a girl in the street, and they moved off past her range of vision. Some tourists wandered by, looking disappointed at the inactivity in the area. She had thought long and hard, and the beginnings of a plan had formed in her mind.

The door opened, and René came in with a sandwich and a bottle of wine. She wore a silk, kimono-like dress that was slit up the side to the black rims of her stockings.

"I brought your lunch, little one," said René sweetly, and put it down on the washstand.

"Thank you," said Lisa. "What's your name?" She smiled warmly.

"René. And I brought the wine 'specially for you." She smiled back coquettishly.

"It's lovely," Lisa exclaimed and went to work on the food to avoid the hunger that dulled both body and mind.

"My name's Lisa. Do you work here?" she asked between bites.

"I work here," said René, bitterness in her voice.

"You don't like it?" asked Lisa.

"It's better than the streets. The owner took me in. He likes me, but he's a pig," René said.

"Then why stay?" Lisa asked.

"But where would I go?" asked René.

"There are other places," Lisa su ggested.

René shrugged. "It's all the same. I do okay."

René sat on the bed beside Lisa and stroked her hair. Lisa permitted it for a while. She reached over and took a long drink of the wine. It helped to calm her disquiet at the girl's touch. She steeled herself and thought of Ben. Everything she was about to do depended on him. She hoped he could be trusted to help her now when she needed him most.

Lisa handed the bottle to René, who drank gladly. It seemed to put some life into her eyes.

"Do you like girls?" asked René.

"I like you, René," said Lisa.

René's hands moved down Lisa's neck, massaging the muscles in her back. Lisa let her head hang free but frowned. She pointed to the mirror.

René understood. "There's no one there, my sweet. Relax."

Lisa placed her hand on René's thigh and stroked her stockinged leg. She could feel the play of sinewy muscles, and René's breathing quickened.

A long time before, when she was thirteen and puberty had given her drives she hadn't yet learned to understand, Lisa had had a friend named Ruth. Ruth was dark-haired and pale-skinned, and Lisa thought she looked like Rebecca in the novel *Ivanhoe*. Ruth was a gifted pianist, a child prodigy. Ruth was also a lesbian.

For a short while, Lisa had thought she was in love with Ruth. She seemed so much more sensitive and mature than the boys at school who giggled and tried to look up her dress if she bent over. For hours at a time, Lisa would sit in Ruth's living room and listen to her play long, soaring pieces on the piano. While Ruth played, Lisa forgot about being afraid or lonely. There was just the music, and Ruth.

Lisa let Ruth touch her the first time she stayed overnight at Ruth's house. Though it was her first and only experience, she couldn't find it within her to return Ruth's passion. Ruth had been kind about it rather than bitter.

"It's just the way you're built, Lisa. Don't be upset. I'm not," she had said.

"Can we still be friends?" Lisa asked.

"Best friends," said Ruth, and they had spent the night sleeping in each other's arms.

Years later, Lisa still got a postcard every now and then from Ruth, sent from some city in Europe or America in which she was playing. Homosexuality had never frightened Lisa after her experience with Ruth. It was, to her, just a choice she was not built to make.

As such, René did not frighten Lisa now when she felt René's hand slip inside her shirt to fondle her breast. Lisa moved her hand over René's legs and felt the heat rising from her. A moan escaped René's lips, and her back arched. René tried to pull Lisa onto the bed. Her face was imploring with need. She was totally unprepared when Lisa leaped off the bed and ran to a chair in the corner of the room.

"I can't," Lisa cried, burying her face in her hands. "I'm sorry. I want to, but I just can't. I'm sorry."

René came over to her and sat by her feet.

"What's the matter, little one? I thought..." she said.

Lisa forced tears into her eyes. "I want to," she touched René's hair, "but I can't. All the other times I...I had something. Something to help me."

René was confused. "What do you need? Don't you find me pretty? Is it me?" she asked.

"Oh, no," said Lisa. "It's not you. I want you. I need my..." Lisa paused. "Do you have any cocaine? I can't... without it I can't...I always..." Her voice broke up into sobs.

René understood. She had been with people like Lisa before. Ones who needed drugs to release what they were. But cocaine was so expensive, and she had none.

"I have some grass in my room. And we have wine. Will that be okay?"

Lisa looked miserable. She shook her head. "It's no good. I

need cocaine. I can't without it. Everything gets so confused in my head, and I can't think," she said.

"I know, little one. I know. But what can I do?" René asked, sadly. "Can we try anyway?"

"I just can't." Lisa put a bitchy tone in her voice. "I thought you said you understood. But you don't. Leave me alone."

René was devastated.

"I would do anything for you. Just tell me," said René. Her hand wandered up Lisa's leg. Lisa let it remain.

"Can I leave?" she asked.

René shook her head.

"It's not possible. Come back to bed. Let me try," said René.

Lisa let René lift her from the chair but broke away halfway to the bed.

"I want to, but I can't, René," Lisa cried and rushed back to the chair.

"But how can I get what you want? It's just not possible," René said. Her eyes were still pleading.

"I have some in my room. A whole bag full," said Lisa, carefully. "My connection is there now." She tried to sound matter-of-fact. "You could get it for me. And we could both do it up. Then we could"—Lisa walked to René and kissed her—"make love," she whispered into René's ear.

René deliberated for a long moment. Cocaine and Lisa were just too much to turn down.

"You won't tell anyone I went for you?" René asked. Lisa shook her head.

"I promise, René. And when you get back, we'll get high, and I'll do anything you say. Anything you want."

René nodded. "I'll go," she said.

"My connection's name is Ben Davidson, and he's at the Pulitzer Hotel, Room two-thirteen. Tell him I sent you and to give you the cocaine. Tell him I need it desperately . . ." René nodded while Lisa explained to her what to tell the dealer.

Ben stripped off his clothing as soon as he got to his room. He felt feverish, and he had a case of the shakes. It was a reaction both to the fear and the violence.

He called the front desk.

"This is Mr. Davidson in two-thirteen. I'll be checking out. Please prepare my bill."

"Right away, sir. It'll be ready when you come down."

Ten minutes later Ben was dressed in jeans, sweater, and sneakers and was almost done packing. He kept checking the time. It was 1:30.

Then a knock at the door spun him around. He went to the window, but there was no ledge, and the drop was too far.

The knock came again, longer and louder this time.

"Who's there?" Ben called out.

"A friend of Lisa's," responded a female voice. "Let me in."

Ben hesitated. A gunshot might be waiting for him. Like in New Orleans.

Ben waited until the girl knocked again and threw open the door. She was alone, hand raised to knock again. In one quick motion he stood, grabbed the girl by the arm, and pulled her into the room using his full strength. She went sailing onto the bed and collapsed in a tumbled heap as he slammed the door.

He was on her as she hit, groping her body for hidden weapons. Suddenly, Ben realized she was giggling.

"You're tickling me," the girl said between breaths.

"I'm sorry," he said, lamely. "I thought . . ."

The girl got up and straightened her dress.

"It's all right," the girl said. "I understand. In your business you have to be careful. My name is René. Lisa sent me."

Mention of Lisa captured Ben's attention. But he didn't understand the meaning of her references to being careful in his business. If Lisa had sent this girl, her purpose was unclear. He tried to be vague, hoping for more information.

"You never know who's on the other side of the door," he said, offhandedly.

"I know. I'll bet a lot of people try and rip you off," said René.

Still confused, Ben ad-libbed. "You've got to be careful who you trust. Do you have a message from Lisa?"

René nodded.

"She said to tell you to remember the deal you made last night, and that she'd be here to pick up the stuff herself, but she got held up. She said you can give it to me, and I'll give it to her."

"Stuff?" Ben asked.

"Cocaine, Ben. She says she paid good money for it last night, and you owe her." René's tone was indignant. "She said to remember your deal."

Ben was still confused. He could make no connection.

René frowned. "Lisa said you might try to play dumb. But she said it was hers. She said to tell you she needs it desperately, that she can't live without it. Please, Ben, don't be a prick about it."

None of this makes sense, Ben thought.

"Where is Lisa?" he asked.

René looked away. "I can't tell you. What difference does it make? It's her stuff, right? Just give it to me, and Lisa'll get it. She said she would have come herself, but she couldn't."

"When did you see her last?" he asked.

"About a half hour ago. She was fine, Ben. Really. Look, she said you don't give a shit about her. Well, I do. Just give me the stuff and let me go. Okay?"

Everything was confused here, Ben realized. He and Lisa had never talked about drugs. She knew he cared for her. The only deal they had made last night was to see each other again. Today. But René said Lisa couldn't come.

"There is no coke, René," he said and moved closer to her. "Where is Lisa?"

Rene's eyes grew wide with disbelief. Understanding followed, slowly. It made her face ugly.

"She tricked me," she gasped and tried to run.

Ben grabbed her and threw her back onto the bed.

"Where is she?" he yelled.

"Please," René begged. "I can't. They'll hurt me if I tell. Please."

Ben wanted to force the truth out of the girl, but tried to bluff, first. There had been too much violence already. He picked up the phone.

"Get me the police."

René grabbed at the phone, but Ben pushed her away.

"Wait. Please!" she said.

Ben hung up the phone. René cowered on the bed.

"Now you'd better listen to me real well," he said. "The girl we're talking about is someone I care about. Her uncle is also one of the richest men in Amsterdam, Pieter Van Dyne. There's a lot of money in it for you if you tell me where she is. If not . . ." He let the implication dangle in the air and turned the full force of his rage on her. She tried to draw further away, but he held her arm. It must have hurt.

"But," she gasped, "Van Dyne was..." and then she shut up.

"Van Dyne was what?" Ben growled at her. He increased the pressure on her arm. René winced.

"He was there. He knows!" she said.

Ben felt the blood drain from his face. Had they taken Lisa to get at him?

"Is she being held somewhere?"

René nodded agreement.

"When did they take her?"

"This morning. Around eight," answered the girl.

Too early, Ben thought. It couldn't be connected to him. His face hardened into harsh lines.

"Tell me all of it," he said and released her arm. René started to speak, rubbing at the growing bruises.

"Stangl..." she began.

Van Dyne tried to stop his hands from shaking as he sat behind his desk.

It's falling apart, he kept thinking as Rikkers told him of Ben's attempted break-in to the file room, the Adlerkinden card, and the attack. The guard had been taken to the hospital. How could this happen? First Lisa and now Ben Davidson. It's all falling apart, he thought again. The shaking in his hand increased. He hid it under the desk.

"Go to Stangl. He must be informed. He'll take care of Davidson," Van Dyne said.

"I can't," moaned Rikkers. "Look at me. I can hardly breathe." Van Dyne tried to call up some authority from his shattered nerves.

"You have no choice. If we fall, you fall."

Rikkers nodded miserably. He stood up to go.

"Where will you be if you're needed?" he asked.

Van Dyne looked at the digital clock on his desk. It was half past one.

"I'll be home. Now get going. Davidson already has an hour lead on us. Tell Stangl he was staying at the Pulitzer. He's surely relocated by now, but it's a start."

Van Dyne watched Rikkers leave. He pushed the call button on the intercom.

"Come in here," he said to Mrs. Stoelin.

Mrs. Stoelin came into the office and sat on the couch. She, too, looked worried.

"I'm sorry," she said. "He was so casual when he left, and Rikkers had said it was a mistake. I didn't think to stop him."

Van Dyne shook his head and walked over to her. She took his head in her hands as he tried to draw strength from her. He had too little left.

"It's coming apart. The whole thing—forty years," he said weakly.

"Maybe Stangl can stop it," she said to give him something. He looks so tired, she thought.

"Maybe," he said. "And maybe we'd better take a vacation. I don't want to be here if he can't. Go home and pack; we're flying out tonight. Dismiss the staff. Give them a two-week holiday."

"Will they let you go?" she asked. He saw her fear.

"If what we've been doing gets out, I'll go to prison. A prison sentence would kill me. They can't do any worse," he said. "Go home, and I'll join you in an hour."

Van Dyne sat back in his chair after she left. He had appointments to cancel and arrangements to make.

Lisa sat and waited. There was nothing else she could do. She hoped Ben would understand that she needed him.

She realized the danger she was exposing him to. He was a journalist, not a police officer. Perhaps she had made a mistake. Her reflection in the big mirror looked small and lonely. Ben will be here soon, she told herself. Again and again till she began to believe it.

Stangl listened intently to Rikkers's report. He saw no reason to worry unduly, although Davidson's possession of the Adlerkinden card confused him. Why didn't Lisa Smith know about the Adlerkinden if, as he suspected, they were part of the same attack.

"What could Davidson have wanted?" wheezed Rikkers. "There was nothing in those files but business records."

"Davidson's purpose is unclear. But, then again, so was Lisa Smith's until we looked beneath the surface," said Stangl. "Remember that they are only tools. Nothing more. And it's not the tools but the worker behind the tools that knows the final design."

"Then you think the two incidents are related?"

"Two such incidents within the same twenty-four-hour span cannot be a coincidence. I refuse to believe that. Not after forty years of security.

"It would be odd," agreed Rikkers, nursing his bruised windpipe.

"I don't know who or what connects them yet, but we will soon. My whores are on the street. They'll do their job and find the people who sent both of them to us. Tell Van Dyne to stay calm and not to panic. Where is he now?"

"Home," said Rikkers. "Can I go now? I need a doctor. That bastard almost tore my throat out." Anger blotted out the pain momentarily.

"Very soon," said Stangl, and he smiled at Rikkers. "You've done well. Don't worry. It was Van Dyne's error, not yours. He's getting very old, you know."

The implications were not lost on Rikkers. Stangl watched him sit up in his chair. Like an overeager puppy, he thought.

"He took me by surprise. Van Dyne told me to roll out the red carpet for him," said Rikkers, by way of defense.

"I understand, Herr Rikkers," said Stangl, in a soothing tone. "Go home and rest. You'll need your strength to assume new responsibilities," he paused, "should anything happen to your employer."

"Whatever you say, Herr Stangl. I'm always ready," said Rikkers.

Apparently his throat felt better, Stangl saw. "I'll call you in a few days," he said.

After Rikkers had left, Stangl called Erich in. He described Ben Davidson.

"Find him. Start at the Pulitzer. He's probably checked out by now. If you can't find him by dark, come back. I'll need you tonight."

Erich nodded and left. Stangl permitted the first bit of doubt to enter his mind.

What if Davidson and Lisa Smith are two isolated incidents? he wondered. Impossible, he answered himself. Anyway, he had done all he could. Van Dyne was obviously the weak link the enemy, whoever he was, had chosen to exploit. Well, weak links needed to be replaced, he thought. Bormann had taught him that.

Eight

Ben had just finished paying his bill when René grabbed his arm. She thrust her chin at the entrance doors.

"Those are Stangl's men," she hissed and turned her face away.

They hadn't been seen yet, and Ben reversed direction. At the rear of the lobby was the entrance to the hotel restaurant. He pushed René with his suitcase toward the door. She moved ahead obediently. He wasn't worried about her betraying him. If Stangl knew she'd disobeyed him, he'd kill her. That, and the money he had promised her, were as effective a bond as he was able to forge.

They left the hotel and walked quickly to the Westermarkt Square. He hailed a cab, which came screeching to a halt.

"Take me to the nearest sporting goods store," he told the driver.

René stayed silent through the short ride.

Inside the store, he went immediately to the arms' section. A clerk in a gray cotton jacket stood behind the counter. He had a revolver broken down on the counter and was cleaning it with gun oil. For a moment the smell took Ben back to Vietnam and his stomach dropped, a remembrance of old fears, old violence.

"I'd like to buy a shotgun," he said to the clerk.

The clerk reached into the wall case behind him and brought out a gun. He handed it to Ben.

Ben hefted the gun in his hands. Apart from its sport purposes, the shotgun was the deadliest weapon ever made for close antipersonnel work. In Vietnam, some rangers he knew had preferred it to their M-16's. Others had used them "sawed-off," in place of a .45. Yet gun stores all over the world sold them over the counter, and they could be sawed off by any amateur. No permit or license was necessary to buy one.

"I'll take this one," Ben said. He paid cash for it and bought two boxes of 12-gauge shells. The clerk brought a new gun in its box out to him, and Ben left the store after buying a box of road flares at the counter.

Ben put the package in the back seat. René looked at him quizzically, but he shook his head.

Ben made one more stop at a hardware store, and then he asked the driver for a hotel near the Red Light District.

The hotel was an old building with paint peeling off its woodwork. It was called the Hotel Treza.

The clerk barely looked at their faces, and Ben paid in advance for two nights. The carpets were stained in the hallways, and there was no elevator. The room, like the rest of the hotel, was ugly. An old spring bed with an iron grille headboard, a table, two chairs, and a bathroom with a shower that Ben had paid extra for. René dumped packages on the bed and took off her coat.

"What are you going to do?" she asked.

"It doesn't concern you, René. It's over for you," he said.

"You love her," René said matter-of-factly. "And you're going to get her out."

"I think I do," Ben said. "And yes, I'm going to get her out."

"You'll have to go against Stangl. He's not like other people. He enjoys it, the hurt and the killing," she said.

"I've known people like him, René," Ben said. "In Vietnam. They die just as easily as anybody else. The only difference is that most of them are dead already. You don't really kill them; you exterminate them."

"You are upset at having to do this," she said, perplexed.

Ben tried to put it into terms she would understand.

"I'm not going to be their victim, René. Or let Lisa be one either. People like Van Dyne and Stangl, from what you tell me about him, depend on your being too scared or too civilized to fight back. So they get away with too much because decent people let them." He looked intently at René to see if she understood. "You've let them, René. And you don't have to."

"There are Stangls everywhere. I know all about them.

Since I was ten," she said bitterly. "What choice did I ever have?"

"Bullshit," said Ben angrily. "If you don't want to control your life, that's okay. But don't fool yourself into thinking someone made you give it up. It's your choice. Do whatever the hell you want. If you like being what you are, that's fine. But if not, it's still your show, every single day."

René was silent. Ben had given his best shot. The rest was up to her. He began to unwrap the packages.

"I'm hungry," said René.

Ben wondered if he could trust her alone. He reached into his pocket and gave her some bills.

"Go get some food. And some bottles of wine or water. I saw a grocery store a few doors down," he said.

René took the bills and began to button her coat.

"Will you come back?" he asked her.

René smiled. "It's my choice. Isn't it?" As she walked out of the room, Ben smiled at her back.

He mounted a two-way clamp on the wooden table, fastened the shotgun, and sawed away at the barrels at the point they emerged over the front stock.

He was almost finished when René came back with the food. They sat on the bed and ate.

"I think Lisa is lucky to have you," she said.

"We're both lucky to have found each other," Ben answered. "We've waited a long time thinking we'd never find anyone."

René didn't quite understand, but Ben didn't try to explain. One lesson a day, he thought. I'm beginning to sound like a goddamned missionary.

"Tell me again how the house is laid out," he said.

The motorized Nikon clicked steadily as Pilsten held the button down. Since he used a 500-mm telephoto lens, the people on the street appeared through the viewing aperture to be only five feet away. He had been taking pictures all day, and the constant squinting was beginning to hurt his eyes.

Leander stood by another window scanning number 96 by telescope from the street to its rooftop. The room was greatly darkened by the cardboard Dreyer had placed over the windows. Only small holes had been cut for viewing.

A carton of food lay in one corner of the loft, the remains of sandwiches and empty coffee cups nearby. A radio-telephone, no larger than a small suitcase, lay on a table. Every few minutes, Leander glanced at it and checked his watch.

"How long overdue is Gerroff's report?" he asked Dreyer.

"Almost nine hours," said Dreyer. Leander seemed unconcerned.

"That's not all that unusual for Gerroff. He has never been very disciplined," he said.

"He's a bloody pain in the ass. If you want my opinion, he should be put down. I wouldn't tolerate it," said Dreyer angrily.

"You don't have to," said Leander mildly. "Let's give him one more hour before we call in the troops."

"Whatever you say, sir," said Dreyer stiffly.

Leander smiled inwardly. Dreyer could say "sir" nastier than most people could say "shithead."

He went back to his telescope and surveyed the brothel again. The amount of street activity by the prostitutes seemed to him to have increased as the day dragged on.

A man had just emerged from the brothel and was holding a conference with a group of prostitutes. Leander frowned. There was something about his youthful-looking face that prodded a long-buried memory. The feeling nagged at him as he watched the man.

"Have you got a shot of that man with the ascot?" he asked Pilsten.

"Several," Pilsten responded, and the whirring clicks of the camera supported his statement. Leander motioned to Dreyer.

"I want those shots transmitted as soon as possible to Central. I want an I.D. as quickly as they can."

Dreyer's reply was interrupted by the buzz of the radio-telephone. Dreyer grabbed for it and listened. He looked over to Leander.

"It's Gerroff. No problems. He's still got Davidson under surveillance," he said.

"Put him on the speaker," said Leander.

Dreyer pushed a button. A slight hiss of static filled the room.

"Report, Gerroff," ordered Leander in a crisp tone of voice. "This is Leander speaking."

"Leander?" Gerroff's voice held surprise. "What are you doing in Amsterdam?" he asked.

"Waiting for a report that's hours overdue from an agent who should damn well know better."

Gerroff's voice was a bit more subdued when he spoke again.

"It couldn't be helped, sir. The subject has had me all over the city. He's had quite a day. His name is Ben Davidson, or at least he was listed that way at the Pulitzer."

Leander interrupted. "We have verified his identity. Report on his actions." His tone was crisp.

"Yes, sir. Subject left his hotel at eight-fifteen A.M. He had no breakfast nor called room service. He proceeded on foot to a business establishment, A. Heinrich & Sons, on the Kalverstraat. Subject spent one hour looking at filing cabinet systems. Subject made no purchase.

"Subject's second stop was a business establishment selling hardware..."

Leander listened intently to Gerroff's report on Davidson's movements throughout the day: Van Dyne's Diamond Exchange, the visit by an unknown woman, the trips to the sporting goods store and again to a hardware store, and finally, to rest not five blocks from Leander's surveillance site.

"And he's been in the hotel room for the past half hour. The girl brought in some food. There's been no movement since then," Gerroff finished.

"Very well then," said Leander. "I want you to stay with Davidson. Are you up to it? You haven't had much sleep."

Leander's tone was less harsh. Given Davidson's jumping about, his failure to report was not a major incident. Yet Leander knew Gerroff too well to let it go by unnoticed.

"I'm up to it, sir. No problem," said Gerroff.

"We're close enough for a portable unit to operate. I'll send one over with Pilsten. I feel it will help with communications from you. Don't you agree?"

"Yes, sir," said Gerroff.

Leander signaled Dreyer to cut the connection.

Dreyer handed a radio unit to Pilsten who, having heard Leander's wishes, was already putting on his coat.

"Don't draw any attention," warned Dreyer as Pilsten went out the door.

"He's a good boy, Jan," said Dreyer. "More training and he'd work out fine, I think."

"Make a note of it for later on," agreed Leander absently. Elements of Gerroff's report bothered him. Davidson was close to the Red Light District now. And, Gerroff's description of Davidson's visitor matched with that of a girl who had left the brothel a few hours ago, down to her coat and kimono dress.

"Should we authorize Gerroff to pick them up?" asked Dreyer.

Leander shook his head. "The benefit isn't great enough to outweigh the risk. See what we flush—that's what we're here for. When Davidson makes a move, we'll know."

Dreyer went to take up position at the camera.

"Sure, Jan," he said, not wanting to communicate his fears. Something was wrong here. But the camera couldn't tell him what it was as he continued to expose frame after frame.

Max Pilsten made contact with Gerroff outside the Hotel Treza. A quick brush of their bodies, and the small unit changed hands. Gerroff disappeared around the corner.

Pilsten was a little afraid of Gerroff. The older man seemed so tough and sure of himself. Even to Leander, though Leander had put him into place easily enough. Pilsten smiled at the thought as he reversed direction and started back to the surveillance site.

At the rear entrance to 93, a prostitute was looking inside the van. Pilsten's first thought was to shoo her away as he approached. Almost too late he remembered Dreyer's last admonition and shut his mouth. He wasn't even sure she was a prostitute.

He took his eyes off the girl and kept walking. He hoped she hadn't noticed his attention. But the girl's voice sang out behind him.

"Hey, where you going?"

Pilsten was in a quandary. Should he stop or go? He tried to ignore her, deciding on the latter, but now she was at his side.

"Don't you want to talk to me?" she asked sweetly, and her arm went around his waist.

Pilsten stopped walking. The girl was pretty in some ways. Her wispy brown hair fell over her forehead in a nice way, and her face was pleasantly oval with wide dark eyes. The scars of childhood acne marked her cheeks, but makeup covered most of them.

"I'd like to talk, but I have to go," he said.

The girl reached over to his package and looked inside. Pilsten snatched it away.

"It's just food," he said lamely. The girl laughed.

"You protect it like gold."

"It's for my family. I've got to go," he said.

"Would you like to go somewhere with me? Only fifty guilder. I'm very nice. My name is Marte." Pilsten shook his head and removed her arm from his waist.

"Sorry, no thank you," and he left the girl standing there. A block away he looked back, and the prostitute had left. He doubled back on 93 twice, but he saw no one. He congratulated himself as he walked upstairs.

Across the street, Marte watched him enter the building. "Such a stupid young man," she thought. "Could he be the one Stangl wants?" Marte shrugged her shoulders and headed back to the brothel. She was already thinking of ways to spend the five hundred guilders Stangl had promised.

Nine

Ben walked slowly through the crowds that flowed around the Red Light District. His raincoat was buttoned up, and he had both hands in his pockets, which gave him a slightly hunched over appearance.

"I think this is enough to start over if you want to," he had said to René when he gave her the money he'd promised.

"It could have been less, you know," she told him, surprised.

"I know. Think of it as a down payment on the belief that some people are different."

When he walked to the door, she kissed him. Neither said good-bye.

Ben turned his collar up as he approached number 96. He looked up at the lighted windows in the building and wondered which one held Lisa.

René had told him what Otto had done to Lisa under Stangl's orders. White-hot anger burned through him as the images ran through his mind. He wanted to hurt them back, badly. Ben hated the violence it aroused in him, but savored it, too.

He had learned all about his capacity for violence during the war. At first he had been afraid of it, of the urge to kill. It came from an ugly place inside him, a place he had been taught to repress and deny. Later, he had come to understand it. And to control the fear that was its source.

He passed by number 96. The next building also had windows with girls in them and crowds watching. Ben felt a push from behind and whirled around, hands out of his pockets, ready. All he got was a strange look from a tourist and a hasty "Excuse me" in German.

Relax, he told himself, and breathed deeply. He felt like a coiled spring.

In the brothel next to Stangl's, he was greeted by a middle-aged woman dressed in a pale yellow, floor-length gown. Her gray hair was piled high in Grecian curls and her makeup was impeccable.

"Good evening, dear sir," said the woman in precise English. "I am Madam Langhelm. How can my house serve you this night?"

Rather than fake a calmness he didn't feel, Ben tried to let his anxiety work for him.

"Ah, I'm really not sure. Could you tell me . . . ah, explain what . . ."

The madam smiled at his nervousness, took his arm, and led him through a set of doors into a large room beyond. Someone was playing a piano; and men and women were everywhere. Pairs and groups sat on couches, hands exploring bodies. The unattached stood drinking and watching. The madam reached for his coat, but Ben backed away.

"I'd rather not, if it's all right," he said, an anxious note in his voice. The madam, understanding his tension, acquiesced.

"It's all right. Time enough later to get comfortable. May I tell you what we have to offer?"

Ben nodded enthusiastically. Encouraged, the madam began.

"We have girls from all over the world here—American, Russian, Chinese, African. They are all among the most skilled in Amsterdam. You may have anyone you choose." She gestured around the room. Ben made no response, and Madam Langhelm frowned but then brightened.

"Of course," she said, "if your taste runs to the more exotic, upstairs we have boys, girls who like pain or like to give pain, groups, and other delights. For the more discriminating, my dear."

Ben allowed a smile to cross his face. Madam Langhelm called to a buxom redhead who stood alone nearby.

"Eva. Come here, please." Eva was dressed in a lacy slip, black stockings, and heels. "This gentleman would like to go upstairs. Please escort him, and see that he finds what he wants."

"Yes, ma'am," said Eva sweetly and slid her arm into Ben's. He glanced questioningly at Madam Langhelm and reached into his pocket. She stopped him.

"That's very thoughtful, my dear. But Eva will take care of all that. Have a nice time."

Eva led Ben out of the room to a staircase just beyond. She kept up a stream of questions and a steady effort to grope at his body. Ben pushed her away.

"Don't you like me?" Eva pouted.

"You're very nice, but please don't touch me." Eva continued to pout, so Ben added, "Yet."

"What's on the top floor?" he asked.

"Those are the whipping rooms," Eva said. "Is that where you'd like to go?"

"Yes."

"That'll cost a lot. Would you like another girl, too? I have a friend who likes..."

"Don't worry. I'll pay. And you're fine. All I want is privacy."

They came to the top floor and walked along a hallway. At its end was a closed door with a small bulb glowing over it.

"What is that?" Ben asked, pointing.

"It leads to the roof. But come inside here." Eva smiled seductively. She opened a door and gestured for Ben to follow.

Inside, the equipment appeared to have been imported from a medieval torture chamber. Racks and chains and ropes filled the room. Mirrors lined one wall completely, and even a throne had been furnished for the "master."

"It pleases you?" she asked.

Ben nodded. "It's just what I want."

191

Suddenly, Eva was in his arms. Her mouth sought his, and her hands caressed his body. She took Ben by surprise. He pushed her away, but she was insistent. Finally, he had to grab her shoulders and push her across the room.

"Tell me what you want, Master," crooned Eva.

Ben pointed to a rack set into one wall.

"I'm going to tie you up," he said. Eva smiled, reached behind her, and her slip fell to the floor. Clad only in stockings and heels, her breasts heaving, she backed against the wall.

Ben fastened her wrists and ankles to the rack. Then he took a towel off the washstand and ripped it into strips. A look of concern passed over Eva's face, but she let it pass, beginning a steady sexual chant.

"What are those for, my sweet? Don't you want to fuck me? I'm so hot. Feel me. Feel me all over. I want to..."

Whatever else she was about to say was cut off as Ben stuffed a strip of towel into her mouth. She was afraid and started to struggle.

"Now listen to me, Eva. Calm down. I'm not going to hurt you. I'm not even going to touch you. I'm going to be leaving now." Ben reached into his pocket and took out some money. "Here's two hundred guilder for you. All I ask is that you don't kick up too much of a fuss for about ten minutes. Will this buy me ten minutes? I promise you'll never see me again. Understand? I'm not going to hurt you. Okay?"

Unable to speak, Eva nodded.

Ben put the money inside her shoe. It wouldn't be seen by whoever came to untie her. The gesture calmed her more effectively than his words. Ben touched her on the cheek and left.

He walked quickly to the door that led to the roof. The wood securing the lock was old and rotten, and almost came apart in his hands. He was out on the roof a moment later.

Ben moved to the low wall at the front edge of the roof to get his bearings. Facing the street, number 96 was to his right. He moved silently among the ventilator shafts and low outcroppings on the rooftop. The tar paper made only a soft compressing noise as his feet trod over it. The night was again his friend, black and all-concealing. Like strange jungle foliage, the ventilator turrets turned smoothly in the light wind.

Ben reached the edge. The roof of number 96 lay only three feet away. René's information was accurate. He could only hope that the roof of number 96 would bear his weight. There was no way to check and no way to turn back.

Ben stood to his full height and put one foot on the edge of the roof. He prepared to jump, arms swinging to add momentum to his leap. Suddenly, the darkness vanished, and he was bathed in white moonlight. He dropped to the roof, his hand reaching out for support that wasn't there. His feet slid out over empty space. Desperately, he clung to the rooftop, his fingers grabbing at the soft tar paper. Then it began to tear. He tried to get his trapped arm out from under him. His breathing was short, coming in pained gasps as he swung further out over the edge of the roof. The noise of the tearing increased.

"There he is, sir," said Pilsten excitedly. "On the edge of the roof. I knew I saw someone. God! It looks like he's falling." He adjusted the focus of the camera to get more clarity through the night scope.

Leander stood poised over the telescope. "I've got him. Can you get an I.D.? Peter, take the scope and see what you can make out."

Dreyer bent over the camera as Pilsten moved aside. He studied the scene closely.

"It's him. Davidson. And I don't think he can stop his slide. What the hell is he up to? Where's Gerroff?" He stepped to the radiophone, while Pilsten resumed his watch at the camera.

"In the street," said Leander. "Tell him where Davidson is, but tell him not to move. I think we're witnessing a rescue attempt. If we are, it answers a lot of questions about his activities today."

Dreyer spoke to Gerroff and relayed Leander's instructions.

"And raises just as many," said Dreyer. He hung up the phone.

"I don't think he's going to make it," said Pilsten.

Ben knew he had only a few seconds more. Each rip of the paper loosened his precarious perch by an inch or so. He needed his other hand free. The heavy tar paper ripped again.

He had only once chance. Throwing all his weight through his hips and shoulders, he swung his legs in a scissors motion. It put him on his back, his hands still digging into the paper. He searched frantically with his other hand seeking anything that could hold him. His arms, stretched over his head backward, had begun to cramp. His face grimaced in pain, and his hands grew numb. Another rip.

Finally, stretched almost to breaking, he felt a pipe protruding from the roof. He grabbed for it, again scissoring his legs for a boost upward. The paper started to rip in a long, even tear. With a last desperate kick, he managed to grasp the pipe just as the paper ripped clear of the roof. The pipe held. He swung back, facing down, taking the strain in his wrist.

With sweat pouring from his face, Ben dragged himself back onto the roof. He lay white-faced and panting, while blood flowed back into his starved extremities.

When he could stand up again, he looked at the distance between roofs. He could wait no longer. He put his foot as close to the edge as possible, and in one burst of energy, leaped into the night air.

Ben took the fall on the other side, rolling. He was up and on his feet in a matter of seconds. As silently as a jungle cat, he moved over the roof till he found a doorway.

He knew where he was in relation to Lisa. René had mapped it out clearly.

Behind the door was a short flight of stairs and then another door opening onto the corridor where Lisa was being held.

Before opening the final door, he unbuttoned his raincoat. The sawed-off shotgun hung at his side, suspended from a leather thong around his neck.

Ben draped the coat over his shoulders. He held the gun securely in his right hand, concealed by the raincoat. The inner door was unlocked. "A good omen," he told himself. Ben took a deep breath and pushed the door open.

In a glance he took in the empty corridor and Otto, standing guard. He had to move fast. Otto was forty feet away. He looked even bigger than René had described.

"Hi, Otto," Ben called brightly when the big man turned

at the noise of his entrance. Ben walked toward him, his left hand out and waving freely. Thirty feet.

"Stangl told me you were on duty. Thought I'd come up and say hi, old buddy. Don't you remember me?"

Smile and wave, twenty feet.

Otto looked confused. "Who are you?"

Fifteen feet.

The confusion on Otto's face vanished abruptly. Ben was only ten feet away when Otto reached behind him. His hand emerged with a knife, and he went into a crouch. Otto started for him.

Ben brought the shotgun out from his coat.

"Stop dead," he hissed.

Otto's glance flicked to the gun and then back to Ben's face. An ugly grin spread over his features. He didn't stop. The knife swayed from side to side in his hand, hypnotic in its movement.

The blast from the shotgun caught him square in the chest. It hurled him backward down the corridor, blood spurting behind him as the force of the shell ripped out his insides and tattooed the far wall.

Ben kicked open the door to Lisa's room. She was standing, fully dressed, by the bed. Tears of relief fell from her eyes. He wanted to embrace her, but there was no time.

"Otto's dead. Let's get out of here!"

Lisa was ready. In a moment she was behind him in the corridor.

Ben led Lisa toward the roof exit. When they were almost there, the door to Stangl's office opened, and an armed man emerged. Ben noticed a scar on his cheek. The shotgun exploded again. The man ducked back, and Ben couldn't be sure if he'd hit him. He broke open the gun and reloaded. Smoke hung in the corridor obscuring his vision.

Ben took out the road flares he had purchased earlier. In a few seconds the corridor was filled with thick smoke and hissing flames. The carpet caught fire immediately. Ben grabbed Lisa, and they ran toward the staircase. Passing the office, even in the smoke, was too great a risk.

At the top of the staircase he ignited two more flares and threw them down. More smoke billowed upward.

The fire upstairs had begun to spread, and the brothel became a madhouse. Half-naked people ran down the stairs.

Ben and Lisa raced down to the parlor. The front door was only a room away.

From behind, Ben heard a shout from the stairway. "That's them. Stop those two!"

Ben turned, saw a man raise a gun, and fired at the same moment. The man's face disintegrated, and his body fell over the railing.

"Get out. Now!" he yelled to Lisa.

She ran in front of him. A shot passed by Ben's head, and he turned and fired the other barrel, blindly. He could see nothing amidst the smoke. He ran.

At the front entrance, Lisa was struggling to get past the panicked crowd. Ben cleared a path, powerfully heaving people aside. The clean night air cleared the smell of smoke and gunpowder from his nostrils. They were out.

Fire sirens were screaming in the distance, and a crowd had gathered. The upper stories had flames shooting from the windows when Ben looked up. He motioned Lisa to a walk, hiding the shotgun again under his coat.

The crowd was transfixed by the fire. Ben strolled over to the canal. With one hand, he released the gun from the thong and let it drop into the water. The remaining flares and shells followed.

Lisa turned to go, but Ben stopped her.

"Why aren't we going?" she asked. "What if we're seen?"

"I need to know that everyone got out. It may seem crazy," Ben said to her, "but I need to know how many people I just killed. Can you understand? We're going to have to live with this," he gestured at the fire.

"Was anyone hurt?" Ben called to an ash-smeared fireman.

"Only two bodies recovered. Everybody else seems to have made it out."

Ben nodded. Two bodies. The innocents had been spared.

Ben steered Lisa away from the scene. He felt tired and weak from the past hour. Lisa was still trembling. People flooded past them, attracted by the fire. The smell of burnt wood and ash filled the air. Ben closed his eyes for a moment.

When he opened them, he looked into the face of the man he had tried to shoot by the office. The scar was unmistakable. So was the gun in his hand. Ben sagged with despair. His mind refused to function.

"If you do anything at all, I will shoot her. You've caused

great problems. People are very unhappy." The man motioned for Ben and Lisa to walk ahead.

"What do you want?" Ben asked. Lisa was shaking harder now, and her eyes looked dull. He berated himself angrily. "If I hadn't stopped, we'd be free." The gunman walked silently behind them.

Another man was approaching them, weaving back and forth across the street. Drunk, Ben thought, as they got closer.

Only five feet away, the drunk swerved directly into their path. He seemed to trip over a cobblestone and went crashing into the gunman who, caught unaware, went down in a heap. Ben grabbed Lisa's arm.

"Run," he yelled, and they took off, their feet beating a staccato rhythm against the cobblestones. Lisa fell, but Ben dragged her to her feet. Her breathing came in gasps. She couldn't take much more of this, he thought.

Suddenly, a shot rang out. Almost simultaneously, another shot exploded. Then silence. Ben risked a glance over his shoulder. The street was empty. Quickly he helped Lisa around the corner.

Shadows were everywhere, each one a source of menace. The crowds were thin here on the periphery of the district. Lisa collapsed against the wall of a building.

"We've got to get off the streets. C'mon, Lisa. My hotel is only a few blocks further. Can you make it? Please, Lisa, try. We've got to get off the streets."

Sweat beaded Lisa's forehead. Her eyes were clear and determined as she threw her arms around Ben.

"We'll make it, I promise. I can make it with your help," she said. Together they hurried back to the hotel.

"We've blown cover, you know," Dreyer said to Leander. He was staring at the body of the scarfaced man, which lay in the street across the canal.

"I know," Leander sighed. "But we had to keep Lisa free and clear. This operation is over. The fire saw to that. But they'll come at the girl again. And Davidson, too. Your drunk act was splendid, Peter. Hit him like a rugby forward. Is Gerroff on them?"

"He picked them up after I hit scarface." Dreyer estimated

the distance across the canal. "Almost thirty yards, I'd guess. Your shooting hasn't lost much."

"Pure luck" said Leander. "I knew Gerroff was covering. We'd better clear out of the loft. We'll go mobile till Gerroff gives us a location."

"Right. I'll call in support from the embassy staff. We all need sleep. Especially Gerroff."

"Do that," replied Leander. "I want to be moving in fifteen minutes. We've worn out our welcome in this area. Pilsten can take me to the airport. You're in charge, Peter. Keep me posted every twelve hours."

Dreyer nodded and walked away. No good-byes. Leander knew Dreyer had left much unspoken. It could not be helped.

Leander moved back into the shadows. They had been lucky, he knew, to have spotted Davidson on the roof, and luckier still to intercept him in the street.

It was clear that Lisa had picked up an ally. But what other purpose might he have?

Speculation was pointless. Bormann would assess the impact of today's attack and, hopefully, make some countermove.

"Then I'll be there," he said softly, as he recalled old hatreds and fears. A street in Berlin. The smell of bread.

Ten

Stangl stood in the deserted loft across the street from his brothel and watched it burn. He kicked at a carton of rubbish on the floor and a half-eaten sandwich rolled out. He picked it up and fingered the bread.

"It's still fresh," he said to the two men in the room. "They were here. See that Marte gets her money."

Neither of the two men responded. Stangl had his gun drawn. His mood was vicious and his behavior unpredictable.

"They were here!" Stangl said again. He turned on his men, enraged. "One man!" he yelled. "One single man, and Otto and Erich are dead, and the rest of you are too stupid and incompetent to catch him and the girl. How is it possible?" he demanded. "How?"

The men shuffled uncomfortably. Stangl pointed to the smaller of the two.

"You, Rios, will stay and close the house down. Pay off the girls, and tell the rest of the men they are discharged. Tell them I'll contact them if and when I need them. You got the bodies away before the police saw the gunshot wounds?"

Rios nodded. He was pleased to have something positive to report.

"I spread some money around."

"At least that was done right. Take care of the rest. I'll call you when I get back."

"You're leaving the city?" asked Rios.

"Since when are questions part of our business?" asked Stangl harshly. "Do as you're told."

Rios felt his cheeks flush hotly, but he made no response. Instead, he left the room to carry out Stangl's orders.

"Get out to the airport and charter a jet," Stangl said to the man who was left. "I want to leave as soon as possible." He looked at his watch. "Say, two or three hours. Use the name Rhinehart. Then do the same as Rios. Can you handle that, Garver?"

"I can handle it," Garver said. "Are you sure you don't want me to come with you?"

"I'm sure. Just take care of what I told you."

Garver nodded, and Stangl strode out of the room. He hailed a cab outside.

Stangl gave the driver Van Dyne's address and then lapsed into silence. He would have to face Bormann soon, and the thought made him nervous. One minute he was getting a location from Marte and organizing his strike on the "fishermen." The next minute shotguns were exploding in the corridor. Not a good score to tell Bormann: Lisa Smith free, Davidson free, and no one to put the blame on. Except, and the logic of it made him feel better, Van Dyne.

Stangl was not surprised to see Mrs. Stoelin open the door to Van Dyne's house, but she was surprised to see him.

"Where's Van Dyne?" demanded Stangl.

"Pieter is upstairs," she said, defiance in her voice.

"Then get him. We have to talk," and he walked inside.

Stangl noticed the packed suitcases when he entered the living room.

"What do you want, Stangl?" said Van Dyne's voice behind him.

"We have some problems, Herr Van Dyne," Stangl said. Mrs. Stoelin stood beside Van Dyne, lips compressed and silent.

"Then take care of them. That is your job. Why come to me?" Van Dyne said arrogantly.

"To wish you well on your trip. Where are you going?" Stangl's tone was sweet.

"None of your affair. A business trip. Now get out, and let us finish our arrangements."

Mrs. Stoelin and Van Dyne stood together like saplings braced against a strong wind. Stangl knew they were afraid. He enjoyed the moment and wanted to savor it. But he had things to do.

"Well?" demanded Van Dyne.

"Allow me just to say that I have never cared for your attitude," Stangl said.

With a sigh of pleasure, he brought up his silenced automatic and shot Van Dyne through the head.

Mrs. Stoelin's eyes went wide with shock. Her hands clutched at her chest, fluttering like a frightened bird. Stangl hesitated. Maybe he had enough time to . . .

But Mrs. Stoelin seemed to recover. A look of resignation crossed her face and mingled with a touch of her old dignity.

"Allow me to say," she stated coldly, "that I have never cared for anything about you."

Stangl shot her, enraged. She had spoiled the whole moment. He watched her fall across Van Dyne's body. But his pleasure was gone.

Stangl buttoned up his coat and left the house. A few blocks away he caught a taxi to the airport.

Ben locked the hotel room door as Lisa fell wearily onto the bed. He felt tired in every part of his body.

"You came for me," Lisa said, simply.

Ben sat on the edge of the bed and let his fingers trace the curve of her face. He parted the hairs that clung to her damp forehead and pushed them aside.

"I'll always come for you," he said, and knew it was true.

Then Lisa's arms were around him. After a while, she reached up to brush a piece of soot from Ben's face.

"We're both a mess," she said. "Is there a shower here?"

Ben pointed to the bathroom. "Inside. Do you want to use it?" he asked.

"You first."

"We have a lot to talk about," Ben said. He reached out to touch her again.

"We have time, Ben," Lisa said. "I think we're going to have time."

Ben still had on his raincoat. He stood up and peeled it off. His shirt was sopping wet, and he pulled it off as well. He was acutely aware of Lisa's presence.

He walked into the bathroom and got into the shower. The heat relaxed him, and some of the tension flowed away. He was happy, he realized, shutting his eyes and letting the water soothe him.

Suddenly, there were hands on his chest. Lisa stood before him. The water ran down her face in tiny streams. She looked small and fragile.

The water flowed over their bodies, making small, warm pools where they touched. His lips found hers, and her breasts pressed against him. Excitement spread to his groin, and he began to harden. Lisa felt it and pressed against him more tightly.

She reached for the soap, and he released her. She lathered his hair and neck and then his shoulders and chest. She stroked and caressed him. Ben's knees weakened, and he braced himself against the shower walls.

"Now me," she said.

Ben gathered her hair in his hands to wash it. He studied her, wanting to know every part, wanting to understand every crease and fold. He slid his hands over her shoulders in long, slow strokes. Lisa's eyes never left his.

Ben ran his hands over her breasts, and her nipples stiffened. He smiled. Lisa made a sound that began as words and became a moan of pleasure. Ben soaped her hips. They were strong and firm. Between her thighs, he felt her lips open, as Lisa moaned again.

In bed, Ben felt as if Lisa's touch found nerve endings he hadn't known existed. Each moment seemed to contain a thousand sensations, a thousand emotions. And in turn he tried to tell her, with his fingers and hands and lips and tongue, what he was feeling.

For Lisa, all of the men before Ben were forgotten. Every time she looked at him or felt his fingers gently, tenderly probing her, she marveled at the stirrings of love. She felt him swell within her. She locked her legs around him and rode him harder as orgasm approached. She felt Ben stiffen as his first spasm wracked through his body. She cried out in pleasure as she climaxed, and her cries joined his. Again and again she cried out, and each time Ben held her more fiercely to him.

Afterward, there was only their breathing in peaceful cadence.

"That was wonderful," Ben said when he could speak again.

"For me, too," said Lisa, softly.

He ran a hand over her taut stomach.

"I used to feel sad afterward," he said, "like I needed to get up and leave."

Lisa moved away and propped her head up on one hand.

"I've known a lot of men in the past couple of years. Does that bother you?" she asked hesitantly.

Ben shook his head. "No. I never thought sex was wrong, only that I seemed to be wrong for it. It became easier, less painful, to avoid it."

"I went the opposite route. Same problem, though. I just kept trying, hoping it would mean something, but it never did. So much has happened to me these past couple of days, Ben. I feel like I'm going to be all right."

He reached for her again and she came willingly into his arms. This time it was longer and gentler, a melding of spirit as well as flesh. No ceremony ever performed nor any ritual ever devised could have solidified their union more completely than this act of loving. With long, slow caresses that grew into sharper, unrestrained passion they dissolved the boundaries that had separated them from themselves.

"I think I love you, Lisa," Ben said, absorbed in his newfound happiness. He propped himself up so that he could look at her. She made no move to cover herself. Rather, she stretched with almost feline grace and brushed her hand against his chest.

"You don't have to, you know," she said slowly. "I'd accept whatever you were willing to give. I'm not worried about words or promises, Ben. What I feel, well, it's enough for me."

"That's why I can say it so easily. Because it changes nothing between us. All I want is for you to know how I feel about you."

"Thank you, Ben." There were tears in her eyes. She nestled closer to him, savoring the happiness she felt.

"Is it unromantic to suggest food at a time like this?" Ben asked, grinning.

Lisa laughed. "Thank God for an honest man. I'm famished."

Ben dressed quickly and left the hotel. Finding an open store only a block away, he returned barely ten minutes later with a bottle of wine, cold meats, cheese and bars of rich, Dutch chocolate for dessert.

Lisa had donned one of his shirts, big enough on her to be a robe. She hugged him as he entered the room, and arranged the food on the table.

"Very domestic," Ben noted.

"I wouldn't get your hopes up too high on that score," Lisa said dryly, pouring the wine, "Household chores have never been my strongest suit."

"And here I thought that all girl children were born with instinctive knowledge," Ben joked. "Who's going to build the fire and cook the meat when I return home from a long day's hunt?"

"The servants?"

"Not on my income." He smiled. "Didn't you ever have to take care of your brothers and sisters?"

A shadow crossed her face.

"I have no brothers or sisters, Ben. My parents committed suicide when I was only a few months old. At least that's what I was told by my Uncle Johann. He adopted me right afterward. I've had a lot of emotional problems because of their deaths. Somehow I blamed myself for their abandonment. Fear of rejection was the term the shrinks used. I leave before anyone can leave me."

"So nothing lasted very long," Ben said. "I think I understand."

"I need you to, Ben. Depending on you today was the first time I depended on anyone in years. That's why it mattered so much."

"But I thought Van Dyne referred to your father and said he was in government service."

"He meant Johann," Lisa explained. She realized that Ben would have to be told about him sooner or later. She hoped it would not change his feelings about her. "Government service is true up to a point, Ben. My adoptive father is the Prime Minister of the Republic of South Africa."

"Jesus!"

Lisa nodded. "He was elected eight years ago and is the only blood relation I have. He gave me a life filled with privilege: virtually unlimited funds, servants... It doesn't change anything between us, does it?"

"Of course not," he answered. "Just as it wouldn't matter if you were poor and the daughter of a fisherman. I suppose if I had to choose between rich and poor," he winked at her, "rich is nicer."

"That's what I wanted to hear. So many people I've known were intimidated by it."

"We are what we are, Lisa. We fell in love before we knew anything about each other. I trust that."

"Me too, Ben. Now tell me about your family."

"Both my parents are dead. My father a few years ago and my mother just recently. He was a doctor, a good man all around. My mother and I never got along very well..."

He told her about his childhood; his mother's rage and bigotry, her blaming Ben for his father's refusal to leave his practice, the lonely nights and the hate-filled days. It felt good to let go. As he spoke, Lisa's eyes brimmed with tears of sympathy.

"I wanted to be just like my father. I was determined to go to medical school. I even attended one for two years."

"What made you stop if you wanted it that badly?"

"My father died while I was in my second year. My mother moved away and cut off my tuition. Med school cost almost ten thousand dollars a year, and I was broke. By the time I could arrange loans, I was drafted. With my father dead the whole thing just seemed pointless. Nothing seemed to matter, so I didn't really fight it. Three months later I was in Vietnam with the Special Forces."

"That's where you learned to fight," she said, understanding what she had seen in the brothel.

Ben nodded. "I think it was some kind of strange death

wish that caused me to volunteer for Special Forces' training. I didn't care much about myself in those days. So once I was in, I went all the way. The disillusionment came later. That's when I started writing."

"Maybe you should go back to school."

"I was thinking about that when the assignment came up that brought me to Amsterdam."

"The diamond article?" asked Lisa.

Ben wasn't sure how to begin. Lisa noticed his discomfort.

"Is something wrong, Ben?"

"The diamond article is a lie, Lisa. I ran into something in Mississippi, in the southern part of the United States, that brought me here. I think your uncle, Van Dyne, is part of it. I have some things to tell you that you may not want to hear."

"Don't be afraid. Whatever it is, don't lie to me, Ben. I couldn't live with that."

"I'm afraid of anything coming between us. I'm afraid of losing you, Lisa."

Lisa took his face in both her hands and kissed him hard.

"When I was trapped today and needed someone, needed someone desperately to get me out, I called you. Not Van Dyne or Johann or a hundred others, but you. And you came. What could you say that could lose my trust—or my love? Nothing, Ben. I'm playing for keeps, too. Maybe for the first time in my life. I don't think the truth will ever hurt us."

Ben told her everything he knew. " . . . So I was leaving when René found me at the hotel. Another few minutes and I would have been gone. I wasn't even sure that you weren't setting a trap for me. But I took a chance you were for real. I'm taking another chance now, Lisa. You've got to believe me. There is a conspiracy. At least part of the funding comes through Van Dyne's. I can't even begin to figure out all of its implications, but it's for real. After my fiasco today, I'm out of leads. I don't know where to look for Croft next. But I'll find him. As much as I'd like to sometimes, I won't put it down. The only thing I'm sorry about is involving you in it," Ben hesitated, "unless you're already involved. Lisa, what was today all about? Why were you being held there? Two men are dead, and I killed them. Why?"

Lisa seemed to be mentally computing some total of her own.

"A week ago, a man named Leander came to see me," she

said, "in Johannesburg. He is the Director of External Operations, like your CIA. Leander showed me a document that detailed an agreement in 1936 between my father, Uncle Johann, Van Dyne, two others named Hauptman and Voorstein, and two members of the Nazi party, Martin Bormann and Dr. Ludwig Stumpfegger. Leander said that the conspiracy was still going on. He mentioned the word Adler. I thought it was a man's name. I think he did, too."

"Adlerkinden," Ben said. "The Eagle's Children!" He listened intently to the rest of her story: the possibility that her parents' suicides had been murder, Leander's warning to her, and her trip to Amsterdam to confront Van Dyne.

"What are they up to, Ben?" she asked finally, frustration showing.

Ben looked uncertain. "I don't know yet. Nothing we know adds up to much. It's all bits and pieces. What's almost as incredible is you and I connecting. Each of us found a piece of this madness on two different continents, and we meet on a third. I wouldn't want to calculate the odds on that," he said.

"Everything's against the odds until it happens," Lisa answered. "We were lucky, that's all."

"We'd better go over it all again later," Ben told her. "Now we have to get some sleep."

He rubbed tired eyes. Dawn was beginning to break outside the window. He pulled Lisa closer to him and put his arms around her. She offered no protest as he turned off the lights. For a little while, anyway, they would have peace.

Eleven

Leander picked up another photograph from the dozens that lay on the table in his office. It was a full face view of the man with the ascot. He put the picture next to those of Ben Davidson and Lisa Smith.

The pictures had arrived in Pretoria before he had, and the computer experts in the Identification Section were already assembling dossiers. Interagency requests, in the form of electronic impulses from computer to computer, flew around the world to countries with which the RSA shared information. Leander was satisfied that if data existed, his people would locate it somehow.

Leander's appointment to the director's position had been something of a fluke, based on a series of unexpected events. The former director, who had almost created the agency fifty years prior, was the grim, steel-spectacled General Van Belghurn. Staunchly Afrikaner, he was an avid supporter of apartheid and an advocate of the "mailed fist" approach to terrorism and civil disobedience.

Leander was a section chief when the scandal broke that forced Van Belghurn to resign. For years, it seemed a number of supposedly free newspapers were, in reality, owned and operated by agents of Van Belghurn's. It was enough to break his power, and the then Prime Minister had forced him out of the agency he had built.

Others, along with the director, were fired or asked quietly to resign. Vacant positions occurred, and in the shuffle to replace the top leadership, Leander found himself promoted to an assistant directorship. The Prime Minister put the Senior Assistant Director, John Byrd, in charge, and set out to find a new director.

The search took almost a year. The Prime Minister finally announced his appointment of a university professor named Bernell, an outsider untainted by the scandal, to head Ex Op. Byrd, almost seventy-five, retired. Leander moved up to senior assistant director. It seemed as far as he would go.

One month later, Bernell died of a heart attack. Faced with another year or longer in search of a director, the Prime Minister asked Leander to fill the chair, now thrice vacant, when Byrd announced he was too ill to return to service. That had been almost a year ago. Since that time, a number of successes had brought Leander accolades and the support of many diverse factions. He was seen as a strong, moderate, but effective director with a growing reputation for direct positive action.

But Leander was well aware that his days as director were numbered. The realities of political life were clear to him. He had survived this long only because Smith had not found anyone he preferred to Leander. This was only a temporary situation, at best, for those who stood against apartheid seldom lasted long.

"Are those reports ready yet?" he called to his secretary over the intercom. A delay meant time lost. And he didn't know how much time he had. A new director meant he would again be accountable; and to a man whose allegiance would be to the Prime Minister, Johann Smith.

His secretary, Lana Hunzen, brought in two folders and put them on the table.

In her early sixties, Lana Hunzen had survived longer than the directors she had served. A permanent fixture at Ex Op since its inception, Leander often thought she was capable of running the agency single-handedly. In fact, during times of crises she sometimes functioned with all the authority of the director's office.

"There are some matters that need your attention, Jan. Counter Terrorism is screaming for the source of funding of that left-wing group, and somebody's trying to blackmail Steinhoff again. His deputy chief called this morning."

Leander grimaced. Steinhoff, the RSA's Consul General in Brazil, had a tendency to spend more time in the casinos than in the consulate. The degree of the blackmail demands were usually commensurate with the degree of his losses.

"Send a memo to Diplomatic requesting Steinhoff's recall. Include the file. Send anything at all to Counter Terrorism to get them off my back. Tell them we're close. It should be only a few days till it breaks."

"Right, Jan. Anything else?" Lana asked.

"Call the Prime Minister and set up an appointment as soon as possible. Tell him it's urgent and personal."

Lana's eyebrows raised, but she said nothing.

"I'd like to see him within the hour. Have my car and driver ready," Leander added as she left.

The intercom buzzed ten minutes later.

"Half an hour. In his office. Okay?"

"Perfect," replied Leander.

The Union Buildings were only minutes away. He read through the file on Ben Davidson.

The file was short. He had no criminal record. Both parents dead, mother most recent; father a physician. Military service during Vietnam: rank First Lieutenant, Special Forces; honorable discharge; numerous citations for bravery.

Career, journalist; agent, Bill Gottbaum, New York City. Income, moderate. No other dependents. Full physical description, no distinguishing scars. Age 33. Basis of data— Social Security Administration, Selective Service Bureau, Internal Revenue Service.

Leander frowned. There was nothing at all out of the ordinary here. He opened the file on the man with the ascot. The index noted that the information had been found in the old Military Intelligence files.

Leander's pulse quickened. M.I. was his old outfit. The hunch that he had seen the face before strengthened and then solidified when Leander removed the first photo from the dossier.

It showed a young man dressed in the uniform of the S.S. standing in the streets of Warsaw. The caption underneath the photo read, Heinz Stangl, Captain, Sturmabteilung, S.S., Warsaw Group, 1939.

The dossier listed Stangl's approximate birthdate as 1920. He had been young, only 20 or so, for his rank. It meant that he had been very good at what the S.S. did best—killing and torture.

There were no further entries for Stangl past 1939. Normally, any information, even rumor, that came in would have been routinely added to the files. But it was a blank after '39.

Stangl could have gone on, as inconspicuous as a ghost, had he not been spotted in Amsterdam. Leander put down the file. It was time to go.

The ride to Smith's office took only a few minutes. Leander sat in the back seat preparing for the meeting. In the game of human chess that he was playing, Smith was a vital piece. The delicate aspect was that Smith was not a piece that he could move directly. He had to be manipulated. But unlike his daughter, Smith was dangerous—past master at the same game.

Even Dreyer didn't realize that Leander was using Lisa not only to uncover the conspiracy, but also to create a schism in a group that had functioned undetected since before the Second World War. Lisa was not only a "crystal." She was a wedge. The question was, would Smith protect Lisa or sacrifice her to the group's interest? Everything depended on which Smith would choose.

The Prime Minister sat behind his desk but stood when

Leander entered his office. Smith was still aristocratic-looking at sixty-five. His aquiline features and piercing blue eyes were a politician's dream; his business suit, as always, impeccable.

"It's good to see you, Jan," Smith said. "How are you feeling?"

"Couldn't be better, sir. I trust you're well?"

"Sometimes I feel like a man of twenty. Other times I feel like a hundred. It's the job, I suppose," Smith said tiredly.

"Have you considered a vacation, sir? A bit of hunting, perhaps?" Leander asked.

"God, but I wish I could," sighed Smith. He smoothed down a stray white hair with a manicured hand.

"But tell me," Smith continued evenly, "what is this urgent business that you need to see me about? Sit down, Jan."

Leander leaned forward in his chair.

"With all due respect, Mr. Prime Minister. This conversation concerns your daughter, Lisa. If we're on tape, you might wish to . . ."

The implication was clear enough. Smith was silent for a second, then reached under his desk and flicked a switch. He nodded at Leander.

"Speak freely, Mr. Director."

The switch to formalities was not lost on Leander, who looked directly into Smith's gaze.

"Your daughter was almost killed last night in some kind of riot at a brothel in Amsterdam, sir."

Smith's face underwent a shocking change. The healthy tan turned to white as the blood drained from his face.

"Was she hurt? Is she all right?"

"She's fine, sir. And somewhere in Amsterdam."

"God damn it to hell!" Smith banged his fist onto his desk. "I spoke to the family she was staying with just forty-eight hours ago. How could this have happened?" he demanded. "Where were your people?"

Leander spoke evenly. "Mr. Prime Minister, we weren't even notified she would be out of the country. We came by this information only by chance. One of our embassy people happened to be a . . . a guest at the establishment that night and saw your daughter leaving. He reported it to the security chief, who called it in to me personally. It appears on no official report. I thought you'd prefer to hear it from me this way. I'm sorry if I made a mistake in judgment." Leander started to rise. Smith waved him back into the chair.

"No . . . no. I'm sorry I blew up at you, Jan. You did the correct thing. I'm grateful, in fact. Do you have any other details?"

Leander shook his head. "As we had no one on the scene, and the staff member was obviously pressed by the need to leave the establishment as quickly as possible, we have no current location for your daughter. However . . ."

Leander let his voice trail off as if he thought better of speaking. Smith jumped on it.

"What were you going to say?" he demanded.

Leander continued in an uncertain tone.

"The man on the scene was understandably upset and concerned about his career. He reported some things that seem improbable. Perhaps it might be better to ignore them."

"Tell me," said the Prime Minister, and his tone broached no argument. Leander tried to appear reticent.

"The man reported that he thought shots were fired at your daughter. Please remember, sir, there was a great deal of smoke and fire as the place was burning. It could have been anything exploding."

Leander's explanation seemed to calm Smith somewhat.

"Do you have an address for this brothel?" he asked.

Leander brought his eyes back to Smith's face.

"Number ninety-six Terenstraat. In the Red Light District, sir," he said evenly.

A muscle jumped in Smith's jaw, and his eyes widened. Not much, but enough, thought Leander.

Smith said nothing for a few moments. When he spoke again, there was ice in his tone.

"Do you have anything else to report?"

"No, sir. Other than we are looking right now for your daughter. Coverage will be established when we find her. If she calls you, please tell my office. If you'd prefer, in the future we'll cover Lisa covertly if you authorize it within the RSA borders."

Smith stood up. The meeting was over.

"I don't think that will be necessary just yet, Jan. But find her in Amsterdam as quickly as you can. If anything happens to her . . ."

Leander nodded. "I understand, sir. I hope to see you

again under more pleasant circumstances." Leander turned to leave.

"Jan?" called Smith after him. "I want you to know I appreciate your discretion. I won't forget it."

"Thank you, sir," said Leander, humbly, and he closed the office door behind him.

Twelve

Martin Bormann stood by the window, arms folded over his chest, watching the waves of the Indian Ocean pound against the rocky South African coast below. Mist hung over the rocks, making them glisten like moist, sharp teeth.

"Tell me again what happened, Heinz," he said. He searched for internal calmness and found it. He was too old to become excited, he reminded himself again. And the others would be here soon.

"I've explained it twice already, Martin. And three times yesterday," balked Stangl. Bormann's calm frightened him only slightly less than his previous rages. "It was all Van Dyne's doing. He sent the girl to me. And the man, Davidson, must have come through him, somehow. It can be explained no other way. When I found him, he was preparing to run—to betray us. I did only what I had to do. What you would have done."

Bormann turned back to Stangl. His arms remained folded on his chest, but his features were set harder now.

"How do you know that, Heinz? Do you read minds now as well as make unauthorized decisions?"

"I assumed—" protested Stangl, but was cut off in midsentence.

"That is clear to me," said Bormann. "You assumed." He moved closer to Stangl. "You assumed that I could do without Van Dyne. You assumed that you could act on your own. You assumed that your fishing expedition, or whatever you call it, was of any value to us at all. And you assumed that you had more brains than a common insect. You assumed wrongly, Heinz. On all counts. Do you hear me?"

Bormann was screaming. His face turned bright red, and his heavy jowls shook with anger.

"Please, calm yourself, Martin," Stangl pleaded. "Do you want to risk another attack? I'm sorry. I thought it was best. It will never happen again. Never."

Bormann levered his old body into a chair. His breathing slowly returned to normal. From below, the sound of a car arriving could be heard.

"That will be Hauptman and Dr. Voorstein," said Bormann. "Go down and meet them. I need time to think. Ludwig is already downstairs."

Stangl left the room. He was still uneasy, and Bormann let him remain that way.

Bormann looked at the clock. Smith would be arriving by helicopter any minute. He posed the biggest problem of any in the group. Hauptman could be controlled. Voorstein was a different sort than his father and was young enough to respect Bormann's position and power. But Smith had too much power of his own to bow to anyone else's will.

Smith had steadily eroded Bormann's control for over forty years. When the Reich had fallen and Bormann had run with Stumpfegger for his life, it was Smith who had picked them up on Germany's coast to transport them to South Africa. Bormann had hated his dependence on Smith since that day. And Smith's steady rise to his present power had worsened the situation.

Bormann had been unable to take even the smallest part of the riches of the Eagle's Nest, which he had had to destroy before the Allies found it. He had fought to stay in control since 1945. Only the Project kept him there, the Project that Smith needed more than, or at least equal to, Bormann's need for Smith.

"The damn Israelis," thought Bormann. In the final analysis it was the Israelis that had made escape impossible. His chance to use the old SS escape routes, the ODESSA network, was long gone. And even if he could, then what? The life of a peasant to avoid the death squads that took Eichmann? Or a recluse behind barbed wire, dependent on the mercy of some petty South American dictator, like Mengele? Bormann had decided to remain in South Africa. The world had destroyed the Führer. All that was left was the Project. And the power over men's lives that it gave him.

God, the power had been sweet. He had been Hitler's strong right hand, carrying orders from the throne of the gods like Hermes from Olympus. With the ease of a *hausfrau* doing her spring cleaning, he had swept human garbage from the face of the earth. Jews and Poles and Negroes and Russians; all had felt the power of his decrees. What a world he could have created, bright and shining and pure, had not the weaklings betrayed Hitler.

Europe had been his to play with, a gift from Hitler. Women, he had gobbled up; art, he had taken for his own; and his simplest whims were magically transformed into reality. He had been the puppet master. He had been a king.

Over the years Bormann had read so many accounts of the Third Reich. At first he had been appalled. Did no one understand what we tried to do? he had wondered. Was there no one who could see the plan—the design? We were never racists, Bormann had protested. There was no hate in what we did. Does the gardener hate the weeds he plucks to leave room for the plants to grow straight and strong? Of course not. Does the breeder hate the inferior strain of cattle that he cannot allow to reproduce among the cows? Absurd. Only the best could be allowed to grow. Only the superior should be nurtured. It was love, never hatred; love of the romantic dream of Aryanism that moved us.

That was the true meaning of power. To give birth to a dream! The suffering of those who had to die was as minor as the agony of a weed. How could they not see that? And Bormann had decreed that the dream would not die.

So he had rebuilt the Adlerkinden. And the Adlernest. And the Project had continued; and now, Bormann thought, when I am so close, that fool almost brings it all to ruin. Van Dyne dead. The entire Amsterdam operation ruined. "Damn him," he swore out loud.

It was essential to know who had penetrated the Project. It had to be made safe again. Two years, three at the most, and they would be ready to begin. Bormann had to have that time.

The rhythmic beat of a helicopter's propeller interrupted his thoughts. It was time, he decided, for the Prime Minister of South Africa to learn that even old scorpions can still bite.

He went downstairs to greet the others with a smile on his face that offset the weariness in his body.

The others had gathered in the large central room that constituted most of the downstairs. Smith owned the house and used it as a fishing lodge. Now it served as a meeting place, easily accessible to all, providing Smith with a plausible reason to depart Pretoria and its political demands.

A fire was burning in the large stone hearth. No servants were present; even Smith's pilot waited outside, so the men poured their own drinks and assembled at the large conference table in the room's center.

Bormann caught Smith's eye as he entered. There was hostility written clearly on Smith's face. Bormann ignored it and took his seat at the head of the table. Hauptman, dressed in a business suit, lit a cigar, and a cloud of gray smoke wafted upward. Stangl took a seat, quietly avoiding Bormann's gaze. Piet Voorstein, the youngest member of the group, was dressed in khaki shirt and pants. He sat calmly sipping his drink, unaware of the tensions. Smith sat rigidly, his gaze never leaving Bormann's face.

Ludwig Stumpfegger noted Smith's glare and raised an eyebrow in question to Bormann. Bormann shook his head, and Stumpfegger took his seat, too.

"I've asked for this meeting," Bormann began, "because we have a serious issue to deal with. For the first time in forty years someone has penetrated our security."

Hauptman spat out his cigar, and Voorstein ceased drinking in midsip. Bormann studied their reactions. He saw that only Smith was unmoved by the announcement. One part of his mind digested that information while he continued to speak.

"I don't believe the Project is in danger at this moment. The penetration has been too low level. However, we must find the source and put an end to it. It is for this purpose we are together now," he said.

"Where is Van Dyne? Why isn't he here?" asked Hauptman.

"For a more complete answer to that, I want Herr Stangl to give you his report. Please hold your questions until he is done. It will answer much," said Bormann.

Stangl cleared his throat and mentally cursed Bormann. He was being offered to the wolves.

"Van Dyne was approached a few days ago by Lisa Smith, Herr Smith's daughter, in Amsterdam. She demanded to

215

know the exact nature of her parents' deaths,"—Stangl shot a sideways glance at Smith, but the man showed no emotion at all—"claiming she was in possession of facts that shed new light on their deaths, which she claimed were not suicides."

"What facts?" interrupted Smith.

"She claimed knowledge of the agreement made between South Africa and Germany in 1936," said Stangl, "and she claimed it was the cause of the death of her parents."

His report was met with stunned silence. Stangl was relieved that it had moved the center of attention from himself.

"How could she know?" demanded Voorstein hotly, his first show of emotion. He shot a look at Smith who ignored the implications of his question.

"Van Dyne said she claimed she had found old papers of her father's," Stangl responded.

"Impossible," said Smith flatly. "I took care of that myself. Even the police turned up nothing, for the simple reason that there was nothing to turn up."

"Van Dyne agreed," said Stangl. "It was his feeling and mine that she had been programmed by someone. Thrown at us to serve as a stalking goat."

"By whom?" asked Hauptman. His cigar had gone out from his furious waving of it at Stangl.

"We attempted to find out," began Stangl uncomfortably, "but failed. I have given a full report to Herr Bormann. Van Dyne made serious mistakes in his handling of the matter."

"Is there some reason you're referring to Van Dyne in the past tense, Herr Stangl?" asked Voorstein directly.

Stangl looked to Bormann, but saw no help in his hard face.

"Van Dyne is dead. I shot him when he tried to run from the city."

"How dare you!" yelled Hauptman. "Who gave you that authority? He was our friend and compatriot. A loyal man who never failed us."

Stangl winced at the tirade, but Bormann at last came to his support and cut Hauptman off.

"Stangl did the correct thing, Walter," he said. "Van Dyne risked the entire Project. He panicked during the first crisis we've faced in years. And he was planning to run, despite your feelings about him. His bags were packed when Stangl found him. What would you have had him do?"

"He could have called me. I've known Pieter for over sixty years," said Hauptman bitterly.

Bormann allowed anger into his voice. "Stop being asinine, Walter. Do you think we are the Boy Scouts? His offense was severe, the punishment ineluctable. If you are too old to see that, your usefulness to the Project is over. Go home and tend your garden."

Hauptman lapsed into a moody silence.

"In any event, there were further reasons. Continue, Herr Stangl," directed Bormann.

"Van Dyne allowed another man, an American writer named Ben Davidson, to come close enough to him to break into his files. This Davidson is the main reason we lost control of the operation."

For the first time Stumpfegger looked up at Stangl, deep concern on his face.

"What was that name?" he asked intently.

"Ben Davidson. An American writer. He claimed to be doing an article on the diamond business," said Stangl.

"Describe him," ordered Stumpfegger.

"About six feet tall. Dark hair and eyes. Medium frame. Why, Herr Doktor?"

Stumpfegger looked around the group, his gaze finally settling on Bormann.

"My research station, as you all know, has been in the southern United States. One of my subjects was aided in the delivery of her infant by a man, a writer from New York. It was a freak coincidence. After the delivery, the father killed the infant and assaulted the man. I treated him in my home until he could travel. I thought it was the end of the matter."

"I had the father locked up in my lab, and the mother had been used for data purposes. For some reason, which I think I now know, the father got loose. We were unsure of the circumstances, so we abandoned the station.

"Not wanting to take any chances, I sent a man to follow the writer. He followed him to a medical library in New Orleans. For obvious reasons, I ordered him killed. That was the last I heard of the man I sent, Henry Schmidt. The writer's name was Ben Davidson," he finished.

"Davidson used that name at Van Dyne's when he was

found at the files. Rikkers was taken in. It gave Davidson a chance to escape," said Stangl excitedly. Others had made mistakes, too. He was not totally alone.

"This Davidson saw the infant?" demanded Hauptman.

Stumpfegger nodded.

"Why wasn't I told of this?" asked Bormann coldly.

"I thought it was over. That no connection could be traced to us. Apparently, I was wrong," Stumpfegger admitted.

"Then you returned to the Adlernest under false pretenses," said Voorstein angrily. "Was your data false, also?"

Stumpfegger's piercing blue eyes narrowed. "Be careful, boy. Not even your father could speak that way to me. I was in this while you were still suckling your mother."

Voorstein began a retort but was drowned out by the violence of Johann Smith's fist bashing into the table.

"Enough!" he shouted. "I have sat and listened to this moronic recital of failure and incompetence long enough. Is this an example of the vaunted supremacy we speak of so easily? Men disappearing. Operations blown. Penetration by amateurs. I'm disgusted. All I hear are excuses."

"Johann, be reasonable. These are disconnected events," said Hauptman quickly.

"I have held my peace long enough, Walter. Now I have questions to ask, and they had best be answered. It was reported to me that my daughter was almost killed in your brothel, Stangl. Shots were fired at her!" Smith looked at Bormann angrily. "Did you think to kill the rest of my family? Do you think I will sit idly by and let harm come to Lisa? To hell with all of you, I say, if the slightest harm comes to her. Deal with that, gentlemen."

"No one meant to harm her, Herr Smith," protested Stangl.

"Where did you get your information, Johann?" asked Bormann quietly.

"I have sources, Martin. The people who work for me are not incompetent," said Smith. "Do you deny it?"

"No," said Bormann, his voice still quiet. "No. I don't deny it. The issue is, however, that your daughter is a threat. And threats must be eliminated. Or have you, too, grown too old to act, too happy with your petty throne to finish what we started all those years ago. Think back, Johann. When did you go soft?"

"Save your empty games for the lackeys, Bormann. My

daughter will not go the way of her parents! That is a fact. The day she comes to harm is the day I deliver you to the Israelis. Never forget that. Never." Smith was choked with rage. The space that followed Smith's outburst was pregnant with violence. It was Voorstein who spoke into the silence.

"My father spoke of you all as great men," said Voorstein with emotion in his voice. "Men with a great vision and the strength of purpose to see it through. Willing to try something no one had ever done before. To take on God's work and see it done in Africa. He called you the finest Afrikaners when he first brought me into this group. As he lay on his deathbed and told me what I would have to do, I cried to be part of such greatness." Disgust entered his voice. "You disgrace his memory. In his name I ask you to stop this fighting. We have work to do. I apologize to Doctor Stumpfegger for my prior remarks. He paved the way for all the research I have ever done. All I need is a year, gentlemen. Just a year. Give me that time. My father and I both ask you for it."

Voorstein's speech had the desired effect. Faces, red with anger and fear, returned to normal.

"It seems we learn much from our young colleague," said Stumpfegger, nodding approval. "I, too, regret my outburst."

"I agree," said Hauptman. "We must not fight among ourselves. We need the Project now more than ever. What do you suggest, Martin?"

Bormann was aware that Smith had not relented. His threat still hung in the air between them.

"Stangl was right when he saw the attack as two-pronged," Bormann said. "But wrong when he saw it as the same attack. Further, his attempt to flush the people behind this was an acceptable strategy, even if poorly carried out. Therefore, our strategy will be based on his. This time, however, it will be done correctly." He threw a peace offering to Smith, "And at no risk to Johann's daughter."

Smith thought for a moment, then nodded. "That is acceptable," he said. The group began to re-form around Bormann.

"I have to have funds very soon, Herr Bormann. The construction I direct cannot proceed without a steady cash flow. My research needs it as well. Without cash, the Project itself cannot be completed. The construction of our sites is essential," said Voorstein.

"You'll have it," said Bormann.

"Can we get more information on Davidson?" asked Stumpfegger.

"I'm going to send Stangl to New York."

"Just make sure I've got funds. That's imperative," said Voorstein.

One by one all of the men signified assent; a nod of the head, the raising of a glass. Only Smith remained uncommitted.

"Johann?" queried Bormann.

Smith's face had lost much of its hardness. Now it returned.

"Remember, Martin. No harm is to come to Lisa. If that is understood, I agree," he said.

"You have my word, Johann," said Bormann, and for the next hour he detailed assignments.

The meeting began to break up. Car engines roared to life, and Smith's helicopter took off into the late afternoon sun. Its beat gradually diminished until the room was again silent. Only Stumpfegger remained with Bormann.

"You were right, Martin. Smith has grown soft. To carry on so over a child? It was unbelievable," said Stumpfegger as he poured a final drink.

Bormann stood at a window again, watching the waves beat endlessly against the rocks below. He spoke without turning.

"I know, Ludwig. And his moral rot infects the others. But his softness makes him vulnerable." Now Bormann turned, and a crafty smile crossed his face. "So vulnerable that he's already lost the game he thinks he's won."

Leander spent the day reading reports and dictating memos regarding the various ongoing Ex Op projects. Satisfied that his section chiefs were functioning well and that the agency was running smoothly, Leander left for the Union Buildings as soon as he received Smith's call.

Smith was sitting behind his desk in precisely the same position as the previous day. But Leander saw that his mood had changed.

"Have you located my daughter, yet?" he asked as soon as Leander was seated.

"Not yet, sir," lied Leander.

"How long does it take in such a small city to find her?" he barked.

"I have half a dozen men working on it. Rest assured we'll locate her soon enough, sir," said Leander patiently.

"How do you know what's soon enough?" said Smith excitedly. "I want her located within twenty-four hours."

"Sir? Is something going on that you're keeping from me? Forgive me for saying this, but your daughter has been known to travel on a whim before. Is there something threatening her that provokes your caution? As Director of Ex Op, I . . ."

Smith cut him off, but continued in a quieter tone. "You've done an excellent job at Ex Op in the past year, Jan. How would you feel about accepting the directorship on a permanent basis?" Smith asked.

"I appreciate your confidence in my ability, sir. I would like to remain the Director of Ex Op," he said.

"It could be arranged, Jan. You have few political enemies, and your record is excellent," Smith said.

"Thank you, again. But there is a message here I don't seem to be picking up. Could you be a bit clearer, sir?"

Hesitatingly, Smith came to his point. "I want my daughter covered by your people. But the coverage must be long range. She is not to know about it. And you are not to interfere with her movements unless, and this is imperative, unless she is in direct physical danger. Further, I want you to take direct command of the operation. Can that be arranged?"

"It's difficult, but it can be done. The question is why?" asked Leander bluntly.

"Stop acting like an agent and start acting like a politician if you want the directorship permanently, Jan. I asked if you could do the job, not for you to question my motives," Smith answered sharply.

Leander realized Smith was deeply worried. More so than twenty-four hours ago. He was using Leander despite his better judgment. Only fear or foolishness caused a man to go against his judgment. And no one who had ascended to Smith's position could be considered a fool.

"I can do the job," said Leander.

"You'll profit from your devotion to duty, Jan. Have a good day."

"Good day, Mr. Prime Minister."

Smith sat back at his desk after Leander had gone. He had not been unsure many times in his life, but now he experienced severe doubt. He had deliberated calling in Leander for hours after his return from the fishing lodge. It had come down to basic truths. The source of penetration had to be discovered and eliminated. But Bormann was capable of killing Lisa as easily as blink an eye.

He pondered again his choice to bring Leander. I think I can control him, dangling the directorship in front of him, Smith thought. And Leander was the only form of protection he could think of to give Lisa. Once Leander had served his purpose, Smith decided, he would have to die.

Smith wondered how Bormann would react if he knew he had brought a trained agent into their midst. The thought made him smile in infantile spite. Leander really would have to die, he thought; he was too dangerous an element to leave free with whatever he discovered in the course of protecting Lisa. Smith sighed. Better the devil he didn't know, he thought, paraphrasing, than the devil he surely knew: Martin Bormann. Smith picked up a report on his desk and forced his mind to dwell on pressing state business. A few minutes later he was engrossed in reading.

Outside the office building, Leander reviewed his meeting with Smith. If I've read him right, he decided there's something brewing. Perhaps Bormann's making his move. His mind ranged over possibilities, as if he were playing a chess game against an unseen but powerful opponent. Pieces were being moved and rearranged. Leander turned his thoughts to Amsterdam.

Thirteen

The sounds of noontime traffic filtered up to the hotel room. Ben watched Lisa stretch in her sleep with a greater feeling of happiness than he had ever known possible. Gently, he leaned over and kissed her shoulder. When she failed to awaken, he kissed her again and slid his arms around her.

"We haven't been out of this room in thirty-six hours, Lisa. It's time to reenter the world."

Lisa sat up in bed and brushed the hair from her eyes. Not yet fully awake, she looked rosy and a little vulnerable. Ben felt a rush of emotion overwhelm him.

"Care to try for another thirty-six?" she asked mischievously.

"You're incorrigible," Ben said, grinning. "We have to eat some time." Lisa was forced to agree. She rose, kissed him on the nose, and ran for the shower.

Ben realized that much had changed for him. He had known himself well, like a house whose rooms were old and comfortable. Now it was as if windows had sprung open, a sweet, fresh wind had blown in, and the house would never be the same again.

Sexually, he felt a greater sense of liberation than ever before. Lisa made love with a passion so free and unrestrained that he felt freed to respond in kind. He shook his head. It was all happening so quickly. But how ironic, he thought again, to find her in the middle of all the death that had brought him to Amsterdam. He struggled with the idea of giving up the chase. Lisa was too important to risk losing.

Ben's mood could not tolerate such ominous thoughts. He threw off the covers and jumped into the shower with Lisa, happily startling her. She splashed water into his face, and they began to play like children in the throes of discovery on Christmas morning.

Later, outside the hotel, Ben's conflict emerged more strongly.

"That's something we've got to deal with sooner or later, Lisa," he said. "Part of me, a big part of me, wants to get on a plane and take us the hell out of here."

On the next block, a hurdy-gurdy man pranced around in front of his organ, keeping time to the music and collecting coins from passersby. The music grew louder, the calliope tones reminiscent of a circus, as they approached.

"There's a part of me that wants that, too, Ben. Somehow, what happened to my parents, and all the years I spent hurting over it, doesn't seem as important now. But I can't leave it yet," she said. "I feel reborn because I'm almost sure that it wasn't a suicide. And because of you, Ben. But if I leave it now, I'll always have to live with only being almost sure. Can you understand that?"

"I think so. I think that I'd always know that I gave up something I needed to do. Something of importance," he said.

"And if we gave it up for each other," Lisa said, "we might blame each other someday."

In the city's old section, they came to a restaurant that looked inviting. They took a table apart from the others, ordered, and in the dim light some of the closeness of the hotel room returned. He had been silent for several minutes. When he finally spoke, there was sadness in his voice.

"Then the only way it seems we have a future is to risk the present. Is that what you're saying?"

Lisa took his hand in hers. "I think so. Would you be content now to forget about Croft? And the baby you delivered, or its parents? But you have to decide, Ben. If you say we stop, then I'll stop. I'll go with you wherever you say," she said, her eyes intent upon him.

"I think we're committed," he said finally. "Otherwise, we run. And if we run, I don't know if we can ever stop. They won't let us. I say we keep going, Lisa."

"They can't beat us, Ben," Lisa said quietly. "Either way it goes. They can never beat us."

"I love you, Lisa," he said.

The impishness returned to Lisa's features. "Then you'd better get some food in you. We might not leave the hotel again for days."

Ben attacked his steak.

"What's amazing really," he said between bites, "is that I know so little about South Africa. Other than what I read in the newspapers."

"Do you want a history lesson?" Lisa asked.

"Just enough to understand both sides," he replied.

"You mean the black and white sides," she said, and when Ben nodded, she went on.

"Apart from the native population, the Portuguese explorer, Bartholomeu Dias, first discovered the Cape of Good Hope in 1488. Then Vasco da Gama found it in 1498 when he sailed for India and made the first voyage by a European around Africa to the East. South Africa was first settled by Europeans when the Dutch East India Company founded a settlement in 1652 on the Cape of Good Hope after taking control of the trade routes from Portugal. The purpose of the early settlement was to provision ships and treat sick sailors.

"It took almost thirty years for the colony to become self-supporting, and it was still ruled by the company, not the citizens. Soldiers released from service were allowed to start farming, using imported slave labor. These soldiers called themselves 'free burghers' and really started the agricultural tradition of the country. Am I boring you?" Lisa asked.

"Not at all. So far it doesn't sound dissimilar to the history of the United States. You're well versed," Ben said.

"As the daughter of the Prime Minister, I had to know this backward and forward, to be trotted out on state occasions. Anyway," she continued, "these burghers were mostly of Dutch and German descent. They were fiercely proud, industrious and strong, Calvinists mostly, who believed in predestination and redemption for the elect alone. Later, a group of French Huguenots, also Calvinists from the elite ranks of French society, immigrated to the colony. They strengthened the religious values in the community.

"By the beginning of the eighteenth century, the colonists started to think of themselves not as Dutch citizens, but as Afrikaners, a term used with contempt by the company's local governors. Have you ever heard the name 'Boer'?" Lisa asked.

"It's familiar," said Ben, "but I can't really define it."

"It simply means 'farmer.' The Boers pushed deeper into the interior to farm more land. They also imported more slave labor, rather than more Europeans, which is partly why the white population was so slow to grow. Boer and Afrikaner are two terms for those African-born whites of Dutch tradition.

"At the end of the eighteenth century," Lisa continued her recital, "the British army occupied the Cape. Ownership swung back and forth from the Dutch to the British until the British took permanent control in the European Settlement of 1814. And that's where the country's turmoil began, at least the white part of it.

"The colonists had their own language, Afrikaans, a derivative of sixteenth-century Dutch. The British began a policy of Anglicization and eliminated the Dutch language from government, church, courts, and schools. The Afrikaners were gradually pushed out of any area of importance by the new

English-speaking arrivals. Got it so far? Two peoples with two languages and two political ties."

Ben nodded. Lisa went on.

"Conflict followed conflict, until finally, in 1835, the Afrikaners staged the historic Great Trek to settle the interior away from British rule. Thousands left their homes in ox carts and went north into the jungle. Like your western migration in the United States—and as revered in our history as the Boston Tea Party is in yours."

"What about the folks who already lived in the interior?" asked Ben as coffee arrived.

"The Voor Trekers, as they were called, fought wars with the Zulu tribes and others who lived there and subjugated them," said Lisa.

"Sounds cruel," said Ben.

"Depends on your point of view, Ben. Consider what your westward expansion did to the native Indian population," Lisa continued. "These were people fighting for room and independence. They were, and are today still, racists; but it's important to understand both sides of the issue before you judge."

"I've read of too many atrocities by our white settlers against the Indians not to understand that," said Ben.

"For a while things stabilized in the country. Boers and Britons agreed not to interfere in each other's affairs. The Orange Free State and the Transvaal were formed as Boer Republics, and the Cape and Natal were British. It was in Natal that Indian indentured servants were first brought in to work the sugar plantations around 1860 by the British.

"So now there were four separate groups in the country: Afrikaan-speaking Boers, English-speaking whites, blacks, and Asians, who were called coloreds. It was, and still is, a racial mess aggravated by reasons I'll explain later.

"It all blew up when diamonds were discovered in Boer territory, and the British government moved in to annex the land. In the first War of Independence, the Boers threw them out. The diamond fields brought other European powers to South Africa. Germany annexed a piece one-and-a half times larger than itself—German Southwest Africa. The discovery of gold on land where Johannesburg now stands fueled the conflicts.

"By the turn of the century, full-scale war had broken out

between Boer and Britain and lasted almost three years. Almost every farm in the two Boer republics was burned under the 'Scorched Earth' policy of Britain. Fifty thousand people, on both sides, died before Britain finally won the war.

"The war had two effects. It paved the way for a united republic, and it gave a great push to Afrikaner nationalism. In 1908, the Union of South Africa was formed from the four republics. But you've got to understand the deep, bitter hatred of the Boers for the British South Africans. It is the cause of many of our problems."

Lisa paused and drank her coffee.

"It's like everywhere else in the world. Every side has its own justification," said Ben.

"I think that's important to understand, Ben. Where you stand is often a matter of where you sit, as someone once said. The blacks feel that Africa is theirs by right, and so do the Boers—for the last three hundred years. The British conquered during a time when colonialism was a perfectly acceptable form of geopolitics."

"I'm still not clear on why the Afrikaners would support the Nazis. I thought the British were in charge."

"That's precisely why they did support them. For reasons of history, they were hopeful of a British defeat. Afrikaner nationalism was at its peak. Only a split in the Afrikaner attitude and the leadership of Jan Smuts, an Afrikaner on the side of the British, brought us in on Britain's side. I think you and I are dealing with a group of Afrikaners who refused to go along with that policy in 1936."

"I see," said Ben. "Where did apartheid spring up? From the same group?"

Lisa sighed and continued her narrative. "After the war, Smuts lost favor, and the Nationalist Party came into power. Its platform was apartheid, and it was dedicated to sustaining white rule in South Africa. Apartheid, forced segregation, became even a larger issue than the two major language groups. There are under four million whites in the RSA and twenty-four million blacks. The ratio of six to one scared the hell out of them, and it still does. The basic numbers made them grow more and more repressive. The leaders in the RSA today are mostly men who favored Germany's cause and came to power first in 1948.

"Black civil rights groups, which began in the fifties, adopted civil disobedience techniques. But constitutional rights became a joke. They were thrown in jail or whipped brutally. After every demonstration, the security laws got harsher and more repressive. Pass laws that had blacks issued passes permitting them to be in white areas existed until just a few years ago, and violators were punished by jail terms. Even now we have a ninety-day detention law that lets the police arrest and hold without trial or legal counsel anyone suspected of subversion. Their power has no limit.

"It came to a head in Sharpeville, where police fired on demonstrators and a labor rebellion ensued. It almost crippled the country. Foreign capital fled the country fearing a black takeover. It was finally put down, and things have been tense but manageable ever since because the laws have become more and more strict.

"The government long ago set up homelands for blacks in which they have legal rights. The only problem is that a black in a white homeland has no rights at all. And the black may never see his homeland if he works in a white area. He may live his life in a ghetto, totally disenfranchised. But the whites are too few to run the cities and need the black labor. Without them, it would all fall apart. That's partly why the whites don't want to resort to military action. It's mutual need aggravated by mutual intolerance.

"And the cost is staggering. Separate schools, churches, buses, parks, and everything else for each group. God only knows where it will end."

"And where do you stand?" Ben asked.

"Given where I come from, my family tradition, I'm a radical. I don't think apartheid has a chance. Not with a population ratio of six to one. I think the RSA could be a paradise if we learned social justice. Without it, I think we are doomed. And deservedly so. Mine is not an attitude that finds much favor, I'm sorry to say. But there is progress. I think I'm ready for some air. How about you?"

"Great. And thanks for the history lesson."

Ben paid the check, and they walked along the Princengracht. He thought over what Lisa had said.

"I didn't realize the black population ratio was so disproportionate to the whites," he said.

"I don't think there's a government minister in any position of power who doesn't fall asleep at night dreaming of a way to alter the fact," Lisa said.

"I can't help but feel that they've probably considered Hitler's kind of final solution, given their sympathies to those kind of politics," Ben mused.

Lisa shrugged her shoulders. "In their hearts, I'm sure some would like nothing better. But remember that it would mean the death of the white culture as well. The black work force is essential. The standard of living of the whites depends on the blacks."

"Like the plantation system in the old South," said Ben.

"Exactly," agreed Lisa. The discussion had dampened her spirits. "Let's not talk about it for a while, Ben," she said suddenly. "Let's just be a couple of tourists. I want to forget who we are and why we're here. Just for a little while. Okay?"

"Okay," he said.

"What's that crowd over there?" asked Lisa, pointing to a long line of people waiting to enter a canal house.

"That's the Anne Frank House, Lisa. The place where she and her family stayed during the war. I'm surprised you've never been inside."

"Can we go in?" asked Lisa.

"If you want to. But I have to tell you that it is not a happy place."

They joined the line of people that moved slowly up the concrete stairs to the entrance of the building where the Franks spent two years in hiding from the Nazis. They walked in single file up the almost vertical stairway and passed through the small doorway that led to the Annex, the living quarters, on the top floor. Lisa was silent, wide-eyed. She hadn't let go of Ben's hand since entering the building.

The steady stream of silent faces, each immersed in private thoughts, like mourners passing a grave, paid silent tribute to the memory of a frail, fourteen-year-old girl who had held on to hope in a world gone insane.

"We stay. You were right," was all Lisa could say before her voice broke.

Descending the stairs to the rooms below the Annex, the crowd moved past a pictorial history of the Third Reich. Captions in five different languages told the story.

A picture caught Ben's attention. A German staff car, Hitler in back waving, rode through the streets of Paris toward the Arc De Triomphe. The picture was old and grainy. But what struck Ben so forcibly that he stopped dead was not Hitler but the other occupants of the car. The crowd began to back up behind him, and Lisa looked at him quizzically. Ben could only stare, openmouthed, at the two other occupants whose picture he had seen before, taken from Croft's locked box in the lab in Mississippi.

The short, fat man in the picture he had taken from Croft rode in the car, smile beaming from his jowled face. Next to him sat Dr. Eugene Croft. Younger to be sure, but Croft nonetheless, dressed in the uniform of the Nazi party.

Shaken, Ben looked at the caption. He read it three times to be sure, to be totally sure that it was true.

ADOLF HITLER ENTERS PARIS TRIUMPHANTLY
WITH TRUSTED AIDES
REICHSLEITER MARTIN BORMANN &
DR. LUDWIG STUMPFEGGER

In a trance, Ben pointed to the picture for Lisa to read it. She did, not understanding his concern. People were staring at them, and she led Ben out of the room and back down-stairs to the street.

"What was it, Ben?" demanded Lisa, concerned. "What did you see?"

"When I broke into Croft's house in Mississippi, I took a box that gave me the lead to Van Dyne," he said. "In it was also a photo of a younger Croft and another man. I just saw the same two men in that photograph upstairs, Lisa. The one I pointed to."

"Stumpfegger and Bormann? Theirs are the names in the document from 1936," she said, not understanding.

"Lisa, Dr. Croft *is* Ludwig Stumpfegger! And the man in the picture with him was Martin Bormann. We are after the same thing!

"We've got to see Van Dyne," said Ben, his voice determined.

The taxi sped through the streets onto Herengracht. Ben leaped from the cab at Van Dyne's, caught up in the intensity of his excitement, and Lisa barely remembered to pay the driver.

Ben pounded on the door. A servant opened it, and Ben pushed his way in.

The first thing Lisa noticed was that sheets covered everything.

"I want to see Van Dyne," Ben demanded. Pers seemed to fade back into the wall at his outburst.

"Wait, Ben," Lisa intervened. "Tell me, Pers," she said. "Where is my uncle? Why is everything covered?"

Pers was visibly upset. "I'm truly sorry, Miss Lisa. I thought you'd have heard. Herr Van Dyne is dead. I'm terribly sorry," said Pers.

Ben stood in mute surprise. He felt cheated. Then, he was moved to sorrow for Lisa.

"He gave the staff a holiday, the day before yesterday. He was going on vacation. He and Mrs. Stoelin." Tears filled the old man's eyes. He had served Van Dyne longer than anyone.

"They were shot, both of them. The police have no leads. I'm sorry, Miss Lisa. I've been with him most of my life. I heard it on the radio and came back to see to the family."

Lisa felt drained. "I'm so sorry, Pers. When is the funeral?"

"Today, ma'am. At five o'clock. The body is to be brought back to South Africa. He specified that in his will. Only a service is conducted today. For his Dutch friends."

Ben had no anger left. He put his arm around Lisa and led her from the house.

"Do you want to go to the funeral?" he asked.

Lisa looked up at him. "Is it crazy to want to?"

Ben shook his head. "Not really, I guess. In spite of everything else, he was close to you for a long time."

"But how I hated him for what he did," said Lisa bitterly, "at the end."

"People can hate and love at the same time, Lisa. We can go if you want to," he said. "I do understand."

Lisa nodded her head, and they walked to the corner and flagged down a taxi.

Walter Hauptman sat in the back of his limousine and brooded. All the way from South Africa to Amsterdam he had mulled over Bormann's rebuke. No one spoke to him like that, he thought angrily. He had funded the Project almost single-handedly since 1936. Who the hell did Bormann think he was? Van Dyne was an Afrikaner, a loyal friend for half a century. It was not wrong to display emotion for that bond.

The chauffeur stopped the car in front of the Dutch Reformed Church. Inside, the service was just beginning, and Hauptman sat down quietly in a pew near the front. The cadence of the service gradually drew him into the prayers.

Apparently Van Dyne was well thought of, judging by the number of persons in attendance. The high arched ceilings reflected their voices, which swelled to music from a hidden organ. Hauptman was pleased. He continued to pray for Van Dyne's salvation. And his own.

Ben tried to stay with the service. He kept drifting back to the Anne Frank House. Bits and pieces flowed around in his mind. Diamonds and dead babies; Amsterdam and Mississippi; Van Dyne and South Africa. Too much death and too few answers. James and Annie and Amy and the men he'd killed. Croft was Stumpfegger; Stumpfegger was a Nazi. Over and over again, like a child's nursery rhyme, it sang in his head.

Suddenly Lisa grabbed his arm.

"That man," she said, gesturing across the aisle. "Do you see him? In the fourth row, third seat, next to the woman in the gray coat."

Ben searched the crowd and found the man. He was in his late sixties, Ben judged, and overweight.

"I see him," he said, still tense.

"That man is Walter Hauptman, another of my 'uncles' like Van Dyne. He owns the diamond mine and is on the list, Ben. He's one of them," she said, excited.

Ben thought for a moment.

"I want you to leave now and get a taxi. Wait in front of the church. I don't want him to see you. When he leaves, we'll follow him."

At the end of the service, Hauptman got up and walked out of the church. Ben watched him get into a limousine; then he ran to Lisa in the waiting cab.

When the limousine stopped, Hauptman got out and entered the Gaan Diamond Exchange, a three-story building near the Rembrantsplein.

"I'll be back in a minute. I want to see if I can find out who he's going to see. You wait here with the cab," Ben said to Lisa.

"Be careful, please!"

Ben walked past the limousine and into the building. The receptionist looked up from her message pad when Ben cleared his throat.

"Yes, sir. Can I help you?" she asked brightly.

"Yes, please," said Ben. "I was sent here to meet Herr Hauptman. I see his car is outside. Has he arrived yet?"

"Yes, sir. He just arrived and is in conference with Herr Putten, the Director. Would you like me to call him? Is this urgent?"

"No, thank you. I have a message for him that I can leave with his chauffeur. Don't even bother to tell him I was here. You know how these things are," Ben said conspiratorially. "Some big shot at the consulate wants a message delivered, and I have to go running. It never changes," he sighed.

"Don't I know it," said the girl. "I take messages from rude people all day. God forbid if I get one word wrong. It's like the world is coming to an end."

Ben nodded in weary agreement. "Thanks again," he said, and walked out of the lobby.

On the third floor, Hauptman was ushered into Telf Putten's office with all the respect due royalty.

"Herr Hauptman. What a pleasant surprise," said Putten, a small Dutchman with white hair that grew only on the sides of his head and a small, gray mustache that sprang from his upper lip. His brown eyes were alert and intelligent.

"Would you care for coffee, Herr Hauptman? Or something stronger, perhaps?" he asked.

Hauptman took a seat and laid his attaché case on the desk.

"No thank you, Herr Putten. What I have to say will not take long. I'm here on business alone."

"Please feel free. I'm happy to do business with a man of your reputation. The owner of the Raelord Mine is not unknown to me. Ours is a small business, and your reputation precedes you," said Putten ingratiatingly.

"I represent a group of businessmen," Hauptman began, "who have asked me to come to you with a proposition."

"I am always receptive to new business, Herr Hauptman,"

233

he said. He was the kind of boy who probably licked his lips, thought Hauptman with distaste.

"From time to time," Hauptman continued, "this consortium, if you will, has to establish a cash flow situation. We would like you to handle that for us."

"How?" asked Putten with a slight narrowing of his eyes.

"Like all the exchanges in the city you buy from De Beers, to whom I sell directly. True?" said Hauptman.

"Yes. Of course. You are restating the obvious, Herr Hauptman," said Putten, a frown creasing his mouth.

"In the future, a supply of gemstones will reach you directly from the RSA. You will not include these stones in your inventory, but cut and sell them nonetheless. When they are converted to cash, you will forward it to a bank I will designate in Paris. For your trouble, you may keep five percent of wholesale value for yourself. Is that possible, do you think? My friends would appreciate your efforts greatly, Herr Putten."

"But I can't do that," said Putten. "It's illegal. If I were caught, I could go to jail. How could you ask such a thing?"

Hauptman smiled at the enraged Putten. "Quite easily. It would make you a very rich man, Herr Putten. Won't you reconsider?" he asked.

"Never!" said the red-faced Putten. "Such a scheme is beneath you. I will forget you ever suggested it. Please, leave my office, Herr Hauptman, or I will be forced to call the authorities." Putten stood up, a gesture of dismissal.

Hauptman sighed. Such a foolish little man, he thought. He opened his case, took out a folder, and tossed it casually onto Putten's desk.

"You were very busy during the war," said Hauptman, "I do hope you'll read these copies and reconsider my offer. However, if you do wish to call the authorities . . . well," he sighed, "a man must do what he must do. Don't you agree, Herr Putten?"

Putten looked at the contents of the file. His face went from red to gray as papers passed before his eyes. From the war long past, copies of his memos to the German local command confronted him: reports on the location of Resistance units, of Allied spies, and of Dutch Jews.

Hauptman watched a war of hatred and fear play over

Putten's face. He waited for the inevitable. It was not long in coming.

"Where did you get these?" asked Putten in a shaken voice.

"That's irrelevant, Herr Putten. I ask you for the last time to consider my offer. Once a month a man will come to you. The code he will give you is the word 'Adlerkinden.' The Paris banker is Paul Martisse. You will cable the funds through special account number 5336-17 to his bank, Martisse et Fils, within thirty days of delivery. You may do what you like with your share. Agreed?"

Putten looked like he was about to be sick. He had aged visibly in the last few minutes.

"It seems I have no choice," he said.

Hauptman nodded and closed his case. "Exactly. No choice at all."

Later that night, Ben lay on the bed, listening to Lisa in the shower and thinking about Hauptman. After he left the Gaan Diamond House, he had driven directly to the airport and taken a regularly scheduled flight back to South Africa.

"I've been thinking," said Lisa, emerging from the bathroom moist and naked. "If Van Dyne served as the conduit for diamonds from Hauptman, then wouldn't his death necessitate the need for a new conduit? And wouldn't that conduit be someone like Putten, an owner like Van Dyne?" she said.

Ben nodded vigorously. "That could be it, Lisa. It makes sense with Van Dyne dead."

"I think so. If we can use Putten to find where the money goes, it would give us the next step," she said.

Ben hugged her. "There must be a way. We'll talk over dinner. But there's something I want to do first." He reached for the phone.

"Who are you calling?" Lisa asked.

"Gottbaum in New York. Voorstein was the other name on the document you saw. And you said he was connected to the U.N. before he died. Gottbaum's got more connections than a Mafia chief. Maybe he can get some information that'll help. If not, we lose nothing."

"Do I get to meet him someday?" Lisa asked.

Ben looked at her warmly. "You'll like each other," he said as he asked the international operator to place the call.

"Saved us a lot of trouble their running into Hauptman like that," said Gerroff. "Would have been a bitch to arrange ourselves."

Gerroff sat back in the chair by the radio that received the signals from the bug in Ben and Lisa's room. Their hotel across from the Treza was luxurious compared to the loft and the cramped confines of the van.

Dreyer mused aloud. "Whatever they do it's sure to attract attention. That's what we want. Let's give them enough room. Who's on pick-up tonight?"

"Vancouver. Embassy Staff. He's good, you can relax," said Gerroff. "When is Pilsten due back?"

"Tomorrow. I'd get some sleep if I were you. Things may heat up pretty soon. I've got to send a signal to Leander."

"Good idea," agreed Gerroff.

Like the trained agent that he was, Gerroff was sound asleep five minutes later, unbothered by Dreyer's work at the radio.

At the sound of the helicopter's approach, Ryerson yanked his body off his duffle bag, which insulated him from the heat blistering off the concrete pad. Native workers lay scattered around a pile of boxes from the labs that had been brought by earlier.

"It's about time," he muttered. "Two stinking days of just mucking about."

Since his "reassignment," as Tamely had called it when Ryerson had protested his firing, he had been barred from the construction site. After two frustrating days waiting for the scheduled run to the Congo, watching idly as the hospital continued to rise up from the dust, Ryerson was bitter and depressed. No one had any reasons for him. Sorry, they said, reassignment was not their responsibility. Take it up with the administrators in Brazzaville, they said.

"Stuff Brazzaville," was Ryerson's candid response. It endeared him to no one.

He shielded his eyes from the dust storm raised by the props as the helicopter settled to the earth.

Immediately, the natives began loading the cargo hold with the metal boxes that looked like camping coolers or ice chests. Under the baleful stare of the white foreman, a South African named Paulson, the natives moved quickly, afraid to displease their taskmaster. One stumbled and dropped the chest he was carrying.

"Get up, you lazy bastard," yelled the foreman, and he lifted a stick to strike the man. The native rolled away to avoid the blow, struggling to lift the chest.

Ryerson saw pain on the native's features as he took a step. He thought the man had probably hurt his ankle.

"Pick it up, Kaffir," barked the foreman. But the man was unable to heft the chest and walk. The other black workers ran by, still packing the copter, unwilling to take part in the conflict.

Ryerson noticed that the pilot had descended, removing his flying gear. He took long swigs from a canteen and stared disinterestedly at the man on the ground only ten feet away. Not his problem.

The native looked frightened. He couldn't lift the chest. Again, the stick swung skyward.

Without really thinking, Ryerson found himself in front of the foreman.

"If you hit him with that, I'm going to put your balls up around your ears."

The foreman looked stricken, but stepped back.

"Keep out of this, Ryerson. You've got your own troubles. Get on the copter, and get out of here."

The heat, the boredom, the racism, and the threats all combined. He grabbed the foreman by the lapels of his bush jacket.

"Now would you be explaining those remarks? What troubles have I got? It's flamin' sure you're not going to put me on that copter."

Ryerson shook Paulson roughly. "I didn't mean . . ." Paulson said, choking.

Ryerson released him. It would go badly enough for the native he had protected anyway. A man like Paulson would vent his rage at the humiliation he had suffered on the native.

Ryerson was suddenly filled with loathing. He had probably made matters worse.

He turned and retrieved his duffle bag. To hell with all of them, he thought, and headed for the now fully loaded helicopter.

The pilot eyed him narrowly as he tossed his bag in back.

"Testy bugger you are," he said.

"Only to pricks," observed Ryerson, and he scrambled inside.

The helicopter was small, and the chests took up most of the space. He arranged his bag and pushed some aside to make space for himself. Out the cargo door he could see Paulson poking at the natives. His words were obscured as the pilot revved up the engines, and the long spindly blades began to rotate overhead. Someone outside slid the cargo door shut, and the copter lumbered heavily into the air.

Ryerson occupied his time with idle speculation about the hospital they were building. His mind's eye kept reviewing the blueprints he had seen. When he had gone over them a half-dozen times and still had no answers to the questions that they raised, he turned his attention back to his immediate surroundings.

The light inside the hold was bright, and he could see clearly. All together, he counted thirty chests. Every one was identical, and they were sealed. Then his eyes focused on one whose metallic shine was dulled with dust. The one that had been dropped. Its seal was broken.

Remembering that his curiosity had gotten him here in the first place, as he had no doubt that his look at the prints had cost him his job, he knew it was a bad idea to open it.

But, as he prodded the box a few times with his toes, the boredom of the flight conquered his indecision.

The seal was a kind of rubbery latex that parted easily under pressure having been already ruptured by its fall. A soft pad, almost six inches thick, lay inside as a cushion against breakage. He lifted it aside.

Like thin wine bottles in a miniature wine rack, under the pad were sealed test tubes fitted snugly into a lattice work of metal strips. The only thing of the slightest interest about the test tubes to Ryerson was that they were set up in groups of three, banded together by a metal clamp like three cigars in a package. He lifted one set out.

He put them back in the chest and looked at the others inside. All the same, five groups of three tubes each. The tubes failed to raise his interest at all; he replaced the padding and shut the box. The sticky latex seal fused itself back together.

Like the labs from which the crates full of test tubes had come, he figured as he lay back and stared out at the sky, it no longer concerned him.

"Fuck 'em," he said to no one at all.

Fourteen

Bill Gottbaum woke up the next morning with Ben's phone call on his mind. He wandered into the kitchen of his apartment on Central Park West and made himself a pot of coffee. Manuscripts lay all over the apartment, some recent, others months old; and he had to push some aside to make a place at the kitchen table.

Gottbaum went to his study and took out his private phone book. Forty years of connections and contacts lay within. Rifling through the pages, he found the name he wanted and dialed the phone.

"Mr. Knowles's office," answered a secretary in a precise but nasal voice.

"Good morning. This is Bill Gottbaum calling. Is Ted in yet? If so, I'd like to speak to him."

"Just a moment, Mr. Gottbaum. I'll check."

Gottbaum heard the flat silence that meant he had been put on hold. Ted Knowles was one of the senior permanent United States staff members assigned to the Ambassador to the United Nations. Gottbaum had met him years before, representing a work of fiction Knowles had written using the U.N. as a setting. Though it had sold reasonably well, Knowles was basically a dilettante, committed to his job, and had never written another.

"Hi, Bill," Knowles's voice broke onto the connection.

"How are you? I haven't heard from you in two years. What's up?"

"I need a favor, Ted. Do I have enough credit for one?"

There was no hesitancy in the reply. "If I can swing it, you've got it. What's the favor?"

"I need as much information as you can get on short notice about a man named Franz Voorstein, a South African who worked for the U.N. till his death in '68."

"W.H.O.," said Knowles.

"Who what?" said Gottbaum, confused.

"No. I meant the World Health Organization, W.H.O. for short. Voorstein was the Director from 1964 or so until his death. He was one of its main developers. He was rather well known in our circles. Do you want more than that?"

"A bit more would help. And maybe something on the W.H.O.," added Gottbaum.

"Are you free for lunch today?" asked Knowles. "Voorstein is easy. It shouldn't take too long to put something together. I can have my secretary do it in an hour."

"Lunch is fine. When and where?"

"Noontime. VIP Restaurant on the fifteenth floor. You can buy."

"See you then. Thanks, Ted."

"Thank me after you see the prices." Knowles laughed and hung up the phone.

Gottbaum decided he would go into the office. He finished dressing and called the desk to get him a taxi. Grabbing coat and manuscript, he locked the apartment, and the high speed elevator had him in the building's lobby minutes later.

The doorman opened the lobby doors for him and stood waiting to help Gottbaum into the cab. It was a bright spring day, and the wind brought the smells of grass and trees from the park across the street. Gottbaum switched his raincoat to his other arm, but dropped the manuscript.

"Damn," he swore and bent to retrieve it. As he did so, he noticed a well-dressed blond man watching him from across the street. At least he thought the man was watching him, though now he had turned and walked down the street. Most New Yorkers, with an inbred fear of potential muggings and street violence, have an instinct for this kind of personal contact. Gottbaum was no exception. The man's eyes had locked with his own, he was sure.

The doorman opened the door of the taxi when it arrived. As it moved down the street, Gottbaum turned back to his building. The man he had just seen was talking to the doorman. The cab turned the corner, and his view was cut off. After a moment Gottbaum dismissed it as the type of thing that happened a hundred times a day in New York.

The VIP Restaurant at the U.N. building was only half full when Gottbaum arrived. A maître d' escorted him to Knowles's table.

"It's good to see you again, Ted," said Gottbaum as he sat down opposite him in a leather-lined, cushioned booth. They shook hands warmly.

Knowles passed a folder across the table to Gottbaum. "This is what we put together," he said. "There was enough on Voorstein to write a book—if you'll excuse the expression. You can keep the material. I can add some personal notes if you like."

"Please do," said Gottbaum.

"Voorstein was brought into the U.N. by Jan Smuts, a South African Boer general turned politician who was the Prime Minister of the RSA during the war. Smuts was one of the people who helped found the U.N. in San Francisco in '45 and even drafted some of the preamble to our Charter. An interesting sidelight to that is that Smuts got so much shit about apartheid from the U.N. he had helped to set up, that it helped to remove him from power in the RSA and paved the way for a far more racist party to take over, the Nationalists, who still hold power over there.

"Anyway, Voorstein, who had no medical training, was one hell of an administrator and politician. He was a Member of Parliament in the RSA and decided to help reorganize the various international health organizations, like the League of Nations Health Organization and the Office International D'Hygiene Publique, and put it all together into one body under U.N. Charter."

"What does W.H.O. do exactly?" asked Gottbaum. Knowles took back the file and leafed through it.

"Their purpose is, and I quote, the attainment by all parties of the highest possible level of health. Which they define as, and I quote again, a state of complete physical, mental, and social well-being and not merely the absence of disease or infirmity," he read from the file.

"On a worldwide basis?"

"Absolutely. Their main headquarters are in Geneva, but it's a decentralized authority. It's too big and diverse to control from one spot. Regional headquarters are in New Delhi, for Southeast Asia; Alexandria, for the Mediterranean; Manila, for the Pacific; Washington, for the Americas; and Brazzaville, in the Congo, for Africa." Knowles put the folder down and continued to eat his lunch.

"There's very little press about them. Do they accomplish much?" asked Gottbaum. "I'm surprised I've heard almost nothing about them."

"You'd know all about it if you didn't live in a country like the U.S.," said Knowles. "They've all but wiped out smallpox and malaria, two well-known killers. They've built hospitals, trained doctors and nurses, introduced new vaccines and drugs all over the world, purified water supplies, and were leading a fight against air pollution years before it was fashionable. They've developed public health facilities in countries just emerging into the world community and have countless research stations all over the globe researching everything from trachoma to cancer. Do you want me to go on? You obviously pick up on the fact that we're very proud of the job they do. It offsets the criticism that we are a useless façade," said Knowles.

"Voorstein directed all that? He must have been quite a guy. Did you know him?"

"I met him at parties once or twice. He directed two or three of the regional centers before going to Geneva to run the whole show. He was a pleasant enough man. I did hear that his politics were ultra-conservative, but that's not all that unusual for the RSA bunch."

"I suppose not," agreed Gottbaum. A thought struck him. "Do members of the W.H.O. have diplomatic privileges?"

Knowles nodded. "They have immunity from personal arrest or seizure of their personal baggage, or a search of any kind. And they have immunity from legal process, as well. In short, they have the same rights, under the Charter, as officials of foreign governments."

"Couldn't that be used for some nefarious purpose?" asked Gottbaum. "Has there ever been any scandal?"

"You're thinking comic-book style, Bill. These people are dedicated. If you want to spy or smuggle drugs, there are lots of easier ways than wading through a swamp in Malaysia or immunizing natives in the Amazon region. It's true no law enforcement agency or government can touch them, but no one, to the best of my knowledge, has ever needed to.

"Oh, I almost forgot to mention," said Knowles. "If you want more on Voorstein, you might want to contact his son, who followed in his father's footsteps. His name is Piet Voorstein, Dr. Piet Voorstein. Got his M.D. somewhere in Europe. He's now the Regional Director for Africa of the W.H.O. Young man, too. Just like the father, sharp and strong, I've heard. Well, Bill, I think that wraps it up." Gottbaum signed the bill and smiled warmly. Knowles stood up to go.

"You've been great, Ted. I owe you one. I mean that sincerely," said Gottbaum.

"Glad to do it, Bill. Thanks for lunch," said Knowles.

Outside, the day was still sunny and mild. Gottbaum grabbed a taxi and headed back to the office when he remembered he had promised to water Ben's plants. He redirected the cabbie crosstown.

Gottbaum had the driver wait outside the restored brownstone on the west side where Ben lived. The landlady, a middle-aged eccentric named Mrs. Rose, who fancied herself an artist, knew him well and gave up the key to Ben's apartment without question.

Gottbaum went upstairs, opened the door, and stood in mute shock.

Ben's apartment looked like a tornado had swept through it. His first thought was that Ben had been the victim of thieves. But the objects of such an entry were untouched. The television stood safely on its stand. Silver and gold jewelry lay on the floor. Yet every drawer had been opened and its contents scattered around the room. Ben's file cabinets had been ransacked.

"Ben hasn't been robbed, he's been searched," Gottbaum realized, speaking aloud.

He locked the door to Ben's apartment, a gesture that now seemed futile, and returned the key to Mrs. Rose.

Instead of returning to his office, Gottbaum went home. Ben would be calling again tonight.

Fifteen

"The question is," Ben called out to Lisa who was still in the bathroom, "where can we get uncut diamonds? And in a large enough quantity to make it seem legitimate?"

Lisa stuck her head out. "I know a few of Van Dyne's jobbers. We can use one of them," she said.

"Jobbers?" asked Ben, getting off the bed and joining Lisa in the bathroom.

"The people at De Beers Central will not sell to just anyone, Ben. The jobbers buy uncut stones in large quantities called lots, and resell them to the various wholesalers like Van Dyne's exchange and Putten's," Lisa said.

"And then the wholesalers sell to retailers like jewelry stores," said Ben. "The markup on gemstones must be incredible."

"Several thousand per cent, from mine to showcase," said Lisa. "Hauptman is getting tremendous profits from moving his diamonds directly through Putten. It's a direct sale, skipping all the middlemen."

"If we're correct in our assumptions," reminded Ben. "The only problem is that we're almost out of money." He made a mental note to have Gottbaum wire funds.

"That's no problem at all, Ben," Lisa said, smiling without guile, "I'm very rich."

"We've got to put more pressure on the situation," said Leander. He was deeply tired—the effects of jet hopping from Amsterdam to South Africa and, finally, back to Amsterdam on Smith's "orders." Dreyer nodded absently.

"You're the Director."

"But you're unhappy," prompted Leander.

"I'm unhappy because you've got some plan that you're setting up, and I don't know what it is. We've run constant surveillance on Lisa Smith and Ben Davidson, and we've even bugged their hotel. You're running around two continents playing a game I'm not privy to. Now you can do that because you're the Director, but don't ask me to be happy about it, Jan," said Dreyer angrily.

Leander thought for a moment. They were alone in the hotel room. Gerroff was with Lisa and Ben; Pilsten on an errand. The rest of the team rested at the embassy, awaiting orders.

"We've been friends for a long time, Peter. Perhaps I owe you an explanation," said Leander.

"You don't owe me anything, Jan. Friendship isn't lend-lease," said Dreyer flatly.

"You're bitter," said Leander mildly. "And I don't blame you. But for the sake of that long friendship, and the things we've shared, let me tell you a story. After I'm done, if you want out of this, I'll release you. You can go back to South Africa. No questions asked. No hard feelings. Deal?"

Dreyer nodded, "Deal."

"Well, then," began Leander. "It concerns a twelve-year-old German boy, visiting his relatives in Berlin..."

Dreyer listened, and his expression changed from disbelief to compassion to outrage as the story unfolded. When Leander was done, Dreyer shook his head several times.

"All these years," he whispered. "All these years I never knew. How could you keep it in so long? I always wondered what drove you so; why you never married. I'm sorry, Jan. I understand now."

"Then you understand how important this is to me. I'm going to find Bormann—if he's still alive. I think he is. The way to do it is through Smith. That's why we use Lisa," said Leander.

In a few sentences Leander told him about Stangl and the meeting with Smith.

"Then you want to drive a wedge between Bormann and Smith," said Dreyer, understanding. "You cast blame on an unknown, Stangl, indirectly, and hoped Smith would see Bormann behind it."

"Exactly. Smith is jumpy as hell and ordered me to protect Lisa at all costs. I think he's going against the group in doing so," said Leander. "It's too dangerous a move to be their idea."

"It's also too dangerous a move to leave you alive afterward, Jan. You must know that."

"I do, Peter. But apart from personal reasons, there is something going on, and we've got to know what it is. I've spent my entire adult life in service to my adopted country. Paying it back, in a way. I won't sit back and see it placed in jeopardy. Regardless of the personal costs, we have a job to do," Leander said.

"I agree, Jan," said Dreyer. "Let's do the job."

The receptionist did not remember Ben from the previous day.

"Would you tell Herr Putten that Mr. and Mrs. Schmidt, friends of Herr Hauptman's, are here to see him?" he asked.

The girl spoke into her phone briefly. After a wait of only a few minutes, she said, "Herr Putten will see you, Mr. Schmidt."

Putten remained seated behind his desk as his secretary ushered Ben and Lisa in and made no move to shake hands.

"You are friends of Herr Hauptman?" Putten asked. There was no warmth in his voice. "What can I do for you?"

Ben laid the Adlerkinden card on Putten's desk. "You understand the meaning of this?" he asked, more statement than question.

"I do," said Putten. "I hadn't expected anyone so soon, though."

So far, so good. Ben nodded to Lisa to proceed.

Lisa reached into her handbag and brought out a suede pouch containing the diamonds she had purchased earlier: fifteen carats of uncut stones. She placed it on Putten's desk.

"Then you know what to do with these," she said flatly.

"Do you think I'm some kind of idiot?" exploded Putten. "You want these converted to cash," he said angrily. "Fine! I'll do it. But don't ask me stupid questions and add insult to injury. Hauptman explained it all. I know what to do, damn you."

"Lower your voice, Herr Putten," said Ben icily. "Do you want us to report your outburst to Herr Hauptman?" He was ad-libbing, guessing from Putten's outburst that he was not a willing participant in this scheme.

Putten grew anxious. "No," he said in a softer, cowed tone. "You don't have to do that."

"I am sure that Herr Putten has control over himself," said Lisa, picking up on Ben's intent.

"I agree," Ben said to her. He turned back to Putten. "Review your instructions, Herr Putten. Now."

"I don't..." protested Putten, but Ben cut him off.

"What kind of game is this?" Ben demanded. "You said you were tired of being treated like a fool. Do you think our patience is infinite? We are leaving. Hauptman will not be pleased."

Ben let his threat hang in the air.

"Wait. Please," said Putten nervously. "I'm sorry. It's just that I'm new to this."

"Review your instructions," said Lisa. Her tone matched Ben's.

"I'm to convert these to cash and send the money to Pierre Martisse, of Martisse et Fils, in Paris. Within thirty days to account #5336-17. All right? I said I would cooperate. There's no need to be angry."

"Very well, then. See that you do," Ben said, and he took the Adlerkinden card from Putten's desk. He and Lisa walked to the door.

"Good day, then, Herr Putten."

When they had gone, Putten picked up his phone and dialed a local number that Hauptman had given him. After the connection was made, he heard the hiss of a tape recorder.

"Report on the tone," said a prerecorded message. With the new answering machines, the recorded message could be received from any place in the world simply by calling the number and activating an electronic beeper. Putten would never know who collected his report from the device. The "record" tone sounded.

"The man and woman were here. They brought diamonds for conversion," he said. "I did what was requested."

Gottbaum spent the rest of the day staring absently at the television, not focusing on the picture or hearing the sound.

It had taken him only a few minutes after he'd gotten home to realize that Ben was not the only victim of a search. The file that Ben had given him on Croft was gone.

He had no doubt that whoever had searched his apartment was connected somehow to Ben. He had gotten his old Army .45 from a shoebox in the bottom of his closet, cleaned and loaded it, and sat with it on his lap like some criminal spinster with deadly knitting. He had resolved to put it back in the closet when the phone rang.

"Hello?" he said sharply.

"Bill? This is Ben."

"Where the hell have you been?" snapped Gottbaum, tension plain in his voice.

"What are you talking about?" asked Ben, confused on the other end. "I said I'd call you around now. Did you find anything useful?"

"Look, Ben. I've got to talk to you, and I want it to be in person. Both our places have been searched, and the Croft file's gone. I'm coming over. My mind is made up," he said in a rush.

There was a long moment of silence from Ben's end.

"Fly to Paris," he said at last.

"Where can I meet you?" asked Gottbaum.

"You remember Norm's book? The one we talked about that time we all met for dinner? I'll meet you there," said Ben's disembodied voice.

Gottbaum thought for a moment.

"I understand, I'll be on the morning Concorde. Take care of yourself, Ben."

Gottbaum hung up. Norm was a friend of theirs who had written a book called *The Napoleon Consideration*. Ben had to mean he would meet him at the Tomb of Napoleon in Paris.

Gottbaum packed a suitcase and double-checked his door locks before going to sleep with the gun wisely back in the shoebox. But he slept fitfully, tossing and turning until morning.

Sixteen

Ben handed their suitcases to a porter at the departures terminal. There had been no problem getting seats, and the flight to Paris left in half an hour.

Lisa shrugged off her coat, the terminal warm after the chill of the morning air. They joined the line of people waiting for their boarding passes.

The terminal was crowded. Car-rental kiosks were doing a booming business, and the public address loudspeakers were incessantly calling out departure information and paging traveler after traveler. Porters hustled baggage-laden carts around the floor at breakneck speeds.

Lisa stood in front of Ben on line. He watched her blond hair lift lazily on the nape of her neck, stirred by some air current. He gently intertwined his fingers in her hair, and she inclined her shoulders to keep his hand there as the line continued to surge forward.

A man standing on the next line saw their play and gave Ben a friendly smile. He pushed his suitcase forward with his foot as his line moved. Ben made no response and started to turn away when the unmistakable sound of a gunshot rang out, distinct over the busy noises of the terminal.

The man who had made the signal clutched at his shoulder, whirled around, and fell to the ground.

In one movement Ben flung Lisa to the ground. A second shot rang out, and pandemonium burst through the crowded terminal. People dropped to the floor, putting their suitcases over their heads. Some ran for cover behind the counters.

There was a spreading pool of blood under the fallen man.

The big terminal grew quieter. A few people were crying in fear, and some were cursing. Armed guards were everywhere, eyes alert and watchful.

One guard called out to the crowd in English.

"Please stay where you are! The terminal is secure. Stay just where you are until we tell you it is safe to rise."

He repeated the message in Dutch and French. Another guard called it out in German. Someone helped the man who had been shot to his feet. Ben watched them disappear and heard the wail of an ambulance siren in the distance. Guards still ran frantically throughout the terminal.

A half hour later, the guard announced that all was safe and boarding could continue. By now reporters had arrived. Questions flew at the "eyewitnesses."

Ben moved off Lisa. He realized he was shaking. She rose unsteadily to her feet.

"That was for us," she whispered, her face frozen.

Ben took her arm and spoke softly into her ear. "I think so. But we're okay. Don't blow up. I don't want the police to notice us or ask questions."

Lisa regained control. The lines began to re-form. Ben heard nervous laughter from many in the crowd.

At the desk he got their tickets, and they walked to the boarding gate. Once through the metal detectors and security gates, Ben felt safer. Television cameras and crews had already invaded the terminal. The word "terrorists" was on everybody's lips.

The airport security guards helped the wounded man into an ambulance along with the man who had helped carry him from the terminal.

A Dutch police lieutenant ran over to ride in the ambulance and take a statement from the man who'd been shot. He was surprised at the diplomatic papers that were shoved in his face.

"This is out of your jurisdiction, Lieutenant," the man said in sharp tones.

"Yes, sir," said the lieutenant, forced to step back as the ambulance doors slammed in his face.

"Goddamned diplomatic bullshit," he swore angrily.

In the van, Dreyer helped Gerroff off with his blood-soaked coat.

"The stage lost a great one when I went into the spy business," said Gerroff smugly.

"A bloody ham, that's what you are," called Pilsten from the driver's seat.

Gerroff was pulling off the apparatus that lay under his coat. Wired to a small battery in his pocket, the device was a leather-strapped harness holding two small charges of powder over a bag of red fluid—in this case, blood from the embassy's infirmary. When Gerroff had triggered the device, the charges exploded, the force going through the cloth jacket. His body was protected by the thick leather.

"It went perfectly," Dreyer praised Gerroff. "I watched Davidson, and I'm sure he thought it was meant for him and the girl."

The ambulance drove to an airfield a few miles north of Schiphol Airport. A fueled and ready Gulfstream II stood waiting with Leander at the entrance hatch.

"From the blood all over you, I expect it went well. Clean up in the plane's washroom, Gerroff. We'll be leaving in a minute," he said.

"It should make the media news by tonight. The TV crews were just getting in as we left," Dreyer said.

"Fine. I'll be in shortly. Send that cable to Smith right away."

Leander signaled to the pilot to begin his preflight check. He looked at Pilsten, still dressed in hospital whites.

"You've done a good job, son. And Peter speaks highly of you. I'm very pleased," Leander said.

Pilsten flushed with embarrassed pride. "Thank you, sir."

"You'll return the ambulance?" Leander asked.

"Yes, sir. First thing, sir."

Leander smiled, paternalistic at Pilsten's enthusiasm.

"How long since you've been home, son?" he asked.

"Over a year, sir. On my last leave."

"That's too long. You'll be home again in two weeks," Leander said benignly.

"Sir?" said Pilsten, confused.

"We can't very well train you long distance. Can we, son?"

The implications suddenly hit Pilsten.

"No, sir!" he said smartly.

Leander took the hatch door in one hand and began to pull it closed.

"Take care, sir," said Pilsten abruptly, emotion overwhelming him.

"Why thank you, son," said Leander mildly. The hatch door closed as the jet engines roared into life.

In Pretoria Smith read Leander's cable for the third time. Each time his fury grew till it threatened to burst into violence. He looked at the cable again.

L.S. ATTACKED SCHIPHOL AIRPORT/SHOTS FIRED/
NO DAMAGE/NO DAMAGE/COVER REESTABLISHED
                                                                    L.

This had to be Bormann's handiwork, thought Smith. No one else could be behind this. He had warned Bormann, and still he persisted. The man was insane to think he could oppose him.

Smith began to wonder if the Project could do without Bormann. The notion pleased him.

He decided a showdown was at hand. Bormann would have to be deposed once and for all. He could no longer be left to act with impunity. Smith was sure the other Afrikaners would side with him.

Smith called a secretary in and began to dictate the coded cables that would assemble the Adlerkinden—some of them, he figured, for the final time.

Ben went to check the Concorde's arrival time while Lisa rented a car. She met him at the arrivals desk with keys in her hand.

"The Concorde got in an hour ago, Lisa. Bill will be waiting."

"The car is in the lot. A blue Renault," she said.

The main highway led straight into the city from the airport. Lisa spread a street map the car-rental desk had given her and called out directions to the Tomb of Napoleon.

"It's such a beautiful city," said Lisa. Parisians walked the streets carrying wine and loaves of bread; she remembered the French word for them: *baguettes*. Thin girls with long hair dressed in high fashion, and men in tapered suits, trim and lean, seemed to be everywhere.

"It is," agreed Ben. "I only wish we could enjoy it."

The memory of the airport attack was still with him, and he drove carefully, looking constantly in his rearview mirror.

The old buildings sparkled white in the sun. Ben saw the gleam of brass plaques that recorded the deaths of Frenchmen during the Nazi occupation. Somehow, here, and all through Europe, the Nazis were more real than in the States. Europe had not forgotten the Nazis as easily as America, three thousand miles away, her soil untouched by the brutality of invasion, the remembrance of rape.

"I love this city," said Lisa. "I wish we could just wander through it together, Ben. I'd buy you crepes from sidewalk vendors, and we could sit and watch people pass by, and drink wine in the cafés. Wouldn't that be nice?"

A wistful tone had crept into her voice. She was tired of

the running and danger. They had put it far away for a time in Amsterdam. Until the airport.

"Oh, Ben," Lisa sighed. "We could go to the Designer Houses, and I could try on new dresses while you watched. We could go on a shopping spree, my darling, that would break the bank. We could eat in Maxim's and go night boating on the Seine. And you could love me every morning and every night. We could go to the opera and be so sophisticated." Lisa's voice turned high and nasal, and he laughed along with her. It was good to hear her laugh.

"I hate opera," Ben objected.

"Then we could go to Pigalle and be truly decadent," Lisa said, her voice low and throaty. She put her hand in Ben's lap.

"Now you've got me," he grinned. "I'm a sucker for decadent."

Lisa kissed him and consulted the map again.

"Make the next left," she said.

The top of the church dome that stood over Napoleon's Tomb emerged from beyond the stone wall that ran parallel to the Avenue Tourville. A high courtyard lay before the entrance to the Tomb, and hundreds of tourists stood around photographing the old, imposing structure. Ben scanned the crowd but didn't see Gottbaum.

"I'll go look for him. Wait with the car."

The courtyard sounded like it had been invaded by crickets with the constant sound of camera shutters opening and closing. Ben heard Gottbaum before he saw him.

"Now you move to the left. No, the left! That's right. Now you move down a little. No, not you. You!"

Ben walked around the corner just in time to see Gottbaum taking the picture of a Japanese family, all beaming. The father bowed gratefully to Gottbaum who handed back the camera.

"*Arigato*," said the father.

"You're quite welcome," said Gottbaum.

Ben put his hand on Gottbaum's shoulder. "Setting up a new business?"

Gottbaum turned so quickly that Ben threw up his hands in self-defense.

"Easy, Bill," he said, stepping back.

"Ben!" There was relief in Gottbaum's voice. "You scared the hell out of me."

"I'm glad to see you, Bill." It felt so good, in fact, to see his friend that Ben threw his arms around Gottbaum and hugged him. The hug was warmly returned.

"You've got a car?" Gottbaum asked when they broke apart.

"Lisa's in it waiting."

Ben was too glad to see Gottbaum to bring him up to date on recent events. He introduced Lisa, who climbed into the back seat with his friend as Ben drove to the Paris Sheraton. He felt safer in a large hotel, where they could rely on hotel security as a first line of defense.

Lisa's frequent laughter and Gottbaum's jovial tones indicated that the two had begun a good relationship. Ben was pleased. It was important to him that they like each other. It would be a kind of parental blessing, he realized.

At the hotel, Lisa took Gottbaum's arm, their conversation continuing.

"Why don't you get a table in the restaurant. I'll check us in," Ben said.

"Given as how I am totally captivated by this young lady, I accept," said Gottbaum.

Lisa let go of Gottbaum long enough to kiss Ben and whisper in his ear, "I like him, Ben. It's like finding another part of you."

Ben asked for adjoining rooms as he checked in, had their bags sent up, and went to find Lisa and Gottbaum in the restaurant. They were already seated, and a bottle of wine was open on the table.

"You don't deserve her," said Gottbaum flatly.

"It's her money I'm after," Ben retorted.

"You can have it all, my love," said Lisa, squeezing Ben's hand. Gottbaum watched them, warmly amused.

"I've never seen you look like this, Ben. It's good."

"I've never felt like this. Something happened inside me that I still don't understand. But I never want to go back to the way I was. You, of all people, should understand that."

"I do," said Gottbaum. "Now I think it's time to fill me in. From the beginning."

*　　*　　*

"... So the next step is to find out where Martisse sends the money. Sooner or later we've got to come across a pattern that we can trace to the source. We think we know who is involved, Bill; but we're still as far as ever from knowing why," Ben said.

"Diamonds from South Africa turned into cash in Amsterdam that flows to Paris. And you came across one recipient in Mississippi. You're sure Croft and Stumpfegger are the same man?" Gottbaum asked, "And that the Nazi factor is real?"

"Absolutely," confirmed Ben. Something Lisa had said in the past days nagged at him, but he couldn't bring it to the surface.

"Can you make any sense out of it?" asked Lisa.

"No, not yet," said Gottbaum. "It's like a puzzle I think I should know the answer to but don't. It's frustrating."

"For us, too," Lisa agreed. "Even more so when you remember that these men are from my country."

"How do you intend to approach Martisse?"

"We haven't discussed it yet," said Ben. "You have some thoughts you'd like to share?" He was nagged again by some thought trying to emerge, but still it escaped him.

"I don't relish the idea of playing cops and robbers. We haven't the resources or expertise," Gottbaum said.

"I agree," said Lisa. "It's too easy to out-trick ourselves. Whatever we do, it's got to be simple."

"One phone call should suffice," continued Gottbaum. "Call him and say that you've got a deposit for the account that's too large to bring in. If he tells you to go to hell and that he has no idea what you're talking about, we can assume he's just a banker and only involved on that level. If, on the other hand, he doesn't balk at the request, he knows the nature of the account. A French banker consorting with Nazis should be pretty vulnerable, if that's the case."

"It might work, Bill. It's certainly worth a try. Are we all agreed then?" asked Ben. Both nodded assent.

"Then I'll do it now," he said and left to find a phone.

"Do you think this will work, Bill?" Lisa asked a frowning Gottbaum.

"I'm an agent; Ben's a writer; and you're a reformed jet-setter. And you ask me if it'll work? I'll tell you honestly, Lisa. I haven't got the slightest fucking idea."

Gottbaum's expression was so honestly hapless that Lisa

tried to hide her worry in silence. But Gottbaum noticed it and took her hand.

"He's tougher than you think, Lisa. Tougher even than he knows. I don't think these people realize what they've taken on. You saw him at the brothel when he came for you. I've seen him fight all his life. Any fool can shoot a gun. He's tough where it counts. In the guts. Believe in him, Lisa. If anybody can do this, it's Ben."

Tears came to Lisa's eyes. "I believe in him, Bill. So much that it hurts. But I want us to be safe."

Gottbaum put an arm around her. "Ben wants it, too. That's why he won't stop, Lisa. I know him. He won't stop till you're both safe. Now, no tears. He's coming back."

Ben sat back down at the table. Lisa looked at him expectantly.

"I called Martisse," he said. "He'll meet us at an inn north of Paris called Le Jardin at seven tonight. He knew exactly what account #5336-17 was all about."

Seventeen

Ben tossed his shirt on the bed angrily. Lisa stood glaring at him from the other side of the hotel room.

"It's not protective bullshit," he said hotly.

"Then what the hell do you call it?" she demanded.

"I can move more freely if I don't have to worry about you."

"Worry about yourself, you conceited son-of-a-bitch," she yelled. "I'll take care of myself. I have just as much a stake in this as you do."

Ben was exasperated. "It has nothing to do with that, and you know it. I'm trained and you're not. It's just that simple."

"That's crap too," said Lisa, equally as exasperated. "Your training won't stop a bullet any more than mine."

"You're acting like a spoiled brat," Ben dug at her.

"Brilliant debating technique," Lisa said sarcastically. "It surely addresses the issue to call me names."

Ben bit back further remarks.

"You're right. That's unfair," he sighed. "It's just that I'm frightened for you."

"Then why can't I feel that, too?" she demanded. "How could I sit here and let you go, knowing you might not come back? I won't do that, Ben. Whatever we face, we face together. I don't want to be protected. I want to be with you. Can't you see that?"

Unfortunately, he did. And he had to accept it.

He engulfed her smaller body with his own. Regardless of risk, they would go together or not at all.

"It's almost time, then," he whispered, not wanting to let go. Lisa turned her face up and kissed him deeply. Then Gottbaum knocked on the door, and they had to disentangle themselves.

Gottbaum was dressed in faded corduroys and an old tweed jacket. "I'm ready," he said.

Knowing that to object would only repeat the argument he had just lost to Lisa, Ben gave in. He felt a fierce pride in the loyalty that existed between them—though a small voice, the voice of the Vietnam-hardened soldier, warned of recklessness and bid him beware. He ignored the voice. They would refuse to understand it. He shrugged a sweater on over his shirt and jeans, put on a jacket, and locked the door behind them.

Le Jardin was located in Contres, a town about thirty miles north of Paris. Only Lisa had been close-by—in Chantilly for the racing season. She had described the region's endless forests and fields and the towns she had visited with their white houses, colored roofs, and cobblestone streets.

She directed them through the streets of Paris. Lights were going on all over the city as darkness set in. They found the main road, N16, and Ben accelerated smoothly.

Headlights from cars going south to Paris on the other side of the road flashed by. Ben was silent as he drove, wondering if that was not the wiser direction. The darkness insulated them, and for a while, no one spoke, each absorbed in private thoughts as they sped down the long highway.

"How much longer?" said an almost forgotten presence from the back seat breaking the silence.

"Fifteen minutes, Bill," Lisa said.

"I had lunch with Ted Knowles," Gottbaum said, "a friend at the UN."

He repeated Knowles's information on Voorstein almost word for word. "His son is a doctor and still with the W.H.O."

"I forgot he had a son," Lisa exclaimed. "He was always away at school or living with his father out of the country."

"We'll talk about it later," said Ben as he saw a road sign for Chantilly and took the exit ramp. The tree-lined, local road was narrower and unlit, and they passed no other cars. A few miles further a sign proclaimed that they had entered the village of Contres.

"Bienvenue," read Lisa out loud.

The inn looked like a converted barn. Two stories high, it was made mostly of wood. Its peaked roof was slate-covered, and ivy grew up the walls. Potted shrubs were set against the inn next to the small portico that covered the entrance.

"He who hesitates . . ." said Ben, and he gestured for them to follow.

Henry Gerroff turned off his car's engine a quarter of a mile away from the driveway he saw Ben turn in at. His eyes were tired from the strain of driving without lights. A hundred yards from the entrance he pulled off the road and continued on foot.

The lights of the inn showed Ben's car parked in the lot, and he caught a glimpse of Lisa as she entered the doorway. Gerroff relaxed. He unzipped his light jacket and took out a radio. Leander and Dreyer were only a few miles back.

"They've stopped at Le Jardin Inn. Under surveillance. Will report. Over."

"Roger, Unit Two."

Gerroff turned the radio off and put it back in his jacket.

Avoiding the open parking lot, he crept through the bushes on the other side of the inn. He moved low to the ground on a soft carpet of moist, mossy earth.

Inside, he could see the three seated at a table. They were alone. Something struck him as odd, though he couldn't quite put his finger on what. The night was still and quiet, and only an occasional breeze stirred the foliage around him. He let his eyes roam around the inn trying to discover the cause of his sudden ill feelings. There they are, he said to himself.

The girl and the two men. There was no one else inside but a maître d'. No one at the bar. No others at tables.

The nagging feeling suddenly burst into full realization. No local inn in France had a total absence of patrons any night of the week.

He reached for his radio with fingers stiff with anxiety.

"Do not move," said a steady voice behind him as a gun barrel was jammed into his back. Gerroff tensed his cramped muscles, preparing to leap, but the world disintegrated into fragments as something crashed into his head, bringing a darkness deeper even than the night's.

Inside, Ben watched the unsmiling, elderly maître d' go behind the bar to fetch a bottle of wine. The interior of Le Jardin was old and rustic-looking, with barn-sided walls and plants hung from the rafters.

"They're certainly not doing a booming business," commented Gottbaum. "I wonder where everybody is?"

"It is odd. People should be congregating here," agreed Lisa.

The maître d' returned with the wine and began to open it. He made an attempt at smiling, but it lay on his face like a cheap mask.

"Where are the other guests?" Ben asked in French. The maître d' had poured too much, almost filling the glass.

"C'est trop tôt, monsieur," said the maître d'. Ben looked at the old man. Too early for guests? he said to himself. Unlikely in France.

The maître d' poured for Lisa and Gottbaum and walked quickly away.

"Our maître d' seems jumpy," Lisa observed.

"Sure does," Ben said, his misgivings growing.

"You'll have to excuse me but nature calls. A long ride and a glass of wine don't mix at my age," said Gottbaum. He walked off to find the men's room.

"What time is it? Martisse must be late," said Lisa.

Ben looked at his watch. The sweep second hand crept around the dial.

"Seven-thirty," he said. His doubt was stronger now, more insistent. He leaned closer to Lisa.

"As soon as Bill gets back, we're going. Too many things here don't feel right."

"For instance?" queried Lisa.

"No customers, a nervous maître d', and no Martisse." A new thought struck. "Lisa, we haven't even seen a waiter. I think the four of us are the only ones here. Get ready to go."

Lisa draped her coat over her shoulders. She scanned the room nervously, waiting for Gottbaum to return, willing him to hurry.

In the men's room, off the kitchen hallway, Gottbaum zipped up his fly and washed his hands at the porcelain sink. He studied his face in the mirror.

"C'mon, old man," he said ruefully to his reflection, "let's join the children."

He passed the kitchen, where the double doors were closed, and heard low voices coming from inside. Curious, he pushed the door open a crack and peered in—and froze.

On the floor was a dead or unconscious man. He saw another man who had a gun. Terror caught him. It was the blond man from New York! He realized instantly that there would be no Martisse and that they had walked into a trap as willingly as naïve, trusting infants. He eased the door shut.

His first impulse was to race into the main room, but he stopped himself. Cautiously, he peered around the corner. Ben and Lisa were still sitting at the table. The maître d' had his face buried in his hands. Ben's face was icy and rigid, and Lisa's held fear. A very large, brutish-looking man stood menacingly over them with a gun.

Conscious that the blond man might emerge from the kitchen behind him at any moment, and conscious of the gunman ahead of him, Gottbaum looked around for a place to hide. There was none.

He contemplated a mad rush at the gunman. He would surely die, but Ben and Lisa might escape. His life for theirs. It made the only sense he could find. His breathing quickened as he prepared himself. Forgotten shards of boyhood prayers raced through his mind. Now was the time. Now or never.

"Don't do it, Mr. Gottbaum. Rios would kill you before you got ten feet into the room," said a voice behind him.

Gottbaum deflated like a punctured balloon. The blond man, gun pointing, stood in the kitchen doorway. His chance was over. He went mutely as the blond man motioned him to enter the room. A third man dragged the body out from the kitchen.

Ben's head jerked up as they walked in. The hope in his eyes died. Gottbaum sat down at the table, feeling a thousand years old.

"Put him over here, Garver," said the blond man, and Garver dragged the body over. He stood opposite Rios and drew his gun.

"How nice to see you again," the blond man said. "My name is Heinz Stangl, and I'm sure we have all been in each other's thoughts quite a lot lately."

Ben stiffened at the name. "Is that man dead?" he asked in an even tone.

"Dead? No, Mr. Davidson. He's only out for a short while. We don't want him to be dead," Stangl said. He was enjoying himself. Three other men came into the inn, thugs like Rios and Garver, Ben saw.

"Wait by the road. They should be here soon. I want them alive, if possible," Stangl ordered.

The men left obediently.

"Who is this man?" Ben asked Stangl.

"You don't know?" Stangl laughed. It was an unpleasant sound.

"I've never seen him before," Lisa said, speaking for the first time.

"That's because he is very good at what he does, I think," said Stangl. "Though my men outside are better. This is one of the men who has followed you since you left South Africa, Miss Smith. And you, Mr. Davidson, since you joined Miss Smith in Amsterdam."

"I don't understand. What are you talking about?" Lisa said.

Stangl spoke distinctly, hammering home each word. "You were programmed, Miss Smith. You were sent to us under the pretext of your parents' death. To see what would happen. You were bait to catch us, the Adlerkinden you know so little about. This is one of the men who sent you. The people he works for are the ones I want. The three of you mean nothing at all."

Ben heard the words. If it were true, it was a bitter truth. Pawns in some game they only barely understood. Stangl had no reason to lie. It was unnecessary to lie to dead people.

"We saw no one," Ben said wearily.

"Do you think it's difficult to follow such amateurs as yourselves? In this day and age? They did it as easily as you would drive a car. You never saw them. You would never see them. They used you to get at me. I used you to get at them. You're less than bait. You're nothing at all," Stangl said.

"What is this place?" asked Ben.

"It's an inn, I assure you. It just happens to be owned by the man you called today. It is most unfortunate we had to get Monsieur Viant here out of bed during the inn's closed season. We have been waiting for you, Mr. Davidson, since Amsterdam. Putten was directed to bring you to Martisse. Martisse brought you here," Stangl said.

Ben found the man's politeness infuriating. But more than that, he cursed himself for having been such a fool. He had played into their hands; walked right into their trap from the very beginning.

"Why did you bring me to that brothel?" Lisa's voice was hollow, defeated.

"To bring out those who sent you, to a place I could get at them." A note of anger crept into Stangl's tone. "It would have worked if not for your intervention, Mr. Davidson. It was only pure luck that you succeeded."

He's like a spoiled child, Ben realized; angry at me for messing up his toys. He still wants to prove that he can beat me.

Out of the corner of his eye, Ben saw a tiny flicker of movement from the man on the floor. So tiny, he was unsure at first if he had moved at all. Time, Ben thought desperately; more time.

"Then you don't know who you're after yet. Do you?" he said.

"Not yet, Mr. Davidson. But soon. When his friends arrive, we'll know. And then we'll end it. You should feel quite proud of the work you've done for us," Stangl taunted again.

Silence hung over the room. Fear drove Ben's mind to greater intensity. Stangl looked at his watch.

"Rios, take charge of the others outside. I want it done right."

Rios nodded and left. New odds, thought Ben. If the man on the floor would only wake up. Another tiny movement caught Ben's attention.

"What about the rest of us?" asked Gottbaum. Lines had etched themselves deeper in his face, and his eyes were sunken.

"With the exception of Miss Smith, who is needed to control her powerful and annoying father, you all die," Stangl said simply.

Ben needed to communicate to the man on the floor. He could handle the guard who stood near him, but the man on the floor would have to take Stangl. Gottbaum was too old and too far away.

"I don't like you, Stangl," Ben said, scorn in his voice. "But even more than you, I don't like this moron of a guard. Do you understand? I'd like to cut off his right hand and shove it up your ass. You hear me?"

Ben looked straight across the table at Stangl.

"You're raving," Stangl said happily. "That's good. I hope you are very frightened."

But Ben saw a slight movement of the right hand of the man on the floor. He knows, Ben thought. Could he count on Gottbaum to react also?

"And you, you stupid old man," Ben yelled at Gottbaum. "I told you to take care of Lisa. And you blew it. You blew it! I'd like to kill you myself."

Gottbaum's head snapped up like he'd been slapped.

"Ben!" Lisa said. "How could you?"

"Shut up," Ben said. "I'm sick of the whole thing."

Lisa looked shocked, and Stangl was pleased. Davidson was falling apart. He thought of Mrs. Stoelin, how she had cheated him at the final moment. Davidson would make up for it.

"I'd like to forget I ever met you," Ben spat at Lisa.

Garver moved closer to him, enjoying his discomfort.

"Stop, Ben. Please stop," Lisa pleaded.

Ben yelled, "I'd like to...", and the man on the floor exploded into movement. Rolling sideways, he caught Stangl in back of his knees with his legs. Stangl went down in a heap. Garver was distracted by Stangl's fall, and Ben got the split second he needed to launch himself from his chair. There was nothing but white hot burning rage in his mind as he threw himself at the guard.

Gottbaum yanked Lisa out of her chair and pulled her under the table. Ben struck at Garver's gun hand with all his strength. But Garver was fast. The gun came up and fired again and again as Ben smashed down with the edge of his hand. One blast caught the maître d' in the head and threw him over backward, crashing into another table. Ben struck again, and the gun went flying; but Garver grabbed at Ben's face and clawed at his eyes. Blinded, Ben struck out at Garver's neck with stiffened fingers. Garver turned and Ben landed only a glancing blow. But it was enough to cause Garver to release him.

Stangl and the other man were locked together, each straining for an advantage. The man had Stangl's gun hand locked in his own as Stangl tried to gain leverage to shoot. Ben could offer no help.

"Get Lisa out of here!" Ben yelled to Gottbaum.

Garver had backed up, wary. Time was on Garver's side. If the others came back, Ben knew he was finished. He launched a kick to Garver's groin to bring his hands down. It worked, and Ben threw the same foot higher, around Garver's hands, and landed a smashing kick to Garver's chest. It drove the breath from him. Ben moved in to kick again, but Garver, faster than anyone Ben had ever fought, caught the foot and yanked upward. Ben lost his balance and tumbled backward, his head smashing into the floor. Lights danced behind his eyes.

Garver was on him in an instant with his hands around Ben's throat. Ben couldn't breathe. Sounds grew distant. He heard a shot. No, two shots. They seemed so far away.

Gottbaum reached down and touched the pool of his own blood. He had just pushed Lisa out from under the table when the bullet ripped into him, and his legs had stopped working. Above, his friends fought on without him. Such a waste, he thought distractedly, to die like this. He wanted to talk to Ben; to say good-bye, absolve him. But he had no voice, and even the light was leaving....

In a last desperate effort, Ben brought both his legs up in a scissors movement and grabbed Garver's head between his calves. He threw all his weight down into his legs, and suddenly, he could breathe again as Garver somersaulted backward. Ben was groggy. Garver wouldn't be stopped for long. He tried to struggle to his feet.

But Garver had found his gun. Ben gathered himself to jump. He saw the gun come up and aim at him. Garver's red and panting face loomed behind it. Ben's mind screamed for action, but his body would not obey.

"I'll shoot," Lisa screamed. "Drop that. I swear I'll shoot!"

Ben turned. Lisa held Stangl's gun on Garver. But his legs couldn't hold him. He sank to the floor. Lisa seemed to be calling from a long distance away.

"Ben? Get up. Please, get up. We've got to get out of here. Please, Ben," she pleaded.

Ben looked around. Gottbaum was under the table, his lifeless eyes stared back at him. Pain lanced through him. "Nooo!" a moan passed his lips.

"Ben! Get up. Please, Ben."

Slowly, his head cleared. He was in the middle of a Mexican stand-off. Lisa on one side, Garver on the other. He dragged himself up. The man who had fought Stangl had a streaming hole in his chest.

Stangl was on the floor, clutching at a wound in his side.

Ben pointed dumbly to Stangl. It's so hard to stand, he thought. Maybe I should sleep.

"No time, Ben," yelled Lisa. "Come on. I shot Stangl. I picked his gun up while they were fighting. Please, Ben. How much longer can we stay like this? Get up, damn you!"

Ben wasn't sure. Sleep called again. His mind cleared, only to wander again. He looked at Stangl, holding his side.

"Please, Ben. I need help," Lisa begged. Her arm shook with the effort of holding the gun.

"Put it down," said Garver.

"Bitch!" Stangl swore. His body was wracked by a coughing fit. "You filthy bitch," he hissed. "I'm dying. You did this, bitch." He tried to reach Lisa but couldn't.

"Ben, please!" Lisa cried.

"Put the gun down," said Garver gently. "You can go if you want. Just put it down."

"No . . ." Ben protested. Lisa couldn't put the gun down. He would die if she did, Ben realized, as his mind cleared for a few seconds.

"You can't . . ." he managed.

"Get up, Ben. You can. Please, just get up."

"I should have killed you, too," Stangl hissed, blood soaking his shirt. "I should have killed you, too. Long ago. I should have . . ."

Lisa's attention wavered from Garver to Stangl.

"Lisa . . ." he yelled. He fought to stand. His body felt disconnected. Lisa swung the gun back, and Garver stopped moving.

"I killed your parents, bitch. Whore! I killed them," Stangl laughed, and red bubbles broke from the wound. "I killed them that fine spring day. Smith knew. Van Dyne knew. He helped . . ." The laugh again, shrill and frightening.

"Put it down," prompted Garver again.

Ben looked at Lisa's face. She was white, pale white, her eyes wide and ghostly.

"Lisa?" Ben said. He got to his knees. His head swam, and blood trickled down his neck. From down a long tunnel that seemed to be closing, Ben saw Lisa turn her gun on Stangl. The tunnel around him grew smaller.

"Don't. For God's sake . . . Lisa . . . Don't!"

As if in a dream, he watched. The first explosion seemed to go on forever as the bullet tore into Stangl's chest.

Lisa pulled the trigger again and again. Loud noise invaded the room. The shriek of a helicopter engine blotted out the last explosions. Lisa kept firing at Stangl, his body jerking under the impact at point blank range till the gun clicked empty.

Lisa stood over Stangl's body. The gun fell from her hand. Her face was blank, drained of all thought or feeling. Ben felt himself slipping.

Garver walked past him and took Lisa's arm. She uttered no protest. Shock had set in. A man in a flying suit ran into the inn.

"Christ. What the hell happened here?" he demanded. "Where's Stangl?"

"All dead. Stangl, too," said Garver.

The man looked around the room. "Bring the girl, and let's go," he said.

"What about the others?" asked Garver.

"To hell with the others. Let's go!"

With an effort of will that Ben found deep within himself, he grabbed at Garver's leg as Garver pushed Lisa past him. The last things he saw were Lisa's blank stare, Garver's smile, and the flash from the gun. Then the tunnel closed, and there was nothing but long, thick silence.

"Look at that, Jan," Dreyer said and pointed to the lights descending into Le Jardin, a mile away.

"Helicopter," said Leander.

"I think Gerroff's in trouble," said Dreyer, and he started the car. Leander took his automatic from beneath his coat.

Dreyer raced down the road. Over the inn he could see the helicopter taking off. As they jumped out, the drone of the engine rapidly faded away.

A shot blasted into the car windshield and shattered it. Leander yelled, "Down," and turned and fired in one smooth, expert motion. A body fell through a hedge to land in the road.

Dreyer moved forward. He heard the sounds of feet crashing through the underbrush. Leander joined him, moving low to the ground.

It took them fifteen minutes to make the final approach to the inn. Their attackers had fled. Leander entered the inn while Dreyer stood guard outside. He went in low and fast.

There was no need. Carnage, he thought, as the scene inside leaped at him.

"Oh, my dear God..." he said out loud. Bodies, blood, and broken things lay strewn about as if madmen had been loose there.

Dreyer came in. "Jesus..." he swore.

Leander bent down to examine Gerroff. He felt for a pulse and put his ear to Gerroff's chest. He was dead.

Leander looked at Stangl. He counted five bullet holes in the body. He looked up at Dreyer, who was checking the old man under the table.

Dreyer shook his head.

"The girl's gone," said Leander.

Dreyer nodded and knelt down by Ben. It seemed hopeless, but he checked anyway. At first he thought what he felt was his own nervous tic. But then he felt it again.

"Jan," he called out. "Davidson's alive. Barely. But still alive."

"Get to the car. Call an ambulance," Leander said. He

knelt by the body and began to administer first aid. Warm blood flowed over Leander's hands.

"I've got more than yours on my hands tonight," he said. "Live, blast you."

It was the second time that night Ben had been asked for something he would have a hard time delivering.

Book Three

One

The first awareness that came to Ben was sound. It came from a long way away, as if he were submerged under water and life was occurring only on some distant surface. It took a while for him to realize that the ever-present, rhythmic beat he felt/heard was his heart, and the loud whooshing, his own breathing.

Other sounds began to penetrate the darkness that changed very slowly from black to gray.

". . . up and around, Doctor?"

"All the vital signs are holding steady. He should be coming around any time now. The EEG's registering an increase in Beta. He's starting to come into conscious thought, but it will be disorganized for a while yet."

"And physically?"

"The trauma to the head is actually more a problem than the gunshot wound. The bullet's angle took it right past the lungs, and it missed the major blood vessels. It will heal quite nicely. The head is another story, though. It was a pretty severe concussion. However, we see no evidence of any hematoma, and he may get off with just headaches and blurred vision. We'll know better when he's conscious."

"Thank you, Doctor. I'll wait here with him if you don't mind. I appreciate all you've done."

"Not at all. I'll station a nurse with him. And remember, when he wakes up, he's going to be weak as a kitten. Don't strain him. Say, forty-eight hours and he can probably walk out of here under his own power. I'll be back to see him when he's awake. Just make sure your security guard doesn't interfere with my nurses."

"You can instruct your staff to ignore him. I'm grateful for your cooperation in this matter."

"It's the least I could do for a fellow countryman."

"Good day, Doctor."

Ben found the conversation only mildly interesting.

Vague, disturbing memories tried to emerge through the fog that shrouded his mind. But they were fragmented; and when he tried to capture a piece, it skidded away back into the fog. He slept again, but it was fitful, filled with dreams.

When consciousness returned, he tried to open his eyes, but they felt glued together, and it took a greater effort to wrench them apart. The brightness of the room was too much, but in the background a blurry, dark shape came closer and loomed over him.

"Mr. Davidson? Are you awake? Can you hear me? Nurse, get Doctor Bertram. Don't try to speak, Mr. Davidson. The doctor will be here in a minute. You've been through a rough time. Just try and relax."

With the return of consciousness, more memories tried to break through.

"Where am I?" he managed to say, but the effort hurt.

"You're in a hospital in Paris. I brought you here after—after you were hurt. Please try and relax. The doctor's on his way."

"Who are you?" Ben asked, the sounds like wind through a torn paper bag. Paris seemed to have some meaning.

"My name is Jan Leander. Does that mean anything to you? I was . . ."

The name brought the pain closer, and he tried to remember where he had heard it. Leander; Paris.

"I am a friend of Lisa's."

And then it was all clear. The memories realigned themselves into one straight, pain-wrenching line. Gottbaum's lifeless eyes stared up at him. The noise of a helicopter. The sounds of gunshots and Stangl's jerking body.

"Oh, God . . ." he moaned, and aching spasms shook him as he cried, remembering it all. A chasm of blackness opened before him, and his tortured mind crawled in.

When he awoke, there was a different man, dressed in hospital whites, standing over him.

"You're awake again? Good. I'm Doctor Bertram. Can you see me?"

Ben nodded, the effort sending sharp pain through his head. Sleep had been only a respite, not an escape.

"How do you feel?" asked Bertram.

"Empty," he said.

272

"I mean physically. Here, drink this. It will ease your throat."

Bertram handed him a cup of some syrupy liquid, but Ben needed help to drink it. It eased the dryness and unstuck his tongue.

"You're American?" Ben asked.

Bertram nodded. "Cornell '51. I was here for a short time after Korea. Married a French girl and set up shop shortly afterward. Now kindly shut up and let me see if you're going to be okay."

For the next few minutes, Bertram tested and prodded and poked, and Ben cooperated lethargically. Finally, Bertram was satisfied.

"I hope you realize how lucky you've been. Either of your injuries, the concussion or the gunshot, could have killed you. But there's no neurological impairment that I can see, and though you'll feel weak for a while as your body heals, you should be in pretty good shape in a few days. You need rest now. I'm going to give you a shot of valium to put you to sleep."

"Not yet," Ben protested. "I want to see Leander first. Is he still here?"

"You're in no shape to see him. You blacked out the last time. Do you want to cause permanent damage?" said Bertram, concerned.

"Please, Doctor. Just for a few minutes. Then the shot. I've got to speak to him."

Bertram looked dubious, but finally acquiesced.

"Only for a short time, then. I'll send him in."

After the doctor left, Ben examined his body. He felt the bandage on the back of his head, secured by a gauze wrapping. Gently, he prodded beneath it and found a great swelling and a rough scab about an inch long. On his left side, was a second dressing. It hurt to lift his left arm, but he strained till he could see the ugly purple bruising of the flesh around the bullet's entry hole.

Leander came in, and Ben had his first good look at him.

"The doctor told me you were awake and asking for me," said Leander, taking a chair next to the bed. "How do you feel?"

"What do you care how I feel, you bastard. You used me.

273

And Lisa. Why the hell didn't you just let me die?" said Ben bitterly.

"Because, regardless of what you may think, I am not heartless. I didn't know you existed until a few days ago. And I didn't force you into this," Leander said flatly. "You acted of your own volition. Lisa Smith is another matter, and I'm doing everything in my power to find her. Will you help me?"

"Help you?" Ben said, shocked. "You used us as bait; my oldest friend is dead, and Lisa has been taken only God knows where. What kind of person are you?"

"The kind that wants to get the job done, Mr. Davidson, regardless of the interference of amateurs like you. Now, do you want to help me find Lisa or cry about life's unfairness? You dealt yourself into this game, Mr. Davidson—play with the hand you've been dealt or fold. All the whining in the world isn't going to help Lisa."

The truth of Leander's words stung him like a slap in the face but didn't mitigate his distrust.

"That's fine for you to say when you put her into this from the beginning," Ben said angrily, and the effort made his head swim.

"If we pool our knowledge, Mr. Davidson, we may hit on some way to find her. Contrary to your belief, I don't know what you know. We've been playing this operation in the dark. What brought you to Amsterdam in the first place?"

"How can I trust you?" Ben demanded.

"That will have to be up to you," said Leander flatly. "We're on the same side in this. I regret what's been done to you and Lisa, just as I regret what happened to your friend. But I tell you that I'd do it all again if it gave me the slightest hope of finding Bormann and protecting my country."

Ben took a deep breath.

"I'm beginning to get the feel of this game, Leander. Knowledge is power. If I tell you what I know, you don't need me anymore. I'll stay dealt in, as you put it, only as long as I have what you need. And either I'm kept in, or you can go to hell."

Leander's eyes narrowed, but he nodded. "One of my people died last night, too, Mr. Davidson. His name was Henry Gerroff."

The memory of Gerroff's fight sobered Ben. It was true, at least, that Leander had lost, too.

"He was a good man," Ben admitted softly, and he gave Leander the details of what had transpired at the inn.

"... I'm sorry about your man, Gerroff. Without him we wouldn't have stood a chance. It was you, Leander, though Stangl didn't know it, that the trap was set for. Gerroff was probably responsible for saving your life as well as mine. I suppose that's something after all."

"In my line of work, Ben, it's almost everything," Leander agreed. "Please think about Gerroff when you wonder about trusting me. And remember also a certain night in Amsterdam when a scarfaced man would have killed you had not another of mine interfered. Again, I ask for your trust, I think we've earned it. There is much to this you don't understand yet. Strategies within strategies; movement and countermovement."

"That means nothing to me unless you explain yourself."

Leander shook his head. "Trust works both ways. Either we become partners, or I tell you nothing else. Think on it. I'll be back to see you in a few hours."

Abruptly, Leander got up and left, and Ben surrendered to sleep. A nurse came in to stand watch over him. Several times, she was on the verge of calling the doctor as Ben tossed in his sleep, dreaming and calling out, "I'm sorry," over and over again in a voice filled with self-torture.

In the hospital lounge, Leander sat down wearily next to Peter Dreyer.

"He told me what happened at the inn, but nothing else." Leander repeated Ben's story.

"I think I misjudged Gerroff," said Dreyer, a note of emotion in his voice.

"It doesn't matter now," said Leander gently. "Move on. Agents have died before. If a man doesn't want to take risks, there are a lot of other professions to choose besides ours. If there is such a thing as dying nobly, Gerroff did."

"I want to find who's responsible, Jan. It's not enough to just say some words. First Koenig and now Gerroff. Will Davidson help us?"

Leander shrugged.

"He knows we used him and the girl. Worse, he knows we failed to protect them."

"We could force him, Jan," said Dreyer grimly.

"No. I don't think we could. He's a strong man, Peter. I could see that in him. We'll just have to wait and see.".

"But what if he won't cooperate with us? Stangl's dead and so is Van Dyne. Hauptman and Smith can't be touched in South Africa. We're back to square one without him," said Dreyer.

"I'd stake my life that Bormann's got Lisa Smith. He took the only person that can be used to control Smith. I should have realized his intent. It's my fault. And now I've got to call Smith and tell him so."

"Wait until we can talk to Davidson again, Jan. Maybe he'll have some answers," suggested Dreyer.

"We may as well," sighed Leander. "But we're in a bind if he doesn't."

"*Allo*," said the nurse when Ben opened his eyes. "I'm Margot, your night nurse. You are feeling better?"

Margot's English was heavily accented. It reminded Ben of where he was. His mind felt clearer, and his body, stronger.

"Yes. The sleep helped. What time is it? he asked.

"Nine o'clock. Would you like some food?"

He was suddenly ravenously hungry. "I would. Thank you."

"*Bien*. I'll be back in a moment."

Margot got up and left in search of dinner.

He thought about what Leander had said earlier. Perhaps it was wisest to throw in with him. He had gotten nowhere on his own. Worse than nowhere, he thought sadly.

But to Leander, Lisa was nothing more than bait. It seemed wrong to ally with a man whose priorities were so different from his own. Leander would sacrifice all of them, Ben decided, to get to Bormann. He made his decision. He would go it alone.

From somewhere in his mind, the bubble of an idea, the interconnection of two elements, suddenly formed. I've got resources too, he realized.

Gingerly, he tried to get out of bed. The initial effort almost caused him to black out. But his vision cleared, and the room steadied after a while.

He tried a few tentative steps and found that the stiffness rapidly subsided into dull aches, which he could stand. His clothing, money, and wallet were intact in the closet. Woozy, he got back into bed.

"I am sorry it could not be more," said Margot when she returned with a dinner tray. "But the kitchens are closed. It is past the usual dinner hour. I made you a ham sandwich. Okay?"

"Just fine," Ben said, eager to eat. "I couldn't handle anything stronger. Thank you, Margot."

"*Pas du tout.*" She smiled and put the tray on the bedstand.

The first bites made him nauseous, but his stomach accepted the food. After a cup of tea, he began to eat in earnest, his body soaking up the nourishment.

"Are you on duty all night, Margot?" he asked.

"Oh, no. Only for another hour or so. Or until you fall back asleep. Then the nurse at the duty station takes over."

Ten minutes later, Ben was snoring peacefully. He heard Margot whisper a quiet "*à bientôt*" and leave the room.

Waiting a few more minutes to be sure she had gone for the night, he turned on the small reading light over the bed. He dressed quickly in the dimness, ignoring the headache that overtook him and the weakness in his left side. Carefully, he peeled away the gauze bandage from his head, leaving only the smaller dressing, half hidden by his hair.

He peered cautiously out into the hospital corridor. Most of the overhead lights had been turned off, and the corridor was silent and shadowy. The nursing station was down the corridor, opposite a bank of elevators. The guard's back was turned, his attention on the night nurse.

As noiselessly as possible, Ben left his room. His sneakers made only small creaking noises as he moved down the hallway. The stairs were difficult to manage, and after two flights, he had to pause to catch his breath and let the pain in his head subside.

When he got to the bottom and pushed open the exit door, the night air was cold. He was on some kind of loading dock, and huge dumpsters of garbage stood near.

The five-foot drop to the ground jarred him as he landed. But no one cried out after him. He walked as quickly away from the hospital as his physical condition would permit and found a taxi only a block away.

The hotel room was emptier by contrast than any he had been in before because it had held so much life just a day ago. Now Bill Gottbaum was dead, and Ben felt like an abysmal failure.

"Dammit, I'm responsible," he moaned out loud. He ran his hands over the tired muscles of his face as pain flooded over him.

He opened the connecting door to Gottbaum's room. Gottbaum's suitcases still lay on the bed, a sweater crumpled on the pillow. He folded the sweater gently, each crease important, and put it back in the suitcase. There were no other last rites he could offer. Loneliness pulled tears from him.

"I'm sorry, Bill," was all he could choke out. "I'm so sorry."

A folder lay on the dresser and Ben opened it. It was the information on Voorstein and the W.H.O. Ben took it back into his room and shut the door behind him as gently as one closes the lid of a coffin.

Margot was in tears; the duty nurse was both embarrassed and hostile; and the security guard tried to avoid Leander's furious gaze.

"When did you leave him?" Leander asked Margot.

"Not half an hour ago, m'sieu. He was sleeping like a child." She paused to sniffle and blow her nose. "This has never happened before to me."

"It's not your fault, Margot. You can go home," he said, wearily.

Margot's sobs could be heard until the elevator doors cut them off.

"Did you see him?" Leander asked the duty nurse.

"If I had seen him, I would have stopped him. I saw no one and heard nothing. *Rien!*" she snorted.

Leander and Dreyer walked back down the corridor to Ben's room.

"There are no signs of any struggle, Jan," said Dreyer. "His clothing and personal effects are gone. He walked out of here under his own power."

Leander sat down, more tired than he'd felt in some time.

"I know. The nurse would have heard something otherwise. Let's go, Peter. There's nothing for us here. I need some sleep. Apparently, Davidson is stronger than even I thought."

"Don't take it so hard, Jan. We've had operations go sour before. The verdict's not in yet," said Dreyer.

"The girl is the key, Peter. Whoever holds her, holds Smith. And Smith holds the power. I should have locked Davidson up," he said bitterly. "Organize a search for him. But I'm sure he's long gone."

"What are you going to tell Smith?" asked Dreyer.

"I don't know yet. I need time to think. I keep going over the whole thing in my head; trying to salvage something; hoping to see a new direction. I just don't know."

Leander lapsed into a troubled silence that lasted all the way back to the embassy.

Ben picked up the Paris phone directory from underneath the pay phone in the café across from the hotel and leafed through it till he found the name he wanted.

There were four Georges Delacroix's listed. He dialed the first one, and someone answered sleepily on the fourth ring.

"*Allo?*"

"Is this the home of Monsieur Georges Delacroix of the Première Banque de Paris?" Ben asked.

"*Non,*" said the voice, and the phone went dead. The second call went the same way as the first except that this Delacroix demanded to know what kind of fool would call so late. Ben dialed the phone a third time.

"*Bon soir, la maison Delacroix,*" said a voice. He repeated his question and was rewarded with a positive response.

"*Oui, de la Première Banque de Paris.* Who is calling please?"

"This is Ben Davidson, and I must speak to Monsieur Delacroix. It's urgent!"

"But it is so late, monsieur," protested the servant.

"Regardless of the hour, this is vital. We met in Amsterdam. Tell him that, please!"

"*D'accord,*" said the servant finally, and Ben waited in silence.

"Mr. Davidson, how nice to hear from you, even at this hour," said a booming voice on the other end of the line.

"I apologize for calling so late, but I must see you as soon as possible, Monsieur Delacroix," Ben said. "Tonight."

"What is so urgent that it cannot wait until morning?" asked the bemused voice.

"A man is dead, a woman kidnapped. Please, you must see me tonight."

"You mean Van Dyne?" Delacroix asked.

"No, someone else. But it involves Van Dyne," Ben said.

Delacroix hesitated for a moment. Ben listened to his heavy breathing for what seemed like a long time. He pictured the phone in Delacroix's huge hands.

"*Bien*," he said at last. "I'll send a car. You are in Paris?"

"Yes. Across from the Sheraton," Ben said gratefully. "I'll be outside."

"My car will be there in five minutes," said Delacroix and hung up.

Ben waited by the café, inconspicuous in the crowd, his wounds throbbing. A dark maroon Mercedes limousine slid to a stop by the curb, and the driver got out.

"Monsieur Davidson?" he called out, and Ben walked over. The driver put his luggage in the car's trunk, and Ben climbed into the cavernous rear seat.

He watched the city of lights swirl around him as the car sped away. But, like gemstones on a black velvet cloth, all he could see were diamonds.

Two

The limousine slid through a gate in the black wrought-iron fence that enclosed Delacroix's mansion. Only a few blocks off the bustling Champs-Élysées, the neighborhood was none-theless quiet and sedate, two-story mansions barely visible from behind their screen of trees and high shrubs.

"I will take your bags, m'sieu," said the driver in English as Ben walked up the steps to the front door, each step a pain-ridden effort. At a touch of the bell, the white, lacquered door swung open, and a servant ushered him in.

Delacroix was dressed in a blue, satin-quilted robe and seated in an armchair in his study. Books lined the walls from floor to ceiling, and a writing desk stood in one corner. A bottle of brandy and two glasses sat on a table next to Delacroix, who noticed his sickly pallor immediately.

"*Mon ami, qu'est-ce qu'il y a?*" said Delacroix, rising to meet Ben, concern in his voice. "You do not look well. Sit down."

Ben half fell into a deep armchair, feeling his bandages cutting into his side.

"Thank you, Georges. It's been a very strange time since I saw you last. So much has happened. I'm sorry to barge in on you this way, but I need help, and I don't know anyone else I can ask."

"Don't talk yet. Have some of this." Delacroix poured some of the brandy into a glass. Ben sipped it slowly, its warmth spreading out through his body, soothing and relieving.

"I don't think I'd better drink too much, or I'll pass out," he said.

"Have you eaten? I can have some food prepared for you."

"Not yet. Thanks, though. I need to tell you why I'm here. Food can wait," said Ben.

"I will admit that when a man I have met for only a few minutes at a party calls at such an hour with so urgent a request, I am more than mildly curious at what that man has to say. We use our given names, I invite you to my home yet we know almost nothing about each other, *n'est-ce pas?*" said Delacroix, mildly.

"In other words, you're asking why you should listen to me," said Ben, putting the glass of brandy back on the table, some energy returning to his body.

"You put it more bluntly than I would have, but that is one of my questions."

Ben lifted up his shirt. "Do you know what makes this type of wound?" he asked, pulling up the dressing.

"You've been shot," exclaimed Delacroix. "I served in the war long enough to know a bullet wound."

Ben closed his shirt. "And a doctor told me I have a concussion. I'm telling you this not to beg for sympathy but to support what I'm about to tell you. I don't blame you for being skeptical."

"People are shot for many reasons. Some noble, some not so noble," Delacroix shrugged.

"I'm not noble. I was shot because I stumbled into something in America that I traced to Amsterdam and now to Paris. By all rights I should have died," Ben said flatly.

"What is this thing you stumbled into?" asked Delacroix, doubt clear on his features.

"First, tell me how you feel about Nazis," said Ben.

Delacroix's face transformed into a brutal, bitter expression.

"You can ask me that? I hate Nazis in a way you couldn't even begin to understand. You are too young to remember the Occupation. I remember people, friends of mine, dragged out and hanged in the middle of the night; French women turned into whores; museums stripped bare; armed Gestapo in the streets. I remember. Who are you to ask me such a question? I fought with the Free French, and I killed Nazis. I would kill them again if need be," Delacroix said angrily.

Ben fished out his wallet and handed Delacroix the snapshot he carried.

"Do you recognize these men?"

"Where did you get this?" Delacroix demanded, his face drawn and tight.

"I asked you if you knew those men," repeated Ben.

"Martin Bormann and Ludwig Stumpfegger, around 1940 or so. We tried for them in the Resistance, but we could not get close enough," said Delacroix, wistfully. He looked closely at Ben. "I agree to listen. No promises. But I'll listen."

"That's all I ask. For now," Ben said, and he began to speak. Delacroix listened silently to it all.

"I am sorry for the death of your friend," said Delacroix when Ben had finished. "But how do you know that the Martisse account is not just another blind? I have known Martisse for over twenty years, and I can't believe he would go along with what you've told me."

"Then you don't believe me," said Ben, close to the edge of his endurance. A clock somewhere in the house chimed four times, and Delacroix twisted the ends of his mustache.

"I didn't say that. But what you've suggested is so incredible that I'm unsure what to say to you."

"Every word is true. I swear it," Ben said. Delacroix held up his hands.

"You don't have to. Strangely enough, at least I believe that you believe it," he said.

Ben was reminded painfully of another man who had used that phrase, in a New York airport, many lifetimes ago.

"Will you help me?" he asked.

"Can you give me any proof at all? Anything to validate what you say?" Delacroix asked grimly.

Ben shrugged helplessly. "What can I give you? Van Dyne is dead. Lisa is being held somewhere. If I call in Leander, I'm forced to work with a man who already set me up once. I can put together again the research I did on Croft, but what would that really tell you? All I have is a photo of two Nazis and a card that could be printed up in any local shop. What proof can I offer except myself? Help me find them, and I'll give you proof enough."

Delacroix got up and paced around the room in agitation.

"What would you do in my position?" he asked. "An exhausted madman comes to my home and tells me the most incredible story I've ever heard and asks me for help. What would you do?"

"Throw him out," Ben said honestly.

"Then why shouldn't I?" asked Delacroix, his struggle evident.

"Because I'm not a madman," Ben said quietly. "And because what I've told you is true."

"I remind you that I have only your word for that."

"And I remind you of your own analysis of Van Dyne's politics. Do you think it so inconceivable that he could have been involved with the Nazis?" Ben suggested hotly.

"I don't want to believe that any man could be involved with swine. Politics aside, Van Dyne was a respected businessman," said Delacroix.

"With his fortune based on Hauptman's diamonds. 'His crowd,' you called them," retorted Ben.

"It does you no good to raise your voice, Ben."

Ben's headache had returned in full force. He tried to repress the shudders that a sudden chill brought.

"I've got no choice, Georges. If you don't help me, I'm through. You've got to understand that I'm telling you the truth."

Delacroix seemed to deliberate for a long moment. He sat back down in his chair and poured more brandy into his glass.

"What do you want of me exactly?" he asked.

"Then you'll help me?"

"I didn't say that. I want to know what you want from me."

"I know that the cash from the sale of the diamonds goes

into an account at Martisse's bank. Account #5336-17. I need you to find out where that money goes next. And to whom. I figured that with your connections, you could arrange that."

"Just like that?" Delacroix snapped his fingers, his tone angry. "I'm now to become involved in spying on a French banking institution? That is no small crime to commit. You are mad."

"Compared to what I've been through, I think it's a small crime," Ben said flatly. "You're going to sit there and tell me it can't be done? I'm not that naïve, Georges. And you're not either."

A gleam of wry amusement shone in Delacroix's eyes. "Well, that is true enough. With the amount of foreign money that's routinely laundered through our accounts, it has become, ah... necessary, shall we say, to have friendly eyes and ears in the system. One likes to have advance warnings about certain things."

"Then it can be done," Ben insisted.

Delacroix nodded and resumed pulling at his mustache. "It can. But what would you gain?"

"The next step. That's all I ask. Just the next step. Maybe it will lead me to the ones in charge," said Ben wearily.

"And the girl," Delacroix added. "That is all you want?"

"Not all, Georges. I need some cash and help with travel arrangements. I can give you my check if you'll cover it."

"That is minor," said Delacroix. "The information is not."

Ben was too tired to protest further. He held out his hands in a gesture of defeat.

"I can't argue anymore, Georges. We each do what we have to."

Ben listened in silence to the steady beat of Delacroix's fingers tapping on the chair's arm. He was too tired to hope, too sick to sustain belief. All he could feel was hopelessness, the burden of the knowledge that he had failed Lisa.

He looked up and found that Delacroix was staring at him, watching him closely. A slow smile spread over his features, and a grinning mouth appeared underneath the mustache. Abruptly, Delacroix reached over and lifted his glass in salute.

"To madmen, my friend. I will help you."

* * *

"I can't offer any better explanation, Mr. Prime Minister," said Leander for the second time to a furious Johann Smith, six thousand miles distant. He could hear Smith's rapid, hostile breathing over the phone.

"And you have no idea of the identities of the men who took her?" Smith said at last.

"We're checking the files now, sir. The photos have been wired to Pretoria for a computer check."

Again, a silence on the phone.

"How could you be so incompetent?" demanded Smith.

"One of my men is dead, sir. Maybe if we'd had more information, we could have saved both him and Lisa," said Leander, but the question hit him hard. He had already asked it of himself.

"You had what you needed. And you failed. Is there anything else you can do in Paris?"

"No, sir. I'm afraid the operation's cold. We have no leads."

"What about her friends or acquaintances? Was she with anyone when she was taken?" Smith asked.

"There were two others. Both are Americans, and they are both dead," he lied.

"I want you back here at once. And not one word of this to anyone. Do you understand? Not one word. Just get back here." Smith was yelling now.

"Yes, sir. I'll come back at once," said Leander.

"I am most disappointed in you," said Smith, and Leander's protests went unspoken as the line went dead.

"Well?" asked Dreyer from the balcony of the hotel room. "I assume he did not take it well."

"As expected. In a way I almost feel sorry for him. I think he knows that Bormann has Lisa."

"Bormann's captured the queen," said Dreyer.

"And maybe the whole game," said Leander.

"I think we should expose them now, then. If we throw enough light onto this, maybe someone else will flush them out," Dreyer suggested.

"We still don't know what they're doing," said Leander. "Even if we expose a conspiracy, all we have proof of is 1936. And if they go underground, then we may never find them. It's not enough to stop Smith, we've got to stop the whole plot. And that means Bormann."

"I don't know, Jan. Is your past influencing your judgment? I'm sorry to say it, but I have to ask," said Dreyer.

Leander was silent for a while. Dreyer knew he had hurt his friend. But this was too important for personal motives to get in the way.

"I don't know anymore, Peter. I don't think so. But maybe you're right. I want Bormann so badly that my stomach is in knots," said Leander.

"Enough to blow what we do have? You're risking it all on finding him," Dreyer said.

"No. Not that much. I still think we've got to know more before we expose them. But I still need your support. Do I have it, Peter?"

Dreyer turned away and looked out over the city of Paris. It was near dawn, and the soft light turned the white buildings rose-colored. It took him a long time to make up his mind. In the final analysis, he realized, it came down to trust. Trust and judgment. And he had backed Leander on both all his professional life.

"You have it, Jan," he said at last.

"Thank you, Peter," said Leander quietly. "Now let's get packed. It's a long flight back to South Africa."

Dreyer nodded and threw their suitcases on the bed. Trust and judgment, he thought, as Leander arranged for a plane to take them home.

The first thing Johann Smith noticed when he got out of the helicopter that had brought him to the fishing lodge was an absence of parked cars. "They should all be here by now," he thought as he walked to the house.

The cables had been sent the day before. No one would deliberately refuse the Adlerkinden summons.

The first chill of apprehension swept through him. Since Leander's report on Lisa's disappearance, Smith had tried to keep his tension suppressed. But suddenly, in the space of a single day, the balance of power had shifted totally into Bormann's hands. If, Smith reminded himself, he has Lisa. But the knowledge that to appear weak to Martin Bormann was to invite slaughter kept his stride long and his posture straight.

Smith pushed open the door to the lodge, half expecting

the sounds of men talking to greet him. But past the creak of the old wooden door, there were no voices, and the conference table was empty. He looked at his watch to make sure he had the time right.

"Do come in, Johann," said Martin Bormann from the staircase. "We are quite alone."

Smith whirled around, caught off guard.

"I thought I was the only one here," he said, recovering. "Where is everyone else?"

Bormann came down the stairs with the casual ease of a man in total control. "There is no one else, Johann. Just you and I. It's time to settle some things between us."

Smith said nothing but watched Bormann take his seat at the conference table and beckon to him.

"Please sit down, Johann," he said.

"What the hell is this all about?" demanded Smith. "I called for a total assembly here. I sent out orders—"

"And I countermanded them," Bormann cut him off. "I may be doing that more often in the future, Johann."

"You are on dangerous ground, Martin. No one ignores my orders. Not even you. Do you think you can oppose me?"

Bormann's expression had remained unchanged, and Smith's fear moved closer to the surface.

"Your weakness opposes you, Johann. You are not the same man you were. Things have gotten in your way. I am going to correct that."

"You're prattling on like an old man, Martin. Since your decaying Reich fell apart, I've been in charge, and nothing can change that."

"But all things change," sighed Bormann. "Even I had to learn that. Life is change. Isn't that what the Adlerkinden is all about?"

"I didn't come here to argue sophomoric philosophies," Smith retorted hotly. "I control the money and power that makes what we do possible and that has made it possible since the beginning. Never forget that. My last threat to you was not an idle one."

"I haven't forgotten your threats, Johann," Bormann said quietly.

"Then what makes you think you can stand against me? The others won't follow you. And without them, you're nothing but a hunted war criminal that every Western power would like nothing better than to get their hands on. You wouldn't last one day longer than your friend Eichmann."

But Smith saw that he had failed to penetrate Bormann's calm or even to ruffle him in the slightest.

Bormann shook his head slowly. "It is sad to see a man so intelligent fail to see the simple realities of his situation. It is you who must think me a fool, Johann. Because it was you who gave me the perfect tool to unseat you from your miniscule throne and your petty politics. You've grown too old to see what lies in front of your face; what you must already know in your heart."

"I know nothing but that you have a death wish, Martin. You are not essential anymore. You can and will be replaced." Smith's hostility was finally in the open.

"So you admit what you want," said Bormann rising from his seat. "But consider this, Johann Smith, and consider it well. I hold the winning hand in this game between us. I hold your daughter, Lisa."

With that one simple phrase, Smith knew that Bormann indeed had the winning hand. His strength seemed to evaporate from within, and he had to put a hand out to steady himself. An oppressive heat closed around him, and he sat down without any of his usual grace.

"If she's harmed, I'll kill you, Martin. I swear I will," he said, but there was little force in his words.

Bormann was smiling now, his wrinkled skin bunched around his jaw. There was a hard edge to his voice.

"You will do as I please, or your daughter will suffer in the thousand ways you know I can inflict. Think hard on what can happen to her."

"The others will never stand for it," said Smith, trying to rally against total defeat.

Bormann laughed, and the sound echoed in the large room.

"The others will never know. Only you and I. If you try to use them against me, Lisa will die. If you refuse to do as I say, Lisa will die. You have no choices left to you, Johann. Accept that with your much-praised aristocratic manner."

"Where is Lisa?" Smith asked.

"At the Eagle's Nest, under guard. There is no way you can get to her and no one who can help you inside or outside our group. You will risk exposure if you try to bring someone in.

How long will you remain Prime Minister if word of the Project leaks out, do you think? Checkmate, Johann. Accept the inevitable."

"What if I tell you to go to hell?" Smith asked bitterly.

Bormann shrugged complacently. "That is the acid test, is it not? You know me too well to think I would bluff. If you refuse to do as I say, she will die; and you would have to expose the Project to get at me. If you agree, however, nothing need change. Only you and I will know of the new arrangement, and I will keep Lisa only till the Project is complete. After that, it will be too late to go against me because you'll have your hands full with your own people. I'll count on the fact that we're too old for childish notions of revenge. I have taken out an insurance policy. Nothing more, really."

Smith felt his years weighing heavily on him. What Bormann said was true enough, he knew. There was no profit in harming Lisa if he were to cooperate. Lisa and the Project safe in return for Bormann's supremacy—or Lisa's death, Bormann's death, the ruination of the Project, and his own political downfall if he defied Bormann. There was no way out.

"You've played this out perfectly," he said.

"I knew you'd see it my way," said Bormann. "It's the wisest course of action. And I guarantee you, no one will be the wiser. Even the cables canceling the meeting were sent in your codes. Only Ludwig knows the truth of what took place here today." Bormann's tone was conciliatory, smoothing over Smith's frustration. But it was time to put Smith away once and for all.

"By the way, Johann. Your daughter had some interesting things to tell me when we spoke. Would you care to hear them?"

"She'd never tell you a thing, Martin," Smith said, "unless you hurt her."

"Quite the contrary. She was not feeling all that well and was very cooperative. After all, she had just killed a man."

Smith blanched, and his voice shook. "What are you talking about?"

"In Paris she discovered that Stangl was the one who killed her parents. Also, that you and Van Dyne were involved. Because of a very quick turn in circumstances and the continued interference of Ben Davidson, she had a gun and shot Stangl. She is still a bit disoriented but perfectly healthy. Stangl, unfortunately, is quite dead."

"She needs help. I've got to see her. Lisa is a sensitive girl, and this could unbalance her. Please, Martin, I've got to see her." Smith pleaded with no regard for his position.

"I'm sorry, but that is not possible. And I think you should be aware of what else she told me. I know who programmed her to go to Van Dyne, who has been responsible for the attacks on us. You may find this interesting. Pay attention, Johann," Bormann snapped.

Smith swung his eyes back to Bormann. He was consumed with worry over Lisa and knew that Bormann had planned it that way. He intertwined his hands in his lap to keep them from shaking.

"What else is there?" he asked. "If you know who it was that used Lisa to get at us, tell me. No more games, Martin. You've won. I accept that. But the Project still has to go on. Who was it?"

"Jan Leander," said Bormann without a trace of emotion. He let the name itself make the impact. "He has been crawling up our backs from the moment Lisa went to Van Dyne. There is no doubt that he sent her there."

Smith hardly heard Bormann. He was thinking back to his first meeting with Leander about the attack in Stangl's brothel. At each turn Leander had been there, ostensibly to help. Smith began to see the pattern emerge.

"Why did you attack Lisa at Schiphol Airport?" he asked bluntly.

"I did nothing of the kind."

"It was Leander, then," muttered Smith.

"What did you say?" Bormann craned his head closer.

"Nothing, Martin." He refused to give Bormann more than he had to. How clever Leander had been, he thought. But Bormann was still more clever. He had used them all.

Smith had never before experienced the kind of hatred he now felt for Martin Bormann. What a fool he made of me, he thought. What an absolute fool. He wanted to leap on Bormann and smash his old wrinkled face into pulp.

"I never suspected Leander," he said, covering his hatred. He was a beaten man, and all he could do now was survive.

"Something must have gone wrong. Perhaps it was when

290

we killed his agent in Copenhagen. We may never know," said Bormann.

"He's on his way back here. I can have him replaced, but he will still be dangerous," said Smith.

He watched Bormann smile again. It was not the smile of a predator. It was the smile of a man who appreciates only the special beauty of cold logic; the smile of a man who has subordinated all passion to the great god of what is expedient. How I underestimated him, thought Smith, with self-loathing and sadness.

"Leander will die," Bormann said simply. "I will arrange it. Would you like a drink before you leave?"

Ryerson sat in the Staff Cafeteria in Brazzaville, bleary-eyed from the previous night's drinking bout, thinking that the W.H.O. center's food was even less palatable than its administrators.

He had gotten no satisfaction at all when he tried to get someone to explain his abrupt transfer. The administrators simply said it was a project foreman's request; and every foreman he ran into told him it was an administrator's. He was ready to explode, his hangover shortening an already short fuse.

He spotted an administrator named Striker, a middle-aged, white South African who was one of the assistants in personnel. He was seated at a table with some of the medical staff. Unable to sit idly any longer, Ryerson strode over and barged into the conversation.

"I need to see you," he said without preamble.

Striker looked up at him dismayed. "It will have to wait. I'm having my lunch, Mr. . . . ah . . . Ryerson, isn't it?" He turned back to his table.

"Lunch can wait, Striker. I can't. I've been getting the runaround for days."

"I'm not surprised, with your lack of manners. I'll be in my office later. Now go away."

The faces of the rest of the people at the table were turned on Ryerson. He read name tags without registering faces: Tsumari, Crandall, Lagose—staff doctors. No use to him. He put a hand on Striker's shoulder.

"Listen, you silly prig. I need some answers. I spend six

months in South Africa building your flamin' project and get yanked off it like some ruddy, snot-nosed kid. Somebody's going to tell me why."

Striker hit his hand away brusquely. "Go away or I'll call security."

Suddenly, Striker found himself yanked from the chair and suspended in midair, one of Ryerson's huge hands on his collar and one on his belt.

"You're crazy! Put me down," he shrieked. The whole cafeteria turned.

Ryerson saw someone race out the door.

"Who ordered my transfer?" he yelled.

"I don't know. Put me down. I can't breathe!"

"You know," bellowed Ryerson.

"I don't know. Please, I don't know."

A soft voice from the table, one of the female doctors, said, "I think you're going to hurt him. Please don't do that. It appears he truly doesn't know, young man."

Ryerson felt his mood turn sour as his fury drained away. He dropped Striker heavily back into his chair. Everyone was staring at him, and he felt foolish at his outburst.

Striker was doubled over, cursing him bitterly. There was no sympathy on anyone else's face either.

He turned away and walked quickly from the room. He wanted to avoid the security guard who was surely on his way. Outside he took a taxi back to the bar. The drinking would start early today.

Three

Ben was already awake when one of Delacroix's servants brought him breakfast. He watched the man pour steaming coffee from a silver pot into a china cup and felt relatively clearheaded.

"Good morning, M'sieu Davidson. You are feeling better today?" the man asked in heavily accented English.

"Yes, thank you. Much better."

"M'sieu Delacroix left for the bank at his usual hour. He called just a few moments ago with instructions to serve your breakfast and to tell you that he would be here at one o'clock. It is now ten minutes past twelve, m'sieu."

Ben hoped that Delacroix would have some news for him, and he wanted to be up and dressed.

"Where can I bathe?" he asked the servant who still hovered at the foot of the bed.

He pointed to a door across the room. "In there, m'sieu. Your clothing has been cleaned and pressed, and I placed your things on the dresser. Do you require assistance in the bath?"

"No, thank you," said Ben quickly.

The servant nodded and left. Ben ate breakfast with relish. The coffee was strong and delicious, and after drinking his second cup, he pushed the tray aside and crawled gingerly from bed.

He felt much stronger than in the hospital. His head was clear, and the muscle aches had diminished. Ben was ready when the servant returned and told him that Delacroix was waiting downstairs.

"You look well rested," Delacroix said as he entered the room.

"I feel much better," Ben said. "No headache, and my side isn't as stiff."

"I'm pleased. You looked like death last night."

"That's close to what I felt, Georges. Were you able to find out anything?"

"It has been a morning of great profit," said Delacroix.

"Then you were able to trace the account?" Ben said excitedly.

"I was. But let me explain first so that you understand, Ben." He produced a piece of paper from his jacket pocket.

"This is called a Wire Transfer. It is used when funds deposited in one bank are sent for deposit into another. One would do that if one were moving one's residence from one part of a country to another, or even from country to country, or arranging payment of large sums for business purposes."

"As I told you last night," he continued, "it is always wise to have friendly eyes and ears among one's competitors. I have such a friend at the comptroller's office in Martisse's bank. For his usual charge, I was able to have him photocopy the records of Account #5336-17 and deliver them to me.

"They arrived a short while ago, Ben. It is a simple account and verifies at least part of the story you've told me. The account is a dummy; its only purpose is to receive and transfer funds to another bank."

Ben received the paper and scanned it eagerly, translating out loud from French as he read. His hands trembled with excitement from Delacroix's words.

"The money goes to the Banque Leveque in Brazzaville..."

"The capital of the Republic of the Congo," Delacroix said.

"And look at this, Georges. The money is credited to the account of Piet Voorstein! Voorstein is the African Regional Director of the World Health Organization, and his father was one of the original Nazi collaborators in 1936. The money starts in South Africa as diamonds and returns to Africa as cash. This is proof, Georges."

"But of what, my friend? You may have traced the money, but you don't know what it is used for."

"I don't know yet. But I'd bet my life it has something to do with Africa—South Africa, more than likely. That's where it all started, and that's where it will end. I'm sure of that now."

Delacroix sat back and lit a cigar. He peered at Ben through the smoke.

"I've got to get at Voorstein," Ben said. "The money is unimportant now. What I must know, is why he needs it."

Delacroix nodded. "But that may not be so easy."

"To hell with easy," Ben said. "I'm going to see this through. You don't think I could abandon Lisa?"

"What if Lisa is dead?" said Delacroix in a quiet voice. "I am sorry to say that, but you must consider it, my friend."

"Then their destruction is all I've got left," Ben said in a voice just as quiet. "Either way, I'm going to the Congo."

"You have some plan in your head or a notion of where to begin?"

"At the W.H.O. Center in Brazzaville. I can get a lead to Voorstein there. I'm a pretty fair journalist still."

Delacroix blew out a chain of smoke rings and sighed. "All right. I'll help you. Though I don't know if I'm doing you a favor."

"You know how grateful I am, Georges."

"You'll need money, transportation, and an identity. You are lucky, Ben. All three are easy in the Congo. France has been their major trading partner since we established control of the area in the nineteenth century. Their independence did not change economic realities, and my bank invests heavily there. As an official of my bank, you will be shown every courtesy if you get into trouble, and a French passport will give you easier entrance than an American."

"I thought the Congo was Belgian," Ben said.

"You're thinking of what is now Zaire, on the other side of the Congo River."

"You continue to amaze me, Georges. I don't know where I'd be without you. I'm in no position to reject your help," he said reaching out to touch the other man's arm.

"As I said before, I'm not sure I'm helping you. If what you say is only partly true, I think you're in way over your head. But it's your own life, and every man does what he must. Now come, we have things to do if you are going to be on a plane tonight."

The mixed smell of oil and fuel radiated from the pavement of the runway as Leander and Dreyer crossed to the waiting limousine. Neither had spoken much on the flight back to South Africa.

"I don't think Smith will move against us quickly," said Dreyer getting into the car.

"Quickly enough," said Leander, "if the girl tells Bormann about us."

He slammed the door behind him and told the driver to go directly to his office.

"We might block Smith by letting him know we have the document. He can't risk our exposing that," suggested Dreyer.

Leander watched the landscape roll by ten feet below the raised four-lane highway as the airport concrete gave way to sandy barrens.

"But that results, at best, in a stalemate," he said.

"Better that than a checkmate."

Idly, Leander noticed a car pull alongside them to pass.

"I suppose," he mused, "but what if—"

The rest of his sentence was cut off as a blast of automatic weapon fire hit the car. The driver, whose window was open, was caught full in the head, which disintegrated like a burst piece of fruit. The gunfire from the car alongside continued along the limousine but failed to penetrate the bulletproof glass as the driverless car skidded wildly out of control toward the embankment.

Dreyer was flung against the door by the violent swerve, but Leander managed to throw himself over the front seat and grab at the wheel. His legs hung over the back, and he could see nothing as he tried to keep the car straight. The dead driver lay under him, his foot jamming the accelerator.

Leander pulled at the wheel of the big car as their attackers made another pass. He heard Dreyer's gun go off rapidly and felt the impact of return shots. Suddenly, the wheel turned to mush in his hands as bullets ripped a tire to shreds.

A hail of bullets spun in through the open window as Leander tried to pull the rest of his body over the seat, but the dead man blocked him.

Again, Dreyer's gun barked violently, and Leander risked a glimpse above the dashboard. The road was empty, the other car almost alongside again.

"Get off the road," yelled Dreyer. "They'll get the gas tank sooner or later."

Leander risked another look, straining to keep the violently vibrating steering wheel under control. Up ahead, the road lowered to flat space in the embankment that led down to the plain beyond, a drainage canal of some kind.

The wheel spun frantically in his hands as he felt a second tire blow, but it failed to reduce their speed. The car began to turn sideways, fishtailing down the highway. With a last desperate heave on the slack wheel, Leander steered for the opening downgrade. If he missed it at this speed, they would go sailing over the embankment and flip over in midair. He kept his head up, ignoring the bullets.

Dreyer wedged his way past Leander to grab at the wheel. Both men fought the screeching vehicle as it threatened to race over the embankment. Their wild motion left the other car behind briefly.

The limo careened through the drainage canal sideways, slapping into the walls of the embankment. Great clouds of sand filled the air and choked them inside, but in the rearview mirror Leander saw the other car flash by on the road.

Dreyer pulled at the dead driver under them, trying to clear the accelerator pedal as the car spun out from the passage onto the flats beyond. He managed to pry the driver back against the seat.

Leander could barely see through the thick dust that swirled around them. His hand felt along the dashboard for the ignition key. A cigarette lighter came loose in his hand. His fingers reached over the steering column, and he had it. Then a shift in the car threw him aside, and he was blind again. He tried to reach again down the column. He had it again. He fought the wild motion of the car.

"She's tilting! Turn it off," yelled Dreyer, steering the car into the opaque dust.

Leander levered himself forward and turned the key. Abruptly, the huge engine died. The car slowed almost at once as the wheel locked and the power systems cut off, and a hundred yards later they came to a halt. Leander thought his back was broken and on fire at the same time as they scrambled out of the car.

The dust had died down, and they were perhaps a half mile from the highway. In the distance, they heard a car engine approaching. Leander pointed to a grassy hillock that would provide cover fifteen feet away, and they ran to it.

Out of breath, with pain spreading across his back in waves, he took out his gun while Dreyer shoved a new clip into his. They shared the silent communion of professionals, working out distances and angles, knowing that their first shots would be crucial, not knowing how many were in the car that had attacked them.

The other car approached slowly and Leander saw it clearly for the first time. A Land Rover, its engine whining in low gear, stopped twenty feet from the limousine.

Dreyer slithered away from cover on his belly, moving like a snake below the slight ridge. Leander tried to steady his hands and slow his breathing to normal.

Two men emerged from the Land Rover dressed in khaki bush clothing. One, the taller of the two, held an automatic rifle, and the other held a .45 automatic.

The smaller man reached into his jacket and removed a grenade. It marked him as a professional. Only an amateur would approach the limo directly. Their goal was to kill the car's occupants, and the most direct way was to blow it up. No risk, no chance of return fire.

The man pulled the grenade's pin and hefted it in the air preparing to throw. Three seconds elapsed; the man wanted it to explode on impact. Four seconds.

Leander held his breath and fired.

The taller man looked dazed as his friend's chest turned into a red mess. He failed to realize that the grenade had fallen, and when it exploded, he died instantly, hurtling ten feet into the air.

Leander heard the Land Rover roar into life. Then two shots signaled in quick succession as the motor died again.

"Jan?" called Dreyer, emerging from behind the Land Rover.

"Still here, Peter."

They searched the pockets of the dead men, but failed to produce anything useful. The men carried no identification.

The stench of the burned skin and clothing of the man killed by the grenade rose around them. They put the bodies into the limousine to be safe from predators until a clean-up squad could be dispatched.

"We were lucky, Jan. I think we both know that. In South Africa itself, they have more resources than we have. It will take us time to build up strength here, to recall operatives..."

"Time we don't have," finished Leander. "I know, Peter. We've got to go on the offensive soon. If they keep us reacting, we're finished."

"Only a matter of time," nodded Dreyer, finally replacing his gun.

They drove back to the highway in the Land Rover.

"Good-bye, Georges. And thank you for all you've done," Ben said as he stepped out of the Mercedes. The lights of the private airfield cast different colors onto their faces. Delacroix smiled and pulled at his mustache.

"Not good-bye, then. À bientôt. We will see each other again, I think. You are a strange sort of man, Ben Davidson, and I am glad we met. It is almost a pity I am too old to go with you."

The sound of jet engines filled the night air.

"You'll never be too old, Georges. And I'm just continuing

something that people like you started a long time ago. À bientôt."

"À bientôt, mon ami."

Ben walked to the private Lear jet that Delacroix had leased for him. In his pocket he carried papers that showed him to be Andre Bouvin, a trusted employee of Delacroix's bank and a French citizen.

The pilot had been given his instructions, and a half-hour later they were airborne. Ben watched Paris grow smaller beneath him until he couldn't see its lights any longer.

He had confused feelings about the city. The loss of Bill Gottbaum was still so recent and painful that tears filled his eyes when he thought of him. It was like losing one's roots, a link to the past. He realized how much love he had felt for the man, the love his dead father could no longer receive and his mother had chosen to avoid. Gottbaum's loss was devastating.

Ben could not escape the feeling that he was responsible for Gottbaum's death. How easy it had been to race off in search of Croft, he remembered, like a maniacal angel. How easy—until someone died. The grim reality of the pain he had caused tore at his belief in himself. It's not a novel, he reminded himself bitterly. People die. With unmitigated conceit, he had led all of them into a trap, and he had lost Lisa. It must have hurt her as deeply to kill Stangl as to find him. He hoped the shock of taking a life, any life, would pass for her. If not, it was a scar that might never heal. How quickly their short life together had fallen apart.

Yet in Paris, he had come to know and depend on Delacroix, a man who had backed him totally on only his word. It was a strange world that could contain both Stangl and Delacroix. And an even stranger balance sheet that let a man find a new friend while taking from him an old one.

The muted roar of the engine droned steadily through the hours of the flight. Conflicts and tensions made his mind tired and his body weak. He thought dark thoughts all the way, through the refueling, until the pilot came back to inform him they had arrived.

Four

The W.H.O. building was a low three-story structure of white concrete on a red-brick base. Three times as long as wide, it had an institutional, efficient look about it.

In the main lobby a kiosk served as both an information center and a bookstore. Copies of *World Health*, the W.H.O. monthly magazine, were free for the taking, along with other pamphlets on health care. Medical books for both laymen and staff were for sale, and Ben browsed through a few.

"When is the next tour?" Ben asked the saleswoman in French.

"In a half hour, sir. The group will assemble here, and the tour guide will meet you."

He sat on one of the couches provided in the lobby and watched the human traffic. White-jacketed medical staff bustled in and out, and nurses escorted patients with a variety of maladies so diverse that Ben could name only a few.

A young Congolese child, no more than a year old, Ben guessed, ran through the lobby despite the protestations of her mother in a language he couldn't translate. The mother had her arms filled with a second child, her face a mask of concern. The child in her arms was unconscious, limp, and feverish.

Suddenly, the little girl tripped and fell flat on her face. Tears poured from her eyes, and loud wails tore from her throat.

Unsure of custom but hoping that certain things were universal, Ben picked up the child and tried to calm her.

"You're causing quite a ruckus, princess. And mama's got to take care of your brother. Yes, princess, I know it hurts. Yes, I know..." he crooned to her, knowing that not a single word made sense. He was rewarded by a pause in her tears, three huge sniffles, and a look of curiosity on her face. He beamed back at her, and she giggled.

A yanked ear and poked eye later, Ben saw the sick child

removed from the mother by a doctor. The mother, very aware of her other child, descended quickly upon her, followed by a young doctor. But her expression softened when she saw the child's smile and heard her contented cooings. Ben delivered up the child at once, almost losing a tuft of hair the baby had latched onto in the process.

"*Merci, m'sieu. Mon fils est malade. Je devrais partir. Le docteur...*"

"*Je comprends, madame. La petite est très belle. Pas de quoi.*"

The mother smiled at the compliment to her daughter, took the girl's hand, and moved off after the waiting doctor.

A group of people had assembled at the kiosk. Ben joined them as the tour guide started by explaining basic facts about the W.H.O.

Going upstairs to the first floor, they were shown labs and classrooms, a brief film, and numerous displays. Pictures of poverty so devastating that malnutrition and disease were dynastic were paraded before them. It was a sobering experience for Ben.

But apart from familiarizing him with the building's layout, the tour told him little that he did not know.

On the third floor the tour passed a room marked Staff Cafeteria. Ben hung back, as the group moved forward, and slipped away unnoticed.

Inside were a few dozen formica-topped tables and groups of people eating and talking. No one objected to his entrance, so Ben picked up a tray, selected some food, and sat down at a vacant table, wondering how to start a conversation with someone.

"Nice of you to tend to the little girl. You seem to have a way with children," said an English voice over his shoulder.

Ben looked up and recognized the doctor from the lobby.

"I could never resist the tears of a child," Ben said, smiling.

"Then we have something in common. I like kids myself. Mind if I join you?"

Elated, Ben gestured to an empty chair.

"I'm Phillip Crandall, on staff here in Pediatrics. English, as you can probably tell."

He offered his hand, and they shook.

"Andre Bouvin. Journalist. Just flew in from Paris."

"You're French? You speak English like an American," said Crandall.

"I did graduate study there. The accent stayed with me. I've worked there several times over the years."

"I see," nodded Crandall. "What brings you to Brazzaville? Which, I might add, is as different from Paris as anything you're likely to find."

"I'm thinking of doing a series of articles on the regional centers. Pick up the contrasts here to the Orient, the Americas, that sort of thing. See how the problems and the approaches differ."

"Could be interesting," agreed Crandall. "You've taken the tour, I suppose."

"I just finished it. I came in hoping to interview some of the staff. Would you mind?"

"Not at all. That's two l's in Crandall."

"I'll remember," Ben smiled, fishing out a pad and pen from his jacket pocket.

As they talked about the problems peculiar to practicing medicine in Africa, Crandall called others over to the table to meet Ben. Soon a doctor, two nurses, and a project foreman, were seated with them discussing material for the "article."

Gradually, he was able to introduce Voorstein's name into the conversation.

"A dynamo. Just like his father," said Dr. Reegan, an Irish woman in her late fifties.

"He's always in and out on business. A program in Kenya, a clinic in Uganda. The man never stops. Dedicated."

"He's South African, isn't he?" Ben asked, and put a deliberate tone of doubt in his voice.

"Indeed," said Crandall. "But don't let that get in your way. He's devoted to the tribespeople."

"Does the W.H.O. do much work in South Africa? The country is much wealthier than other African states." Ben continued to probe.

"Not the native population," said Gamal, the project foreman. He was Egyptian, of swarthy complexion and solid build. "Some do better, around the cities, but most are as bad off as the rest. We're building a series of hospitals there right now. It's a major project, and Voorstein is directing it personally."

Ben wanted more but came at it slowly. "That's an interesting slant," he mused out loud. "Goes against the media stereotypes."

"It does that," agreed Reegan. "And it's the kind of thing we all would like to see in print. Voorstein's a great man. He deserves it."

"Didn't that chap Ryerson just get back from there?" asked Crandall. "Maybe he's still around. He was in only yesterday."

Ben caught Gamal's uneasiness.

"Who's this Ryerson?" he asked.

"He was on one of the construction crews in the RSA. I did his physical check-up when he came back for reassignment. He wasn't too happy about the change, though, and he's been doing a lot of drinking lately," said Crandall.

"Maybe it would be better to pass him up," said Gamal. "I don't think he's too reliable."

Ben decided not to push. He came at it from another angle.

"Where do you all go to relax? There must be some favored watering holes."

Laughter greeted his question.

"In the city, everybody goes to Jacot's," said Shuan, a very pretty Asian nurse.

"Or Le Styx," chimed in Crandall with a leer that made Shuan giggle. "That's about all the city has to offer."

"I'd like to meet Voorstein," said Ben.

"He's not at the center now," said Reegan. "Probably be back from South Africa in a few days. It's been good to meet you, Bouvin, but I've got to get back to work. Best of luck with the article."

Ben stood up to take her hand. Crandall and the others stood as well.

"I think we'd all better go. Call us if you need anything. Right?" said Crandall.

Ben thanked them all as they drifted away and put his pad and pen back into his jacket. He wanted to meet this Ryerson who had just returned from South Africa. And returned unhappy.

Le Styx was aptly named, for, akin to the mythical river, most of its patrons looked as if they drank to forget. It smelled of sweat and beer and people. Couples groped each other in booths on which old leather was patched with tape, and a few soldiers danced with women Ben was sure worked, rather than frequented, the establishment. Old, slowly rotating fans barely disturbed the thick, smoky air.

"Scotch," Ben told the thin, lanky bartender whose white apron, incongruously, was spotless. The man was built like a spider, long arms, neck, and legs, and he prepared the drink in quick separate motions and set it on the bar.

"Do you know a man named Ryerson?" Ben asked. "I was told he does his drinking here."

The question failed to animate the bartender. Ben put a fifty-franc note on the bar and watched it put some interest into the man's features as he reached for it.

Ben put his hand over the money. "Ryerson."

The bartender inclined his long neck toward a corner of the bar where a man sat alone at a table with a bottle in front of him. Ben took his hand away.

He studied Ryerson for a while. Hunched over a glass, the tense set of his broad shoulders seemed to indicate hostility. No one approached him, and even the lone, fat waitress skirted his table. He's nursing that bottle like a grudge, thought Ben, walking over.

"Mr. Ryerson? My name is Andre Bouvin. We have acquaintances in common."

Ryerson looked up, a sullen glaze on his face. "I don't know you, mate."

"You're just up from South Africa. I'd like to hear about it," Ben plunged ahead.

"Not a flamin' thing to tell. I got canned. Just as well, maybe. Rotten flamin' place, that was." He lifted his glass and downed another shot.

Ben sat down opposite Ryerson without being asked, and he felt the other man tense.

"Bug off," said Ryerson, low and deadly.

"I've come a long way, Mr. Ryerson. I need to talk to you. I'd appreciate the time."

"You don't hear very well. I don't want to talk."

The man's menace was almost tangible. At this distance his breath was heavy and sodden. Ryerson measured him with a long stare, and his hand moved toward the bottle.

"Don't even think it," said Ben quietly. Ryerson's face showed nothing.

"Are you good enough to stop me walkin' out of here, though? That's the question, mate."

Ben put both hands on the table. "It's a long way to the door."

Suddenly, Ryerson's face cracked into a huge grin, and one big hand slapped the table.

"It is that, mate. It is that."

Ben relaxed and made a peace offering.

"I'm sorry to intrude. But Crandall said you were in South Africa on W.H.O. business constructing a new hospital. He also said you were unhappy. Gamal said not to bother with you, but I'd like to know why."

"Gamal talks too much. Why are you so interested?"

"I want to know more about Voorstein's projects in South Africa."

Ryerson shrugged. "That doesn't answer my question."

Ben ordered another drink from the waitress. "It's very complicated. I think something is happening in South Africa. Maybe your project is connected. Maybe not. Why was Gamal uneasy when your name was mentioned?"

"He's a foreman." Ryerson made it sound like a dirty word.

"That's not a crime," Ben said.

"Listen, Bouvin. There is something going on down there. And the foremen, at least some of them, are in on it. But I'll be blasted if I can figure it out."

"Or you're just pissed off because they fired you," prodded Ben.

"I was never fired from a job in my life," Ryerson said belligerently. "And sure as hell not for looking at a set of prints. How could I work blind? And when I did see 'em, they made no sense. How could . . ." His annoyance faded. "You did that deliberately."

Ben nodded. "I'm in a hurry."

"You are a slick bastard. I'll grant you that," grinned Ryerson, appreciatively.

Ben returned the grin. "And you're not a man I'd ever fire, I think."

"Let me buy you a drink, Bouvin."

"Ben. Ben Davidson," he said, making a sudden, intuitive decision to trust him.

Ryerson lifted an eyebrow and raised the bottle to Ben's

glass. "My pleasure, Ben. It's Craig to my friends. You have more names?"

"You said you were fired because you looked at the prints. I take it you mean blueprints. It strikes me as odd they would be kept secret," Ben said.

"Odd as hell. That's what stirred up my curiosity. My foreman got bitten by a snake, and I got a chance to see them. What we were told we were building and what the plans really called for were two different things. Whatever it is, it's no hospital like I've ever seen."

"Can you be more specific?"

Ryerson explained detail after detail where the blueprints were coded in error: the large rooms, the huge wards, down to the classroom sizes and kitchen facilities.

". . . And the place is built like a fortress. Double perimeter fence all around." A stray memory struck him. "Do you know what a P4 designation is? It was on the prints in what they coded as office space. I've never seen it before, and it might not even mean anything."

Ben shook his head. "It's vaguely familiar. I think I may have heard it sometime. But I'm not sure; P4. Shit, that does sound familiar."

"Another foreman came in while I had the prints. I thought I put him off. Next day I was reassigned. It still sticks in my craw."

Ben was only half listening. More pieces, he thought. And now the puzzle extended back to South Africa to where it had begun. P4, whatever it meant, tugged vaguely at his subconscious. A hospital that wasn't a hospital. Annie's baby. Croft is Stumpfegger and Stumpfegger is a Nazi sang in his head again.

And somewhere in all this was Lisa. I'll always come for you, he had said. His hands balled into fists. I should be able to put it together, he thought, and it was maddening. Ryerson was still talking.

". . . With wards that size you could raise a flamin' army. Classrooms big enough for hundreds of blokes. Nothing fit. Voorstein must have something up his sleeve if he's putting it up. Always hanging around poking into things . . ."

Raise an army, Ben mused. Funny thought. He watched the big fan blades turn slowly, and the steady beat of loud music from the jukebox hammered at his mind. He had found more pieces but still no pattern. Raise an army. Damn funny thought. P4 on the charts. He had heard that before.

"Even the labs were restricted. Guarded night and day. Terrorists, they claimed." Ryerson was still talking. A dam had burst releasing long pent-up rage. "Never fired before..."

No pattern. There had to be a connection. The moisture on his glass slid to the table top in tiny beads. Idly, he traced meaningless designs in the film of moisture. P4, each one looked like. He tried to recall something Lisa had said in Amsterdam. Something that had prodded other memories; a sense of connection.

"I don't think we..." Ben began when suddenly the whole world exploded in his head. In a blinding flash of intuition, all the pieces fit, and the jigsaw puzzle locked into place.

"What's wrong? Ben? Are you all right? Your mouth is hangin' open. Ben? Hey!"

He knew where he had seen P4 and what it meant. And like a puzzle where one piece led inevitably to the rest, locking together in a fixed pattern, he saw it all, the implications, remembered Lisa's words. He saw it right back to Croft, all the way back to 1936.

"What is it, Ben?" Ryerson's voice held concern, worry.

"Raise an army, Craig," Ben said. "You were right. They're going to raise a goddamned army."

Ryerson was totally confused. "Who's going to raise an army? Make sense, mate. I don't follow you.

"P4, that's what it means. I remember from med school. Tell me, did the prints have anything in them near the P4 designation that looked like double doors or a sealable entry?" Ben asked excitedly.

"They did! It looked like an airlock. I thought it must be a misread on my part," said Ryerson.

"Airlocks. Oh, my God. They *were* airlocks. You weren't wrong. That's what P4 is all about."

"I don't follow. You don't need an airlock in a hospital."

"No you don't. But you need them in a Microbiological Containment Area if you're working with the most virulent bacteria. There are four levels of P, which stands for the physical aspects of containment of deadly life forms. P1 requires nothing more than standard microbiological practice, cleanliness and anticontamination procedures. P2 is roughly

the same, but protects against the dispersion of aerosols."
Ben was breathing hard, racing ahead, seeing the pattern.

"P3 requires negative air pressure in the lab to prevent the
escape of any airborne life. And P4 is needed only with the
most dangerous pathogenic disease carriers. It requires airlocks,
protective clothing, and even showers for the personnel.
Those weren't offices, they were labs! That's what P4 means.
And I know what they're doing in them."

"Labs aren't out of place in a hospital, Ben," Ryerson said.

"But it's not a hospital. You even said that you'd never seen
anything like it before. It's not a hospital, Craig. It's a
nursery! A place to raise an army. An army that they're going
to create to solve a problem that's three hundred years old."

"Who's they?"

"A group of Afrikaners in South Africa. In one shot they're
going to take care of their racial problems. And what they
plan to do makes the apartheid policy seem kind by comparison. I've got to trust you completely, Craig. I need your
help."

His words flowing out in a torrent, Ben told Ryerson about
Mississippi and what he had found there. He told him about
Van Dyne and the diamonds, tracing the flow back to Brazzaville,
to Voorstein. He told him about Leander's manipulation.
Finally, he told him about Lisa.

"She had the answer, Craig, only I didn't see it till now.
There are twenty-four million blacks and four million whites
in South Africa. She said there wasn't one government official
that went to sleep at night not thinking of how to change that
question of balance. Do you see it? That's what they intend to
do. Just like in Mississippi. In one stroke they plan to
decrease the blacks by creating whites! What you were
building in South Africa isn't a hospital. It's a nursery! A place
to take white children born of black parents and raise them
by the state. That's why there was so much space. That's the
need for classrooms and kitchens of such size. To teach the
children. The new Afrikaners."

"It's not possible," protested Ryerson. "No one could do
that. It's crazy."

"No it's not," insisted Ben. "It's called Recombinant DNA.
In the States we're just beginning to understand it. But these
people have a head start, a forty-year head start. The
Adlerkinden—the Eagle's Children. *These* are the children

they mean. And what better partners than the Nazis? It's staggering, but so was the genocide of six million Jews and twelve million Eastern Europeans. It's a second Holocaust, but this time for the blacks."

"It's insane if what you believe is true. But I don't see how it's flamin' possible, Ben."

"I don't know how they're going to do it. But the W.H.O. is involved, that's for sure, through Voorstein. His father was an original member of the conspiracy. I need to get into his office. He may keep some records there that will give us something to work with. I can't even venture a guess as to their delivery mechanism for changing the genetic structure at long range. But you can bet that they've got one."

Ben turned it over and over again in his mind. It was clear; so obvious in retrospect.

"It would be easier just to kill the blacks, I would think," said Ryerson.

"Without the blacks to do the manual labor, the dirty jobs, the whole system falls apart. Kings have to have subjects. Royalty doesn't want to take out the garbage or sweep streets. They need their servants. No ruling class has ever been without them. They don't want to kill the blacks, Craig. They want to outnumber them."

"It's insane." Ryerson's mind refused to accept.

"But it's real. I saw my friend die because of it. And Lisa is gone because of it. I'm going to find her, Craig, but I have to find where those people operate from, because that's where I'm betting she is. They'll hold her, I think, and her father's position will keep her alive. That's all I've got, and no one is going to stop me. No one!" Ben raged.

Ryerson looked at him strangely. "I don't expect they will, Ben. You ever do construction?"

"Never. Why?" asked Ben, confused by the change of direction.

"You've got the balls for it, mate," he said quietly.

The W.H.O. Center was almost empty at night. Moving silently over the lawns, bushes screening their progress, they reached it unseen, and Ryerson led them to the side door.

"I want you to consider what you're getting into, Craig," Ben said. "People have already died. You've got to understand that these men are insane; not frothing at the mouth insane, but the kind of insanity that just plots the shortest distance between two points and goes that way. They have no regard for rules or ethics or costs, and if you are perceived as an obstacle, you'll die. Logical and precise. That's a whole different kind of insane."

"Quiet down. I can't work with your jabbering. We've been all through that already. Chalk it up to the cactus bush theory if you like."

In the complete dark, working mostly by feel, Ryerson was methodically breaking the locks. One security guard patrolled the building, and only a small staff worked the night shift.

"Cactus bush? What are you talking about?" Ben whispered.

Ryerson put pressure on the screwdriver he had inserted into the doorjamb, grunting with effort. He whispered hoarsely, "I'm here for the same reason the man jumped naked into the cactus bush."

"Which is?"

"Seemed like a good idea at the time."

Ben was past the point where he could refuse Ryerson's help. The man seemed strong and sure of himself, and a relationship of sorts was growing between them.

Whether it was simply resentment about his firing that caused Ryerson to join him or something more—he hesitated to use the word, noble—didn't really matter. Unsure and feeling desperate, Ben was glad to have his support. All he could do was warn Ryerson. It was his right after that to choose for himself.

The doorjamb separated from the wall it was set into. Ryerson pried at the crossbolt, and the door swung open.

"Voorstein's office is on the top floor. There are only administrative offices up there, which should be empty," he said.

The carpeted hallway on the top floor smothered noise as they walked. Senses alerted for the slightest sound of another presence, they detected no one. The polished wooden doors to other offices on the long dark corridor were smooth and cool to touch as they felt, rather than saw, their way along the dark corridors.

Ryerson repeated his performance with the screwdriver, and thirty seconds later they stood in the anteroom of Voorstein's office; thirty seconds after that in the office itself.

Ben experienced a strong déja vu. He had been in Van Dyne's office only days before and could only hope that the sophisticated detection equipment of a Diamond Exchange had not been installed here. In almost total darkness, he heard Ryerson closing the window blinds. Abruptly, Voorstein's desk lamp was turned on.

Ben saw Ryerson's satisfied look as his vision cleared, growing used to the light.

"Do you know what we're looking for?" Ryerson asked in a hushed voice.

"Only vaguely," Ben responded, and took his first look around the office. Standard institutionalized furniture, a desk, chairs, and a table were set up in front of the single, wide window. The walls were painted an ugly beige color, and a glass cabinet full of African carvings and ivory figures stood against the far wall, next to the door and a bookcase full of medical tests. Two file cabinets and a Xerox copier were in the corner.

"I'm going to go through his files. You check the room for a hidden safe or cabinets."

Ryerson nodded and began probing and tapping his way through the room.

The cabinets were unlocked, either a sign of arrogance, he decided, or an indication of valueless contents.

He moved through the files as fast as he could read them. Personnel folders, purchase orders for medicines and supplies, public relations materials, correspondence with other regional centers, minutes of staff meetings, cost overruns, nothing of value to him. No sign of DNA experimentation, and no mention of the Adlerkinden.

"Ben!"

Ryerson's voice was excited.

A section of paneling had slid aside, revealing a set of folder boxes within. Together, they transferred them to the desk.

Ben felt his heart racing in excitement and elation.

"Stand watch outside," he told Ryerson. "I'm going to look these over."

"You got it, mate. Just be right quick," said Ryerson, and he left the room.

One ear cocked to hear any signal from Ryerson, Ben spread the contents of the first box on Voorstein's desk.

Records of experimentation on human DNA, coupled with experiments using bacteria, virus, and an array of techniques and information he could barely grasp without close further study.

He turned on the Xerox machine and waited for it to heat up. In the meantime, he brought the papers over and then the rest of the file boxes. When the machine was ready, he copied each page and replaced them into the folder box. It took over two hours to copy the full set of four boxes in all.

Finished, he reset the counter on the machine to where it had been, carefully replaced the file boxes back in their niche, and closed it. He checked for any sign of their entry, took the sheaf of copied papers, and turned off Voorstein's lamp before reopening the shades.

Ryerson was seated in the anteroom, alert and nervous.

"What in flamin' hell took so long?" he asked anxiously.

Ben held up the papers. "Let's go. I need time and quiet to look at these. Can you put the locks back as they were?"

"No problem. Just have to bang back the jambs and reslide the bolts. It won't stand up to real close inspection, but there shouldn't be one."

The office relocked, Ben followed Ryerson back down the corridor to the stairs. He clutched the papers as if they contained the secrets of life. And if what he had surmised from the little he'd seen was borne out, it was a likelihood not altogether farfetched.

Five

Ben worked through the rest of the night, Voorstein's papers strewn about the room along with dozens of crumpled yellow paper balls: the remains of notes he had made. Empty coffee cups from the hotel's bar lay piled up and overflowing from the wastepaper baskets. Ben had sent Ryerson out twice to the W.H.O. Center itself, to buy medical and biological texts that he needed to refresh his memory of studies done years before and to update his knowledge.

Ryerson returned to see shock and disbelief etched into Ben's face as he pored over the records, deciphering what lay within. Grunts that Ryerson could only identify as horror escaped Ben's throat regularly.

In the late morning Ben fell asleep at the desk. Ryerson hefted him easily onto the bed and went down to the restaurant to buy breakfast. After a brisk walk outside to clear his head, he returned to find Ben back at the desk slumped over a new section from the files.

"You've got to rest," he said later in the day, looking at Ben's sunken eyes and hollow cheeks.

"Later," was the only response.

"Then at least eat something. It will do no good if you collapse. You've been at it for over twelve hours."

Ben accepted the logic of his statement and paused only to eat a sandwich. Then he went back to his notes.

In the evening he finally fell onto the bed for a few hours of restless, tossing sleep.

Ryerson watched him grimly and went and got more food. It, too, lay untouched after Ben awoke until he again insisted that it be eaten.

The only real response that Ryerson got was on the morning of the second day. He had slept part of the night and found Ben still at the papers when he awoke.

"How about a shower, mate? Take the kinks out. I think you could use one."

"Can't. Not yet," mumbled Ben.

"She must be quite a woman, this Lisa of yours," he mused aloud.

Ben looked up, the harsh lines of strain clearly evident, his voice raspy and tired.

"It's past that, Craig. She and I are only a small part now. They'll have to kill me to keep me from her. I have to—need to—find her. But compared to this," he gestured at the papers, "we're unimportant. There's no other word for what they intend but evil. Evil on so grand a scale that it's difficult even to conceive of it. I've almost got it all. Just a few hours more. I'll rest later."

"Okay, Ben," he said. "Get on with it."

Ben hadn't even heard him, lost again in the graphs and charts of Voorstein's files.

It was Ryerson who fell asleep, exhausted by the tension of

his vigil. His respect for the stubborn tenacity of his new friend had grown along with his affection. He recognized a similar breed of man. Like himself, Ben stubbornly fought with every resource at his command until there was nothing else left but will alone. The sound of the shower woke him, and by the light streaming in the windows, he knew it was morning. His clothes were wrinkled and sweaty, so he stripped them off and waited. The papers were piled neatly in a pile on the desk.

Ben emerged, dripping wet with a towel draped around him

"You look better," Ryerson observed.

"I got a little sleep. I finished it last night."

"You look frightened when you say that."

"I am. I understand most of what they intend to do, Craig. Even so, it's hard to believe. Go wash up, and I'll order breakfast. Then you can have an explanation."

"But it's not good, I'll bet."

"We have, my friend," Ben said tiredly, "jumped right into the flamin' cactus bush."

They put the food on the table by the window and ate slowly. Sleep and hot water had restored some of their energy and erased much of their fatigue. Ben reached for the coffeepot.

"How much do you know about DNA," he asked, "or genetics?"

"Not enough to pass a high school biology test. If that's what this is about, you'd better start from the top," said Ryerson, noticing Ben's hand shake as he poured the coffee.

"Think in terms of construction, Craig. For every project you are going to construct, there is a blueprint that indicates which materials are going to be used and in what order to put them together. If you follow the blueprint, you build the correct structure. You are, in effect, 'slaved' to the blueprint, carrying out its orders; a messenger and a constructor."

"Not very flattering the way you put it."

"But accurate nonetheless. The human body works the same way. In every one of our cells there is a set of blueprints that contains the instructions for the use of materials and the order they are to be put together in order to keep the body growing and functioning from birth to death. The food we eat is broken down into its components and used as raw materials in the cells according to the blueprint. The name for this blueprint is DNA, and it is found in the nucleus of all our cells.

"A gene, the biochemical unit that determines our heredity and how certain processes will take place in the organism, may contain as much as one hundred thousand molecules of DNA; and the human cell has about one hundred thousand genes. Genes are linked together like a string of beads to form units called chromosomes. Like a blueprint, the instructions are all in a kind of code, a chemical code. Every human's cells, with only some exceptions, have forty-six chromosomes."

"Sounds like one helluva blueprint. All that in every single cell," exclaimed Ryerson.

"And yet the whole package is so small it can only be seen under the most powerful of microscopes.

"Now, the body is composed almost entirely of protein, large molecules made up of amino acids, which are smaller molecules composed of carbon, oxygen, nitrogen, and hydrogen. Though there are only twenty or so different amino acids occurring in the proteins of living matter, twenty can be arranged in an endless variety. The enzymes in our system are made of proteins; the organs are made of proteins; even our hair is protein. There are around a hundred thousand different proteins in our bodies. The DNA in our genes directs the production of the protein from the basic building blocks of amino acids.

"Again, in terms of construction, iron and carbon and other chemicals are put together to make the more complex compound—steel—which is then used as part of a building. Still with me?"

Ryerson nodded. "As long as you use construction terms."

"Fine. Here's how the process works. DNA in the genes of the cell makes a copy of itself, like a photocopy of a blueprint. The copy is called RNA, and it has a slightly different chemical structure. The RNA picks up the genetic code and carries the instructions to a part of the cell, the ribosomes, where it supervises the protein manufacture—analogous to the foreman telling you to go over to the site and build a brick wall of some design and dimension."

He sipped at his coffee while Ryerson tried to digest the

complicated picture he had drawn. He had only scratched the surface of the complexity of genetics, but it would suffice as a background for the other man's understanding of the horror that was yet to come.

"DNA is the foreman with the prints; RNA is the assistant who supervises construction, and the ribowhatevers are the construction site. Yes?" asked Ryerson, like an eager-to-please schoolboy.

"Ribosomes. Yes," agreed Ben. "But now you have to understand heredity, the inheritance of traits from parent to child.

"You get twenty-three of these chromosomes from each parent. That's why you have the characteristics of both; tall like your father, fair like your mother, and so on. Since each chromosome is a string of genes, you now have a new set of coding instructions for every part and process of the body. Every sperm carries twenty-three chromosomes, and every egg, twenty-three. They pair up when sperm meets egg to fertilize it and form the forty-six you get in your cells. So every individual inherits genes in pairs, two genes for every trait. The pair is called alleles; one, an allele. This way your biological and physical traits are inherited from your parents. Two whites mate and produce a white-skinned child; two blacks marry and produce a black-skinned child. Eskimos produce Eskimos and Orientals produce Orientals. People can intermarry and produce a child with racial characteristics of both parents, a hybrid.

"Now here's where we get to the state of the art. There is a branch of medicine called genetic engineering. It hopes to be able to surgically, or otherwise, remove one or more genes and replace them with another. Up till now, it's only been theoretically possible."

"I don't see the purpose in that."

"Think, Craig. The possibilities are endless. On the positive side you could eliminate all birth defects. Anyone with a chemical deficiency—like diabetics who don't produce insulin, a protein—could be genetically altered to be able to produce it. You could control every process and every trait of a human being. Decide on what you want your children to be, and they will be it. No more bad teeth, no more retardation, no more cancer or genetic diseases like Tay-Sachs or sickle cell anemia. It's staggering, Craig."

Ryerson stared at Ben, shaken. "We could be . . . gods," he whispered. "Perfect."

"But flawed human gods," Ben said sadly. "That's the catch. Who defines perfection? Is blond better than brunette, or tall better than short? Should we make some people stupid so they can be happier sweeping streets? These are old arguments, and no one has the answers; only the questions, and not even all of them have been asked. Possibilities we can't even foresee may arise. Think of the applications to biological warfare: genetically altered supergerms immune to all vaccines. Like every coin, there are two sides. Gods can destroy as well as create. We could build an Eden or a Hell. Given our history, I'm not inclined to believe easily in the former."

Ryerson shook his head to clear it. "It's unbelievable. It could change everything, the whole world. Could you do it with plants as well? And animals?"

"Sure. You could produce stronger, better-yielding grains or cattle that could survive in the Arctic. Remake bacteria to produce chemicals we need as a byproduct . . ."

"Or on the opposite side, create bigger and better soldiers or animals with enough intelligence to be trained to kill," Ryerson finished. "Tell me, Ben, what the Afrikaners are going to do. Tell me what you've found."

"The opposite side, Craig. That's what I found. It's all there in Voorstein's papers. They're way ahead of the rest of the scientific world. Not more than ten years ahead, probably, since they couldn't publish and share their experimental results. But they haven't had any ethical restrictions either. I told you about Annie."

He wanted to avoid saying the words. The Nazis and the Afrikaners—the Second Holocaust. The coffee was cold and bitter, like the meaning he had found.

"They've found a way, Craig, to initiate long-range genetic splicing. The offspring will not resemble its parents—the ultimate final solution. *No more blacks*, Craig; that's what they're after! A white South Africa where black parents produce white children, raised by the state in giant nurseries. Racial genocide, where every birth ends a part of a race.

"Lisa explained it. It's the balance: six to one. They're going to correct it. My dear God, they're going to correct it."

"It's not possible, Ben. I can't believe it. No one would allow it."

"Like no one allowed Nazi Germany. And no one allows apartheid. With the kind of censorship they have here, no one will even know about it for years. And even if they did, then what? No country is going to go to war over it. Protests, that's what there'll be. Protests and outrage."

"Do you know how they intend to do this long-range changing?"

"It's all in the notes. If it wasn't so totally malevolent, it would be brilliant.

"It's a three-stage process. The DNA in bacteria is simple and in the shape of a ring, a plasmid, it's called. They've altered bacteria plasmids by splicing in a new gene, which causes the bacteria to produce a new enzyme. The bacteria is site specific; that means it attacks a specific site in the body, just as you get a chest cold or an eye infection. These bacteria infect the testes in men and the ovaries in women. They will infect the spermatogonia, the site that produces sperm, and all of the half million eggs in the ovaries.

"The bacteria invading the cells attacks the sperm and eggs producing an enzyme, a 'cutting' enzyme site specific to the genes that control racial characteristics. Within five days, these genes are 'cut' from the strands of DNA in the black person's cells by the intrusion of the enzyme."

"Doesn't the body fight the infection?"

"It does. It ultimately kills the bacteria and restores health, but the damage is done. It's too late. Those cut genes are dead. Then comes the second stage.

"A virus is released. Now a virus is nothing more than a protein shell packed with DNA. In this case the DNA, the blueprint, for the creation of white, European-featured children. It, too, is site specific and invades the same cells that have already been attacked. The viral DNA replaces the cut-out DNA, and a new set of genes in the sperm and egg are present. The process is called transduction. New blueprint—new building. It's already been done in America on a small scale.

"Again the infection is killed by the body's antibodies, but again it's too late.

"The process is completed in stage three. Just like stage one, a second altered bacteria is released, which is site specific, and produces an 'annealing' enzyme that closes the splice. Again it is killed, but the process is over. The whole thing, from start to finish, takes two weeks. And every black who survives it will carry the seeds of white children."

"But people will be sick and come for assistance. It will be spotted," insisted Ryerson.

"They'll come to places like the W.H.O. Remember who controls that. For Christ's sake, it's the W.H.O. that developed and transports the diseases! Voorstein's section, at least did.

"With their diplomatic immunity no one can even stop or search them. They're going to use the water supply to distribute the diseases. Every reservoir and every river in the country will be contaminated. In a country where people use water directly from the rivers, it will infect almost every native man, woman, and child."

"If that's true, it will infect the whites as well. They can't want that, Ben. But it's unavoidable."

"They've worked that out, too. Almost all the whites live in the cities. Those who don't are in communication by radio and phone. They'll announce that the supply of water is not drinkable, tainted, and to use bottled water. The whites escape uninfected."

"Then so do the city blacks."

"Some. Those who can afford bottled water that will be restricted and sold only to whites. And that's fine with them. Remember, they don't want to eliminate blacks completely— just outnumber them forever. They'll have city-trained blacks who are still a slave labor force.

"The demographics are all there in the papers. They estimate a death rate of blacks at five to ten percent, a successful infection rate of seventy to seventy-five percent, and a no-success rate of fifteen to twenty-five percent due to natural immunity. In raw figures, that's over two million dead, eighteen million converted, and six million unchanged. Better odds for the racists."

The thought of a helicopter ride back to Brazzaville suddenly leaped into Ryerson's mind.

"Ben," he said excitedly. "I think I know where they make the stuff, the diseases. I know where they come from. I've seen the test tubes that contain the diseases. They're packed in groups of three just like you said."

He told Ben of the metal boxes being shipped and of the incident that broke open the seal of one case.

"No wonder the foreman was upset," Ben said. "The bacteria will work over short distances airborne as well. If the tubes had broken.."

"I don't want to think of that."

"Do you think you could get us into the labs in South Africa?" Ben asked. "If we could get to the production center, we might find out who controls the whole project."

"And where Lisa is," Ryerson added.

Ben nodded. "A sample would also be proof enough to go to the U.N. I don't hold out much hope of their being effective, but it's a beginning, Craig."

"I think I can wangle us a flight on the next copter back. No reason the pilot should refuse. I've still got my papers. But they'll know we've arrived."

"Then we'll rent one ourselves. I've got enough money."

"I'll be back in an hour," said Ryerson, his face set and grim.

Ben sat for a long time in silence. Car horns blared in the street, signals of frustration echoing his mood. Though the air was stale, he made no move to open the shutters.

Now I understand, he thought, what I saw in Mississippi. They must be very close to beginning. Very close. He wondered where Lisa was, and pain followed the thought, ripping through his chest. He was grateful for Ryerson's presence. Alone, he might have broken.

Six

The remainder of the day they spent preparing to leave for South Africa, after Ryerson had returned to announce he'd procured a helicopter and pilot.

Ben packed his possessions in the suitcases he'd brought and locked them in the hotel's storage space. Then he and Ryerson had purchased supplies and equipment for the jungle. Everything went into two knapsacks: extra khaki pants and shirts, canteens, ground cloths, hunting knife, hiking boots, assorted camping gear, even a small metal box that Ben hoped to fill with captured specimens from Voorstein's lab. Last, he had been able to buy a .45 automatic that rested, with spare clips, inside his pack, a reassuring weight. Voorstein's papers lay alongside.

Ryerson had declined a weapon. "Never used one," he had said, holding up his large, strong hands.

Ben watched as Ryerson purchased the tools he felt they would need. A taxi took them to the private airstrip a few miles south of the city.

"Have you thought about what you'll do with the papers? If you release them, then everyone will know how to do genetic splicing. I thought about it, and that may not be such a good idea," Ryerson said while they waited for the pilot to finish his preflight check.

"No one person can make that decision. There will be progress whether or not we bury the research. It's only a matter of time till the rest of the world knows how to do it anyway." He paused for a second to frame the words. "I wouldn't outlaw guns just because some crazies use them to kill people in the streets. Or cars because some people drive them into brick walls. Nothing is inherently good or evil—it all depends on who does the using. Progress is going to occur in spite of any attempt to stop it. All we can hope is to be mature enough to live with it."

"Maybe some things aren't possible to live with. Maybe there's a too far," Ryerson objected.

"Change is painful, Craig. Old ideas mean security, and we look back and say how great it was way-back-when. But kings used to die of syphillis, and castles were drafty because they had no central heating. You can't go backward, even if it was better back then—which it wasn't."

"He's ready," Ryerson said, catching the pilot's signal.

They crawled into the four-seater helicopter, its engine already revving, and stowed their knapsacks.

Ben felt a rush of adrenaline rip at his heart as they lifted off.

Leander strode into his office causing a cry of dismay from Lana Hunzen at his torn, dirty clothing. She followed him inside, but he had already plunged into the bathroom.

"Lana?" he called out.

"I'm here, Jan. What happened?"

"Dreyer and I were shot at coming from the airport by three men, now deceased. Dispatch a team to clean it up. Ten miles north of the airport and a half mile or so off the R twenty-one; four bodies in the limousine. I want any possible I.D. on the three gunmen. Have my driver prepared for burial services and notify his family. I'll do something personal later."

"Is that all?"

"No. Call the doctor. My back feels like I caught something in it. And send for Dreyer as soon as he's able to come up."

Lana Hunzen ran off to comply. Word of the attack by now had reached the other section chiefs, and her phone lines were ablaze with incoming signals. She gave out a standard reply that there was no danger and put them off till later. Then she completed the rest of her instructions.

She ushered the doctor in when he arrived and waited nervously for the half hour he was in with Leander. When the doctor left, she went in.

Leander was naked from the waist up, strips of adhesive holding gauze in place on his back. He heard her sharp intake of breath.

"Nothing to worry about. A few creases and some cuts from flying glass and metal. Surface wounds."

Her words of concern were cut off by Dreyer's entrance. He too had cleaned up, but his face, she saw, was a mask of tension.

They sat at the conference table. Leander motioned to Lana Hunzen.

"I want a complete record of this meeting taken down. We are on very dangerous ground; and if it blows up, I want it to be my sole responsibility. I'm going to give you a set of documents that I want assembled into a file. Code mark it: Adlerkinden.

"Peter, assemble a list of agents to be recalled here at once. We're going to need men we can rely on to stay quiet and do their job. Assign a covert three-man team to every name on that document including the Prime Minister and Putten in Amsterdam. Make sure they're armed. And assemble an interrogation team as well."

"I've got to know what you're planning if I'm to select personnel," said Dreyer.

"You were right. We have no options left. Today proved that. The Adlerkinden know about us, and our crystal operation has been blown.

"If we cannot establish within the next twenty-four hours the location and the purpose of their group, we will give the document to the state president. Having already set up our teams on Smith and his cohorts, we can claim jurisdiction as the conspiracy involves citizens of a foreign power and take them into custody before any other branch can move. Then the I-team goes to work.

"If we move fast enough, we can get the required information and act upon it before Bormann has a chance to move."

"You are engaging in a most dangerous game. Kidnapping the Prime Minister! It's going to tear the country wide open," Dreyer said, "if it gets out."

"Neither the state president nor either party will want that. We may be able to survive if we present them with a fait accompli."

Lana Hunzen was appalled, fingers still poised over the tape recorder.

"Besides, we'll need their cooperation to go against Bormann. He could be anywhere, and we may not have the manpower alone," Leander finished.

"There's a simpler solution, Jan, if it's really Bormann in charge; inform the Israelis. They can take the brunt of the outrage produced by an attack and shrug it off. We help to cover. Historical justification and all that."

"It might work," mused Leander.

"I'll be in my office," said Dreyer. He left hurriedly.

Leander sat back in his chair and looked at Lana.

"Steady now. I want you to know it all. Just in case. Start that file with what I'm about to show you." He went to his safe and took out the document from 1936.

"Read this," he said.

The jungle reminded Ben of 'Nam, though without the fetid mugginess that rotted cloth and turned skin into a fungoid mess. Broad-leafed vegetation swung indolently in the night air, and sudden, rapid scurryings jerked his head around anxiously every few seconds.

Since he was unfamiliar with the wildlife of the region, vague shapes in the blackness became creatures of fantasy. He stayed close behind Ryerson, walking where he walked, the sounds of their boots crushing into the dense plants on the jungle floor mingling with the incessant cries of birds and insects.

It wasn't until they broke through the jungle onto the plain where the construction site was that Ben could unclench his shoulders, which he'd tightened reflexively with instinctive caution. He crouched alongside Ryerson in the tall grass.

"Over there," Ryerson pointed, and Ben followed his finger. "The fencing starts there, then it's about a hundred and fifty yards to the hospital. The labs are on the other side about a quarter mile or so away. If we circle the perimeter, we can get within two hundred yards of the labs."

Ben nodded, figuring approximate distances in his head. The compound had a diameter of over a mile, the eight-foot outer perimeter fence was almost four miles long and the area of the compound itself was about five square miles. The W.H.O. budget could not possibly underwrite the staggering costs for such a project. The costs had to be borne by South African diamonds returning home—Hauptman's diamonds.

From his pack he withdrew the .45 and slipped it into his belt. Ryerson took out a pair of heavy wire cutters.

The chain link strands parted one by one as Ryerson used his strength. Patiently, they waited for signs of detection when he was finished, but there were none, and they moved through to the inner perimeter fence, eight feet away, crawling on their stomachs. Ryerson cut the second fence, and they were inside the compound, still wary, alert to any movement.

Ben had Ryerson's description of the labs, but he could now see them clearly for himself. The quadrangle of low, white buildings were silvery-gray in the moonlight, and most of the lights were dark at this hour. They moved off again slowly, using whatever cover they could: an upturned tree lying on its side, a high shrub, a pile of sand.

Fifty yards from the labs, Ben motioned Ryerson to stop behind a bush and wait. He moved cautiously from concealment and looked around the area for signs of guards. He saw nothing. Turning back, he crouched low and began to move to Ryerson. Then he froze.

A guard, rifle slung over his shoulder, was walking toward them. Ben could stay hidden, but if the guard continued in the direction he was walking, he would surely see Ryerson whose back was turned away. The guard must have been circling the perimeter and had passed unnoticed behind them. Now he was heading toward the labs, straight along the same path they had taken.

Without hesitation, Ben began to circle around the guard who sauntered slowly, lulled by a boring duty. Ben slid behind a pile of brick, and when he emerged on the other side, he was behind the guard, who was now no less than fifty feet from Ryerson's back.

Praying that Ryerson wouldn't move, for the slightest motion would call the guard's attention, Ben ducked low and moved closer. If he could make it to a low bush some twenty feet away, he would be between the guard and Ryerson. He slithered on his belly, head down and noiseless.

He slid his hand forward in the dark grass and felt something alive and slimy. Every instinct screamed to react, to roll aside. His mind shrank away, and his skin crawled, but he moved slowly, removing his trembling hand and continuing toward the bush. Cold sweat sprang out on his face and trickled down his neck and back. He made it to the bush, shivering in tight spasms.

Still the guard had taken no notice. But Ryerson would not stay still forever. Sooner or later he would move off to look for Ben.

Ben judged angles and trajectories, but had nothing to throw, and gunfire would alert the compound. And, as close as the guard would come to the bush, he knew it was too far. A run over that distance would give the guard time enough to shoot him or to warn others. Out of the corner of his eye he saw Ryerson stir.

Abruptly, the guard stopped. Ben tensed to race for him, his fingers searching for a projectile of some kind.

The guard was making odd motions with his hands. He reached into his shirt. It took a moment for Ben to interpret what he was doing. A cigarette!

He heard the rasp of a match against the strike pad of its box and was up and running as it flared into brilliant light.

Momentarily, the guard's night sight was blinded, and Ben covered the distance like a sprinter.

Every pound of Ben's weight caught the guard full in the chest, and the breath burst out of him like a popped bag. Ben clamped an arm across his windpipe to stifle the guard's cry and brought the butt of his gun down hard. The guard died, the back of his head a glistening wet pulp.

Ben rolled over and threw up, his retching hoarse and restrained. He felt Ryerson's hands on his head, holding and supporting. When it was over, he cleaned his hands on the grass and his mouth with water from his canteen.

The darkness still enveloped and concealed them as Ryerson pulled the guard's body into the brush.

Ben fought for control of his disjointed emotions. The guard was one of the enemy, he reminded himself. There was an undeniable logic to that. But some small part of him was surprised and gladdened that he could not kill with impunity. In this war, at least, he might retain his humanity. The soldier that he became in 'Nam, or that surfaced to fight for Lisa in the brothel, was forever gone, he realized, a casualty sacrificed to his ability to love.

At the labs, Ryerson pulled him to a stop. "Building Three is for construction people, and Four is a warehouse for supplies. Two is a dorm for the medical staff. What we want, the labs themselves and Voorstein's quarters, are in One. This way."

There was no telling, Ben thought as he followed Ryerson, how long the guard's disappearance would be unnoticed. They might have hours or minutes, depending on the duty schedule or check-in times.

Ryerson stopped by a window and cut it away with a glass cutter. He had it open within seconds, and both men slipped into the thicker darkness inside, closing the window shades before flicking on pencil-beam flashlights.

The lab was a maze of equipment, some familiar and some whose function Ben could only guess at. At the far end of the lab was a sealed door. He played his light over it and saw it was secured by a wheel not unlike the door of a ship's watertight compartments. They had found the P4 containment facility.

Shining the light through the inset glass window, he saw the inner door of the airlock. Beyond, on table after table, were rows of small, round Petri dishes used to culture bacteria. He heard Ryerson behind him.

"You were right. Look inside. Those dishes contain colonies of bacteria. But I can't risk cracking the seal because I don't know if the rest of the room is sterile," Ben said in hushed tones.

"No need to," said Ryerson. "I found boxes like the ones I saw loaded in the 'copter. I broke the seal and found these."

In his hand was a set of three tubes held together by a metal clamp.

"There's no way to be sure, but I'm guessing that's it." Gingerly, Ben took the tubes and transferred them to the metal box in his pack.

"Do you have any idea where Voorstein could be?" he whispered.

Ryerson shook his head.

"I didn't pay any attention to his comings and goings."

"His quarters could be close to the lab. Check those doors." Ben pointed to one at the center and one at the far end of the lab.

"That center one leads into the hall corridor. The other, I don't know," said Ryerson.

Ryerson moved to it and found it unlocked. Gently, he opened it a crack and peered in.

"Voorstein. Asleep and alone," he whispered after closing the door.

Ben nodded and withdrew the .45 again. This time he had to feel no sickness. He had been too young to help end the first Holocaust; he would not allow the second.

He moved past Ryerson and opened the door. Voorstein did not stir, and Ben saw his face for the first time. Sleeping in his shorts, there was nothing to indicate the man's real nature on his peaceful features: tousled, curly blond hair, high forehead, flat nose, and a pointed jaw. Ben closed the door quietly.

He thought for a moment, decided on a course of action, and then explained it to Ryerson. In the lab he found what he needed.

Moving as quietly as they could, they reentered Voorstein's room and Ryerson moved into position.

In one quick flurry of action, as smoothly as if it had been rehearsed a hundred times instead of not at all, Ben grabbed

Voorstein's head and rammed it into his pillow. Voorstein woke at once, but his shouts were muffled into low, incoherent sounds.

At the same time, Ryerson grabbed Voorstein and flipped him over on his stomach in one great heave. In thirty seconds, Voorstein was helplessly gagged and hog-tied, and Ryerson flipped him over on his back.

Voorstein's features were contorted with hostility and shock, and the gag was wet with spittle from his furious attempts to yell. He thrashed violently on the bed, and Ryerson had to prevent his falling off.

Ben put the muzzle of the .45 under Voorstein's nose.

"That will be enough," he said, menace as clear in his tone as the gun in his hand.

Voorstein quieted. Fear replaced hostility in his eyes, the only feature not distorted by the gag. His breathing was heavy through his nose, and his color had grown pale.

"Put him in the chair," Ben directed Ryerson, who lifted the bound man effortlessly.

Ben placed a pencil in Voorstein's right hand and paper under it.

"That is how you're going to answer my questions. If you don't answer, I am going to kill you, and no one will hear me because I won't use the gun."

He unsheathed the hunting knife and placed it on Voorstein's lap. It lay across his groin, the silver finish unmarred by use, like a thing alive.

The pencil scribbled briefly against the paper.

"WHO ARE YOU?" Ben read.

"My name is Ben Davidson. Consider me a friend of Lisa Smith's."

He saw the shock of recognition Voorstein tried to conceal, and it pleased him in an odd way. Voorstein scribbled again, and Ben read.

"DEAD!"

"No," Ben said, "not dead. Garver shot me, but I didn't die. I'm here to find Lisa, and you're going to tell me where she is. I know what you plan to do."

There was crazed fury in Voorstein's eyes. He strained against the bonds, but Ryerson held him from behind. Quieted, he wrote on the paper.

"YOU KNOW NOTHING."

Ben smiled and told him what he knew. It left no doubts.

". . . And now it's your turn. No more questions, Voorstein, only answers or death. Where are the Adlerkinden? Where is Lisa?"

Voorstein dropped the pencil onto the floor and closed his eyes.

Ryerson replaced it and cuffed him angrily in the head. It brought tears of pain.

"Where are the Adlerkinden? Where is Lisa?" Ben repeated.

Again, Voorstein let the pencil fall, and again Ryerson replaced it.

Ben picked up the knife and held its blade against the tip of the little finger of Voorstein's left hand. The small room had grown tight and hot, and they could smell Voorstein's fear. Ben's face was sweaty and drawn, and Ryerson looked away.

Voorstein let the pencil fall.

Ben filled his mind with thoughts of Lisa, thoughts of the two million that would die if Voorstein had his way. He remembered the pictures of Dachau from the Anne Frank House.

With the half-remembered skills of a medical student, he sliced off the first joint of Voorstein's finger.

Bile flooded his throat, and it was all he could do not to throw up. He saw Voorstein wince in mute, searing agony, and blood spurted on both their clothing. He put the pencil back in Voorstein's pain-clenched fist.

"Where is Lisa? Where are the Adlerkinden?" he hissed.

Voorstein jerked his head from side to side in spasms of pain and protest. The pencil dropped from his fingers.

Ben summoned visions of Annie's corpse; of Amy, who would never know why she died; of the men who had tried to kill him in New Orleans and Amsterdam; of Otto, who had violated Lisa while her uncle watched. He put the knife over the second joint, held it against the bone and swollen flesh . . .

And knew he could not do it again. It didn't matter, all the pictures and the emotions they summoned. He could not become an animal.

He saw contempt burn in Voorstein's eyes. He knew, Ben realized, had known all along. Helplessness washed through him. He looked up dismally into Ryerson's face.

"Not even for Lisa?" Ryerson asked softly.

It stung him sharply, but he shook his head. "It would

. . . pervert it. I can't do that. Not any more." He cursed his weakness.

"Then there has to be another way. Stay here. I need something I saw in the lab."

Ben saw Voorstein's smugness and wanted to beat him senseless, but his new emotions were at war. He might never forgive himself if Lisa died because he hadn't the stomach to get what he needed from Voorstein.

Ryerson came back holding a glass-stoppered bottle of clear liquid and a metal mixing bowl.

"I can hear what you're thinking, Voorstein, even though you're gagged. I can see it in your eyes. They tell a story. You think you've won because people like Ben don't have the guts to be as rotten as you are. Well, maybe you do win sometimes. And maybe we can't play by the rules you do. But don't ever confuse that with weakness, mate. I think you're about to find out what we're all made of."

Ben had not heard Ryerson make such a speech before. He watched him pour liquid from the bottle to the bowl and wrinkle his nose at the vapors.

"Do you know what's in this bottle? It's labeled H_2SO_4. I studied enough chemistry in engineering school to know that that's the formula for sulphuric acid. And I know what that acid does to the metal of this bowl—it dissolves it. Should take about five minutes, I suppose."

Ryerson placed the bowl on Voorstein's lap.

"Now don't struggle, mate. If that bowl turns over, you're in for a bit of a rough time. Doesn't smell too nice, does it? Rotten eggs."

Voorstein was utterly rigid, the acrid fumes stinging his eyes. But he dared not tip the bowl in his lap. He was sweating profusely.

"Four minutes or so, I'd guess. Then the acid gets to what's underneath. You thought you'd fool around with the children. Well, I hope you've had all of yours. Maybe you could join the priesthood. I hear tell they like blokes to be sexless."

He put an empty test tube in Voorstein's stiff, clenched hand and pushed Ben from the room.

"Just drop that when you're ready to give my friend what he needs. We'll be waiting outside. Don't wait too long, though, because in four minutes we leave. My friend and I are the squeamish type, remember."

He closed the door on Voorstein's frantically imploring eyes.

"I don't know, Craig," said Ben outside.

Ryerson's countenance was stony. "I'm not going to let that grinning bastard get away with it. I don't blame you, Ben. You saved my life outside when you had to. But that flamin' whore's son has got to talk. It's up to him now. Either he's got the balls, or he doesn't."

"But..."

"But my ass. Either he's got the guts to take it like he plans to give it out, or he doesn't. It's not your responsibility. It's his now. And I say the bastard burns if he must."

Ben thought of what genocide meant and said nothing.

They both heard the sound of the test tube shatter.

Ryerson held him back. "Not so quick. We want him ripe."

Thirty seconds passed, while Ben's pulse raced, until Ryerson opened the door.

Voorstein was panicked, white froth sprayed out from around the gag. He took the pencil and wrote on the paper as Ben questioned him.

"Where's Lisa? Where are the Adlerkinden? Who is in charge? How long till the diseases will be released?" He asked the questions a second time before taking the paper to read the answers.

Ryerson removed the steaming, malodorous bowl almost casually, and Voorstein cried with relief. The first drops of acid had eaten holes in his shorts. The smell of excrement was rank.

Suddenly, a siren blasted through the compound, and lights flashed on outside leaking through the window shutters.

"It's the guard," Ben yelled over the din. "They've found him. Grab Voorstein. Move! I've got the packs." Then he disappeared into the lab.

Ryerson swiftly retied the unprotesting Afrikaner, slung him over his shoulder like a sack, and ran out in search of Ben.

Slipping out the lab window they had entered, Ben gestured for Ryerson to follow. Outside, Ben waited to receive the semiconscious Voorstein, staggering under the weight Ryerson had barely noticed until Ryerson climbed out and took Voorstein back.

Moving like broken field runners, they raced from the lab

buildings to cover afforded by a pile of lumber. Armed men raced from the buildings and spread out in a search pattern. Doctors, lab personnel, construction workers, all flooded out from the buildings, indistinguishable in nightclothes, anxiously searching for signs of intruders.

Ryerson pulled at Ben's shirt, puzzled. "We've got to get back to the fence. They'll see us if they get any closer."

"Not yet. We'd never make it."

The guards were becoming more organized, methodically searching the buildings and poking into the brush alongside. From the other side of the compound they heard gunfire.

"They mean business, Ben. If we don't go now, they'll cut us off."

"Not yet," said Ben stubbornly.

Voorstein was coming awake, the shock of his collapse fading.

The guards had almost reached the lab. Only thirty yards away their rifles were lowered and pointed purposefully, their features clearly visible in the spotlights.

"This is crazy!" Ryerson blurted through clenched teeth.

Ben took no notice but brought up the .45 and took aim at a lab window, resting his arm on the lumber.

"You can't shoot them all!" Ryerson said in disbelief. "What do you—"

His words were lost in the blast of the .45.

Ben dropped beside him behind the lumber as the lab building exploded in a paroxysm of violent fury. An orange fireball leaped a hundred feet in the air, and particles of glass sprayed over them. The shock wave rocked their hiding place.

Screams of injured men rang through the darkness.

The lab was in ruins, fire spreading from end to end. The roof had collapsed as the sides had blown out. Sparks flew in the air like fireworks, igniting the other buildings. The attention of most of the personnel, those that the explosion had not killed, was turned to containing the fire.

Ben's grin was grim but determined. "Labs have gas jets to operate Bunsen burners and the like. Someone must have carelessly left them all open. One spark and the whole works go. Damn careless."

They moved out from cover, Ryerson still carrying Voorstein. A few hundred yards away they cut back to circle the perimeter toward their entry point. Ben caught Ryerson's arm.

"No good. Look, they found the cuts and posted guards. Go back the other way; we'll cut another section."

Running back in the opposite direction, they used any cover available. But again armed guards were in their path.

"How many of the bastards are there?" said Ben, chagrined.

He noticed the strain Ryerson was under. Voorstein's weight was becoming too heavy a load, using up even his enormous resources of strength. Ryerson could not go on running like this much longer.

They moved deeper into the compound. The construction site loomed ahead, steel girders weblike against the moon. The flames from the labs cast flickering shadows, and still the sounds of men screaming could be heard. Someone shouted rapid orders in the distance.

A guard yelled, spotting the fleeing figures, and shots followed, ringing off the steel around them.

Ben turned and crouched, the gun a part of his arm rising in fluid motion as he fired. The return fire stopped as the guard tumbled over, but others had been alerted, and more shots rang out.

He vaulted a low brick wall after Ryerson. He fired at a group of approaching guards, and they scattered as two of their number fell. Ben jammed a fresh clip into the gun.

"We can't stay here, Craig. We've got to get to the perimeter fence. Forget Voorstein." He raised his head above the wall and fired again.

"Voorstein's dead," Ryerson panted. "The guard you shot . . . would have been me if I hadn't . . . been carrying . . . him."

The guards' fire had increased, and bullets ricocheted through the structure. Ben realized they were running out of time.

He looked around, helplessly. Machinery lay abandoned from the shift's end. Cement mixers, great oval tubs, bulldozers, trucks, shovels, stacks and mounds of equipment. No help. They would need a tank. Hold on—not necessarily a tank.

"Do you need a key to start those machines?"

Ryerson shook his head. "They're ready to go. No need for keys in a closed site. Just turn 'em on."

"Grab Voorstein and c'mon."

They ran to the line of heavy equipment.

The guards were approaching, made bolder by a lack of return fire.

"Now listen. I want you to start every damn piece of equipment here that will ride or roll out. Just start 'em and lock 'em in gear. Then point them at the perimeter fence. Put Voorstein in the first one to go. In plain sight." He winced as a bullet smacked into a pile of sand. "Go!"

"Wedge a brick on the gas pedal, or it will stall when in gear," Ryerson called.

Ryerson ran to the first machine in line, a bulldozer, and dumped Voorstein in. Pressing the start button, he threw it into gear, locked the shift and with a moan, the dozer moved off on its steel treads. He steered it for the oncoming guards, propped up Voorstein, and jumped off as it picked up speed.

A pickup truck was next in line. He started it up, rammed it into gear, and set it off in another direction. Just for good measure, he blared the horn.

Out of the corner of his eye, he saw a cement truck take off and Ben jump out. He flashed him a thumbs up and moved down the line.

The guards were thrown into complete confusion as vehicle after vehicle rumbled out from the site. Someone, in panic, blew up a truck, which only showered the others with burning gasoline and flying debris. Their charge became a rout.

Ryerson had just leaped off a truck when Ben found him.

"Hold the next," he yelled. "We go on that one."

Ryerson nodded and leapfrogged the cement mixer with its metal bell-shaped rear. He sent out another bulldozer and a tractor while Ben managed to get another pickup truck rolling.

"Get this thing moving straight out, then get in the mixing bell with me," Ben yelled.

Another truck blew up in the distance.

Ben scampered into the open mouth of the bell as the big mixer moved off into the darkness. He heard screams and more yells. Some of the vehicles had stopped, and guards cautiously approached. He prayed the mixer wouldn't stall.

Ryerson's head appeared in the mouth of the bell, and he somersaulted in. The bumpy ride jarred them into the walls, and they huddled at the bottom, blind to whatever was outside as gunfire rained against the metal sides.

Not even daring to peek out, they rode the mixer as it rambled across the compound. Smoke and the smell of burning rubber filled the chamber.

With a jarring crash, the mixer hit the inner perimeter fence. At almost ten miles per hour, it burst through like a fist striking wet paper. Ben was thrown over on his back and Ryerson to his knees. The fence had slowed them down. With one last heave, the mixer rammed across the outer fence and crushed it. But the motion was spent, and the big engine stalled.

"Out," called Ryerson, helping Ben to stand, and they scrambled over the fallen outer fence to the ground beyond.

Seven

With the sounds of the melee in the compound far enough behind and both men close to their limits, Ben and Ryerson sprawled out in a clearing whose soft, mossy ground provided some relief. They passed the canteen back and forth, and succumbing to the aftereffects of adrenaline shock, rested, marshaling strength.

"We're not out of it yet, Craig. When they find we've gotten out of the compound, they'll come looking. And they know this area far better than we do. Let's get going."

Ryerson got a map out of his pack and studied it under his flashlight.

"You still set on Pretoria?" he asked.

"More than ever. Look at this." Ben handed him the crumpled piece of paper.

"Hmm . . . Voorstein answered the same way twice. The Adlerkinden and Lisa are at the same place—Kosi Bay. He called it the Eagle's Nest."

Ben looked at the map. On the eastern coast of South

Africa, on the Indian Ocean, was a clearly marked nature preserve—Kosi Bay. Notations indicated that only the use of four-wheel drive vehicles was permitted, and that a ranger had to be contacted for permission to enter.

"We need to find out more about it. Neither one of us has ever been there. Pretoria has libraries and tourist bureaus— it's still our best shot. We knew what waited for us here and had your experience to guide us. Paris taught me not to do anything unprepared, and Kosi Bay is too important to make a mistake."

Ben took back the paper. Voorstein's answers had confirmed other things as well: The name Martin Bormann stared up at him. He had no doubt left that the Nazis and the Afrikaners had planned the Second Holocaust.

The target date was over a year away. But Ben had seen the plague itself and knew from Ryerson that large batches had already been shipped to the W.H.O. Center in Brazzaville. That could mean that much was already in place, and there was nothing to prevent its release earlier if the Adlerkinden were threatened. A partial success would affect the lives of millions, and there was no reason to believe that if desperate enough, they wouldn't begin prematurely. Fifty percent effectiveness would still be murder, no . . . genocide.

Ben felt the pressure of time and events bearing down on him as they pushed off, Ryerson leading.

Before they had left Brazzaville, they had worked out the problem of transportation if they could successfully get in and out of the compound. Scanning area maps, they had seen that the Tshipise health spa was only some twenty miles distant. One phone call later, a room and car were being held for M. Bouvin who would be arriving within the next day or two.

At dawn they broke off to rest and eat a breakfast of dried food, choosing to avoid a campfire. Wearily, they trudged off again as the sun began its slow ascent across the clear blue sky.

The more they walked and Ben reviewed the events of the past days, the more convinced he became they could not succeed unaided.

There was only one person in power in this country who wanted the destruction of the Eagle's Nest as much as he did—Jan Leander.

If he could bargain with Leander, using his knowledge as a lever to get him to help save Lisa, they stood a chance.

Memories of Lisa were sharp in his mind. He thought of the rich texture of her skin and the way she had reached for him as she slept. He missed her with an ache that persisted and grew stronger.

They reached the spa, an older hotel built around a mineral springs, as the sun began to set. A large trailer camping park was on one side, small guest cottages on the other. Ben brushed off as much dust as he could, ran dry fingers through his hair, and walked into the large, ornate lobby.

"Je suis Monsieur Bouvin. J'ai une rèserve," he said to the clerk behind the desk. The man's professional smile turned to confusion.

"I am Mr. Bouvin, and I believe I have a reservation," Ben said. The confusion vanished.

"Oh yes? Let me see. Mr. Bouvin."

The clerk turned away from the long marble sign-in desk to a wall of pigeonholes wherein keys rested. Then he consulted his ledger.

"Yes, indeed. Mr. Bouvin, cottage for one, number thirty-six. Been having a hike, I see. Well, the baths are just the right sort of thing for muscle aches. Sign here, won't you, Mr. Bouvin."

Apart from the fact that he disliked such cheery pretension, there was something vaguely disturbing in the clerk's manner. A middle-aged man, he wore a short-sleeved white shirt and tie; his brown hair was slicked back with not less than a pound of grease, and a pencil-thin mustache grew under his large nose.

"Is the car I ordered ready?"

"Oh yes, it is. Parked right in front of your cottage. Keys and petrol are in it. The four-wheel drive is automatic and perfect for exploring the area. You'll turn in the keys when you check out."

"Certainly," Ben lied.

"Good idea, that. Wish more folks would catch on. Silly to smash up the axles when a four-wheel drive is just the thing here. Cottage thirty-six is right on the left-hand path. Can't miss it."

"Thank you," Ben said and walked away still uneasy.

The cottage was only three rooms: a sitting room, bedroom, and bath. As the clerk had promised, a Land Rover stood parked outside. There were others in front of cottages down the line. Ryerson, inside, had already thrown himself into one of the beds.

"You can shower first. I'll guard the bedroom," he groaned.

"You're a prince," Ben said dryly, but Ryerson's snores were already beginning.

It wasn't until after he'd showered and changed into an extra set of khakis that Ben realized the clerk had not looked him in the eyes once during their entire conversation. Not once.

"Get up, Craig."

"Wha . . . ?"

"I'm uncomfortable. This place is beginning to feel like Paris. And I'm not going to get caught flat-footed again."

"And here I was dreaming about an amazing woman I knew once in . . ."

"Be serious for a minute. Get washed, and I'll explain what I want you to do."

Half an hour later, Ben stood concealed in a group of high hedges twenty feet from the cottage watching a much distressed clerk come shambling up the walk.

It wasn't so much his agitation, Ben decided, that was wrong, but that he kept looking around as if expecting to see something. He slowed to a stop not twenty yards from the cottage and wiped the palms of his hands on his black trousers. Stepping up to the cottage door, he gave the Land Rover a wide berth, again as if expecting something.

"Mr. Bouvin?" he called and knocked at the door.

Ben could hear Ryerson's voice faintly but clearly through the door. "He stepped out for a minute, mate. What's the problem?"

"Problem?" the clerk snapped. "Why, he called me! He said the water pressure was gone and demanded I come over to see to it."

"Are you a bleedin' plumber?"

"That's what I said. You tell Mr. Bouvin that I'm a busy man, and I don't—"

The gun pressed to the back of his head stopped the clerk immediately.

"Inside," Ben said. "Craig?"

The door opened, and Ryerson grabbed the clerk in his big hands and tossed him easily onto the bed.

The clerk looked panicky, his head darting around like a tormented turtle.

Ben closed the door and leveled the gun. "There's something you're not telling us, my friend. I want to know what it is."

"You're out of your minds. I'm just a clerk here."

"You do seem nervous."

"You have a gun!"

"Please try and remember that," Ben said softly. "Is it customary to ignore an unregistered guest in a room?"

"But you signed the register. I knew..." and the clerk stopped.

"Precisely, my friend. In my haste I forgot to book a room for two, and I signed in alone. Someone else had to tell you I wasn't alone." The last question was fired sharply.

"I didn't know; I assumed when I heard the voice you were... don't shoot me... please... I assumed you were a bit queer."

"You think very quickly. Especially for a man so nervous."

"It's true. I swear it."

"And I believe you," soothed Ben. "Let's take a ride in our new car."

"No!" It was out of the clerk's mouth before he could stop it.

"Why you bleedin' little..." Ryerson cuffed him hard, and the clerk tumbled off the bed.

Ben leaned very close to the clerk. "Tell me now, or he'll do it again. What good is a desk clerk without a face?"

"I was told!" the man cried, trying to stem the blood with a handkerchief. "We got the call this morning asking about some men; Bouvin or Davidson or Ryerson. If they showed up, we were to call a number. Well, we already had your reservation. They told me to put that car in front and leave it with the keys, and someone would be out to fix it. They said no one else should drive it."

Ben looked at Ryerson. "It's rigged to blow."

"I'd guess. But how could they know?"

"They didn't till he told them. Probably alerted every place in this region. It's so damn sparse that's not hard to do. They could rule out cars. And no 'copters took off. They guessed

339

we walked and lucked out here. My name they got from the W.H.O. Center; yours was a possibility. And someone could have recognized you last night. Then they sent a team in to rig the car before we got here."

"Very neat. You're learning fast, Ben."

He turned to the clerk. "Are there keys in the other Rovers?"

The clerk looked at Ryerson again. "No. But I have a master."

"Very good. You're learning too. Put him in one of the other cars and start it up. I'll be there in a minute."

Ryerson paused only to pull the cords off the window shades.

Ben watched Ryerson push the desolate clerk out the door. Then he threw everything into their packs but their dirty clothing and went outside.

The windows of the Rover were open, and Ben tossed in the old clothing, keeping out a shirt. Then he carefully unscrewed the gas cap and fed in the sleeve till it was soaked. With a quick motion, he ignited the shirt and ran.

"Get going!" he yelled jumping in the Rover.

A hundred yards away the heat wave hit them with a blast of scalding air. Then a second explosion followed, even more violent. When Ben looked back, both the car and cottage were smoking ruins.

The clerk was white with shock, tied up in back.

"The clothing won't fool them for very long," Ryerson observed as the Rover hit the artery to N1.

Ben inclined his head to the rear seat.

"He comes along. I do believe he would say nasty things about us if we let him go," said Ben.

"Pretoria?" questioned Ryerson.

They were exposed and open to attack, and the enemy was aware they were in South Africa. Ben nodded. It was time, he knew, to call in the troops.

Leander rubbed his tired eyes and stretched again in his chair. The minor pains in his back had grown into full-fledged annoyances the longer he sat.

Dreyer's shirt sleeves were rolled up, and he had long ago

discarded his jacket and tie. Lana Hunzen looked worn out by her constant activity during the long night.

A phone rang, and Dreyer reached across the conference table to get it. He listened intently for a few seconds.

"Right," he said. "Stay in touch. Half hour reporting schedule. Code for go is Blue," and hung up.

Leander looked up from the papers spread before him.

"That's it, Jan. All teams in place. Coverage established."

"Okay, then. Keep the radio linkage open. As soon as I get through with Carlysle, I'll send word, and you can send Blue to the teams."

He got up, shrugged into his jacket, and adjusted his tie. "You've both done a superb job. Get some rest, but don't move from this office. We should have an okay within the hour."

The long night had been one of constant activity. Dreyer had assembled the list of men who would form the teams to cover Smith, Hauptman, and Putten, and those who would be the interrogation team. Agents were pulled from duty all over Africa, and some from as far away as India for the reassignment.

Briefings were sent out, contingencies planned for, and leaderships assigned in each team.

Hauptman and Putten were not exercises of great difficulty. Abductions were relatively easy to arrange for private citizens.

Smith was a different matter altogether. A corps of bodyguards from Internal Security surrounded him at all times in Pretoria. Further, Leander's information on Smith's habits and life-style was incomplete; he had never come under their scrutiny before.

The operation to place Smith under their control had been complex to say the least as a new file had to be built up almost exclusively for this plan. All night they had labored, putting bits and pieces together, running computer checks and cross-checks, and working on information hastily supplied through investigation, bribery, and blackmail.

One by one the complexities and problems had been ironed out through the night and early morning until finally the computer had given them a positive reading on success/probability indexes. Teams were sent into place to wait in readiness.

"My appointment with the President is confirmed?" Leander asked.

"Twenty minutes from now," Lana nodded.

It was the State President who would take control of the reigns of government during Smith's absence—Adam Carlysle.

Leander held two files as his car took him to the Union Buildings. The first was on Carlysle; the second on the Adlerkinden. He reviewed them both, knowing that if he failed to convince Carlysle of the truth of his accusations, then the operation he had mounted was as finished as his life would probably be.

He entered the Presidential Offices only a minute before his allotted time. Due to his rank, he was ushered past banks of secretaries, assistants, and liaison officers directly to Carlysle without the usual delay.

The office itself was ornately furnished in the colors of English Wedgewood. Blue-gray walls with white trim, elegant French-style furniture, and an antique desk that stood in front of windows over which velvet brocade curtains swept to the floor.

Carlysle had little de facto power in South Africa. Though his office was the seat of the Executive Branch, Leander knew, as did every South African, that he was little more than a figurehead who signed into law the dictates of the Parliament.

However, as the Head of State of the Republic, he could step into the breach and hold the country together. Further, he could authorize Leander's operation against Smith.

"Good day, Mr. Carlysle," said Leander, taking the offered hand.

"And to you, Mr. Leander. It's not often I have a call from External Operations."

"It's not often we have such need, sir," Leander replied.

Both men sat, and coffee was served by a male secretary. Leander waited until he had left.

"Responses such as that pique the curiosity of an old man."

"You do yourself a disservice, sir."

"I'll be seventy-one next month; I don't think 'old man' is totally inappropriate. Now what brings you here?"

Leander looked closely at Carlysle. He saw an impeccably dressed, white-haired man whose skin was wrinkled and still leathery tough from his years in the Bush. Descendant of

British stock, Carlysle was a political compromise to the English-speaking whites by the ruling Afrikaners.

Though seventy-one, his dark brown eyes sparkled with intelligence that, associates held, had enabled Carlysle to take his family's two-century-old farm, modernize it, and create one of the finest agricultural producers in the country. He had compiled his first fortune when he was twenty-three.

His business career began in mining stocks and spread to such diverse enterprises as tire manufacturing, precious metals, and hotels.

By the time he reached fifty, there was little else to conquer but politics. A member of the Provincial Administration for ten years, and then of Parliament for six more, he was currently in the fifth year of a seven-year term. His reputation for shrewd business dealing combined with a sharp, incisive political sense made him a respected, if not adored, figure in government, though some felt he saw profit before people.

"We have a serious crisis of international import, sir, which has disastrous implications for the country and its present government. Ex Op has been investigating this matter for some time. It is now the moment to act."

Carlysle picked up a pen and pointed it at Leander. "Have you been to the Prime Minister? This is more correctly his area. But then, you know that, don't you?"

Leander winced internally.

"Yes, sir. I know that. However, the nature of this matter is such that it cannot be solved by the Prime Minister. I have judged that I must consult you directly."

Carlysle's gaze never wandered. "This would be serious indeed, Mr. Leander. And there are implications for your welfare in this judgment."

"I am aware of that, too, sir. I would not be here if the situation did not merit it. It's not a course I take lightly," said Leander.

"Very well, then. I'm willing to hear you out."

Leander passed the Adlerkinden file across the desk. He watched Carlysle read it and then read it again. He closed it with an angry gesture.

"This is an outrage. A pact with the Nazis! Diamond smuggling! Do you have any reason for these things?"

Briefly, Leander described the course of their operation.

". . . But we have not been able to penetrate far enough to understand what purpose they serve. Only to document that the conspiracy still exists and to identify its members."

"Can Martin Bormann be a part of it? He would be very old."

Leander hesitated but plunged on. "He would be only a few years older than you, sir. Not too old."

"Well put, Mr. Leander. I suppose it is possible. What do you want to do?"

"Ex Op has jurisdictional rights as this involves a conspiracy between the RSA and Germany. It is an international matter. I have a team ready to pick up Mr. Smith . . ."

Carlysle broke in, "You would arrest the Prime Minister?"

"He will not be arrested. It can be kept quiet, and no one will know save you and me. He will be questioned. Then we will have the rest of it," Leander responded.

"There has to be another way. You can't control security on a thing like this. If it gets out, the whole country will panic. Think of the racial tensions and what it could do to inflame them."

Carlysle's face was set into hard lines, but Leander pressed the attack.

"Think of the tensions if the newspapers get it first and we have done nothing! Even within Ex Op I can't guarantee security over a course of years. This way it's over and done quickly. A resignation; ill health. It could be done smoothly."

"You are certain of your charges, Mr. Leander?"

"It's all there, sir, and can be verified. You hold the document in your hands. A simple audit would implicate Hauptman and the Dutchman, Putten. There are certainly others within Van Dyne's exchange, and Smith will tell us who they are. The others will be picked up as well."

Abruptly, Carlysle got up and left the room without further comment.

Leander waited in silence. It was no longer in his hands.

When Carlysle returned, there was a second long silence while he tapped a pencil against his desk.

"I have spoken to my staff," he began, "and they assure me that if you can move as quickly as you've indicated, they can keep it from the press. It will be treated as a heart attack, hospital unreported for security reasons."

"Then I have your approval?"

"Mr. Leander, conditions in this country are difficult at best right now. We must deal with this—this treason, if we are to keep it stable. Like a financial market, the conditions in a political entity must be kept stable. You have my authorization to question Mr. Smith, and I will do my best to maintain an orderly transfer of power. When will you move against him?"

"In two hours. At his residence."

"Very well, then, Mr. Leander. Good day."

"Thank you, sir."

Carlysle said nothing more as Leander rose and walked out of the office.

For a long time, Carlysle sat and reflected on years gone by and the changes in life that one must face. Then he picked up his phone and dialed a number that he had used only rarely in three decades.

"Ivory," he said when the connection, routed through a private exchange, was made.

"Steel," came the response.

"There is a complication," Carlysle said, memories surfacing with the voice.

"Then we will have to deal with it, won't we?" said Martin Bormann.

Two hours later, Leander looked up from his desk.

"Signal Blue," he said to Dreyer. "All teams."

Eight

Johann Smith entered his townhouse, a mile or so away from the Union Buildings, weary from the day's exertions. It was harder lately to keep up a front, and he had begun to see ill-concealed looks of concern on the faces of his staff at the changes in mood that overcame him. Mentally, he felt sluggish, and his fears for Lisa's safety had turned into numbing dread.

345

He was a fighter who had closed for the kill and been defeated. The shock of that defeat had crippled him as thoroughly as power had sustained him. To one like Smith, there was no middle ground. He knew that about himself, but he had no defense for the lethargy of spirit that Bormann's victory had thrust upon him.

He dismissed his bodyguards at the front door, and they took up their usual places of deployment. The servants took his coat and hat, and he motioned them away, preferring the solitude of his library and the solace of its liquor cabinet.

He poured whiskey into a tumbler, sat in one of the high-backed, stuffed chairs, and looked at the books and at Pretoria through the French windows. He drank deeply.

I am second, he thought, and I must be first. I am unable even to protect my family. Keeping up the deception in front of the others will be painful. A jester is what Bormann's made of me, in a court where he will be king.

Hatred and self-pity brought the glass to his lips again.

The evening air was normally cool and sweet. But tonight he felt unusually warm. He mopped at his sweating forehead idly.

The Project would go on, he was sure of that. For so long they had labored. Such good men, strong men. Afrikaners—committed to an ideal. But Bormann had soured even that.

God, he was tired. And sweating profusely. Where was the breeze? he wondered. It was such an effort to turn his head.

Strange to think that what they had planned so many years ago would soon come to fruition. "No more blacks," he heard himself say to Hans in comfort that day at the airfield. He wished Hans were here now. But Bormann had taken him, too.

He beat us both, Hans, he thought. Why is it so hot in here?

It seemed to take a long time to decide to move. An odd fuzziness clouded his vision, and his limbs felt heavy.

He stared at the tumbler of whiskey for a long while, its amber color quite pleasing. Then it fell from his grasp, and a stain spread onto the carpet.

From somewhere in the recesses of his mind came the realization that he had been drugged. Panic tried to assert itself but could not replace the creeping lassitude. He tried to think which one of his servants had sold him out.

His last thought before the poison stopped his heart was of how much he hated Martin Bormann.

The three Ex Op agents did not speak to each other, and the tension in the car was almost palpable. Powell, the leader of the team, sat behind the wheel and watched Johann Smith's house, though part of his attention was fixed on the radio under the dashboard. He had been back in South Africa only eight hours, having flown in from Ghana under Leander's urgent directive.

He was uneasy with the operation. This was the Prime Minister they were going to snatch. Training was hard to overcome, and he hoped the Director knew what he was doing. The sharp clicks of an automatic weapons check came from the backseat. Powell knew that Remson shared his unspoken distress. Jogin constantly complained.

None of the three had ever worked together before. Remson had been stationed in Rhodesia; Jogin, at the embassy in Bombay.

When Powell received the Code Blue, the team moved out to start the diversions that would draw off Smith's bodyguards. Jogin began it at the front door; Remson began it at the rear.

Powell slipped unnoticed through the French windows into the library during the melee.

One minute later he scrambled back out to recall his group and report to Leander.

Ben wiped clotted dust from his neck and tried to hold his voice steady into the phone.

"Tell him Ben Davidson is calling. He'll speak to me."

"Please hold, sir."

It had already taken ten minutes and four secretaries to reach this stage of discussion. But he was prepared to wait and would speak only to Leander.

He visualized the endless chain from higher to higher-up that his call would be taking.

Ryerson was still in the Rover finishing the last bit of food purchased from the roadside restaurant next to the Strijdom House. The house was a local landmark, having been lived in by a prime minister, and it was open to tourists. They had looked disinterestedly at its thatched construction caring only for the food and phone it provided.

Ryerson made a questioning face at him, and Ben shrugged negatively.

The clerk was still tied in back of the Rover, having been untied only long enough to eat and defecate under Ryerson's stern watch.

"How nice to hear from you again, Mr. Davidson. This is Jan Leander speaking."

Ben thought he remembered the voice but was unsure.

"What was the name of the doctor who treated me in Paris?"

"Bertram" was the unhesitating reply.

"What is his native country?"

"America."

"What did I call you when we last spoke?" he questioned again.

"A bastard, among other things," said Leander, "and I took exception."

Ben realized that even now there was no way to be sure. He had learned since Mississippi that there were no truths; only better guesses separated those who lived and those who died.

"Okay, Leander, I want to come in. I know the answers. All of them."

"Where are you?" Leander asked.

"North of Pretoria."

"You're in South Africa?" The voice held surprise. "You have become a very resourceful man."

"A very untrusting man," corrected Ben. "Here's how we're going to do this. The maps indicate a Tribal Handicraft Center twenty miles north of the city on N1. You will bring two cars. In one you can put as many bodyguards as you wish. You alone will drive the second. At the Center will be a Land Rover parked with its lights on. Get out of the car and walk to it. I will not be inside, but someone will who'll take you to where I am. Now listen carefully. I am armed and will not under any conditions be disarmed. If I see so much as one weapon, I will start firing. You either trust me or the whole thing's off. Decide, Leander."

"Agreed" came the response, and again there was no hesitation.

Ben hung up the phone.

As he drove, Leander thought that he had never before believed in either luck or fate. But Davidson's phone call had come like a Divine Sending in the aftermath of the operation that had produced one dead Prime Minister, whose heart attack was obviously murder; one dead Diamond Exchange owner, analysis the same; and failed totally to find Hauptman at all.

Carlysle had betrayed him. There seemed no end to those embroiled in the Adlerkinden conspiracy. Steadily, they had eliminated his leads as quickly as he could evolve them. There could be no doubt that he would be a high priority to die next.

The scenario for his demise could not be simpler. Removed from the directorship of Ex Op, no longer afforded access to its protections, he could be singled out and removed. Probably only his aggressive movement against Smith had forestalled that. In an indirect way, Leander knew that he was responsible for Smith's death. He was only sorry that the information he had held was lost.

And then the incredible phone call from Davidson.

He checked the odometer and saw that the Center was only a few miles further.

This way of meeting was melodramatic. But perhaps Davidson knew that. Leander realized that it was a gesture, a way of saying that he understood the rules now. It would be accepted as such. And if Davidson had somehow stumbled on the truth, then he was entitled to his gestures.

He spotted the Land Rover, parked a short way from the Handicraft Center, a one-story frame house with a red roof. Tourists' cars were parked outside, and people browsed through the rather unimpressive collection. He checked the rearview mirror and saw that the second car, with Dreyer and four other agents, was still right behind him.

Dreyer had been obstinate in his insistence on protecting him from a trap. And it was just possible that Davidson could have been turned. Leander's rationale had been quite simple—it was worth his life to find out.

He pulled to a stop and got out of his car. Dreyer had stopped a distance away.

He approached the Rover with hands held clearly in sight of the man who sat at the wheel.

"I'm Leander. You're to take me to Davidson?"

It was then that he understood the man's frightened expression. His hands were tied to the wheel. Reflex almost took over at the unexpected sight.

"I'm here, Leander. Just stay put," said a voice from the back seat, and he saw Davidson throw off a blanket that had covered him, the .45 pointed unwaveringly.

"Not bad at all," Leander said, admiringly.

"I'm going to come close and put this gun in your back. Turn around."

"As you like," said Leander, and he stood stock-still while Ben moved behind him. "Who is that man?" he asked.

"A clerk from Tshipise. Have one of your men drive the Land Rover and follow us. Tell a second man to drive your car, and inform the others that we will be stopping two miles down the road."

Dreyer was much relieved to find it was indeed Ben but anxious at the gun.

"It's all right, Peter. Put Powell in the Rover and have him follow us. You drive with Mr. Davidson and me. We'll be making one stop on the way back."

When the cars roared back onto the highway, Leander sat in back with Ben's gun pressed into his side. He would speak in his own time, Leander knew.

They stopped to pick up Ryerson.

"'Lo, mates. It seems that everything worked out according to schedule. Ryerson's the name—a friend of the family, you might say." He got in the front seat.

Ben sighed and put the gun back in his pocket. "There is an old American saying, Mr. Leander, that we must all hang together or we will surely hang separately. We each have need of the other, I think."

"It's a good saying, Mr. Davidson. We have another old saying in Africa: you kill a snake with whatever is in your hands."

The discussion at the conference table grew more intense. "That's what we have, Mr. Davidson," concluded Leander.

"The conspiracy reaches to the highest level of government. No fewer than the leaders of the majority party and the President himself are involved. Even here, a Prime Minister cannot be killed with impunity.

"Further, the press has been carefully fed the heart attack story. It is completely credible, certified by doctors, and national mourning will commence. The political ramifications are clear, though. The next man in that office will be one of the Adlerkinden. At that time, I am certain I will cease to head Ex Op, and my own heart attack will surely follow.

"We have no time left if we are to act in concert. I urge you to give us your information freely and without restraint."

"There is one condition. And it isn't negotiable," Ben said gravely.

"What condition?" Dreyer asked.

"I know where the Eagle's Nest is, and that's where Lisa Smith is being held. Before anything else, we go in and get her. If I weren't convinced I needed help for that, I wouldn't even be here."

"I don't like veiled threats. And please remember that you *are* here," said Leander.

"And I'm still armed. We may not get out of here alive, and only a fool would try and kill us; but either way, we go. If you force it, you have nothing."

"It's a bluff," said Dreyer.

"Don't bet on that, mate," called out Ryerson, listening closely. "I've seen him work. You won't stop him where the girl is concerned. Not alive, that is."

"There are broader considerations here—" Leander started, but Ben cut him off.

"Bullshit. You worry about them. That's my point, Leander. In a pinch, the only one who gives a damn about her is me. I don't have to care about your interests or those of any damn country. Just Lisa's."

Mrs. Hunzen spoke for the first time. "Mr. Davidson, this is our home you're speaking of. Would it be the same if this were America? Wouldn't you care then?"

"Maybe," Ben admitted. "And I do understand your position. But let me ask you—if it were you being held by Bormann, possibly tortured, certainly brutalized, what would you want my priority to be? Sitting there alone and afraid,

351

would you be consoled to think you were being sacrificed on the altar of 'national interest'?"

Lana Hunzen looked away, her silence eloquent.

"That's it, then," Ben said wearily. "Lisa first, or have Mr. Dreyer call my bluff."

"What is it you want exactly?" Leander asked.

"A small team goes in first. We'll need weapons, transport, advance information on the site, and sufficient time to get Lisa out. After that, you can do as you wish."

Leander's voice was neutral, but Ben sensed a hidden agenda.

"Is the Eagle's Nest in South Africa? I ask only because logistics will prove difficult if not. Your presence here indicates that you found what you know in this country. You didn't want our help in Paris."

"The Eagle's Nest is in South Africa," he said.

"Who is in charge?" Leander asked, and Ben heard the change in the neutral tone. This was a question Leander wanted badly to have answered, he realized.

"Martin Bormann," he said clearly.

Ben saw it flick over Leander's face, a mixture of pain and fear and rage. But it passed quickly, controlled by a hard will. What is he to Bormann or Bormann to him? he wondered.

"Do you agree to my terms?" Ben asked as he continued to study Leander closely.

"Have you thought how to enforce them after we have the information?" Dreyer asked.

"I hadn't really. But now I don't think I'll have to," Ben said, subconscious cues forming a sudden judgment as he watched the subtle play on Leander's face.

"And why not?" Dreyer asked.

"Because I think what I want to do is just the way Mr. Leander wants to play it," Ben said. "I think he wants to come with us."

"Jan!?" Dreyer sputtered, but he was ignored.

"In some ways you are really quite remarkable, Mr. Davidson," Leander said quietly. "I agree to your terms."

Ben reached into his pack, brought out Voorstein's papers, and tossed them onto the table. "It started for me in Mississippi, in the southern United States. I took a wrong turn..."

When Ben had finished, he studied the reactions on each of their faces. Dreyer's surliness had been replaced by a grudging respect. Lana Hunzen was stricken by the insanity of the conspiracy revealed.

Leander sat deep in thought for a long while before sending Lana Hunzen for maps of Kosi Bay.

"It all fits together," he said at last. "Every piece. The only thing they didn't count on was the freak accident, a single, determined man with an odd combination of abilities falling into it. I said before you were remarkable, Mr. Davidson. I was wrong. What you've done, what you've been through—remarkable doesn't do it justice."

Mrs. Hunzen returned and spread the maps out before them, surveys and topological charts.

Ben read and began to build up a picture of the area.

"It has to be here," Leander pointed. "The only structures are on the island in the bay, save for the ranger station on the mainland. The rest of the park is wilderness, mostly swamp."

Dreyer flipped through another volume.

"The buildings are listed as an Ornithological Research Station. Total of three labs, a main house, a barracks for native workers, and assorted supply shacks. Good cover for the flow of scientific supplies and equipment," he said.

"The ranger has got to be in on it," Ben said.

"I would think so," agreed Leander. "He would be the first line of defense and keep the limited number of tourists away."

"Judging by the terrain," Ryerson threw in, "we could land a small boat here," he pointed, "or here."

Leander looked surprised. "By 'we' do I understand you intend to come, Mr. Ryerson?"

"I sure as flamin' hell do."

"But is that wise?" Leander asked. "I know you survived Voorstein's compound, and Mr. Davidson attests to your physical prowess. But you aren't trained for this. Please understand that I do admire your courage, but perhaps it's misplaced."

"Balls," spat Ryerson. "It wasn't courage. Nobody fires me from a job. I signed on, and I stay till it's over. You know that, Ben."

"Leander's not totally wrong, Craig. You've done a great deal. I couldn't have gotten here without your help, and I couldn't have put it together till you gave me what you knew. I would understand if you wanted out now. Do you?"

"Nope." Ryerson grinned expansively. "Partly because I

take friendship very seriously, and you pulled me out of a bad spot in Brazzaville. And partly 'cause I don't like Afrikaners, and I think what they're trying to do stinks. But mostly, as the man said who jumped naked into the cactus bush—"

"I know, I know: It seemed like a good idea at the time," Ben finished. He looked at Leander and gestured helplessly.

"He's incorrigible. But I'd trust him over any man I ever knew."

"Same goes for him," said Ryerson.

"The free spirits of this world are growing increasingly rare," Leander mused. "They do not often give their loyalty and then only to special people. Treasure it, Mr. Davidson. In the end it's what defeats the Bormanns of this world."

"Then we three go. Who else?" Ben asked.

"Three of my agents. Powell, Jogin, and Remson. Remson and Powell have operated in Africa for years. I brought them back to work Smith's operation. Two come with us; one takes out the ranger."

"I'm part of it," said Dreyer flatly.

"I'm sorry, Peter, but you have to handle other things. Someone who has this information has to stay clear if we muck it up. And I need someone to handle the air strike. Someone I can trust not to jump the gun."

Dreyer took the rebuff with barely stifled annoyance.

"What air strike?" Ben asked quickly.

"I'm giving us twelve hours from the time we push off to the island to get in and out with Lisa Smith. But you said yourself that the plague has got to be stopped. Exactly twelve hours after we land, Peter will send a wing of planes to bomb the island in Kosi Bay. We can't afford to fail. This guarantees we won't."

"If you do that, you run the risk of scattering the plague microorganisms," Ben objected.

"Didn't you yourself run the same risk when you exploded Voorstein's lab?"

"I was sure the fire would kill the germs. Any microorganisms adapted to live in the human body are also adapted to its temperature range. Extreme heat or cold will kill them. It's why the body develops a fever when infected."

"We can use napalm," Dreyer suggested.

Ben suppressed a shudder. He had seen firsthand the effects of napalm bombing in Vietnam, had seen people writhing in agony as the flames that could not be put out consumed them. He had watched, sickened, as children ran screaming for the water of the rice paddies as the burning fumes seared their lungs.

Then he thought of Martin Bormann's long history.

"It would work," he said finally.

"Then I suggest you and Mr. Ryerson get some sleep. We have quarters here in the building. Another few hours and we should have the rest of the details ironed out." Leander looked at the charts before him. "Before dawn we'll fly by helicopter to the coast and rendezvous with a fishing trawler. We'll make the final approach by rubber raft."

"Then we kill the snake," Ben said, and Leander nodded.

Bormann sat at the linen-covered table in the dining room of the main house and finished eating his lunch. Black servants hovered attentively nearby, local tribesmen he had "trained" for domestic service. The training course had been brief, but its effects lasted a lifetime.

Ludwig Stumpfegger walked in and tossed his bush hat to a servant who placed it in a teakwood armoire with a reverence usually reserved for religious relics.

The other servants hurried to serve his lunch.

"I trust the loading is going well," said Bormann.

"Another forty-eight hours and we'll be done. The labs will go last."

"I'm going to miss this island. It's been home for so long," confided Bormann.

"We've had others before," said Stumpfegger. "One forgets them in time. Carlysle had no trouble arranging a new location?"

"None at all. An alternate site was readied years ago and given to the Weather Service. They were relocated a few days ago."

"I assume he has his hands full maneuvering the political situation right now. Has he made a choice for the new Prime Minister?"

"One of the M.P.'s, Malthinus Goosen, will be elected. The votes are not a problem. We also have a splendid forgery of Smith's, written after his doctor told him of his heart condition, asking Goosen to carry on his work if he is unable to," said Bormann happily.

Stumpfegger began to eat the lunch the servants had brought.

"And the situation with Leander and Ex Op?" he asked.

"Goosen will remove Leander as Director of Ex Op. Then we can easily isolate and kill him." A frown crossed Bormann's face. "Davidson will be killed as soon as he can be located. That man has cost us too much. He was responsible for Voorstein's death."

"I have punished the men who allowed him to escape Tshipise. There was no body in the wreckage when it was checked. And a clerk is missing," said Stumpfegger. "We assume a correlation."

"Davidson is still in South Africa. He must be! I want the opportunity to kill him, slowly. When we find him . . ."

"Your blood pressure, Martin. Please remember your condition," cautioned Stumpfegger. "Calm yourself. He will be found."

"I suppose." The redness faded from Bormann's face. "Now that Smith is dead, you may kill the girl if you'd like. She is unnecessary."

Stumpfegger's smile was a leer. "When I tire of her. I grew rather . . . ah . . . fond of her during her initial questioning. She is an amusing distraction."

"Is she still in shock?"

"Most of the time. She is more pliable that way, eh, Martin?"

Both men laughed hoarsely.

"I think you are too old for these games, Ludwig. And what does your Heidi say about this?" asked Bormann.

"She frowns and pouts. Jealous little creature. I gave her to some of the guards as punishment. You know, I think she enjoyed it and forgave me," said Stumpfegger.

This time Bormann literally shook with mirth, his fat jowls bouncing.

"I don't see why you keep her. The brain is defective," he said.

"She has other compensations, Martin. Because she was one of our first experiments in the Project, I have a professional fondness for her, even if she represents failure. Call it a

Pygmalion-like urge, though his statue had more brainpower. I will get rid of her eventually. All things must pass."

The thought sobered them.

"We have seen a number of our colleagues pass of late," Bormann said, and Stumpfegger nodded.

"Van Dyne, Stangl, Voorstein, and Smith. We do have a great deal to repay Davidson for."

"Hauptman, too, if we hadn't gotten him here to safety. He can't emerge until after Goosen's election."

"I spoke to him before. He's very frightened of you, Martin; afraid he'll be killed like Smith. The man is a coward," said Stumpfegger disgustedly.

"I know. He came in to see me to complain about his quarters in the lab building. I do my best to ignore him," said Bormann idly. "Send him back to Pretoria."

Stumpfegger stood up, and a servant quickly brought him his hat.

"Where are you going?" asked Bormann.

"To supervise the loading." His face took on its earlier leer. "And then to see Lisa Smith. Our conversation has sparked my aged imagination."

Lisa remembered Stumpfegger's visits only as dim, fading memories, like the remembrance of childhood nightmares. Her clothing had been ripped until there was little left but tatters, and she huddled in her locked, windowless room with only the cot's blanket for warmth and protection.

Since Paris, there had been only emptiness. She seemed to be seeing the world through a layer of haze that made everything diffuse, indistinct. The haze lifted sometimes, and she found herself wondering if she was slipping down the long slide into insanity, never to return.

Lately though, she had discovered a place inside her where there was no fear, no pain—where Ben waited. It was her only escape, a refuge she fled to when she couldn't let herself think about what was happening to her.

The sound of the key in the lock was unmistakable.

The fear on Lisa's face was replaced by blankness, as she took what little of herself remained inviolate and withdrew from the horror.

The blanket fell from her slack shoulders, and her bare breasts rose and fell with her slowed breathing.

Stumpfegger reached for her.

It didn't matter. Lisa was in her internal world, where what was left of her might survive untouched by the cold, moist hands of the Nazi.

Inside that place, what was left of her waited for Ben.

Nine

The fishing trawler bobbed restlessly at the dock, as if anxious to get under way. Or so Ben imagined, projecting his tense urgency onto the craft. Unable to remain still, he picked up a crate and helped stow it under the tarpaulin cover on the front deck with the rest of the ammunition and supplies.

An hour or so before dawn, a hazy gray light had spread over the Indian Ocean, making the white froth of the waves just visible beyond the trawler. Ryerson, Jogin, and Remson had formed a chain, and the rest of the gear was being stowed rapidly.

Remson was short and stocky, his dark hair cut close to the scalp in contrast to the thick beard he wore. Dark eyes stared out from his face giving him the look of a medieval acrobat or an English highwayman. His T-shirt bulged with powerful muscles as he picked up crates and tossed them easily to the others.

Jogin was fair-haired and light-complexioned. Taller than Remson and thinner, his thick lips and large ears gave him a pouting, boyish look.

Both men were in their midthirties, Ben judged. Powell seemed older. There were touches of gray in his hair, but his build was trim and fit. He seemed more relaxed than either Jogin or the energetic Remson, more observant as well.

Leander and Powell stood off to one side. It was Powell who would hold Kosi Bay's ranger until the rest of them had gotten in and out. There was no opportunity to establish the ranger's guilt or innocence. He would simply be held under guard. Formal apologies, if needed, could wait till later. No one thought they would be necessary.

The men were clothed identically in combat dress of army design, camouflage-colored. Loose-fitting pants tucked into heavy combat boots, green T-shirt, and a heavier hip-length jacket.

Ben noticed Ryerson pulling at his clothing, unused to the fit and design. Ryerson had been given a crash course in the weaponry they would carry, and even Ben had to brush up earlier that day.

They were introduced to the Israeli Uzi machine guns at the firing range in the basement. It took Ben only a short time to rehone his skills and become familiar with the new weapon.

Ryerson's natural strength and coordination allowed him to attain considerable skill with the Uzi in a short time. However, it was decided, when he demonstrated a total lack of ability, that a pistol would be useless to him.

Leander had explained the two types of grenades they would carry very clearly.

"The usual type, with which I know Mr. Davidson is familiar, operates like this. Pull the pin, release the handle, and six seconds later it will explode. Do try to toss it away from you, Mr. Ryerson."

"Right you are, mate," he had conceded.

"This, however," and Leander had held up a six-inch disc with a knob on top, "is a limpet grenade based on the limpet mines used during World War II. You peel off the vinyl backing to uncover the adhesive, set the timer for up to four hours, and affix the grenade to whatever you wish to destroy."

"Sounds easy enough," Ryerson had commented.

"One of the problems with limpets was that, if discovered, they could be turned off. These cannot. Please remember that. Once activated, they will explode in the set time. They will feel turned off; that is part of the design. One hopes the target will take it home. But it is still active. When the dead seal is broken, it will explode at the preset time."

"Why do we have these?" Ben had asked.

"To destroy their transport and to serve as diversion at a prearranged time. We've used them here and in Europe for the past few months. They are quite effective."

Later, Ben had been given extra clips for the .45, which

now hung properly holstered next to a hunting knife on his web belt. The Uzi was suspended from a shoulder strap.

Except for the crew of the helicopter and fishing boat, this concrete dock on the South African east coast was deserted. It was no longer used commercially, the endless fleet of fishing trawlers that worked the Indian Ocean having moved to the larger southern ports.

Leander walked over with a man whom Ben had seen supervising the boat's readiness. He had long limbs, rough skin, and his neck and face were those of a man of sixty, filled with lines. His thick turtleneck sweater was old and stretched in many places under his rain slicker. But there was life in his eyes, animation in his features.

"This is Captain Vries, Mr. Davidson. He'll take us to Kosi Bay. We have contracted his services before, when he could be persuaded to miss the day's catch."

Ben shook hands with the captain, who then walked back to the boat, noting the placement of their gear and supervising the crew's preparation. Ryerson's easy banter with Remson as they worked drifted back to them.

Ben noted Leander's stance, a way of leaning into the wind that blew in from the sea, almost savoring its saltiness as one inhales fine wine.

In the gray darkness, they stood together. There is strength in him, Ben thought, a quiet watchfulness. He could almost see a younger man beside him, whose lean body had not yet been betrayed by age, whose hair was still brown. He wondered if, under different circumstances, they would have been friends.

"I'm sorry we didn't have more time, Mr. Davidson," Leander said, as if aware of his thoughts. "When you look at me, what do you see?"

"It changes," Ben said carefully, choosing his words. "I feel like I've known you for a long time. When Lisa first told me about you, I was grateful that you had given her something to believe in, that her parents were not suicides. Later on, when I realized how you had used us all, I hated you.

"When you saved my life by getting me to a hospital in Paris, the hate lessened; but I decided you couldn't be trusted. That's why I left to find Lisa on my own."

"And now, Mr. Davidson?"

"And now I think I understand that in your position I

would have used anyone and anything to unravel the conspiracy." He gestured toward Ryerson. "In some ways I already have."

"Mr. Ryerson is here of his own choice," said Leander.

"No one is here of his free choice," said Ben wearily. "My choice ended when a baby was born the wrong color; yours, when you found a document with the name Martin Bormann on it."

"And the others, Mr. Davidson?"

"Ben. The agents are here under orders from you, and Ryerson is here because he finishes what he starts. Not a sane one among us."

The wind picked up sharply, and they tugged their coats closed against its bite. Leander looked out to sea with an expression Ben couldn't read.

"You were right when you guessed that I wanted it this way, Ben," he said. "My choices were made long before the document was found—on a street in Berlin a long time ago. I'd like you to know why."

Ben listened. The salt spray crashed up beside the boat as the wind tossed it.

The trawler plowed steadily northward, hugging the rugged coast and often sending flocks of outraged pelicans or flamingoes screeching skyward. The gray light had begun to give way to the gold of true dawn.

The water ahead was remarkably clear, and Ben could see different kinds of unnamed fish. On shore, above the rocks and brief sandy beaches, hills covered with subtropical trees and bush rose upward in an unbroken, undulating coastal line.

Kosi Bay was almost on the Mozambique border. The charts showed it to be part of an extensive lake system, relatively free of wildlife save for a large population of aquatic birds and a few hippopotamuses. Further inland, crocodiles and other dangerous animals were numerous. Ben understood the wise choice of Kosi Bay for the Eagle's Nest. Free of deadly predators and only minutes from the border, it was ideal both for safety and escape.

Ryerson's voice broke him out of his reverie.

"Ben? Leander says five minutes to the drop-off point." He

pointed to a protruding spit of land in the coastline ahead. "Kosi Bay's beyond that. Any further and the boat's noise might carry. We'll swing in on the raft to the eastern side of the island."

Joining the others in the quiet of the now silent engines, they helped Powell into the smaller of the two rubber boats.

Powell took up his gun, pack, and radio and paddled to shore with a hasty "Good hunting" from Leander.

The trawler began to drift further north with the morning current. By the time they reached the desired position, Powell had collapsed his boat and disappeared over the hills on the mainland.

They slung the packs over their shoulders and carefully arranged the Uzis on top. Leander stepped into the precariously bouncing rubber boat first; then, Remson and Jogin; last, Ben and Ryerson. Paddles were taken up and dipped in unison into the clear water.

There was no talking in the rubber raft. Each man strove to see further ahead, nervously aware of the Uzis on their backs, hoping they would not be necessary as they rounded the spit of land that hid the trawler and paddled into Kosi Bay.

The island sat in the middle of the huge bay, taking up most of the area with its large mass. On either side, the water was forced into channels that ran beside it before joining and reentering the ocean. Oval-shaped, the island was two miles from north to south, three from east to west. High trees and scrubby underbrush made thick foliage, and flocks of birds nested in and around it. Gulls flew screaming around the sky; a flock of flamingoes stood sleeping one-legged on the nearest shore, and frequent splashes marked the dive bomberlike fishing of the terns.

The rocky edges of the island were harsh and uninviting. As yet undissolved by the coming dawn, mist hung in many places over the water, diffusing the bird sounds and making their direction difficult to tell. The effect on the men's nerves was both the product of their imagination and their fears. Kosi Bay was an unlovely place.

"To the right," said Leander, the first words anyone had spoken, and they pulled to obey. The island loomed closer, and the wind carried the smell of bird dung to them. The current increased in strength.

With each man pulling at his paddle countervailing both

the sea and his fear, the raft grounded onto the gritty shore of the Eagle's Nest.

Their disembarkation was rapid. Leander and Remson leaped from the boat and scrambled up the beach into the woods, each with weapons unslung to take a position to cover their landing.

They moved through the woods single file down the island's center, using compass and map. There were no paths in the dense brush. Remson took a machete from his pack to hack away obstructions they could not go around.

Early morning sunshine penetrated the tree cover only in shafts of light. The forest floor was still damp with dew. Their clothing was soon wet from the vegetation and their own sweat as the heat of the day increased.

After a mile, they came to a small clearing where Leander ordered a rest.

They sat on overturned logs and drew close together.

"The closer we get to their compound, the greater the danger of sentries," said Leander. "From here on we'll avoid bunching up. Remson goes first, followed a hundred feet behind by myself and Jogin; Ryerson and Davidson last at the same distance."

Leander took a map from his jacket.

"If we can safely approach the compound, we'll regroup and set up fire positions. Then Davidson and Ryerson will attempt to ascertain Lisa Smith's location."

"Assuming all this goes well, when do we make our moves?" asked Jogin.

"Forty-five minutes before the air strike," Leander checked his watch. "Eight hours from now, we'll blow the transport as a diversion, and you and Remson will provide fire cover for Davidson, Ryerson, and me to get the girl out."

"I'm still no flamin' good with that machine gun," said Ryerson ruefully.

"You're good enough," said Remson. "But you won't be on the cover fire anyway."

"I want you all to understand something," Ben said, hesitantly, "that if this blows up in our faces, I can't give a damn about transport or Bormann. I'll go straight for Lisa. Alone, if that's the way it goes."

"We're quite clear on your feelings. Why do you need to tell us that again here and now?" asked Jogin angrily.

"For the record, Mr. Jogin. I want to know you understand."

"It doesn't matter," cut in Leander. "We all have a job to do. Let's just do it and get the hell out."

Remson moved out of the clearing. A few minutes later, Leander and Jogin followed into the forest.

"You do have a way of getting on people's good side," Ryerson observed when they were alone.

"Dammit, Craig. I wanted him to know where I stood. If it comes down to it, he can't depend on me. It's important they all understand that."

"Should I understand it, too, Ben?" Ryerson asked soberly.

It took Ben a while to answer.

"I lost a good friend in Paris. I won't let that happen again, Craig," he said at last.

Ryerson's reply was lost as the woods swallowed them up.

Once, a group of birds took off from under a bush, flushed by their passage. Ryerson had his gun aimed and would have fired had Ben not clutched frantically at his arm. To ease the strain, he told Ryerson about Leander's past.

The weight of their packs grew heavier as they walked.

"I wonder how Leander is holding up," Ben whispered. "This must be taking its toll on him."

"Beats me how he could do it," agreed Ryerson in a low voice.

Obsession will carry a man a long way, thought Ben in response. Leander had spoken of the street in Berlin as if it had happened only yesterday.

He clutched the Uzi more tightly and walked on toward the Eagle's Nest.

They came to Leander, Remson, and Jogin standing in the path.

"Smell and listen," Remson whispered to their unspoken query.

There was salt in the wind. And like a low bass rumble, the sound of the incoming surf pounding on the beach could be heard.

"The bush ends in a hundred yards. Then the clearing starts and goes all the way to the shore line, maybe half a mile," Remson whispered. "I took a look and doubled back."

Leander took out a diagram of the compound and handed it to Remson. He spoke in hushed tones. "Is this accurate?"

Remson looked at the map. "Fairly, but there are some additions," he said. "The front end of the island extends a half mile down to the bay from the tree line. I'd estimate it's a mile or so wide at that point.

"On the north side of the compound is a fenced-in series of shelters that have a number of native blacks walking around; probably their quarters. In the center of the compound is the main house, a white, two-story wood-frame building. In front of that is a helicopter pad that right now has two big Sikorskys on it. I think they're loading them up. Guards and natives are all over them, and there are stacks of crates alongside.

"On the south side of the clearing are three one-story buildings, a hundred feet long and fifty wide. I assumed they were the labs. They're set up in a U-shape, the open end facing the bay. There are three garage-type buildings to the north of the main house and another barn-type building alongside it, on the south side.

"There is a concrete dock on the beach straight out west from the helipad, and there are three boats moored—a cabin cruiser and two small motor outboards."

"Number of armed guards?" Jogin asked.

"Around a dozen that I could count. Automatic weapons on a few. The rest with sidearms only. Their building seems to be in front of the labs toward the beach. There could be more inside or in the main house."

"Well done," Leander congratulated him. "We'll corroborate that with your report," he said to Ben as he made corrections on their map of the compound.

Remson pointed to the map. "I think she's probably in the main house here, or the labs here. But I don't know how the hell you're going to find her with all those guards walking around."

Ben made no reply.

"Where are we now in relation to the compound's buildings?" asked Ryerson, and again Remson pointed to the map.

"Here. About four hundred yards due east in line to the back of the house. Behind the house it's open ground with guards patrolling it."

"We'll set up fire positions by the labs, the main house, and the native compound," Leander said.

Ben and Ryerson tossed their packs to the others and unslung their guns.

"Let's hope that won't be necessary," Ben said. "How much time do we have?"

"It's six hours to the air strike. Be back in one hour if you can. That gives us ample margin to work with," said Leander.

The others moved off to their positions, but not before Leander had pressed something into Ben's hand. Their eyes locked briefly in understanding. "Three seconds," Leander whispered. Ben and Ryerson walked away. They moved in a low crouch to be as noiseless as possible. They made the final approach crawling on hands and knees, both grateful for the absence of wildlife on the island. Abruptly, the trees ended. They moved away from the house toward the natives' shelter. Raising binoculars to their eyes, they scanned the compound before them.

The helipad in the center of the compound was the scene of feverish activity. Native porters carried crates to the pad in an unending stream from the labs and the main house. Armed guards in khaki uniforms watched over them, their uneasiness evident in rapid turns and quick motions.

"I think they're getting ready to move from here," Ryerson said after a few minutes.

"Those Sikorskys are big 'copters. We used them in 'Nam to transport tons of equipment and personnel," Ben agreed.

"How the hell are we going to find Lisa? We can't saunter in there and ask a flamin' guard in broad daylight," muttered Ryerson.

"I know. Leander knew it, too. He gave me this."

Ben removed a gray metal pistol from his pocket and broke it open at the breech. The feathered tail of an anesthetic dart showed in the barrel.

"He said it would work in three seconds. Now we wait for a guard. Let's move to a spot protected from the view of the house."

They waited in the shade of the bush, watching the compound for signs of Lisa. Suddenly, Ben jerked on Ryerson's arm.

Walking calmly across the compound were two men. One was short and old, bullish-looking and thick-bodied. The other was tall and thin, his bushy white eyebrows unmistakable.

"Stumpfegger!" Ben whispered hoarsely. "I think that's Bormann with him."

They tracked the two men until they were lost to sight.

The blood pounded in Ben's ears. All he had to do was make a dash across the open compound, and they would die. Gottbaum's killers, Annie's killers, James and the baby and Amy and Leander's family. He could stop it here. God, how he ached to do it.

"Easy, Ben. Not yet," came Ryerson's voice from a long way off. "First things first. Look here."

Ben hesitantly swung his vision over to where Ryerson pointed. A lone guard approached.

"Go back fifty feet and make a bit of noise when I whistle," Ben said. Ryerson disappeared.

The guard's walk was careful and measured, his automatic weapon held in an easy grip.

When he was twenty feet away, Ben turned and sent a low whistle to Ryerson. Almost at once, the sounds of a bush rustling came back.

The guard heard it, too. Only ten feet from Ben, he paused and turned toward the woods. He took one hesitant step. Then another. On the third, the anesthetic dart caught him in the neck, the hiss of the gun unnoticed.

His hand reached up to brush away the offending "insect." Then, with an odd look of surprise, he collapsed.

They dragged him deeper into the bush.

"Take off his uniform. Tie and gag him," Ben said. Then, under Ryerson's pained gaze, he took his knife from his belt and waited for the guard to revive.

Jogin's face was strained into an annoyed grimace, which only intensified his pout. Ben Davidson was the object of his annoyance.

Even Leander caters to that nasty bugger, he thought. And Davidson just about told us he'd sell us out if it came to a bloody crunch.

Jogin resented that Davidson seemed to know more about the operation than he did, and a bloody amateur at that! He snorted as a fly brushed past his nose and shifted his body into a new position.

"Serve him right to get caught. I'll be buggered if I'm going to come running," he mumbled. "Get my ass shot off, for what?"

He parted the bush in front of him and stared at the labs.

The rear of the building closest to him had vines growing up its exterior. The casement windows were caked with dirt.

Ryerson isn't so bad. A regular kind of guy, he thought. But Davidson irks the shit out of me.

The mental cursing pleased him, and he hoped Davidson would screw up. Then Leander would have no choice but to call in the pros. He wished he had Powell's assignment.

The heat and boredom were getting to him. He took out one of the limpet grenades and looked at it idly. He had not used this type before in India. Like the older models, he saw that all one did was to rip off the vinyl cover on the adhesive side, set the timer, and push it onto a surface.

Jogin hadn't seen anyone in all the while he was sitting there. A little action, he decided; that's what's needed.

Leander wanted the grenades to go off at 5:15, he'd said. Jogin looked at his watch: 4:15. Okay, he thought, I'll set this baby for an hour. He grinned at his boldness. Fuck Davidson.

He grasped the timer's knob and turned it sharply. He felt the small "crack" as the dead seal was broken and the timer began. The grenade hummed sweetly in his hand.

He pulled off the vinyl cover, tested the adhesive that pulled at his skin, and prepared to run for the lab wall. He looked right and left. No one.

Then a piercing thought stopped him. It can't be 4:15!

Jesus fucking Christ! I'm still on Bombay time! I didn't reset my watch, he realized wildly. Jesus! I'm three-and-a-half hours later than RSA time.

He would have ruined the operation. What a bleedin' fool, he mentally kicked himself. The grenade would have gone off at 1:45. Not 5:15 as they had planned.

He fumbled at the grenade and replaced the vinyl backing onto the adhesive.

Carefully, he reset the timer to zero. There was no crack, but the timer's hum stopped. His fingers were unsteady, and his hands shook. Jesus!

Then he settled down to wait, his decision to be daring destroyed by the near disaster. He put the grenade back in his pack.

It took some time for his anxiety to subside, and he could be angry at Davidson again.

*   *   *

Ben dumped the guard's uniform and weapons at Leander's feet. He was pale, and Ryerson stood quietly by his side.

"We might need these," Ben said tonelessly.

"It will make moving around possible," Leander confirmed. "You know where they're keeping Lisa." It was more a statement than question. The empty uniform spoke volumes.

"She's in the first lab building, closest to the main house. Rumor among the guards has it that she's insane. Also that Stumpfegger has hurt her."

Leander looked closely at Ben. There was an inhuman coldness about him, as if he had gone past emotion. Leander could understand such hatred.

"We spotted Stumpfegger and Bormann with him," Ryerson added as Remson and Jogin entered the clearing from opposite directions and sprawled on the ground a distance away.

Leander smelled warm baking bread.

"It seems we have come to the right place," he said.

Ben walked away having no response.

"I think we have some time," said Ryerson to fill the gap. "They're not planning to leave till tomorrow. In all the confusion, the guard probably won't be missed."

"The information," Leander said. "It was hard for him."

Ryerson shrugged. "He did what had to be done."

"But he's suffering for it."

"He told me that before he met Lisa he wouldn't have. In the long run, then, maybe it's a good thing," Ryerson said pointedly.

"A very complicated man, this friend of yours," Leander mused.

"That's a fact, mate," Ryerson agreed.

"It doesn't seem to bother you as much as it does him, though."

Ryerson looked around him. The lush jungle was a lonely place, cut off from the rest of the world. Sweat dripped down his sides. He watched Remson open his canteen and sip water, aware that Leander was still looking at him.

"I didn't have to hold the knife," he said finally, and walked away to sit by his friend.

They ate the lunch that was in their packs, dried food such as climbers use.

Ben and Ryerson sat hunched close together on the ground

on the opposite side of the clearing from Remson and Jogin. Leander sat alone pondering old debts.

From time to time Ben looked up and would catch Jogin's harsh stare, clearly discernible fifty feet away.

Jogin pushed his pack behind him and took out his knife. Methodically, he threw it over and over again into a soft tree trunk. Each time it made a dull thunk as it penetrated.

Ben checked his watch: 1:30. Soon, he thought, soon I can get to Lisa. The time goes so slowly. Let's do it now, he wanted to shout.

Jogin's knife went thunk. The birds screamed insanely in the treetops.

When Ben looked at his watch, it was only five minutes later. Maybe the rest was good for Leander, but he could feel his toes tapping nonstop in his boots.

Jogin's knife went thunk.

"I'd like to put that where it belongs," Ryerson muttered. "What time is it?"

"One-forty," Ben said.

Every insect in the forest seemed to add its noise to that of the birds. He watched a large, gray caterpillar work its way up a tree, one inch at a time. Each motion was clear and distinct: first the back, then the front, then the back, then the front. It was irritating in its slow, steady crawl.

The tension in the clearing was becoming almost tangible.

Thunk went the knife.

Leander poked at the earth with a stick.

Remson flicked pebbles.

Ryerson began whittling at a piece of bark.

Ben thought of Stumpfegger, and his hands knotted.

At exactly 1:45 P.M. South African time, which was 5:15 in Bombay, the limpet grenade in Jogin's pack blew him into infinity.

Along with the other explosives in his pack, the explosion ripped through the clearing and turned the jungle upside down.

Ten

Dazed and bleeding from the explosion, Ben tried to push the debris off his body, but his strength failed. The loud noise in his ears refused to go away; nor could he clear his vision. Tendrils of smoke curled upward from charred foliage and hurt his lungs, which were laboring painfully to breathe.

He felt a weight pressing on his chest and reached up to pull it off. Vague impressions of a soft tube with fingerlike appendages reached his brain, and he panicked thinking his arm had been severed by the blast.

But both of his arms were intact. This was someone else's, and vomit roared out of his stomach in revulsion. He thrust it from him weakly.

The roaring would not cease. He floated in and out of a twilight sleep where dreams and reality mixed confusingly together.

Later, he heard a voice commanding that "they" be taken to the machine shack and tied up. He had no idea who "they" were, nor who spoke, nor could he correctly interpret the sudden jostle and bounce of his transport over the shoulder of a guard because he blacked out again.

His arms hurt. That he knew when consciousness returned for the third time. The pain in his shoulders was excruciating. The feeling grew slowly that he was being crucified, and he cried out in the guilty knowledge that he was being punished for failing at something he couldn't quite understand.

Then he opened his eyes, and he realized that his arms had been tied to iron hooks set into the wooden wall and that his limpness put all of his weight on them. He found he could support his weight with his feet on the earth floor, and the pain began to subside.

He was glad he hadn't been crucified, but the feeling of guilt and failure still gnawed at him in his confusion. He felt awareness begin to slip away again.

"Stay up, Ben. Come around."

The voice was familiar.

"Open your eyes, Ben. I'm right opposite you."

He opened his eyes and saw Leander similarly tied to the other wall. Next to Leander, Ryerson hung like a limp rag suspended from identical hooks.

"What happened? I can't remember..."

Leander shook his head sadly. "One of Jogin's grenades must have blown. I don't know why. Or how. But it ignited the others in his pack. Killed him and Remson immediately and knocked the rest of us out. I was farthest away and woke up soonest."

Ben could see blood on Leander's clothing, and his left arm lay on the wall at an odd angle.

Leander noticed his gaze.

"I can't feel it. I think something hit me and broke my shoulder."

Pieces moved back in order in Ben's mind. Full consciousness returned.

"How's Craig?" he asked.

"Got a bloody awful gash on his head. He's been out all this time. I can't seem to rouse him."

Smells of gasoline and oil permeated the air. Ben looked around and saw workbenches laden with tools and small engines. In the far corner of the shack an engine had been lifted from a jeep and hung suspended from a block and tackle. Dark oil stains spotted the floor, and five-gallon cans of gasoline were stacked nearby. One dirty window and a half-glassed back door let in dim light.

"What is this place?"

"A garage or repair shop of some sort, I'd guess. Seems as if they store fuel here as well," said Leander. "From what Remson said, we're on the north side of the compound between the main house and the native compound."

A sudden frightening thought struck Ben. "Oh my God, what time is it?"

"Four o'clock," said Leander. "In two hours this part of the island will be reduced to cinders. I'm sorry, Ben."

"Four o'clock. They're in position by now, Captain Jansen."

Dreyer spoke to the commander of the Air Force wing that would bomb Kosi Bay. "In what stage is the fueling?"

"Almost completed, sir. According to the timetable, we'll be ready to begin our run at seventeen-thirty. Kosi Bay's only twenty air minutes from here, so we'll have ample margins."

"It is clear to you that you will be over Kosi Bay and make your run at eighteen hundred hours precisely? We have to give our people time to get out."

"Yes, sir. No problem. The napalm's already been loaded. Eighteen hundred hours, sir."

Dreyer sensed some discomfort in Jansen. He paced around the Operations Room at the airfield like an expectant father.

"You have a question, Captain?"

Jansen seemed reticent to speak.

"Well, sir. It's just that... Some of the men are, well, curious at an air strike of this kind within our own borders. It is odd, don't you agree, sir?"

Jansen was young, but he had been recommended highly by General Rawlings when Leander had set up the mission, Dreyer knew. His question was both foreseeable and understandable.

Leander had had to use every bit of credit he had with Rawlings, a man with whom his relationship went back to the Second World War. When Leander had been in Intelligence, he had provided the information that gave Rawlings, a very young brigadier promoted by the exigencies of war, a high success rate and low casualty reports. Now Air Force Chief, Rawlings had listened to Leander where few would have.

In the final analysis, past Voorstein's papers and the 1936 document and all the other "proof" that could be offered, it was Rawlings's trust in Leander that had made him give the mission a green light.

"It's four o'clock, Captain. You'll be leaving in an hour," Dreyer said.

Jansen took it as a sign of dismissal and started to walk away.

Dreyer called him back.

"Captain?"

"Yes, sir?"

"If a body had gangrene in a limb that would kill the whole body, what would you recommend?" Dreyer asked.

Jansen's response was immediate. "Amputate, sir. To save the rest of the body."

Dreyer clapsed him lightly on the shoulder.

"Think of your mission that way, Captain. To save the rest of the body."

The more Ben struggled, the deeper the ropes cut into his arms. Rivulets of blood ran down to his shoulders. He slumped back against the wall.

"I can't break them," he said bitterly.

"They threw our packs over there, but I can't reach them with my feet," said Leander tiredly.

Chains and saw blades hung over the workbenches on pegboard. Any of a dozen implements in the shop would cut the ropes, but they were all out of reach. Ben yanked again at the ropes in frustration.

"It won't help," chided Leander. "Save your strength."

"For what, Jan? In ninety minutes we're going to be either cooked by napalm or suffocated by a lack of oxygen as it burns," Ben said harshly.

"All I can offer by way of consolation is that they burn, too. That's all we have left."

"I hope Jogin fries in Hell!" Ben cursed.

"In ninety minutes you'll have the chance to find that out for yourself," Leander said sardonically.

There was quiet after that.

"I don't understand why they didn't just shoot us in the jungle," Ben said.

"I'm sure they will. They just want to make sure we're the only ones who know about them."

"Look, Jan. If for any reason they untie us, I'm going to go for a gun first thing. No waiting, no talking, maybe by surprise—"

"C'mon, Ben," Leander said sharply. "These people are pros. They are not going to untie you and give you a chance to be dangerous. Accept that. They will outlive us for less than an hour. That's the only break we're going to get. No heroic last stands, no blazing gunfights. Just a single shot, and you die. If there were any other way, don't you think I'd be trying it?"

"I know, Jan," Ben said, sobered. "It ends here."

"It ends here," Leander agreed. "And if your friend Ryerson were up and around, he'd shrug and say, 'Well, it did seem like a good idea at the time.'"

"I suppose he would," Ben agreed. "I always thought that if this time ever came, I could make some profound remarks." His voice softened. "I can't think of a damn thing to say, Jan."

"There is nothing you can say about dying," Leander said, equally softly.

The wooden door of the shop swung open, and a shaft of light reflected the dust in the air. Martin Bormann and Ludwig Stumpfegger walked in.

Ben took his first long look at Bormann and his second at Stumpfegger.

Leander saw only the Bull.

They stopped in the center of the room, pleased expressions on their faces.

"Welcome to the Eagle's Nest, gentlemen," said Bormann. "You have both been severe annoyances who, I am glad to say, will now be put to rest."

In the light of the doorway, Ben found himself staring at them. Here was the reason for all that had happened, all the killing that had taken place. These were the reasons he had come from Mississippi to die in South Africa. No leering monsters, no horns or tails, just two old men with sagging flesh. A clerk and a doctor—two old men.

In the midst of a confrontation with the madness that had spawned the Second Holocaust, Ben could only do one thing. Improbably, impossibly, he laughed.

They turned to him, staring.

"What amuses you? Does death terrify you so?" asked Croft/Stumpfegger with obvious relish.

"It just occurred to me how small you are," Ben said. "It must be horrible to be so ordinary."

Stumpfegger's face turned crimson. He took two quick strides and struck him full in the face. Ben lashed out with his foot, but Stumpfegger had already moved back out of the way.

"You continue to offer proof," Ben said easily.

Stumpfegger began a retort but was interrupted.

"Enough, Ludwig," said Bormann. "You may do as you wish later." He turned calmly to Leander. "Mr. Davidson is an amateur, a gifted amateur to be sure, but still an amateur. You understand that I must know certain things. The choice is yours. I can use torture if you wish."

"And under torture I will break, as everyone does sooner or later," Leander said.

Bormann nodded. It was only logical.

"I want to know who else knows about the Adlerkinden and what measures have been taken against us. As you know, you will die anyway; the choice is up to you. We'll confirm it with drugs."

"Don't, Jan," said Ben angrily.

"I will be killed immediately after?" asked Leander.

"My word on it. One bullet."

Leander studied Bormann for a time.

"Very well. I need some time to compose myself."

"How long? I am very busy just now," Bormann said easily. "An hour?"

"Half," said Bormann. "I will be back. It was a pleasure doing business with you." He turned to leave. "Ludwig?"

"I'll be along in a moment, Martin."

After Bormann had gone, Stumpfegger turned his hostility back to Ben.

"Because of you I had to leave the United States. You killed Henry Schmidt and caused the death of Heinz Stangl and of Piet Voorstein during the destruction of his labs. I am going to repay your insults, Mr. Davidson, before I kill you. It will please my smallness, as you put it.

"I hope you will enjoy what you are about to see. I am going to have your woman while you watch. Here, in the dirt. And then I'm going to allow the guards to have her, one at a time or in groups. Will you enjoy watching that? I hope you will. You will know how it feels to be helpless, to have lost all control, as she writhes in the dirt in front of you. Think about that, Mr. Davidson."

Ben's rage strangled words in his throat. He tore at his bonds in sick fury.

"I'll be back shortly, Mr. Davidson." Stumpfegger walked out the door.

Ben pulled at the ropes and cried in helpless anger. Leander tried to comfort him.

"It's five-thirty. In half an hour it will all be over. It won't matter then. Please. It's transitory, Ben; all pain is. Don't give him the satisfaction."

Ben went limp against his bonds. It was no use. He wished he could pray.

The Air Force jets rolled down the runway, one by one, igniting their engines and roaring into the sky.

Dreyer walked off the runway toward the Control Tower.

Leander, he knew, would be out of the Eagle's Nest by now, the operation over.

He wondered if Leander had found Bormann and, if he had, how he had killed him.

It didn't really matter; in half an hour the Eagle's Nest would be only rubble.

Someone giggled.

At first Ben thought he hadn't heard the noise, but then he heard it again. He looked around the shop, searching for the source.

It happened again. Someone giggled. Leander heard it, too, and his head spun sharply around.

"From the back, I think," he said softly.

Ben strained to see what lay in the back of the dimly lit shop. The window, the workbenches, the door. The door was partly open. He was sure it hadn't been before. And a vague shape of darker color seemed to move when he stared at it.

"Who's there?" he called out hoarsely.

He heard the giggle again before unseen hands stifled it.

"Please. Who's there?" he called again, pleading.

Suddenly, a small figure darted out from the shadows. She was beautiful, young, and her amber skin was almost translucent. He had seen her before.

"I remember you," the girl said sweetly, and giggled again. "You were at our house once. You wouldn't play with me."

Ben's brain went into high gear. He forced Stumpfegger out of his mind.

"I remember you, too, Heidi. I'd like to play now if it's okay."

Leander was tense and silent, watching their byplay. So far, Heidi had ignored him.

"I don't know," she pouted and chewed at her finger.

"But you're so pretty. And you said I was handsome. Please, Heidi?"

"Doctor says you're bad. I shouldn't play with bad men."

"Oh no, Heidi. I'm good. Just like the doctor. I'll give you nice presents. Would you like that?"

"What presents?" she asked eagerly.

Ben bit back an oath; Stumpfegger would be back any minute. He forced calm tones into his voice.

"I'll give you candy. And jewelry. Anything you want," he said. Please, God, don't let him come back yet!

"That's nice. I like that," she said.

Leander had closed his eyes, not yet daring to hope.

"Would you untie me so I can play with you? Just take a saw and cut the ropes. Then I can give you candy and nice things. Okay?"

"Not supposed to. Doctor would be mad." Her pout had returned.

"No, it's okay," Ben said quickly. "He won't mind; and when we're done, you can tie me back up, and he'll never know.

"Can't," she said simply and chewed at another finger.

Ben tried not to cry. Frustration overwhelmed him and made it hard to think. There had to be a way to use her. There had to be. He couldn't have much more time.

He looked around frantically and came up with an idea borne of desperation as he watched her light a cigarette. She smoked contentedly.

"Heidi, can I have one of those? Please?"

"Sure. We can still play?"

Heidi came over and put her cigarette in his mouth. The smoke burned his eyes. He felt her hand reach into his pants.

"Soft," she said in childish annoyance.

"We can make it hard for you. It's my hands that hurt too much. If you could take some of the liquid in those cans and splash it on my wrists, I won't hurt; and then I can get hard. You do that, and I'll give you candy and make you feel good. I promise."

Time, just give me time. Please, God, let her do it. Please.

Heidi looked undecided. "For candy?" she asked.

"Oh, yes, I promise. All the candy you want. Any kind."

"Okay," she said brightly.

The gasoline on his arms burned into the open cuts.

"On the rope, Heidi. That's where it hurts most. On the ropes. Try not to spill it on the rest of me. Please."

Heidi splashed the gasoline on his wrists and arms.

"Smells," she wrinkled her nose.

"That's a good girl," he said. "Good girl."

A stream of gasoline ran down his arm. He tried to keep it from his shoulder and away from the cigarette, which he puffed into a burning, glowing ash.

"You can't scream," spoke Leander, quietly, for the first time. He saw the glaze of terror in Ben's eyes.

"Now we can play?" asked Heidi stepping in front of Ben. He steeled himself for what was to come. No other way, he said over and over again. No other way. Lisa. No other way.

In one movement he brought up both legs and drove them into Heidi's chest. She careened over to the other wall, smashing into it with her head, and fell unconscious onto the ground.

Then he swiveled his head around and touched the burning end of the cigarette to the moist gasoline on his arms.

Pain engulfed him. There was no place in the world where pain was not. Burning, tearing, screaming pain shot up his arms now covered in flames. Jerking and pulling at the ropes, he felt his hair being singed and his skin crackle. The fumes made his eyes burn and his lungs a searing agony.

Again and again he pulled at the burning ropes. He would go mad with the pain, the excruciating, terrible, agonizing pain. His arms had a thousand needles ripping at them; his hands turned black as skin popped and blistered. He had to scream, had to yell in blind panic at the endless searing pain. He couldn't bear the pain. Yanking desperately like an insane marionette, he fought, and the pain grew worse, charring his wrists. A scream that would have no end began in his throat as the torture of the flames drove him to flail and cry and burn . . . and the ropes broke.

He fell on the ground and beat his arms into the sand to put out the flames. It was reflex alone working, for his mind had been driven to its limit by the agony he had endured.

But he had won. He was free. And the small piece of sanity that was left forced him from the dirt and to his feet.

He lurched to the workbench and grasped a saw blade in hands that had no feeling but pain. He felt his skin tear off as he sliced at Leander's ropes.

"Just a bit more, Ben. Just a bit. It's coming. That's right. Let the tears come. Good. Just a bit more. You've got it. Now!"

Ben grinned dumbly as Leander's right arm fell free grabbing the saw blade from his hand.

"I didn't scream," he said, and then he fainted. The cool black void was sweet and took away the pain.

When Ben awoke, he found Leander hunched over him wrapping his arms in gauze bandage. The pain was only a constant dull ache.

"Stumpfegger...be back...soon." His voice was a whisper.

"I know. You first," said Leander. "Together we make one whole person."

He saw that Leander worked one-handed.

"I pumped you full of stimulants and painkillers. That and shock could and probably will kill you, but that's certain if we don't get out of here. You're going to spend a long time in the hospital after this is over, son."

"S'okay," Ben slurred. "Lisa."

"We'll get her, Ben. I swear it. Now try and get up, and we'll see if you can use your hands at all. Your head should clear up soon, and you can crash later."

Ben did find his senses returning. Pumped up by the stimulants, he grew clearheaded. He looked at his arms wrapped from fingers to shoulders.

"Time?" he asked.

"Fifteen minutes. Now listen..."

Ben nodded agreement, struggling into Leander's jacket to cover the gauze.

When the door opened, Stumpfegger grabbed Lisa by the hair and shoved her into the room. She sprawled headlong into the dirt.

"I hope you remember your insults, Mr. Davidson, when the guards start on her," he said, his face twisted and brutal.

Stumpfegger dragged Lisa to her feet and pushed her face to Ben, still bound to the wall.

"Look, Lisa. See who's here? Look!"

"Lisa," Ben whispered.

Her face was bruised and dirty. There was no recognition in her eyes. She was still waiting.

Stumpfegger dropped her to the floor. He reached down to loosen his belt.

"Watch, Mr. Davidson."

"I never believed Nazis had sex organs," said Leander behind him. "Least of all little pompous ones."

Stumpfegger spun around hotly.

"Be careful, Leander. I can—"

He never finished. Ben drove the knife into his back with all the rage he could call forth. It flowed out of his arm and exploded out, and the thrust of the blade went its full length into Stumpfegger. He died, his face shocked, as Leander came off the wall and jammed his hand into the Nazi's mouth to stifle his scream.

Ben gathered Lisa into his arms and held her.

"I'm here, Lisa. I said I would come, and I'm here. Please come back. It's Ben. No one can hurt you anymore. Please come back."

He rocked her gently as Leander worked on restoring Ryerson to consciousness.

"Come back, Lisa. It's all over. I'm here. No one can hurt you anymore."

Her face was pale and rigid, but slowly some color returned. Her eyes blinked.

"Ben . . . ?"

"Yes, darling. It's Ben, come back to me. It's over. You're safe now. Please, Lisa."

Suddenly, her body convulsed in a series of terrible wracking spasms.

"Oh, Ben . . ." she cried, and threw her arms around him, clutching with all her strength.

"I love you, Lisa," he said, and her tears burst forth from the pent-up anguish of her ordeal. He held her till it was over.

"I think Ryerson's coming around, Ben," called Leander. "Help me. We've got less than ten minutes."

Ben draped his jacket around Lisa's bare shoulders. "Can you make it?" he asked her.

She looked at Stumpfegger's dead body, then up at Ben and drew a great breath that almost caught in her throat.

"Now I can," she said. She stood and brushed the dirt from her and her clothing.

"His pulse is steady," said Leander as Ben helped him lift Ryerson to a sitting position so he could be injected with a stimulant.

"Wha . . . ?" moaned Ryerson as the drug took effect.

"Get up, Craig. We've got to get out of here. The planes are coming in ten minutes. Get up," Ben urged.

Ryerson came awake and struggled woozily to his feet.

"Flamin' headache," he complained.

"Help Lisa; I'll take him," Leander ordered, handing out packs and Uzis. "We've got to make the beach."

Lisa was on her feet already. "Give me a gun, Ben," she said clearly. Her eyes were bright with released anger.

He gave her the .45 with no question.

They stood by the door, each holding pain back, the remains of a mission that should have killed them. Briefly, they touched, knowing these were the final moments. They would make the beach and its life-saving water, or they would die.

"Now," said Leander, and they burst into the sunlight.

A group of guards stood on the right. Ben cut them down with a burst of fire. He heard the sharp bark of the .45 as Lisa fired to their rear.

The main house was on their left, and the helipad, straight ahead. Ryerson launched a grenade at the house that demolished a side, and the wood frame caught fire. A second grenade scattered the workers and guards at the helipad as one Sikorsky exploded.

Guards screamed at each other to locate the intrusion. Smoke poured from the burning 'copter. Weapon fire was like hail in the compound, and native workers raced for cover.

Weapons blazing, they fought their way toward the helipad and the beach beyond. But they had been spotted now, and the guards' resistance mounted as they reorganized. The element of surprise was lost. They had to get to cover. The guards were advancing on them, cutting off the beach.

"The native quarters!" yelled Leander.

Firing as they were pushed back toward the northern edge of the compound, Leander caught a bullet high up in the chest. He fell painfully to the ground, but Ryerson scooped him up and supported him as they ran.

The clear blue water beckoned like an oasis only a hundred yards to the east. The scream of jet fighters passing overhead filled the area and overshadowed the melee of the firefight.

"Next pass they'll come in!" Ben yelled, firing as he ran. "Get to the water." He grabbed at Lisa to help her run.

But a group of guards had made it to the beach in advance of them. Dug into the soft sand, they fired on the four as they advanced.

Bullets whined into the air around them.

"Cover!" yelled Ryerson, as he shoved Leander behind a pile of crates. Ben and Lisa dived after them as fire from the beach smashed into the soft wood, trapping them against the compound fence.

Suddenly bullets tore at them.

"By the garage. Bormann!" yelled Leander, his gun firing wildly as he held it one-handed. Blood covered his shirt.

There was no way to make a run for it. Guards on the beach blocked their way forward. Bormann and his guards held off their retreat to the west past the garage. The native compound stood at their backs, fenced in and impenetrable. Before them, the helipad blazed.

"We can't move," panted Ben. "Both sides blocked."

"Got to," Leander grunted, his face white and drawn.

Ryerson tossed a grenade at the guards on the beach with all his strength, but it fell short, exploding and throwing the sand high in the air. They continued firing. His toss at Bormann suffered the same fate.

The scream of the jets was louder now, the first bombing run beginning. Silver specks, they came in low and fast, smoke pouring from their engines.

"Down!" Ben yelled, and the planes dropped their first load of napalm.

The lab buildings on the far side of the clearing burst into a sheet of fire a hundred feet high. Burning guards shrieked and ran amok as the jellied gasoline ignited their clothing. Smaller explosions followed as fuel combusted near the buildings. The jets roared by, circling over the horizon. The air was full of the stench of gasoline.

"Last chance," wheezed Leander. "Split up...only way ...Ryerson covers...with grenades. Ben and Lisa...attack beach...I'll take...Bormann. Ryerson...my back-up. No time to argue...Do it!"

Ben clasped Leander's arm, and looked deep into his face. A look of recognition passed between them. Slowly Ben nodded as Leander struggled to stand.

"Go for the water . . . if you can get past the garage, Craig. Go for the water . . ." he finished, rasping.

Ryerson pulled the pins on two grenades and waited before thumbing off the handles. His face broke into a mad grin. A berserk rage welled up in him as he stood and cocked his arm back.

"Now!" Ben yelled.

Ryerson launched a grenade toward the house, and Leander was up and running with the last of his strength.

On the second toss Ben and Lisa raced out from cover. The grenade exploded fifty feet beyond them, creating cover in its explosion of sand. Their weapons blazed into life, and they attacked.

Leander's first burst of fire went true and caught the two guards next to Bormann. They spun backward, red blotches appearing on their chests. Leander ran forward, firing at Bormann, who ducked behind the side of the burning house and fired back.

A bullet caught Leander in his useless left arm. There was a hatred in him so intense that it barely stopped him. He ran on, firing wildly, immune to anything but the violence that filled him. The smell of gasoline mixed with the odd smell of bread.

It was a morning in Berlin, and a twelve-year-old boy yelled obscenities as a man killed his family. He had needed a weapon, and now he had one.

Bormann burst from cover and fired again.

Leander's legs went out from under him as he took a shot in the thigh.

Bormann's gun steadied, and Leander could see a smile come over the aged, sagging features.

Then the wall around Bormann burst into fragments as Ryerson, coming up on Leander, fired into the burning structure.

Leander was up and crawling. He saw Bormann again, and he fired at him. The gun clicked empty. He tossed it away and crawled faster, kicking at the dirt behind him, blood pouring from his chest and thigh, spots dancing in his eyes.

He reached the corner of the garage and waited for the Bull to show himself. But he collapsed in the dirt, feeling the loose planks of splintered wood under and around him.

Racing up to the garage, Ryerson fired as he saw Leander sprawled ahead of him.

Suddenly, Bormann stepped out, and Ryerson fired again. But his gun clicked empty.

Bormann's smile was wholly malicious as he stepped out of the burning building and steadied his gun. He looked at Ryerson and his weapon burst into life.

Ryerson knew he was as good as dead when the first bullet caught him in the leg while in midleap to the ground. He looked up, rolling awkwardly in the sand, expecting the death he could not avoid.

Bormann took another step forward. Ryerson could see Bormann's hand tighten against the stock of the automatic weapon to steady the fire that would kill him.

But Leander leaped from the dirt in one last, all-out effort. The burst that would have killed Ryerson caught Leander full in the chest as he swung a piece of timber at Bormann's head in a last desperate act to get the man who had killed his family.

With a crack that was audible even to Ryerson sprawled in the dust, the plank burst into Bormann's skull. Oozing gray matter mixed with blood showered Leander as Bormann died, collapsing onto the ground.

Ryerson limped over to Leander's bleeding body.

"Bormann?" hissed Leander.

"You got 'im, mate. He's dead."

"Tell . . . tell my father . . . I . . . ." and Leander died.

"I will, mate. That I will."

Tears leaked from Ryerson's eyes as he limped past the garage and the native quarters, toward the bay beyond.

The second napalm run exploded the helipad, and the 'copters burst into flames. The guards died horribly, burned to death racing for the water. The jungle behind the compound was already ablaze.

*   *   *

Ben and Lisa ran through the sand spray caused by Ryerson's grenade, their guns firing at the unseen guards beyond.

The planes roared overhead heading out to sea to turn and make their final run. It would be on this side of the island. They had perhaps two minutes left.

As the sand settled, Ben saw the guards rise to shoot. There were three of them, their weapons spraying bullets.

He fired with all the hatred he had ever felt at the men who were trying to kill him.

Lisa ran at his side. The .45 barked again and again. A guard fell over in the sand dead.

Something burst in Lisa's leg, and the .45 flew from her hand as she fell.

"Ben!" she screamed.

He looked over and saw her fall. His gun was blistering hot in his hands as he saw a second guard die, head snapping backward when the bullet caught him in the neck.

The third guard rolled to the side and fired up at Ben who fired the Uzi again, knowing it was kill or die. Then suddenly the gun sprang out of his hands as the guard's bullets smashed into it and pulled it away.

He didn't stop or swerve away. Yanking the knife from his belt, he leaped on the guard, blocking his gun, and stabbed desperately. An audible snarl broke from his throat in fury.

The jets' engines grew louder as he struggled with the guard. Somewhere inside he called on strength he never knew he had as the jets roared closer. His hands and arms were aflame with agony as the gauze ripped away.

Ben kicked at the guard who had rolled on top of him grasping at his knife hand. Skin on his arm came away, and his grip loosened as his burned fingers grew weak.

The guard forced the knife back toward his chest. Ben fought till his face was contorted into a grimace of pain and fury. He levered his legs under the guard and, with all his remaining strength, thrust the guard away from him.

The guard twisted in the sand to retrieve his weapon, sending sand into Ben's eyes. For a moment he was blinded. When he could see, the jets were almost overhead, and the guard was turning, his gun in hand.

Lisa's first shot caught the guard in the stomach, and he doubled over in agony. The second caught him in the legs, and he fell. She emptied the gun at the guard until he was dead.

The jets roared overhead for the last pass.

"The water," Ben yelled, pulling at Lisa to stand.

They ran together, their blood leaving a trail in the sand to the bay. They dived into its cool, clear depths as the jets released their final load of burning death on the compound and the jungle beyond.

When they surfaced, treading water to stay afloat, the entire compound was burning. Dead guards lay in flames everywhere. The helicopters on the pad were a pyramid of flaming debris. The buildings were gone, charred rubble glowing red. The Eagle's Nest would produce no second Holocaust. It was over.

The planes raced over the island a last time and then roared off back over the mainland.

Ben and Lisa swam back in to where they could stand, chest high in the smooth water that had saved their lives.

Ben felt Lisa move next to him, and he drew her close. Her blond hair was wet against her face, droplets of water falling from her cool skin.

They held each other tightly, and his mouth sought hers. She cried a little as they touched.

"I knew you'd come for me," she whispered, her tears stopping.

"I always will," he said, the pain far away.

Without moving, they watched the Eagle's Nest burn.

Epilogue

Paris, December 1974

Through the large glass windows of Lucas-Carton, a restaurant on the Place de la Madeleine, they watched Parisians dressed for winter trundle through the lightly falling snow outside.

"I'm glad you could come, Georges. Both Ben and I wanted you to be here."

"I was delighted to be asked, Lisa. You have not seen this man since . . . ?" Delacroix paused.

"Since a few days after Kosi Bay," Ben put in. "We were flown to a hospital almost at once. This puts the final touches on it, you might say."

Delacroix shook his head. "It is still hard to believe. When you returned, I was, well, shocked really. But I never doubted you, *mon ami*," he added quickly.

"Of course not," Ben said.

The maître d' brought Peter Dreyer to their table.

"Please don't stand," he said. "I must be going shortly. It is good to see you both looking so well."

"Georges has been very kind to us these last few months," Lisa said.

"Mr. Dreyer, this is Monsieur Georges Delacroix."

"*Un plaisir*, Monsieur Director," said Delacroix.

"Thank you," said Dreyer. "A pleasure also."

He reached into his coat and produced a sheaf of legal papers bound in a leather folder.

"The matter of your estate has been settled, Mrs. Davidson. These papers contain a list of your assets and holdings. As I'm sure you are aware, they are quite substantial."

"So you will need a good banker, *bien sur*," said Delacroix with an elfin twinkle in his eyes.

Lisa smiled and took the papers, slipping them into her handbag.

"Craig Ryerson said to send you his, uh...flamin' best, when we spoke to him last," Ben said mildly.

"Where is the free-spirited Mr. Ryerson these days?" asked Dreyer.

"On a W.H.O. project in Pakistan—building a bridge. We couldn't convince him to take more than a week off after he got out of the hospital. He's flying back here for Christmas, though."

"I'm sure his work will seem tame after what you went through," Dreyer commented.

"On the contrary," Lisa answered. "He claimed he had to do a great deal of 'head-knocking' to get his crew into shape. He's not sure he likes being a foreman."

Dreyer laughed politely and then grew serious. "You have a right, of course, to know how it all ended, and I must be going soon. If you don't mind, I'll come straight to it."

"Yes. We'd like to know," Ben agreed.

"The Director General of the W.H.O. in Geneva was able to find the rest of the plague and the members who were to spread it. They were released from office, and the plague destroyed. Fortunately, only the African Regional Office was involved. There is a new director there, and a rather large turnover in staff resulted.

"With respect to the government in the RSA, Mr. Carlysle proved to be very cooperative once the conspiracy was destroyed. He furnished a list of those involved. The result is that there is now a new majority party in the Parliament and a new Prime Minister. Malthinus Goosen proved to be susceptible to the...ah...same political flaws as Mr. Smith."

"What happened to Hauptman?" Lisa asked, the mention of her father hurting, but far less these days.

"It is unfortunate that several of the RSA's leading citizens, including Carlysle and Goosen, had bad hearts. The country is in a period of mourning." He shrugged. "Some things do not change overnight; expediency is one of them.

"The Adlerkinden's scientific discoveries have been turned over to the United Nations to be shared among the community it represents. I am told a revolution in the field of biology is about to occur. The world owes you a great deal, Mr. Davidson. I am sorry it will never know of your sacrifices. How are your arms?"

"Better, Mr. Dreyer. A bit more control each day," Ben said.

"Thank you for coming, Mr. Dreyer," Lisa said as he stood to go. "We appreciate being able to put an end to it in our minds."

"Will you live in the United States?" Dreyer asked.

"We don't know yet about our plans. We have very few ties," Ben said.

"It is changing in our country. Slowly, but change is possible. Someday, perhaps." He shrugged. "A pleasure to meet you, Monsieur Delacroix. Good-bye, Mr. and Mrs. Davidson."

He considerately did not offer to shake hands as he walked away.

"Remarkable," muttered a subdued Delacroix.

Later, over the wine, Ben turned to Lisa.

"Would you like to visit the States, now that things are settled?"

Lisa put her hand on his arm. "We'll see after Craig comes for the holidays. After all, darling, we have all the time in the world."

Ben smiled and reached awkwardly for his wine. It was true.

ABOUT THE AUTHOR

BART DAVIS is a native New Yorker, a graduate of the Bronx High School of Science and of the State University of New York at Stony Brook. He holds a brown belt in karate and is a licensed hypnotist, a reasonably good shot, and a seasoned European traveler. He has traveled extensively throughout the United States and has lectured frequently on education, social work, and writing. Married to an attorney, Bart Davis now resides in Port Washington, New York. He is also the author of *Blind Prophet*, his first novel, which was published in October 1983. He is currently working on a new novel.